A TABERNACLE FOR THE SUN

A TABERNACLE FOR THE SUN

A Novel set in Florence
in the time of
Lorenzo de' Medici
1472–1478

LINDA PROUD

First published in Great Britain in 1997 by
Allison & Busby Ltd
114 New Cavendish Street
London W1M 7FD

A catalogue record for this book is available from the British Library

ISBN 0 74900 365 0

Designed and typeset by
N-J Design Associates
Printed and bound in Great Britain by
Redwood Books
Trowbridge, Wiltshire

TO MY TEACHER

ACKNOWLEDGEMENTS

According to the law of the octave, there are two intervals that require an extra input of energy in order to cross from one note to the next; one of these is between si and top doh. This book might have lain becalmed at this interval but for those who arrived like zephyrs to help it across with the breeze of their spirited enthusiasm. Even then, completion may not have been achieved but for a *deus ex machina* in the surprising form of Southern Arts and a bursary award. Grateful thanks, therefore, to both gods and friends

NOTE

There have been tremendous contributions made to the knowledge of the Renaissance, in all its facets, by scholars of recent generations, and to them profound gratitude is owed. Every effort has been made to stay true to the facts, but doubtless some errors have crept in; also, there have been occasions when for the sake of the story deliberate changes have been made. Although these are slight, perhaps even inconsequential, one senses the disapproval of Poliziano and all who continue in his noble tradition of exact scholarship. And so the author craves forgiveness for any mistake, deliberate or otherwise.

The best general accounts of the period are regrettably long out of print. Of modern general works, the following are outstanding: *The Florentine Renaissance* by Vincent Cronin (London 1967), *The Rise and Fall of the House of Medici* by Christopher Hibbert (London 1975), and *The Companion Guide to Florence* by Eve Borsook (London 1966). For a full account of the bridge that was Oxford between the age of the Renaissance and the Reformation, see *The Oxford Reformers* by F. Seebohm (London, 1911).

Regarding Italian pronunciation, *Gi* has the sound *J*, so Giuliano sounds as Juliano. Also the stress is often on the penultimate syllable, so Tom-*mas*-o.

CONTENTS

THROUGH LOVE, WE NOT ONLY MOVE TOWARDS THE DIVINE BUT WE ATTAIN TO WHAT IS MOST HUMAN IN OURSELVES.

MARSILIO FICINO

To Desiderio, dearest of friends

By now you will have received Colet's injunction not to speak to me. We may continue our lessons in Greek, but I am not to tell you about anything other than grammar and syntax. Apparently I have pagan leanings and my company puts your soul at risk. Pagan! Me? Born and raised in the heart of the Holy Roman Catholic Church, how am I leading you from the path of Christian virtue? Colet seems to think that Italians are wine barrels where the contents do not correspond to the labels. He says we are not to be trusted. He is right of course.

You are to come no more to my house, you are to hear no more tales of the gods and heroes, no more of that story of mine which you have been begging me to tell you. I will speak no more to you of anything but Holy Scripture. My lips will be as thin as Colet's. I shall spurn you in the street or, if you prefer, I shall allow you to spurn me. However, as Colet has made no injunction against my putting pen to paper, I have decided to write it all down. (We Italians are nothing if not devious.) The choice will then be yours, Desiderio, whether to read it or not.

Fate has consigned me to a wattle and daub cottage, a house of dried dung and spit. My exiled eyes gaze out through a small window on to a bleak vista of English mist and sodden, flowerless fields. I seek beauty and find none. You assure me that flowers will come in time. Why should I believe you? This country is one of perpetual winter.

In my empty house that sighs in the wind I am crowded by the shadows of friends I have been told to forget. I long to dwell in grander places, in greater halls, to be able to stride across marble floors without knocking into things, to hear my voice echo as if in eternity rather than boom as if in a box. If Colet will deny the pagan world of the ancients he must realise that he will deny this country of England knowledge of arts such as fine architecture and true proportion, to deny, that is, men space in which to flourish and to know their own true stature. O Dio! Did I go through all that pain of self-knowledge only to become confined in a mud hut?

John Colet, that man of dark robes, firm jaw and profound wisdom, warns my pupils against me. Why? Because the source of my learning, which is ancient literature, contains as much evil as good. And Colet, like any true philosopher, will have only the good. As I love language, but am not a grammarian, so I love wisdom, but am not a philosopher. However it was as an historian, as an eyewitness of history, and as an Italian, that I cried into my cups last night, shocking my English companions. You philosophers! You tell me not to consider the past or the future but to find happiness in the present. In two weeks' time you will sit quietly and meditatively as the bell tolls the passing of a century, while I shall be crossing a gulf as precipitous as any Alpine pass, to leave my world behind me forever. How can I do that without speaking of it, that iridescent burst of light from the sun of Creation? Colet visited Italy, took what was good and left the rest. You always wanted to go there but never reached further than England; do not pretend to me that it has not caused you deep regret and hungry longing.

Ha! Is this the voice of temptation? Am I drawing you out to speak the truth as it is rather than as you – or Colet – would have it be? Admit it! Florence has been the scene of a Golden Age. I was there and through me, you would drink of its cup to the dregs. Fine man, I believe that under your austere Augustinian robes hides a poet, therefore drink, drink, drink! Besides, was it not your Augustine who said, 'Lord, make me celibate, but not yet'? Desiderio, dance in your soul to my tunes and then, when I have done, confess to Colet and proceed with the good work.

May Minerva, goddess of Wisdom, attend your days, but do not forget Venus. She is the goddess of Love, both divine and human; if you would love God, you must also love Man and all creation.

Tommaso dei Maffei da Volterra
March 11th 1499
Oxford

THE FIRST BOOK

THE BISHOP'S WARD

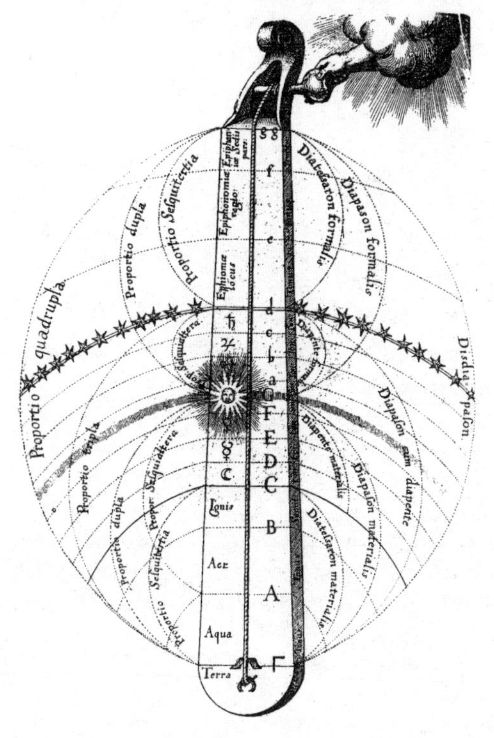

It needs but a little to overthrow and destroy everything –
just a slight aberration from reason.

Epictetus

ONE

WHEREVER a man is born, he is born under the laws of nature. He grows up, fulfils a meagre destiny, dies; passes either into limbo, to hell or to heaven; and there is an end to it. But God chooses some for another destiny, a destiny which is divine, which is His own. These men move beyond the laws of nature, beyond even the influence of the planets. Why are they chosen? God alone knows.

My people were short, black-haired, and had skin the colour of the best oil. They had thin faces with high cheekbones, ears set higher and further back than is usual, and almond-shaped eyes as black as olives. They were taciturn. Strangers took their silence for hostility, but it was merely a caution bred of generations: my people, who had occupied this city on the high ridge long before the Romans came, had small reason to trust others. The round tombs of their ancestors swelled under grass on the slopes beyond the walls, and their abandoned gods still dwelt on the acropolis.

Our city was built on rock and I lived on the highest point. 'Acropolis' was a word I enjoyed long before I knew its meaning. I savoured its consonants and vowels as I ran on lanes of stone laid by an ancient civilisation, or played among the rubble of Etruscan temples. With a child's awareness of the present and none of the past, I was oblivious to the record of ages held captive in the stones with which we built our new houses, but enjoyed instead their subtle colours and enormity, measuring my growth against the massive walls that encircled a space far greater than that in which we lived. If you picture Volterra's plan as the head of a roaring lion, then our Christian city was but its mane, for my people had declined after Sulla besieged and sacked the city in 88 BC, after which the Romans had dominion over us.

My city was high and proud and commanded extensive lands as far as the eye could see in each direction, a territory rich with minerals. Hot sulphur springs bubbled in the valleys; there also salt was panned and copper mined, while the alabaster caves provided us with the stone for which we were famed. Naturally when a city is so rich, other cities desire it; and so our history was a repetitive one, of battle, siege, foreign occupation and rebellion.

On the acropolis was the fort, the prison and the church of San Pietro. Here the nobles of a previous age built their houses, around the Palace of the Bishop. This is where I lived, near the Selci gate. From our battlemented tower I could watch the sun rise on misty valleys and juniper-blue hills; I could watch it set and the clouds marble the evening sky; I could watch Venus rise with the sickle moon, or thunderstorms form in the distance. It was easy to presume that this place was the highest point on earth, that here there was nothing between me and the angels but the darting swifts. The elements were my closest companions. The wind in my hair, the sun on my face, the rain, the stones, the beloved rolling hills of the Volterrana, this was the world of my childhood.

I lived in the Bishop's Palace with Mariotto, a man who I called 'nonno', though he was not my grandfather. He was the steward of a decrepit estate, its walls mottled with lichen, moss and small flowering plants, a palace which had not seen a bishop resident for generations. Each day I swept the courtyard under the tall pointed arches and dusted the painted escutcheons which were set in its walls, the arms of bishops who had never been here. I collected and chopped logs for the kitchen fire; drew water from the courtyard well to nourish our pots of herbs. In the autumn I went down to the woods to gather a harvest of mushrooms and pine kernels. Such duties were easily accomplished and the rest of the time I was free to run the streets with my friends, lanes so steep and labyrinthine that often one could stand below an orchard and above a roof; it must have been thus in the hanging gardens of Babylon. With my friends I played at Etruscans and Romans, or Guelfs and Ghibellines, and we fought with wooden swords. Sometimes we would linger in the half-barrel workshops of the alabaster carvers and in a cloud of soft, choking dust see them create magnificent urns and statues in a white stone which, when polished, became transparent. The artisans were so covered in dust that they appeared as shrouded ghosts chipping their own funerary monuments in whitened sepulchres.

Sometimes we would gather lower in the town, on the piazza before the Palazzo della Signoria, which was the first town hall to have been built in all Tuscany. There we would look out for strangers, merchants arriving from Pisa or Siena, and taunt them (sea-pissers! wolf-sucklers!), but the Florentines we dared not insult. Instead we mobbed them, trying to earn a few soldi by looking after their horses.

This was my life in winter and spring, that of an orphan who lived in a palace, but each June, around Saint John's Day, when the view from the walls was of a limitless terrain of poppies and cornflowers, my relations would arrive from Rome to spend the summer in the cool hills. They came in a line as long as a merchant's train, bringing their furniture, their horses, servants and slaves with them. Then I became a Maffei.

They had a fine tower house below the acropolis, close to those of the Inghirami, Minucci and other families of the town who were once noble but had long since relinquished their titles (for in a republic it is the merchant, the banker and the guild master who has power, and so the nobles had turned to trade). The Maffei had Florentine sympathies, as did their neighbours, and when they entered the main piazza from the acropolis lane, they represented the rich and governing element of Volterra, as opposed to the artisans who entered by the Street of the Prisoners, and the poor people who came in from the boroughs by the narrow alley on the opposite side of the square.

My earliest memories are vague; as a newborn baby I was put out to a wet nurse, the wife of a farm-worker near San Andrea, and stayed with her longer than the usual two years, so my first recollections are of an aloof cat, arrogant cockerels, grubbing pigs (killed each winter and screaming as they died) and a patient cow; of wild asparagus, ripening olives and corn; of curing hams, dripping cheeses and bread soup; of a soft woman who I will always confuse in my mind with images of Our Lady. When I returned to the city, it was as the 'grandson' of the Bishop's steward – Mariotto was my nurse's father – and as the orphaned son of the youngest brother of Ser Gherardo dei Maffei.

In the summer, therefore, I had to comb my hair, be dutiful in the Bishop's Palace, to go quietly to scripture classes and await the annual summons to dine at the fine tower house. There I would sit at the long table amongst an extensive family: Ser Gherardo and his wife Mona Lucia, a woman as porcelain as a Della Robbia figure, his brother Roberto and his wife, and a multitude of sons and daughters who were my cousins. We would eat fine food beautifully presented and drink the best wines. I would gaze in wonder at the friezes and painted arches of their home, and miss the lizards of my own.

Ser Gherardo had four sons. The eldest, ten years my senior, was Antonio. With black hair falling straight to his shoulders, modelled cheeks, pointed chin and watchful eyes, he was without doubt an Etruscan. A kind youth, he was well-known for acts of mercy, such as slipping coins into the baskets of old women when they were not looking. Such acts worried his father, who thought that Antonio might, like Saint Francis, give away all the land and possessions that he, Ser Gherardo, had struggled so hard to acquire.

Raffaello, the second brother, was somewhat fairer, with hair the colour of the pine forest floor, the same as mine. He was studious and had to be torn from his books to dine. While he and Antonio seemed grown up and remote, Mario was at that age when a boy can become insufferable and is best avoided. I might have turned to the youngest, Gianbattista, for friendship, but he was so sickly that he required all attention and could give none. Therefore it seemed that I looked in upon my relations as a leper peeps in through a squint in the church to a congregation which he may never join.

My uncle was a lawyer and apostolic secretary who had been favoured by Pope Pius with many ambassadorial duties to Florence. A man of such learning, he was therefore naturally interested in my education, and I would tell him how I progressed well in Latin and badly in arithmetic under the tutelage of the local priest. My aunt Lucia was more concerned about my soul (she was of the unwavering opinion that I needed much more help in this respect than most) and I would speak knowledgeably of the life and passion of Our Lord, voluble with information I had gleaned almost entirely from Mariotto's commentary on the wall paintings to be found in chapels throughout the city. Apart from these sharp inquisitions, Mona Lucia spoke to me not at all.

I was glad when the supper was finished, when I could escape to being myself again and no longer have to play the role of the grateful beggar. I would leave the Palazzo Maffei with an armful of opulent but cast-off clothes, mostly Gianbattista's, which I would store in a chest, not to be required for another year. Uncle Gherardo would accompany me alone to the street and there present me with a golden florin – a single coin sufficiently valuable to provide for all my needs in the coming year – and then he would call upon San Lino to protect me and seem most moved, in a way that I could not understand.

My cousins spent the summer hunting in the forests of the Volterrana, training falcons, perfecting their riding, practising archery and sword play. I swept the Bishop's courtyard of pigeon droppings and made oblations to the old gods of the acropolis, asking them to speed the time to harvest when I could be free of the Maffei and not have to comb my hair.

It was amongst the grassed-over rubble of the temple that Antonio found me one day, and astounded me by saying, 'I envy you.' I was about six years old and had no answer to this. The westering sun stretched our shadows to the length of pine trunks, but Antonio's was twice as long as mine. I stood abashed at his side but then began cautiously to imitate his movements as he transformed his shadow into a variety of shapes, of gods and demons, angels and beasts. At last, as the sun disappeared and the colour drained from the terracotta roofs, as the swifts rose to renew their battles with each other, and the bells on the campanile next to the Cathedral below us rang the hour of Vespers, I turned to him and said, 'Why?'

Antonio's reply was a smile as wistful and enigmatic as that of an ancestor on a funerary casket. He tousled my hair and left me.

On the morning of the following day, as the sun rose over the hills like the ascending Christ and I was laying the dust by sprinkling it with water, Antonio arrived on horseback at the Bishop's Palace and told Mariotto, my grandfather, that it was time for me to learn the true methods of riding (I already knew the untrue methods, which are learnt on the backs of oxen and mules).

That summer Antonio taught me not only how to ride, but how to do so without a saddle; he taught me also the rightful way to fight with swords and how to wrestle to win. I went everywhere with him, stretching my legs to try and match his strides, convinced that being sixteen years of age was an impossible accomplishment of which only Antonio was capable. I think it was this first year of our friendship that he took me to the place where I was not supposed to go.

Our city was built on rock, and also on sand. At the most northerly part of the ridge there had been a landslide which had taken away a section of the Etruscan wall, created an abyss, and left the Camaldolese Abbey stranded on a promontory. It was a long walk from the acropolis to the cliffs, a walk that marked the extent of the ancient boundaries but which, in our time, took us out of our city by a gate in the Christian wall and into the boroughs. Before we left the city, however, we stopped at the monastery of San Francesco, of which Antonio was particularly fond and which he would never pass without entering, for in a chapel within the church was a magnificent cycle of frescoes. I gazed at each wall in turn, and the pointed arches and lunettes – all covered in scenes and figures – but Antonio stood captivated by one scene only, that of the Massacre of the Innocents.

Here, before this vast picture of distraught mothers and dead babies, he pointed out the details to me, of the mother tearing her face with her nails, of the mother who gripped the thrusting sword of a soldier so hard that blood spurted from her hand. To me it was a scene from the Bible, of Herod's iniquity, and my attention was drawn away from the carnage by two women shown hiding in a cave. The bodice of one was open to reveal two full breasts at which her baby suckled. As she reminded me of my nurse, I presumed that her quiet companion – the only woman in the picture without a baby – must be my mother. But Antonio interrupted my thoughts with the startling assertion that this was a picture of the sack of Volterra.

'These gates,' he said, pointing, 'are our gates, through which the soldiers ride.' Volterra had been sacked at least twice in its history, and had suffered many violent upheavals in the politics of power. Sometimes governed by Pisa, sometimes by Siena, the history of the city was a continuous one of a struggle for independence. In these days of my childhood, Volterra was nominally a republic in the territory of Florence, and Florentines held the major offices of Captain of the People and the Lord of the Castles. After a century of rebellion under Florentine rule, my people had at last become content, for Florence itself was a republic, and the Florentine magistrates had the air of protective fathers. Volterra, said Florence, was independent, and as long as we continued to pay tribute to the great city on the Arno, we would be safe to enjoy our freedom. Battles and sackings were of the past. This was a new age where merchants ruled and our working days were governed by trade rather than the whims of castellated lords.

Antonio gazed at the picture of massacre and said, 'I envy you because you are a Volterrano; you live here, you breathe this air in all seasons. For the sake of my education, I have to live in Rome, the city of hypocrisy. As soon as I can, I intend to live here all year as you do, and no longer have to leave this place each autumn blinded by tears.'

As we left the monastery, Antonio paused to give an old beggar a few coins and then – to the beggar's amazement and my horror – he stooped down not only to speak to him but to lay his hand companionably on the filthy rags of the old man's shoulder.

'You do not have to speak to those people,' I said as we continued on our way. 'That is why we have the Confraternita della Misericordia. We give them the alms, and they distribute them.'

In response to this, Antonio bore an expression of such sorrow for mankind that I began to share my uncle's fears, that Antonio would one day walk away with a staff to some isolated, craggy place and pray so feverishly that bloody spots would appear on his hands and feet.

From San Francesco we went down through the boroughs to the place where the ridge had collapsed. Though Antonio might weep at leave-takings, he had no fear. He ran to the gap between the massive boulders of the ancient wall and stood with his feet projecting over the lip of the precipice of sand. I stood back, trying to enjoy the vista of gentle hills, some dotted with sheep that looked like stones placed in mysterious cyphers for the gods to read. Further along, on the bluff of the ridge, was the Camaldolese Abbey, a place of much beauty and tranquility. It stood on a grassy mound which, when swept by anemones, was our first sign that spring had truly arrived. I pretended to gaze at the buildings in admiration but knew too well what was to come, what was expected of me. Everything in me liquefied, my very bones demanded that I remain safely behind the wall and not stand where the wall no longer was; but when you have a cousin ten years your senior, it is imperative not to betray fear. 'Vieni, vieni,' said Antonio gently, beckoning me forward, and against the desire of my palpitating heart, I moved next to him. Below me there was nothing but the drop. I inched my toes over the edge and dared not look down. Antonio raised his arms; I raised mine. To anyone in the eroded valley below, we must have seemed as two crosses on the skyline, one tall, one short. As we stood thus, inviting the elements, the wind came to play with us and larks rose up to greet our appearance in their own elevation. Suddenly Antonio threw back his head and cried to the sky: *'Freedom!'*

'Freedom!', I cried, as an echo.

I did not know then that one word could mean different things, or that what Antonio desired was not the same as the fledgling ache in my own soul.

After that, I began to look forward to summer. Each year Antonio taught me something new and, though I was a poor boy, I acquired the skills of a rich man's son, including playing upon the lute. These were peaceful times, when you could ride in the lowlands and see nothing but carefully tended farms and olive groves, fat hay ricks and plump cattle.

One year Antonio remained behind in Volterra after the family had left for Rome, for he was intent on seeing the harvest. The city was so walled-about and crowded that to leave it by any of the gates was to step into another world, one of space, blue air and green hills. Antonio and I were in the shallow vale beyond the Selci gate, flying his falcon. He was training the bird, a lanner which he loved beyond all things. As we stood watching her circle, ducking as she swooped low over our heads, we began to hear sounds from a lower valley. Drawn by distant music, we called Freccia in and made the long descent to Santa Cristina like two mountain goats who have heard the shepherd's call.

As we went down the hill, the sounds grew, of pipes and singers and drums, of people laughing and the babble of gossip, all amplified by the still air. Soon we could see below the colour of a village festooned for the harvest festival. Even the oxen in the fields had garlands round their horns. I had been to such festivals before, but usually with my grandfather and never with Antonio. He was alight with enthusiasm. The leaves of the chestnut trees and turkey oaks were beginning to turn yellow and red, the corn was cut, the olives picked. Wood smoke curled from the chimney of every farmhouse. Step by step we continued our descent, not only that from the city to the village, but that of the citizen to the peasant, until at last we joined the throng to share their dancing and the new wine.

I do not know where Antonio learned to dance like a contadino, but it came naturally to him, he who had been taught restrained, civilized steps by a dancing master. He joined the circle and drew me in with him. Together we leapt and stamped and hollered in song with the rest, performing a rite that had been celebrated on these hills for thousands of years. We both grew drunk, and the more intoxicated we became, the more love ran in our veins, love for our fellows, for each other, above all, for our country.

I believe it was on this occasion that Antonio met Francesco Caruggi, for I remember toiling back up the hill behind them, two young men in earnest conversation. Feeling neglected, I watched their calf-muscles moving as they walked and wondered how long it would be before I was a man with strong legs and an interest in such conversations, for what they spoke of was alum.

I wanted Antonio to take me to the sea. From our eagle's nest I could often see a sparkling line on the horizon and on a bright day I could even see Corsica. I longed to wade on the shores of the Tyrrhenian sea and to watch the caravels sailing out from

Pisa to unimaginable destinations. Antonio took me instead to Castello del Sasso on the road to the Maremma where a month before a Sienese with a divining rod had discovered that substance for which men had searched for hundreds of years. We found the cave where the precious stone was guarded by Florentine soldiers. They had been hired by the company of merchants who had leased the site from the city. Although we were not allowed in, the captain opened a pouch delicately and showed us one white crystal; it did not look precious, but when ground in a mortar, then it promised riches, for alum is the mineral vital to the dyeing of cloth.

The power and wealth of Florence rests entirely on the cloth trade. Importing the finest English wool, it is Florentine weavers and dyers who turn a natural wonder into something divine; but the dye needs fixing, and that is the property of alum. There was one mine in Italy, at Tolfa, and it belonged to the Pope. Most alum, however, was imported, and its country of origin was Turkey. To the Italians, as to any Christian, this was like having to go to the devil for communion bread.

As Antonio explained all this to me before the mine, I understood for the first time the excitement which had greeted the announcement of its discovery. All the bells in the city had rung, drawing the people into the piazza before the town hall where the Gonfaloniere, resplendent in heraldic colours, declared portentously that alum had been found in the Volterrana. Naturally Siena made an immediate claim on that which one of its own citizens had discovered, but the Signoria of Volterra revoked it. This alum was a rock of our soil; it was ours. Henceforth, Volterra would be rich. And, said men such as Francesco Caruggi, there will be no further need to pay tribute to Florence: Florence can now begin paying tribute to us.

This year of 1470 was marked by another event, that of the inauguration of a new Bishop of Volterra: Antonio degli Agli of Florence. A Mass was sung in his honour at the Cathedral and we looked for a space in the courtyard where we might embed his escutcheon. Other than that, I gave him little thought, though there was some gossip about his being less than orthodox. Some even said he was a magician, and our housekeeper was adamant that he had six fingers on each hand as a sign of his satanic origins.

'I have heard that he reads Plato,' said my grandfather, and at this the others gasped and rapidly crossed themselves, leaving me to associate the unfamiliar name of a Greek philosopher with rank heresy.

It was about this time that I was caught trying to push a boulder from the Etruscan wall over the cliffs, wanting to see it crash into the abyss. A white-robed monk on his way from town to the Camaldolese Abbey grasped me by the collar of my jerkin and marched me to the Abbot. I expected a lashing, a form of punishment I was now practised at bearing with fortitude, but the Abbot was a good man who loved children, even when they reached the age of twelve.

My punishment was to watch one of his monks in the scriptorium writing out an alphabet, and then to write one out myself. It was my first experience of the feel of a nib on parchment, of quill on skin, and it gave a satisfaction that no amount of plummeting boulders could ever give. The next day I returned to confess having stolen a melon, in the hope of more punishment. This was duly given; thereafter, and on the understanding that I could have as much punishment as I desired providing I committed no more crimes, I was allowed to visit the scriptorium whenever I liked. Soon I became adept at cutting nibs and mixing ink, at giving a good surface to parchment with liberal dustings of pounce, and of drawing large letters in the old style, with straight lines as fat as tree trunks, and angled lines as slender as blades of grass. The Abbey, then, became a place of refuge as the clouds began to gather over the town, and the weather of its history darkened once more.

TWO

A YEAR later Francesco della Rovere was inaugurated as Pope Sixtus the Fourth. I waited impatiently for my family to come from Rome to hear at first hand about the Holy Father and the celebrations, for by this time both Antonio and Raffaello had secured places in the Vatican as secretaries. They would have been there when kings and princes gathered for the Jubilee, when all the leading families converged on Rome: Sforza of Milan, Bentivoglio of Bologna, Malatesta of Rimini, Montefeltre of Urbino, Gonzaga of Mantua and the Medici of Florence.

Take any point on our walls and you can see castles. On each hilltop stands the walled keep of a distant age; when I heard tales of Lorenzo de' Medici, I imagined him living in such a castle and enjoying the adventures of Arthur or Roland, those heroes of fireside tales. He had come to power only recently in Florence, succeeding his father who, after a short life crippled by gout, had died prematurely. Tales of this young man (or glorious knight, in my imagination) came to us with the merchants bringing spices, rich cloth and paper from the distant city on the plain; tales of his wedding and the feast which had lasted a week, of his courage when he had saved his father from an ambush laid by rivals for power, of his generosity, benevolence and love of poetry. The story of his joust, which he had won against competitors drawn from all over Christendom, I heard directly from Antonio who had been there, acting as squire to a knight of Rome. Thus in my fancy Lorenzo de' Medici sometimes approached over the hills, dressed in gold brocade, his white horse draped in crimson, to enter our city, very soon afterwards to notice me and engage me at once as his squire. Then together we rode through the forests, clearing them of wolves, wild boar and dragons. I was the lustiest squire ever to serve a knight, and my fame grew with my lord's. Thus I dreamed, standing on the walls at sunset, watching the last rays turn stone castles to gold.

When the family at last arrived, late that year, it was several weeks before the invitation came to dine. Meanwhile I had seen Antonio often in the streets and piazze, but he was always engaged in serious debate with other young men and appeared not to notice me. These men were not from our ward but that of the artisans and they were followers of Francesco Caruggi, who had become the spokesman for those who believed that any riches to be had from the alum mine would not reach the pockets of the common people of the city. Once as I watched from my tower above the Selci gate, I saw these men ride out of the city, Antonio with them, on the road to the Maremma. They rode bareback, with bare legs, and their hair, heavy and shining with oil, was combed behind their ears to fall straight down their backs. Later there came reports of fighting at the alum mine, that a soldier employed by the company of merchants had been killed and another maimed; an attack made, it was said, 'by wild Etruscans'. The Florentine guard, already uneasy at spending night duties in a land of pagan tombs, had been sufficiently frightened to run off. The mine was now in the possession of a Volterrani militia.

The Captain of the People addressed us on the main square: there was to be no fighting and no killing. His own soldiers would ensure peace at the mine. The age of barbarity had passed and in our own civilized times all disputes were to be resolved by negotiation. The Volterrani went away to sharpen their knives and strengthen the militia.

When at last my invitation arrived, I ran to the Palazzo Maffei dressed superbly in Gianbattista's old clothes, longing to tell my uncle that I had mastered the art of writing and that I had determined to become a scribe. I realised that this meant I must also become a monk, but it was a detail and not one I was allowing to interfere with my dreams. Besides, becoming a monk was perhaps all I could hope for as I was not willing to follow my grandfather as steward of an empty house. But then I also knew, for I had been told so by the Abbot, that if one becomes a monk you have no right to decide what work you will do. This too was but a nagging detail: God and San Lino would somehow arrange it so that I could grow up, marry, father sons and make a good living by the skill of my hands. I had heard, after all, that these days there were scribes who were not monks.

That summer night the family was even less aware of me than usual. Antonio took the trouble to welcome me, grasping my hand in the ancient Etruscan manner, but then at once he returned to the conversation dominating the table, which was about the alum mine. Ser Gherardo was adamant: the Volterrani should cease their rebellious activities and accept what had happened, that their governors had leased the mine to a company of merchants, and that this was the only feasible solution. His brother Roberto objected, saying that the company, ostensibly formed of merchants from various city states, was in fact under the control of Lorenzo de' Medici; so, he said, was it not rather suspicious that the man who had been chosen to arbitrate between the company and the people was Lorenzo himself? Antonio agreed and stated forcibly that the wolf was eating the dog's food, that by the duplicity of the governors, who were Florentines, what belonged to the people was being passed from the commune to private hands. 'Francesco Caruggi says ... '

'Francesco Caruggi, Francesco Caruggi,' snapped my uncle. 'Who is he? An alabaster carver! I do not want my sons forming their opinions from those of artisans. Think for yourself, Antonio.'

Antonio darkened with anger. 'All rich men think for themselves; it takes an artisan to think for others. Caruggi says – '

'Enough!' Ser Gherardo banged his hand so hard on the table that the fine silver jumped and the glass tinkled. My aunt protested but too late, for by now everyone was talking at the same time, everyone except Raffaello. He sat there listening and looking troubled. I plucked on his sleeve to gain his attention and ask him which side he took.

'History shows that the Volterrani are in the right; it also shows that those with just cause are unlikely to obtain justice. In the end you must choose what you value most: life or freedom. I have found no record of a time or culture when men have enjoyed both, except perhaps the Greek civilisation, and even then only rarely.'

I had a burning question: 'Is Lorenzo de' Medici our enemy?'

'He is our ruler. If we obey him, he will be our friend. I truly believe he wants the best in this situation, but the Volterrani are making things increasingly difficult. Do not follow this man Caruggi, Tommaso. He is a trouble maker. There is far more happening here than a few scratchings of rock in a cave, however precious. Take heed.' Then he rose from his chair, begged to be excused – a request which went unheard amidst the now clamorous argument – and returned to his study.

This was the last summer of my boyhood, and I did not spend it with Antonio. I saw him often, always with friends from the artisan quarter, dressed simply and looking so grim-faced that I dared not approach him. I longed to reach out to him, to put a bridle in his hands, a sword or a bow; to kick a ball towards him, or to tread on his feet in readiness for a bout of wrestling – by any of these means to draw out from this hardening carapace his living and beautiful self – but he had gone from me.

That year he remained in the city for the winter and on one bright day he called for me at the Bishop's Palace, standing there like a prince of Etruria with Freccia on his wrist. There was no explanation for this reversion to normal, nor did it last for more than one day; but for that day the sun shone and we went out of the Selci gate to fly his bird.

Far below on the road from Florence we saw a party of riders making its way slowly up to the city. For a moment my heart stopped, but even at this distance I could see that it included no knight on a caparisoned horse, only a group of men as black as crows, led by one riding on a mule.

'Who is that?' I asked.

Antonio, launching his bird, spared the party but one glance and shrugged. 'Who knows? It could be the Bishop of Volterra.'

I laughed, for this was a familiar joke made about any unexpected visitor. 'For a moment I thought it might be Lorenzo,' I said.

'What, coming in person to deliver his fair and just decision?'

'You wait and see,' I muttered under my breath.

'Tell me something,' Antonio uncoiled the rope of the lure and attached a dead mouse to its end, 'given the choice between fabulous riches and being just, which would you choose?' With a piercing whistle to his bird, he began to swing the meat in wide circles.

'Justice of course,' I declared. Antonio looked at me scornfully.

'Anyway,' I said, ducking as Freccia flew so close over my head that I nearly received a tonsure, 'that is not the choice. The mine is not Lorenzo's, it belongs to the merchants.'

'It belongs to Volterra!'

'And Volterra rents it to the merchants.'

Antonio snatched the meat away before his bird's talons could close on it, sending her off in another circle. 'The rent is too low. And the merchants are either Florentines or would-be Florentines, such as that lump of dung, Benedetto Inghirami.'

This man was a neighbour and friend of the Maffei who, I presumed, were still themselves supporters of Florence and of the Medici party.

'Anyone can see that the merchants are but pawns in a game being played by someone else,' Antonio continued, again snatching the mouse from Freccia. I wondered why the bird suffered all this frustration and did not fly at her master and rip out his eyes.

'There is something you do not know, Tommaso. When Lorenzo de' Medici was in Rome for the Jubilee ... '

So Lorenzo had been there! I turned on Antonio then, and in a rush demanded: how did he look? what did he wear? what was said?

'He looks like a man of twenty-three, which is what he is, and he wears clothes.'

I felt pained by my cousin's cynicism. It was Antonio, after all, who had fed my dreams with tales of the Medici knight. He it was who had given me the blue and silver ribbon which I wore constantly, tied above my elbow. What had happened to change his mind, and to change him? Must I now alter my colours to suit? I was at the age, however, when it is important to find one's own ground and be loyal to one man. I decided to remain true to the idea that Lorenzo was a brave hero with a good heart. Antonio's recently adopted convictions were robbing him of his grace and beauty; if for that reason only, I hesitated to follow him into a hatred of the Medici.

'What is important,' he said, 'is what Lorenzo was given. Our Holy Father, continuing in the execrable tradition of the Holy See, and knowing Lorenzo to be the richest banker and therefore probably the most powerful man in all Christendom, larded him with gifts. Apart from the usual trinkets, he renewed the contract for the Medici to remain bankers to the Curia and gave Lorenzo the agency for the only other alum mine in Italy. This is the man who our Signoria has asked to arbitrate, the man with the exclusive possession.'

The chivalrous dream can withstand such assaults. 'You wait and see,' I said. 'Just wait and see.'

'Believe me, if, when the herald arrives, he announces that Lorenzo de' Medici has decided in favour of the people, I will be more delighted to be proved wrong than you will ever understand. Meanwhile I shall continue to entertain healthy doubt.' He lured the bird in, allowing her to catch the mouse.

I willed that the approaching party would indeed be the one for which we had already waited a month, that of the man bearing Lorenzo's decision, but when at last they came clearly into view, my spirits plunged like a stooping bird. It was a group of priests. I kicked at tufts of grass, head lowered. The bells on Freccia's jesses tinkled. She sounded as innocent as a lamb, but her eye was wolfish until, the hood drawn over her, she sat on Antonio's wrist in a proud plume of feathers, bobbing harmlessly.

'So,' he said, turning to leave, 'the sun is going down and the annunciating angel of justice has once again failed to arrive.' As if this in itself was enough to prove the worthlessness of Lorenzo de' Medici, he strode off confidently towards the city gate, his long shadow running away in the direction of Florence. Dawdling behind him, I reached the gate just ahead of the priests. They all looked alike except for one, and he was only different in that he rode on a mule. All of them were grey-haired old men and I took scant notice of them, not knowing then that there was something in the world more important than Lorenzo de' Medici, more important even than alum, and that here was its courier.

The Bishop's Palace was a vacant, neglected place tended by a skeleton retinue: the steward, the housekeeper, the cook, the groom, one maid, two scullions and myself. We occupied the kitchen and the servants' quarters while the main rooms of the place were under dustsheets and inhabited by beetles and the occasional scorpion. Mariotto, my grandfather, issued orders as if lord of a domain which had substance and reality, but the cook made salami, the housekeeper made cheeses, the groom looked after one mule and a milch cow, and in the winter we told stories at the hearth as any peasant family.

In those drear months, when the rest of the world was obscured by cloud, I would play with my friends in any one of the six dens beneath the dustsheets – Florence, Milan, Naples, Rome, Venice and Volterra – or in the two underground passages and five secret routes which I had to the roof. I was the best condottiere in all Italy, laying waste to whole cities without opposition, and in between times was the faithful squire of Lorenzo de' Medici. As for any friend who dared question the virtue of the Medici, he was soon overcome and left bound and gagged somewhere, not to be released until a concerned parent came to see my grandfather.

This wilderness was the episcopal seat of Volterra, a city which had once been ruled by bishops. In our simoniacal days, however, no one expected a bishop even to visit his see let alone dwell in it. Bishops lived in Rome or Florence or on their estates in the country. And if, by some miracle, a bishop were to arrive, then surely one might expect not only advance warning, but also the pomp and spectacle of a glorious entourage. Thus, even as I mounted the rocky path within the gate which led up to the palace, and found that the riders were coming the same way, I still did not guess. Only when I entered the courtyard to be greeted by Mariotto, and saw my grandfather's smile transform into an expression of horror, did I turn round and know that behind me, entering through the gate of his palace on a mule, was Monsignore Antonio degli Agli.

There had been much discussion about this man by the household as we gathered by the fire during the cold nights. Once a favourite of the previous Pope, he had annoyed His Holiness by taking up residence at his see of Raugia. I was too young to know the subtleties of human nature, or why a man doing his rightful duty should annoy the Bishop of Rome. Mariotto tried to explain to me that good deeds irritate bad people, but I still could not grasp it. With the simple logic of a boy, I asked my elders why, if the Bishop had lived at Raugia, might he not also live at Volterra? But this was greeted with derision, and it was explained to me that, so far as the rest of the world was concerned, being granted any office related to Volterra was a form of punishment. Loving my land as I loved my very self, this was a subtlety I had no hope of understanding.

'Why?' I demanded.

'Because to great cities such as Florence, Volterra is small and very far away, lost in the clouds.'

Now here was the old man with silver hair who had been punished with the bishopric of Volterra, resting his hand for a moment on my head. I found myself staring into a pair of lapis eyes. Blue eyes were a rarity in my world and this mild gaze I took as a scrutiny. The moment passed, the courtyard filled with a consternation of servants, the air became palpable with guilty consciences – of those who had not swept under beds or been to confession – and I withdrew back through the gate, to run and tell Antonio what had happened.

As I ran down the rock of our foundation, knowing the way too well to be concerned by the gathering dark, I collided with another party entering the Selci gate, this one as glorious as the last one should have been. Knights there were a-plenty, or at least, men-at-arms, and in their midst and under the banners of the lily, the herald of Florence. With a shout I leapt out in front of them, startling the lead horses, and ran ahead like a capering hare, down the lanes to the piazza, shouting all the way, '*Palle*! *Palle*! *Palle*! Lorenzo for the People!' I drew out the inhabitants of our ward with my yells; to summon the rest of the city I fell on the dozing bell-keeper of the Palazzo della Signoria, climbed upon his knees and hung on his rope like a monkey. The great bell of the republic rose, turned over and fell, once, twice, three times. Pigeons left the piazza in an irritable flutter.

The people thronged to the piazza, dressed in furs and heavy woollen cloaks against the cold night air. Leaving the campanile,

I went into the piazza on the eastern side, to stand amongst the people of my ward and represent the Maffei. The square was so surrounded by the flat faces of towers and palazzi that any noise caught by the almost continuous walls was sent this way and that like a tossed ball. Now the noise became deafening, the shouts of the Mediceans colliding in the air with those of the artisans. The swifts left the city in a squeal of protest.

In front of the Palazzo della Signoria was a loggia, the platform of which was reached by a flight of steps. These the herald mounted while officers ran round the piazza, hurriedly illuminating it by setting flaming torches in the sconces.

Drawn by this man who represented Lorenzo de' Medici, I edged my way to the front of the crowd, but I came too close: reality, like too much vinegar, swamped the fine oil of my dreams. The herald's powder-blue hose were saddle grimed; he had stubble on his chin; he had arrogant eyes, the kind of arrogance which hides fear.

He began to speak, coughed and had to start again. The men shouted for him to speak up, but he could not. This was not how I had foreseen things, and I began to be glad that Antonio was not beside me.

The artisans demanded that he come to the point, but he had no point to come to. Where was the lofty speech I had anticipated? Where was the firm, strong voice of Lorenzo de' Medici in these vague, ambivalent words? The herald rambled at length over the history of the dispute.

'Prattle!' shouted Francesco Caruggi. 'Come to the point and tell us the truth!'

The herald's voice faltered.

'What are you saying?'

'According to the law ... ' the wretched herald continued.

'Is Lorenzo for us or for the merchants? What is the answer?'

The herald's voice snapped like a lute string. He stuttered out the vital sentence. Voices thundered for him to repeat himself and to speak up, because he had not been heard.

But I had heard what he said. Amid the rising din I screamed like a stuck pig and a woman beside me gathered me up, thinking I had been trodden on.

It was the Gonfaloniere who finally delivered the message to the people: the alum mine must be returned to the company of merchants, for Lorenzo had not yet reached a decision. He needed more time to consider the matter. Both he and the herald ducked as a hail of soft missiles and hard words rained on them and the other dignitaries. Stinking brown splotches ruined heraldic jackets and signorial gowns. Robbed of all spirit, I could not move but stood there in a rain of animal excrement.

Then the artisans seethed triumphantly across the square to confront the Mediceans with the truth about their man, and I came face to face with Antonio. Gazing at me darkly, he took hold of my arm and pulled from it the blue and silver colours of the Medici party.

THREE

English houses are oppressive. Every time I rise from my chair, my cap picks up cobwebs from the heavy oak beams. These houses, with their low ceilings, small windows, uneven floors and narrow, crooked stairways, are perfect for children, dwarves, or nesting birds. For a scholar they bring on melancholy.

The view from the upstairs window is over watermeadows, flat and bleak. Only the squat osiers along the river bank mark where the river flows in the sheet of water. There is no horizon to mark where the grey sky meets the grey land and it rains all the time.

The English splash down the muddy streets of Oxford on wooden pattens, shrinking within their oilskins, but when they come into a neighbour's house, they throw off their cowls and reveal shiny red faces full of good humour. 'What weather, neighbour! Would that we were ducks.' And their wives hold you by your shoulders and kiss you, once on each cheek. What a fashion! Yet they remain demure. The men may kiss you too, on occasion. I had heard about the English and their labial habits, but I did not believe it until my own cheeks were thus assaulted.

All foreigners laugh at the English. I remember how we met, Desiderio: me catching your eye as I was being kissed, and seeing your face fill with mirth at my expression. Then you caught me by the shoulders and said, 'Will you not kiss me, too?'

I reminded you frostily that you were talking to an Italian.

'Ah, but when in England ... ' you said, and planted your thin lips on my cheek.

It is, I agree, a custom to be preferred to their beer. Red faces, chapped skin, streaky skies, silver rain, I think that here I have travelled as far from Italy as a man can go without leaving Christendom.

FOLLOWING the herald's announcement, artisans surged forward to take the Palazzo della Signoria, and the shouts of the Volterrani became screams. The artisans, having no doubt about the truth behind Lorenzo's ambivalence, interpreted the message as the loss of their cause. It was time to act. At once the doors to the Palazzo were bolted and guards leaned out of windows with crossbows, threatening to shoot if the crowd did not disperse. When the people retreated grumbling to the far side of the square, they were left by their governors to kill each other, if they so chose.

The surge had parted me from Antonio and, left without any loyalties, I was buffeted by confusion. The way back to the acropolis was blocked by two opposing factions shouting at each other, with such lust that I dared not go near, so I determined to find shelter closer to hand.

Our town hall was built back-to-back against the Cathedral and it was to the church that I resorted, entering by a door which opened into one of the transepts. With the exception of various full-sized figures carved in wood, the place was empty; it seemed extraordinarily peaceful compared to what was happening outside. Still not feeling safe enough, I crossed to the opposite transept and a little chapel which had a door so low that most people knew nothing of its existence. I passed beneath the painted wooden statues of the scene of the Deposition of Christ and, being a lost soul without hope of salvation, looked not upon the face of Our Lord, but upon the pair of pliers held by the carpenter who removed the nails from His feet, wondering at the sublimity of this detail. Once inside the chapel, I closed the door behind me and sat against it; oblivious to the message of the scenes of the Passion painted on the walls, I hugged my knees and thought about Lorenzo de' Medici. I went over the herald's words, trying to find something positive in them – perhaps, after all, Lorenzo did need more time – but each such thought was greeted by the acid laugh of a new Tommaso, one who had come to meet me on the threshold of adulthood. Was I then to grow cynical, as Antonio? If so, if henceforth I was to be grim-faced and unable to find joy in simple things, at least I would regain my cousin's good opinion and have him as a companion once more. Thinking thus, I slept a little.

I was woken by a noise in the church, of the sounds of a person moving within. About what business? Feeling suddenly trapped in the little chapel, I opened the door a crack but could see no one. My only way out was the way I had come in, and I tip-toed towards the altar and the opposite transept. Then I saw him, on his knees in prayer before the altar candles.

I recognised him at once, from the fleeting glimpse I had had at the Palazzo. It was rude to stare but I could not help it: he was, after all, the first bishop I had ever seen. And bishops being rare and hazy figures in my dreams, I had never imagined seeing one in prayer.

Raising his head and seeing me, he beckoned. I crossed to him, to his outstretched hand.

'Help me up, young man. My old knees – they creak. I cannot bear it when they creak.' He looked old and yet not old. His face was traced with lines like dry, creased silk but his hair was as fine as a baby's. Though his eyes were blue they had that same lustrous light which had once shone in Antonio's.

'You only have five fingers,' I observed idiotically as I helped him up.

'Strange,' he said, 'I thought I had ten.'

I laughed. 'I mean on each hand.'

'How many should I have?'

'Six, if it is true what they say, that you are a magician.'

I already knew that it was not true: to look in those kind eyes was to see God and not the devil.

He grew severe and said firmly, 'Do you know who I am?'

'The Bishop of Volterra?'

'And do you accuse me, one of the line of Peter, of black arts? Is that what the Volterrani expect of me?'

'We have never had a bishop here before.'

'Not recently, perhaps, but do not forget your patron San Lino. Made a bishop by Saint Peter himself, he brought the Faith to this city, making Volterra one of the earliest centres of Christianity. How could I not follow in the footsteps of such an illustrious saint? The shepherd must always be with his flock, most especially when it is in trouble. Lorenzo warned me there was ... oh, now, what is the matter?'

To our mutual consternation, the sound of Lorenzo's name had brought tears spilling from my eyes. To meet at this moment someone who actually knew my erstwhile hero was an irony too sharp to bear. The Bishop embraced me and the warmth of the gesture dissolved me in a flood of grief. I had picked lightly on Lorenzo as my hero, but what had begun as a whim had become ingrained. For the past hour I had been as a man sitting stunned on the battlefield gazing at the arrow protruding from him, feeling nothing until someone came and tried to pull it out. In the warm, dark, protective embrace of those arms, I thrashed as if I would cry myself to death. The generous folds of his woollen gown were soft and fragrant, but beneath the cloth, against his chest, was something metallic and hot. It hurt my ear as he pressed me to him, and that local pain dredged me up from the deep.

He asked, as he had been asking all along, what the matter was, but how could I explain that I had been robbed of a dream? The Bishop, however, guessed the cause of my distress.

'You were expecting Lorenzo to pronounce in favour of the people?'

'Yes.'

'How old are you my son?'

'Twelve.'

'How simple, to be twelve, when there are good men and bad men, and you know one from the other by the plume on his helm. Ah, to be twelve! For adults, nothing is quite what it seems, especially in the world of diplomacy. There is far more happening here than is apparent. Lorenzo, believe me, meant what he said: he needs more time.'

Hope rose like a faint sun in winter.

'He is only twenty-three, though I suppose that seems old to you, but to me, well ... This callow youth has had the city of Florence thrust on him, a responsibility he would rather not have. Left to himself he would rather be out serenading the ladies.'

I wrinkled my nose in disgust.

'Or competing in tourneys,' added the Bishop hurriedly.

'Instead he has an insurrection on his hands. He must somehow, with no experience to guide him, resolve this dispute. He consults every possible councillor. Do you wonder that he has not reached a decision yet? I could not solve this one myself very easily, and I am a wise old man.'

I disengaged myself, no longer needing his embrace. His eyebrows fascinated me. Extraordinarily mobile, they rose and fell over eyes twinkling in gentle self-mockery.

'Are you wise?' I asked.

'Wisdom comes with age, they say, and I am certainly old.'

'So Lorenzo really does want the mine to go to the people?'

'What Lorenzo wants is justice. Justice may not be the name of what you want, young man.'

'But it is our mine and the merchants are already fat and rich. Why should they become more fat and more rich? It is not fair!' I was surprised to hear myself repeat Antonio's arguments.

'The truth is that your mine was rented out to the merchants by your Signoria for two very good reasons. One, because you do not have the machinery necessary to extract the alum and you are too poor to raise the cost of it. Two, because alum is so valuable that every wolf in the land will be after it and you will need an army to protect yourselves, and you cannot afford that either. Now surely the only solution is to rent the mine to those who can afford such things?'

'And the rich become even more wealthy.'

'And pay back the city through rent.'

'The rent is not high enough. And anyway, the merchants are puppets of the Medici, who want exclusive possession.'

'What ideas! Are they your own?'

'It is what everybody is saying,' I replied evasively.

'The artisans perhaps.'

I frowned, confused. The Mediceans wanted Lorenzo to vote for the merchants. The artisans wanted the mine to go to the people. I wanted the mine to go to the people, and I wanted Lorenzo de' Medici to say so. Which made me a particoloured politician, halved and quartered by conflicting opinions. Suddenly, where all had been clear, I was muddled. I gazed confounded at the Bishop. He smiled and held my face in his hands.

'If Lorenzo was called upon to arbitrate, why should you not think he might arbitrate on behalf of the people? It is an assumption based on a natural faith in the goodness of human nature. Alas, boy, reason and logic are not often seen to rule in this world. Trouble is being stirred up here. Those who most loudly claim the mine for the people are not themselves moved by thoughts of the general good. What they want is trouble with Florence. Stay young, child, and simple.'

He asked me my name.

'Tommaso dei Maffei.'

'Maffei? A fine family. Surely your palazzo is near here? I shall walk home with you; together we may pass through this sea of unreason in safety.'

We left the Cathedral, however, to find the streets quiet and the pigeons roosting peacefully. As we walked up the hill, I explained about not living in the Palazzo Maffei but in the Bishop's own household. We talked as we went of domestic affairs, for the Bishop needed informing of everything, of the relation of the housekeeper to the cook, and of me to the steward, of what street led to which lane, of market day and local festival days, of the best streams for fishing and where to find porcini mushrooms in the woods. Full of self-importance in this new role as guide, I hoped at least one of my friends might see me as I led the Bishop of Volterra through the city, but the streets were deserted. All shutters were closed, all doors barred and locked. The sudden dart of a cat upon a mouse made me jump.

Spontaneously, we both reached out to take the other's hand. Mine was proffered in fear, the bishop's in faith. As I grasped his hand there flowed from him to me a powerful sense of strength and permanence. It was as if I had been bobbing, one helpless reed amongst many on the river of life, and then a hand reached out and drew me to the bank. I thought I was taking the Bishop back home, but he was taking me, back to that place, more certain, more sound, than any construction of stone and mortar. I was merely his guide to Volterra; he was mine to Philosophy.

FOUR

Desiderio, if now I dwell on fine memories of a great man, rather than racing on with my story, it is for two reasons. One is that I believe what I have to say on the matter of true education will encourage you in your work. The other is that it is a balm to my poor spirit to remember my beloved friend. Ah! even as I write this I see at once what has escaped me up to now: in you my Bishop lives on. What is there in common between one old Italian bishop, long dead, and a Dutch monk in the prime of his life? Love. The love I held for him is the love I hold for you. Never fear the loss of a friend, Desiderio, for what is loved in one friend may be found in another. Is that a harsh philosophy? Not when you know, as you do know, what it is that is loved, and who the lover. You, the priest of unity, will understand what I am saying.

UNDER the patronage of my uncle Gherardo and since the age of seven, I had attended the school founded by the Commune to teach boys mercantile practice and the laws of commerce, how to weigh things, calculate exchanges in money, test coins for their value and keep accounts.

'Now we have reading, writing and abacus,' the schoolmaster used to say. 'But the greatest of these is the abacus.' And the beads on the frame clicked off the long hours of our mornings, a desultory clicking of boys calculating set problems, real problems, everyday problems. 'When you are adept in the abacus,' said the master, 'you will be adept in life itself, for no man will get the better of you in the market place, no Jew will have you in his usurious grasp, no Turk will sell you brass for gold. You will be wise men.'

One evening in his first week with us, the Bishop summoned me to his study. 'I am informed that you often play truant from school,' he said. Though he looked fierce, he did not frighten me. When love is real, its displeasure can be met with an open, honest heart. I told him that going to school was a waste of time, for I could not grasp any of the principles.

'You are intelligent enough.'

'No I am not. I am stupid.'

'Who tells you so?'

'The schoolmaster.'

'Does he indeed? Such words condemn the speaker. What is he like? No, let me guess. He seems a clever man, full of scholarly graces, but his lessons have as much vigour as yesterday's soup, his facts are gristle, his principles over-boiled cabbage, his rhetoric a separated grease floating on the top.'

I laughed gleefully at this accurate summation.

'The definition of a fool is a man who thinks he knows when he does not know.'

'But he does know things!' I said. I had spent too many years being baffled by arithmetic to believe my tutor was an ignorant man. I ran through the junk of broken facts that had been stored uselessly in my memory. 'For instance,' I said, 'he knows how to divide circles into equal parts.'

'So? When have you ever had need of such knowledge?'

'Never!' I yelped with relief. 'I asked him once. I said, "Master, why are we learning this?" He birched me and said that it was to be able to divide apples fairly between ourselves.'

'Fruit *pi*,' said the Bishop.

'What?'

'*Pi*. It is the name of Euclid's formula for dividing circles.'

With the mention of this name, his tone became reverent and he went on to explain that geometry, though of some practical use, was a subtle thing of a realm beyond our physical world. A man who taught its applications but not its principles was robbing it of its meaning and its richness. 'No wonder you are bored,' he said finally. 'Do you sometimes wish you could escape this world?'

'Yes, sometimes, especially during the winter.'

'Where would you wish to go?'

All I could think of was the sea, but I said cautiously, 'Heaven?'

'What will you find there? What is your notion of heaven?'

Vague images arose of an unknown mother, of a woman for whom I had no face, only to be replaced by more solid images of my Virgin Mary nurse and painted angels playing musical instruments. These in turn were swept aside by recollections of all my wrong-doings. It is difficult to imagine a place in which you have no right to be; far easier to imagine the other place.

The Bishop laughed gently. 'The ineffable does not easily lend itself to description,' he said. 'Let us not tax ourselves further with theology, but consider geometry. If you wish to escape this world, the realm of number is a good route.'

This to a young Volterrano was confounding. Out of respect I was prepared to take it on faith, but the Bishop preferred being understood to being believed.

'According to Plato ... ' he began.

My eyes started from my head. '*Plato?*' I dared only whisper the name synonymous with heresy.

'You have heard of Plato then?' he asked, surprised.

I nodded dumbly.

'The wisest man who ever lived. Next to Our Lord, of course,' he added, a little hurriedly I thought. 'He knew the virtue of the study of number, which is not to cut up apples or to gauge barrels of grain.'

'No?'

'No. To study number, for the sake of study itself, will lead you to the Divine. Forget heaven. To be honest, I have never met anyone who really wants to go there. The true goal of Man is union of the soul with the Divine, and an understanding of number can lead us to that.'

Something stirred inside me, some waking thing. All my days I had longed for a good and adequate reason why I should study; these were the words I had waited for.

'The Divine,' he repeated. 'What do you think of that for a goal?'

I considered it. No image at all came to mind, but at the same time there was a sense of profound peace, a sense of coming safely home.

'Have you met the Rule of Three?' he asked.

I groaned. 'We use it all the time: if a merchant is selling nine lengths of cloth for twelve florins, how much would seven lengths cost?'

'What if I told you that, by the Rule of Three, we arrive at the Law of the Octave, and that by the Law of the Octave, we can hear God?'

I stared at him. It was as if I had spent twelve years in the dark and now someone was lighting a candle, as if sight was about to be experienced for the first time. And it was happening here, not in church, where one might perhaps expect revelations, but here, in the room the Bishop called his study, a room which had begun to fill with strange charts and models of multi-faceted shapes, a room which only a week before had been covered with dustsheets and had been the imaginary Florence of my games.

'Do you know what your desire is, Tommaso? Do you know that to which your life will be devoted?'

I shook my head.

'Let me put it another way. What will your trade or profession be?'

'I shall work here, and in due time will replace my grandfather as steward.' It was the first time I had given statement to my inexorable fate.

'And do you dream of other futures?'

'Sometimes,' I admitted cautiously.

He did not probe. He merely asked, 'If I were to offer you three things, tell me which you would choose and tell me at once without thinking: wealth, fame, or knowledge?'

'Knowledge.'

'But riches and fame would free you from servitude to this place. Knowledge would not. Nor would it particularly ease your task or lighten your burden. So why have you chosen it?'

As I could not say, he provided the answer himself. 'It is because knowledge leads to true freedom. The rich man and the famous man are not free. Only the wise man is free. You have chosen well, my young friend, and I am not surprised you play truant.'

He told me that if I was willing to work hard, harder than I had ever worked before, I need not return to school. I agreed readily and from then on the Bishop took charge of my education. The task of teaching me Latin – not the Latin of the Church, but the Latin of the Romans – he passed to his secretary, but each evening I joined the Bishop to continue our studies in the science of number.

There was a Persian rug draped over his desk, woven in a geometric pattern of vivid colours. On a high shelf were hung the vital articles of a philosopher's equipment: compass, dividers, rules, scissors, rolled diagrams of the planets and charts of astronomical calculations. Standing freely in the middle of the room on a pedestal was a sphere of bronze bands, a skeleton globe showing the courses of the planets. It was the room of the alchemist, not the kind who tries to change base metal into gold, but a true one, one who seeks the transformation from the human to the Divine.

One evening I was idly turning the wonderful spheres waiting for the Bishop; when he arrived it was with his arms full of carpenter's tools.

'Here we are,' he said, as he neatly laid out saw, plane, chisel, hammer, nails and wood. I picked up a pair of pliers and began to think of a victim of crucifixion. 'The lesson for the day is mathematics,' said the Bishop, and with that display of incongruity he had from me what I had never given my schoolmaster: my full attention. He asked me to state the Rule of Three.

'Multiply that which one needs to know about by that which is dissimilar to it and divide the product by what remains.'

'This, child, is the Principle of Harmony. Now give me the fourth number in the series 6 : 8 : 9.'

'Twelve.'

'How did you arrive at that?'

'Eight times nine is seventy-two, divided by six is twelve.'

'6 : 8 : 9 : 12 – the harmonic scale of Pythagoras.' He went on to explain about the intervals, fourths, fifths and octaves in music. Before long I was lost, and, as lost was not what I wanted to be, I stopped him. 'I do not understand.'

'Excellent.'

'What?'

'To realise your ignorance and to admit to it is the first step on the path of knowledge. You would not believe how few men are capable of that. Let us go back to the beginning.' He took from the shelf one of the many strange ornaments he had there, a tapering column.

'An obelisk, from Egypt. Only a model of course, very difficult to construct. Let this be our Number One. We must always start with Number One, for that in truth is all there is. The entire universe all adds up to One. Never forget that, or you will become lost in the multiplicity of things. Let it stand here as a reminder, while we go straight to number three.'

'What about number two?'

'Ah, therein lies the beginning of all illusion. A complex relationship, best left to another time. Three, then ... '

Between us we constructed a triangle of wire, tying it round three nails hammered into a block of wood at very precise places. The measure of one side was two, of the next, four, of the third, five. We tightened the wire as tight as we could.

'Right,' said the Bishop at last. 'This is the number three, is it not? – in that we have three lengths or sides of wire?'

'Yes, indeed.'

'Would you like to hear the number three?'

'Yes, I would.'

He plucked the wires, all three sides together. I shouted with joy. The triangle is a chord.

At the first opportunity, I raced to Antonio to tell him the wonderful news, that a triangle is a musical chord. He was not only unimpressed, he was annoyed.

'You have given up school to stay at home and pluck at triangles?' he asked as we walked through the city at dusk.

'But it is magical!'

'Maso, take care. Your Bishop has been in trouble for this kind of thing before. Magic is heresy. Do not become involved. If you want to give up school, do it for some useful reason such as weapon practice.'

'Why?'

'War is in the air. Can you not smell it?'

I sniffed. All I could smell was the usual waft of salt. 'There will be no war,' I said in full, if borrowed, confidence.

Antonio gazed at me piercingly. 'You have that on good authority do you?'

'The Bishop says so.'

He grasped me fiercely by the shirt. 'Listen to me, it will come to war, because it must!' He released me. 'Tommaso, Tommaso, do not listen to the blessed peacemakers. They are not what they seem. The Bishop has been sent by Lorenzo to make the Volterrani accept their fate meekly. I will have a word with your grandfather and arrange for you to live with me at the Palazzo Maffei.' He was gentle now. 'I am lonely on my own.'

The city was strangely quiet. I felt as if I were standing on the cusp between two worlds, the line between two spheres of a diagram on the study wall. One world was that of the body, with its persuasive reality of needs and dangers; the other was the world of the soul. Antonio's friendship promised all the wealth and security of being a member of a long-established and noble family. The Bishop promised a different kind of freedom. Which way to go?

As if in answer to the question, four apprentices suddenly leapt out of nowhere waving clubs and crying: 'Death to the Mediceans!'

Punching and kicking with some skill, we sent three of them off clutching their wounds and hollering in protest, but Antonio caught their leader by the jacket, threw him to the ground and pressed his nose into a puddle of pig dung. Then, just before the youth drowned, Antonio pulled his head up out of the filth by the hair.

'I think you have made a mistake,' he said. 'We are republicans like yourself.'

'Oh ... ' gasped the youth.

'Are we not, Tommaso?'

I heard myself answer, 'Yes, indeed.'

Sometimes you do not know what the truth is until you hear yourself speak it. All the Bishop's good opinion of Lorenzo de' Medici had not healed my hurt. But was I a republican? If I were, it was only while I was with my cousin. When I returned to the Bishop's Palace it was by way of the fountain. Washed clean, I was a Medicean again.

Between them, the Bishop and his secretary uprooted every weed sown in me by schoolmaster and priest and replaced it with a nutritious plant, the roots of which were Principle, Law and Ancient Wisdom. My days were divided into seven parts, allocating time to the seven disciplines called the liberal arts. The secretary taught me Latin, Rhetoric and Logic. The Bishop taught me Arithmetic, Geometry, Astronomy and Music. They were busy men and often only had time to start me off on each lesson. Every morning I sat by myself in the library, chanting aloud passages from a textbook of Latin grammar which was written in hexameters. I was filled with conjunctions, declensions and vocabularies until I could rattle them out like a bird scarer. By myself I struggled through Virgil, Ovid and Horace.

The Bishop instructed me in the rules of memory set down by Cicero in *Ad Herennium*. We went through the palace choosing rooms as the 'places' which Cicero recommended. In those places I memorised words, phrases or whole passages. Later I had only to remember the place for everything to be at once recalled. The Naples, Florence and Milan of my dustsheet world had been cleared away. Now I had in their stead Rules of Grammar and long passages from Plato, Aristotle and Boethius. I had only to walk through the palace to realise the compendium of knowledge that the trained mind may become. But I was a late beginner, under the instruction of a man nearly seventy years old.

'There is no time,' said the Bishop, 'to make of you a scholar of *humanitas*. All I can do is to show you the roots of knowledge. You will have the rest of your life to explore the tree for yourself at your leisure.'

As the weeks passed, the main staircase of the palazzo began to fill with the Bishop's collection of antiquities. The torsos of gods and busts of noseless senators, dug up from Tuscan soil, began to decorate landings and niches. One fine figure of Hercules greeted the visitor at the head of the stairs. The Bishop came upon me challenging the hero with my wooden sword. 'It is time,' he said, 'you had a real sword.' By now I had read Caesar's *Civil Wars* and I had heard much about the Greek heroes, but I had assumed that a man who reads about soldiers and heroes does not himself become one. By following the road of learning, surely I had left the way of action?

'A sword?' I echoed, astonished.

'A man needs to defend himself in this world, and to defend himself well. A sword you shall have, and a sword master.'

Thus into a full day I had also to fit an hour of weapon practice. I was proud of my sword, and wanted to wear it. I had new clothes now, brightly coloured hose and a young man's skirted jacket. All I needed as the finishing touch was a sword at my belt, but the Bishop forbade it.

'You may wear the sword when you have mastered swordsmanship and not before.'

Latin, however, I adopted long before I had mastered it. Having to converse with my tutors in the ancient tongue, I thereby alienated myself from the rest of the servants, who continued to speak in the local dialect. All my days were thus spent in study and practice, but still we found time for leisure, when the Bishop would show me how to construct models of the elements. Always beginning with a single unit of measure – usually the length of my thumb – we would draw overlapping circles and within their arcs find the angles for Platonic solids and polyhedra: the cube, the tetrahedron, the octohedron, icosahedron and dodecahedron. Then drawing circles divided by these angles on parchment, we cut them up and folded them and stuck them together. Just as I was beginning to feel childish, with simple shapes emerging from gluey fingers, the Bishop quoted from Plato's *Timaeus* and told me that the multi-faceted ball or pyramid in my hands was the shape of elemental fire, air or water.

I thought we were very clever to make such objects. But one day the Bishop said, 'Look at what God can do ... ' and slipped a rose inside the cup of a pentagon. The five bracts beneath the flower laid exactly on the five folds of the cup. I flooded with joy, to be part of such a well-ordered and magnificent universe.

The element of earth is the shape of a cube. One day as I was being overawed by a handful of cubic salt crystals, a letter arrived from Antonio, inviting me to reside at the Palazzo Maffei.

The Bishop read it out and then gazed at me steadily while his eyebrows moved like caterpillars. 'Well? It is a fine offer, Tommaso, and would free you from servitude.'

I found it difficult to speak.

'Well?'

'Did you not say something about building a monochord?'

Taking this for his answer, the Bishop called enthusiastically for a servant to fetch certain things from the carpenter's workshop. When they arrived, we drew patterns, sawed up pieces of olive wood, and tapped, clamped and planed while the Bishop whistled like a happy artisan. I did all the running, fetching and holding that he required of me. The servants, who were barred from the study, speculated on the curious comings and goings, the knockings and the bangings, while the housekeeper, who considered herself exempt from anyone's desire for privacy, walked in unannounced. She created a storm about the mess and the smell.

'Oh God, what is it?' she cried, pinching her nose.

'Fish glue.'

'What sort of monster are you making?'

'One of scales.'

'Bleuh!'

'Away, good woman, this is man's work.'

'And who has to clear up afterwards, if not woman?'

'True, true,' agreed the Bishop, leading her towards the door. 'Come back in the morning.'

But she was barred in the morning because we had not finished and the Bishop wanted nothing to be disturbed. For two days his visitors had to tread over whorls of woodshavings. Then, on the third evening, we completed the work: a slender soundbox, as long as I was high, with a hook at one end and a tuning key at the other. He took a lute string, fixed it on expertly, then handed me the instrument and said, 'This is for you, your own Pythagorean humming string.'

Although my gratitude was wholehearted, I still did not know what the object was.

'It is the soul, your soul, stretching between earth and heaven.' He plucked the string. It was loose. I laughed at the flabby sound.

'Familiar?' he asked. 'Is this not how you feel, when you are listless and full of dreams?'

I did not like to admit it.

'Tune it.'

'What to?'

'Whatever pleases you.'

I turned the peg and, even as I turned it, I heard the goal of my quest sounding as an harmonic tone within me. The string tautened. When I reached the note itself, I stopped.

'Why there?' he asked.

I did not know. 'It pleases me. It sounds right.'

He turned the peg sharply, tightening the note. I winced.

'Would you not prefer it here?'

'No.'

'Why not?'

'I do not know,' I said. Taking the box back, I retuned the string to my original note.

'That is the tonic note,' he said. 'A musician would say that by choosing it you have displayed a good ear. Of course that is nonsense. Your ears are only couriers. That which hears is the soul itself. In the soul is the "harmonium", a scale of perfect notes. You know this tonic note is the right place to begin, because it has been echoed by – no it is an echo of – what is sounding in the soul. So if I say to you now, sing the tonic note ... '

I opened my mouth and let the note out.

' ... you can. Now I shall sing the same note.' He did so. 'Was that it?'

'Yes.'

'The same as yours?'

'Yes.'

'Exactly the same?'

'Yes ... ' I said, dubious now.

'Well, let us see. Pluck the string.'

I did so, and, as the note sounded, the Bishop put his finger down on the string exactly half way along its length. An aerial version of the same note sounded, only higher. 'That is you,' said the Bishop. He plucked the open string. 'This is me. Both singing the same note, but one is low and one is high. Halving the string doubles the note, and we call both notes doh. Now, remember 6 : 9 : 8 : 12?' He took a piece of charcoal and a measure and carefully marked out the ratios on the soundbox. Then he made me pluck the string while he touched it at each of the marked places. Beautiful harmonic tones began to sound.

'What you are hearing is the perfect beauty of proportion. What you are hearing is number. With this one string I can show you the nature of the universe and the wondrous order of Creation, the courses of the planets and the Music of the Spheres: one string, one note; one note halved, quartered and further divided according to the divine ratios of Pythagoras.'

I plucked the tonic note, he touched the vibrating string, now here, now there, creating bright aerial sounds until it seemed that angels were dancing in the sky.

'The Number One is the source of all other numbers. The Pythagoreans called it "the monad of intelligent fire alone in the dark of the unlimit."'

How could I move to the Palazzo Maffei? I wanted to stay with the angels. I went closer to the old man sitting beside me and pulled on the grey wires of his eyebrows. 'I think I shall stay with you,' I said. His arm came round me and pulled me into a grateful embrace.

'Is it true?' I asked from within the folds of his gown, 'that you are an agent of the Medici?'

'Is that what they are saying in Volterra? No, Maso, it is not true. I am an agent of the One. As are you.' My ear heard the words through his chest, as if it were his heart which was speaking. And the words of his heart went straight into mine.

FIVE

WE DIVIDED the string of the monochord into all the notes of the octave. 'Now the sol–fa scale does not proceed from doh to doh in a simple progression,' said the Bishop. 'If it did, the life of Man would take a simple path from the birth of the soul to its return to God. However, in between the beginning and the end we have something called Creation. It is the work of Creation to keep itself going, and to that end it employs ignorance of the truth. It is just a dream, my son, and we all believe in it. So much so that it is God who we tend to think of as dreamlike and insubstantial, whilst nature appears to be reality itself. We explore it in ships, measure it with compasses, classify it with names and go to war for possession of our piece of it. All this is in accordance with the Laws of Creation. But some of us, longing to return to the source, turn back and peer behind the veil.'

The Bishop played each note of the scale and asked me to define the qualities of the notes. Agreeing that there was something odd about re and ti, he explained: 'These are called discordants. Re comes after the beginning, ti just before the end. Between them they encompass creation, and keep it turning in its cycles. Re starts it off, ti turns it back on itself, and we forget where we came from, which is doh, and know not where we are going, which is doh.'

If the teaching of the Bishop was a joy, his discipline was a torture. My days were measured by a strict timetable and I was not allowed to go out except in his company. Life on the piazza, he said, is creation at its most disorderly, yet what a compelling disorder it was. The tension in the city was tightening like a string going sharp. Several times a week I went with the Bishop and his clergy to the Cathedral for Mass. My place in the choir was next to that of a boy called Michele Inghirami, the son of one of the company of merchants who had possession of the alum mine.

'Make way,' he said to the rest as I struggled past them into my place. 'Here comes the Bishop's puppy dog.' The better part of me took consolation in the knowledge that, for all his wealth, Michele Inghirami did not have a Pythagorean humming string. The worse part of me itched to punch him on his beaky nose. I had always thought that to be good is to be weak; only now was I discovering how much strength it took to behave well, and that I had not strength enough. I was beginning to thrum with the desire to see my friends, to play and argue, to tempt Antonio into a good wrestling match. Protected as I was, I was in danger of turning into a woman.

After a few weeks of this incarceration, the better part of me lost the fight. Sent to bed as usual after my lessons, I rolled up some blankets and put them under the sheet to fool anyone who might look in, then took one of my several secret passages out of the house. The next night I did it again. And so a double life began, of days spent in pursuit of Truth and nights spent with Antonio and his artisan friends.

One evening, when the moon rose full in the sky before the sun had set, when the market was closing and people were leading away their goats and pigs, when workmen came as usual to the piazza to exchange news at the end of the day, a fight broke out among a gang of apprentices standing near the Palazzo della Signoria. On the façade of the Palazzo were embedded the heraldic shields of the major families, including those of the Maffei. While the guard were thus distracted, three other apprentices defiled the arms of the Inghirami.

Michele Inghirami's father, Paolo, had never courted the love of the people. He was not only a member of the merchant company, but he boasted about it. Such was his disdain for the common people of Volterra, and such the extent of his unpopularity, that as time passed he was finding more and more excuses to be in Florence. The people had given him the nickname 'Pecorino', sheep's dung, but it was a bucket of the more sticky pig manure that the apprentices splashed over the Inghirami shield.

'I have heard that Ser Paolo Inghirami is returning from Florence,' said Antonio to Francesco Caruggi.

'We await him with open arms,' said Caruggi.

When the guard realised what had happened, they stopped trying to break up the fight and rushed to clean the shields. Everyone else drifted away towards the acropolis to watch the sun set but Antonio remained to sit on the steps of the loggia and play on his pipe. I sang the words of the song:

'I am a bird without flight, at the mercy of the stars.
I am a seaswept mariner, buffeted by the gods and by fortune.
Careless am I of my destiny, since heaven alone rules that of each one of us.'

I began the song again, but my voice trailed off as Andreas the Greek approached us. Greasy haired and with a face like a ripe fig, he and his chilling prophecies were a recurring feature in my nightmares.

'Well, well, well,' he said in his thick Grecian accent. 'What a picture of innocence. What a sad song. My heart is rented.'

'Only mines are rented; hearts are rent,' said Antonio.

I nodded in dumb agreement. The light of flaming torches on the Palazzo della Signoria picked out the gold in the prophet's teeth and the ring in his ear, and made the moisture on his full lips shine.

Some said he was a pirate, others a brigand from the eastern trade routes. Some said he was a gypsy, others a necromancer. Whatever he was, no one believed he was an honest exile from Constantinople, least of all me. It was reckless to correct him.

'A most heart-rent song,' he said scornfully. 'Careless of your destiny are you?' he asked me. 'Beware, Tommaso dei Maffei. You are careless because you are blind. Blind, like all mortal men. Only I, in my misfortune, have been born with the gift of sight. Your destiny I see as clearly as your face. Take heed – be careless no longer.'

'What can you see?' asked Antonio with interest.

Andreas continued to address me. 'All whom you love on this earth shall perish before you,' he said. 'You will live to see all whom you cherish die, even as it has already come to pass, in the death of your mother before your birth. Born of a dead woman, you do not belong to this world.'

How did he know these things?

Antonio said, 'He is mad. Take no heed.'

'But how does he know ... ?'

'Everyone knows it. Go away, Andreas, you and your stupid prophecies.'

'*Was* my mother dead before I was born?'

'Be off, you smelly Greek!'

'You speak of freedom, Antonio dei Maffei, but you have the seeds of hatred in your heart.'

Antonio flushed scarlet, but whether from embarrassment or rage, I could not tell. Andreas turned back to me and, dodging Antonio's kicks, said urgently, 'Love that which is imperishable, Tommaso, only then will you escape your sorrow.'

'What is that?'

'Do not listen to him,' cried Antonio.

'Do not tempt me,' the prophet thundered in the face of my cousin, 'into revealing *your* fate.'

Antonio sneered in derision, so Andreas grimaced, manipulating his face with his fingers until it was all holes: nostrils, mouth, staring eyes – the mutilated face of a corpse. The vision terrified me but Antonio laughed harshly and pushed the Greek away, cursing him in the rich Volterrani dialect.

'Remember what I said, Tommaso,' said Andreas, walking backwards, neither resisting nor defending himself against Antonio. Then he turned and strode off.

'Leper,' Antonio shouted after him. 'Zodiacal cripple!'

Suddenly boys stampeded into the piazza like bullocks. Their shadows, thrown by the windwhipped torches, lurched around them. They raced towards the campanile and the bell. They had news.

'Attack! Attack! An army is coming!'

The urgent tolling of the bell called everyone to the piazza. People ran pell-mell but the more quick-witted went to fetch arms from the arsenal. The gates of the Palazzo del Capitano opened and the Captain himself ran across the square and up the steps of the loggia.

'Quiet!' he roared. 'We are not under attack! A small armed escort is approaching, that is all.'

'Whose?' shouted Antonio.

'One of your own citizens. Go home now and be at peace.'

There was only one Volterran citizen who required a protective escort in his own city: Paolo Inghirami.

On the Captain's orders, we were herded roughly from the piazza with all the people. The streets were closed by soldiers and the torches extinguished; thus it was to a dark and empty place that the merchant's party came. Inghirami did not return to the comfort of his home; instead he was locked up for his own safety in the Palazzo del Capitano.

Under the lamp of the moon, Antonio and I looked down on the city from the height of the acropolis. We could see our own shadows but below us the city was dark: the darkness of the unlimit. Then came the sound, it seemed, of an owl hooting. Antonio cupped his hands over his mouth and hooted back. Somewhere, in another quarter, came another echo of the sound.

Antonio looked down on me. 'Well,' he said. 'Are you coming?'

At first it was a night of black carnival. Wine from last year's harvest was opened and people were soon reeling about in the dark, singing and yelling. We were under curfew – all torches were out – but the Volterrani lurched about in their impromptu moonlight bacchanalia. Some groups of men collided with the civic guard and, after a scuffle, one or two were arrested, but as more and more Volterrani came out on to the streets, the guard began to retreat back to their quarters. Sensing the power of their numbers in the shadowy night, the people grew more brazen. Inghirami was left to the protection of his own escort as the Captain sensibly took himself and his own men into the refuge of the Palazzo della Signoria.

Confident now, the people began to light torches; the faces illuminated by the flames were demonic. I grew frightened. Suddenly I wanted to be back in the Bishop's fold, but Antonio had a grip on my shoulder. We seemed to be waiting; someone, somewhere, was organising things on our behalf. It was a black vigil. I looked up at the windows of the Palazzo del Capitano and, in sudden sympathy with Paolo Inghirami, felt weak and breathless with fear. I must have shivered.

'Not scared, are you?' asked one of Antonio's friends, a farrier. 'Perhaps it is too late for you to be out.'

'Yes,' agreed Antonio. 'Go home, Maso, before the Bishop misses you.' He was sarcastic. Though he had never met him, Antonio never mentioned the Bishop without bile in his voice.

'Bishop?' asked another, looming in on me with a frown. 'What have you to do with that old woolsack?'

'This is Monsignore's pet Volterrano.'

The man pinched my ear. I cried out: 'What if I am? What is wrong with that?'

'You consort with the devil.'

Even Antonio found that laughable. 'The Bishop is irritating, but harmless; nothing more than Lorenzo's mouthpiece.'

Men from the guild of candlemakers arrived bearing kindling they had collected, miners brought in lumps of sulphur, foresters arrived with a tree trunk and set about ramming it into the wooden doors of the Palazzo del Capitano. The orchestration of the work was as earnest as that for a religious procession; but, as heavy as were the swings, the effort proved vain. Guile was quicker and more successful. Francesco Caruggi knocked on a small window, the shutters were cautiously opened and, after a few words, a deal was done with those mercenaries who had accompanied Inghirami from Florence. Having been paid to ride in escort, not to be locked up and possibly killed, they gratefully accepted assurances that they would come to no harm and opened the gates. The people surged in.

Some fell under the weight of the press. I myself stumbled, propelled forwards by the crowd, but Antonio seized hold of me and hurried me towards an archway and shelter until the worst of the crush had passed. Then he slapped me hard across the face.

'Go home, you little bastard! You are always under my feet. Go home and leave me!'

I ran off crying to the other side of the piazza, there to turn and watch. A fire was started on the third floor of the palazzo, a fire mixed with sulphur; its drifting, acrid smoke made us all retch. As for the proud merchant, he soon staggered choking from his refuge. The artisans were waiting for him.

'Is a man responsible to himself alone or to his family also?'

'To his family I should think, Monsignore.'

'And is the family an isolated unit, or does it intermingle with other families?'

'It mingles, by way of marriage.'

'And would you say therefore that the state is composed of intermingled families?'

'Yes, it must be.'

Socrates, I have heard, was a merry soul, always teasing, but the Socratic humour in the Bishop on the following morning was not merry. He towered over me and thundered his questions. I sat on my hands on a stool and quaked.

'What is the second commandment?'

'Thou shalt not kill.'

'Who is this "thou"?'

'I have not killed anyone!'

'Yet you are a part of a family are you not? And the family is part of the city? Last night your city murdered one of its own sons. Murder is the name, boy, not vendetta nor revenge nor justice. Murder. By your very presence at the act, you are culpable. Thou shalt not kill. *Thou*!' I collapsed in grief. The next thing I knew I was being both consoled and asked to quote the first commandment.

'Thou shalt love the Lord thy God with all thy heart,' I quavered.

'Sometimes the Lord is wrathful, Tommaso, when he sees you err. Love inspires the anger. You have deceived me with your blankets and tunnels. I do not suppose I could block off all your exits even if I could find them. So I am going to ask you, as a man, to promise never to deceive me again.'

I made the promise; and I kept it. For a month I stayed indoors, locked in by my own word, which was as a magic circle drawn around me, protecting me from my own desires.

On the eve of Shriving Day, the Bishop desired a good supper before the Lenten fast and allowed me to choose what dishes we would have, as well as which guests. Besides the housekeeper, my grandfather Mariotto, the Bishop and the Bishop's secretary, I invited Antonio, hoping that at last I could introduce him to the Bishop. Antonio, however, declined the invitation, and cakes were baked, jellies set, fish marinated, crystallised flowers taken from their jars, and the table laid for five. Then, at the last moment, Antonio arrived after all, the worse for wine.

In response to the murder of Inghirami, Lorenzo de' Medici had imprisoned all the Volterrani who lived in Florence, and frantic embassies were passing from Volterra to Florence and back again, trying to secure peace. The Bishop was at the forefront of these efforts and each day wrote a new letter to Lorenzo, begging him to release the hostages. He was confident of success, knowing that many of Lorenzo's councillors were also urging restraint.

Antonio entered, knelt to kiss the episcopal ring and, on rising, surprised the Bishop with the news that the Florentines had engaged the services of the Count of Urbino, the best condottiere in the entire world. 'So much for their desire for peace,' said my cousin.

'There will be peace', said the Bishop, recovering at once, 'as soon as the Volterrani are peaceful.'

'We will be peaceful when Lorenzo releases the hostages.'

'I agree,' said the Bishop.

This unexpected yielding to his point of view threw Antonio off balance. 'You agree? I thought you supported Lorenzo.'

'I support reason, and in so far as Lorenzo is reasonable, I support him. However, though one of his friends has been murdered, though he has every cause for wrath, he is not right to lock up innocent men as hostages simply because they are Volterrani. He is being stubborn and wilful, and I have told him so. I have told him that I want those men back here in time to celebrate Easter in their own homes.'

'Lorenzo is young,' said my grandfather, as we moved to the table. 'This is his first trial. He needs to be seen as strong.'

'That is as may be,' said the Bishop, 'but let me repeat my rule for this house: there is to be no discussion of politics while we eat.'

'Then this is to be a silent meal,' muttered Antonio.

The Bishop considered him narrowly. 'You too are young. To you politics are all important; you think they will change the world. It is commendable in a young man that he wishes to put right the wrongs. The trouble is, when you start with the world, you begin in the wrong place. The change that is required is within us: if only men would look to themselves, there would be no need for politics, in which no one agrees, no one, not even those in the same family. Table is the place to meet together, not to fall out.' So saying, the Bishop said the Grace, following which Antonio stabbed moodily at the pickled fish on his plate. He seemed a little afraid of the Bishop's unquestionable authority, but the fire in him used his fear as more fuel. He looked up and held Monsignore's gaze steadily. His glittering eyes met the soft, unchallenging light in the Bishop's gaze.

'What has brought you to Volterra, Monsignore?' he asked.

'What has brought you? How is it that an apostolic secretary is not at work in Rome but idling in his native town?'

The bluntness of the question drained the colour from Antonio's face. He cleared his throat. 'I care more for my city than my duties.'

'Oh? But it occurs to me that, as a member of the Camera Apostolica, your presence here may indeed be your duty.'

'I do not understand you, Monsignore,' said Antonio, echoing my own thoughts.

'His Holiness, surely, must be concerned about these events, and in need of reports?'

The directness of the accusation shocked us all. Though the arrow hit Antonio, we all felt it. The housekeeper blushed red and complained that the fish was too vinegary. The Bishop heard what was behind her inane words and blushed a little himself. 'Now do you see what I mean about politics at table? No more of it, boy, no more.'

I stared at my cousin. Was it true? Was he here as an agent of the Pope? The prestige of it might have beguiled me except that, in the presence of the Bishop, any prestige always looked more like tinsel than gold.

Antonio said, 'I hear you value the truth, Monsignore. I shall tell you the truth. I have indeed been sent by His Holiness to find out what is happening here and to send him reports. Why should I be ashamed of that? I am serving the Church and my city together.'

'That depends on what you tell him.'

'The truth, of course, that the Volterrani are being cheated of their rightful possession of the alum mine by clever merchants, devotees of Mammon. Lorenzo de' Medici is the undisclosed head of the merchant company. He wants to gain the exclusive possession of all Italian alum and is on the point of achieving it.' Antonio looked as if he would stand by this argument with his life, but the Bishop found such views wearying. He seemed not to think a reply worthwhile. Instead he asked what the Pope's interest in the matter might be.

'When it comes to war, as it surely must, both Volterra and Florence will ask Rome for help. The Pope wishes to determine who is in the right.'

'His Holiness intends to support the right?' The Bishop sounded astonished.

'And lions will live in peace with sheep,' said Mariotto, to which the housekeeper gasped and crossed herself. 'The Pope's only interest,' continued my grandfather unabashed, 'is the alum.'

'He already has alum,' said the Bishop, having forgotten his own rule about conversation. 'The Tolfa mine is his; it is only leased on concession to the Medici. No, it is not the alum. What the Pope wants is a greater prize indeed.' He gazed steadily at Antonio. 'What His Holiness wants is Florence. This could be just the little war he has been waiting for.'

This was too much for the housekeeper. 'Monsignore, are you talking about the Vicar of Christ?'

'Certainly not,' said the Bishop. 'No, no, I am talking about Francesco della Rovere.'

'But he is Pope Sixtus the Fourth.'

'For the sake of our sanity, let us keep name and function separate. In this way we can criticise one and respect the other, as is necessary.'

'Monsignore,' said Mariotto. 'If our guest is a papal agent, are you not being, if I may say so, a touch outspoken?'

At this the Bishop glanced at Antonio and then began to laugh. He laughed until the tears came into his eyes. Antonio grew red with fury. The old man went to speak, to dispel the anger in our guest, but started to laugh again. Antonio's chair scraped hard on the tiled floor as he jumped to his feet.

'I see you have respect neither for His Holiness nor for his servants.'

'Then I am as transparent as you are. Sit down, boy. I meant not to offend.'

To lighten the atmosphere, the Bishop called for the cakes. They were my favourites, honeycakes covered with marzipan. I had made them myself, under the cook's direction, and my mouth had been watering with anticipation ever since they had been taken from the oven. They were offered round to everyone in order of age. The Bishop wiped the tears from his eyes and took one, Mariotto took one, the secretary took one, the housekeeper took one. Five cakes on the plate: six people at the table. I thought, 'They are all taking one to spite me.' But I could rely on Antonio to leave one. He hated cakes. Whenever there were delicacies about, he lectured on starvation in the peasantry. As the plate came past me, I grabbed for the cake.

'Tommaso!' my grandfather thundered. 'Guests first!'

'It is the last cake!'

'Antonio first.'

Antonio grinned and took the cake. 'Thank you,' he said graciously to the servant.

I was on my feet and yelling, 'You hate cakes!'

'Not this kind.'

'Tommaso, sit down!'

'He hates cakes!' I shouted. I swung towards Antonio. 'What about all the starving peasants?'

He sank his teeth into the pastry.

'I hope you choke!' I cried, and fled the room.

If the Bishop came looking for me, he did not find me. I had my lecture from the pulpit on the following Sunday, when he gave a sermon on the causes of war.

'Suppose a child is denied something it desires, some trifling thing such as a cake. He screams in a tantrum. The blood rushes to his head, his heart throbs in rage, his whole body is like a fist clenched, clenched over nothing. He has lost the object of his desire, but will not relinquish the desire itself. He screams, he is racked, he is entirely subject to his passion. Inside him, drawing him to itself, is that lodestone, the desire to possess. That is the cause of war.

'Let go, oh my people. Let go of the alum mine. Whether Lorenzo is in the right or in the wrong, let it go. For in truth it is neither yours nor his, but God's. Let it go. What will you lose? Only that which you have never had. Let it go and have something far more precious than wealth. Choose peace.'

The sermon was a two hour flight of eloquence. Where we usually fell asleep on our feet as we stood before the pulpit, on that evening our attention never wavered. The Bishop unfolded an argument for peace with faultless logic. There was no rioting that night.

But on the next the artisans were out again, shaking their fists, saying that the sheep were following a shepherd in the pay of a tyrant. Many exiles from Florence had taken up residence in Volterra; they joined the republicans in spreading dissension against the Medici. And that was as easy as spreading butter in summer. Rioting began again.

The Bishop mounted the pulpit outside the Cathedral to address the people. 'Concord builds in a sweet bond, discord disrupts even those who are joined by blood. The one builds cities, the other demolishes; the one creates wealth, the other dissipates. Discord turns men into beasts. Concord unites souls after death with God. I do not exhort you, I do not pray you, I implore you, seek peace!'

Following that, the Signoria at last decided to send a deputation to Lorenzo accepting his conditions for peace; and following that the people elected eight different men in their place. The new Signoria sent a deputation to Florence giving Volterra's conditions for peace, a none-too subtle difference which Lorenzo understood. He sent back an order that the people of Volterra prove their words by their deeds.

The sky held its breath.

Not all the artisans wanted war. Those who desired peace subscribed to a gift for our Bishop and it was duly presented to him, a fine chessboard with pieces carved from alabaster and onyx. The Bishop was delighted and in return gave the artisans patterns for making obelisks and Pythagorean solids. He stood the chessboard on a table in his study and made me set out the pieces, then he took the onyx king, which he called Sixtus the Fourth, and placed him before the alabaster king, Lorenzo de' Medici. 'The pawns,' he said, 'are the Volterrani.

They think this battle is theirs, being fought for their cause. It is nothing of the kind. The battle is between these two kings, who will use the pawns.'

I considered the board.

'This is not about alum, Tommaso, it is about Florence, the richest city in the world. It is Florence which is the Pope's desire, and, no matter how generous and friendly Sixtus is, Lorenzo knows it. This is why he is cautious and does not act. He is waiting for the onyx king to reveal himself.'

'And my cousin?'

'An onyx knight, as much a slave to the king's desires as a pawn.'

I went to the roof of the tower, hoping to be alone, but there was someone already there. I crept from the stairway, amazed to see my grandfather studying the clouds and the flight of birds.

'What are you doing, nonno?' I asked.

'Hush, child. Let God make His will known.'

Storm clouds were gathering in the west and, as my grandfather stared at them, his face seemed to wither with age. 'As I thought,' he whispered. When he turned to me, his gaze was harrowing. 'You must go away, Tommaso. Leave this place!'

Even as he spoke, lightning forked in the sky, as bright as burning olive wood. Mariotto cried out as if in pain. 'You must leave,' he shouted above the thunder. 'Go to Rome, Tommaso, to your true family!'

He seemed wild. Reciting every line of prayer that came to mind and calling on San Lino, I tried to draw him back inside the tower. The storm passed over our heads and a sudden deluge brought Mariotto back to his senses. I led him to the stairs and took him down to the nearest fire.

'Nonno,' I said, as he sat gazing silently into the flames. 'Is it true that my mother died before I was born?'

He nodded with a sigh.

'Who was she?'

'You will be told in due course, but not by me. All I can say is that you are a Maffei, and that your father is – was – a noble man. I shall speak to the Bishop tonight, and insist that tomorrow you go to Rome. There is an ambassadorial party due to leave. You can ride with them.'

Mariotto spoke to the Bishop. The Bishop rebuked him for being superstitious and denied his request.

Everything was still, resting in a balance as fine as a money-lender's. Lorenzo had agreed to release the hostages, but first the Volterrani had to prove their goodwill by their actions. May gave way to June and the pale green corn now turning gold was studded with cornflowers of inscrutable blue. Farmers dusted green beetles from the cherry trees and their wives picked the fruit. Days that passed without event we counted as precious coins. The Bishop, when not talking to ambassadors or the Signoria, was in constant prayer. Then the news came out of nowhere: banishment. Families with connections with Florence and the Medici party were sentenced to exile, the Inghirami, the Minucci, the Riccobaldi, the Maffei. To encourage their departure, the Volterrani militia torched their palaces.

'Madonna ... ' my grandfather turned ashen.

'So, there is the deed that proves your heart, Volterra,' said the Bishop. 'This is what Lorenzo expected. Now we prepare for war.'

'We must leave!' cried Mariotto. 'The acropolis is alight. We must leave at once, Monsignore!'

'We will be safe,' said the Bishop.

'Where? In the cellar?'

'No, living as usual. Is it nearly dinner time?'

'Monsignore! Holy Mother of God!'

'Is faith only for times of tranquility? Have the meal served, Tommaso.'

I ran to the kitchen and found it in uproar. 'The Bishop is ready to eat,' I cried, but no one heard. The scullions were howling, the cook was yelling, the groom was filling bags with hams and cheeses, ready for flight. I took a pan from a hook in the hearth and a large ladle. I jumped on the table and rang my makeshift gong with a mighty blow. 'The Bishop,' I boomed, in a voice just like his, 'is ready to eat.'

To my surprise, everyone went back to work, except for the groom, who left us then and was never seen again.

SIX

With the divine spark that is in every creature comes an innate sense of the eternal. Every day, however, that knowledge is challenged by all evidence to the contrary, for everything in Creation is transitory. The philosopher Marsilio Ficino once said to me that, for a man to live in Truth, he must first die to this world. Without doubt I died in June 1472.

All is now healed, and I thank God for the adversities I have suffered because, with each loss of a possession, a man comes a step closer to Truth. So why, you say, am I so melancholy? Desiderio, I shall confess. For all my desire for the eternal, I am victim to the transient. If my soul now flutters with apprehension it is for no other reason than that soon it will be March 25th, Lady Day. Yes, there is my confession. I, the disciple of wise men, am scared of the number twenty-five. For it will not only be March 25th, but the day that the fifteenth century of Our Lord comes to an end. It is my century. Between it and the next is a great abyss of infinitesimal time. As I cross it I shall leave behind almost all my friends – and my wife – in their graves, for the terrible prophecy of Andreas the Greek proved true.

The students of Oxford have already begun their celebrations but I find nothing to celebrate. The next century is theirs, not mine; mine is coming to an end. Indeed, mine came to an end two years ago when we burned the prophet Savonarola. I shall be nothing but a guest in the next century, a relic from the past. I can hear you laughing, Desiderio, a great Dutch laugh at Mediterranean emotion. 'Shall I tell you what will follow the twenty-fifth of March?' you say. 'Why, the twenty-sixth. Remember your philosophy and have no thought for tomorrow.'

THE BISHOP'S faith was proved. We all dined as usual and miraculously the palace escaped the flames. That faith gave me something to cling to within myself while everything else, every emotion and thought was tottering instability. The day war was declared I went to the roof to gaze in the direction of Florence as if trying to catch the eye of Lorenzo de' Medici, but he would not meet my gaze.

It crept towards us slowly, inexorably – nemesis arriving at a snail's pace, flattening the corn and the poppies. One day levelling a fortress, the next razing a village, all the time coming closer to its real quarry, the armies mustered by Florence approached Volterra. They were led by Federico da Montefeltro, the Count of Urbino, a friend of the Bishop.

'A fine man,' the Bishop said. 'We could not hope for a better enemy.'

'We could hope for no enemy at all,' I muttered sourly.

'Such hope is fled. Volterra is in a state of rebellion, and rebellions, being disruptive to the state, must be crushed. Note well that Lorenzo has hired one of the most learned, judicious men ever to take arms. Even *in extremis* Lorenzo is not letting desire for revenge govern his actions.'

The Bishop's words were fair but, falling as they were on the ears of a Volterrano, they were wasted.

The Volterrani were full of hope. Rapid envoys were sent to Siena and Pisa. Now was the time for free republics to rise up against the oppressor. The Sienese granted passage for our soldiers across their territory; but they granted the same freedom to Florence. Pisa remained silent. We sent ambassadors to Venice, Milan and Rome. The last, in particular, must surely come to our aid? But Rome, like the other cities, replied by sending armies to join the Florentines. Diplomatic activity became intense. It seemed that every hour another party of envoys left Volterra to hurry to a smaller, even more remote region of Italy than the party before, in increasingly vain attempts to secure help. Venice alone sent a token force of mercenaries but said it was for us to pay them.

The Florentine armies were still a week away, crossing Tuscany like a plague of locusts. I saddled a fast horse for the

Bishop and rode with him as far as Colle. From there the old man galloped to Florence, to repeat to the Florentines his sermons on peace. Everyone said he would not come back; I knew he would.

There was no longer any mention of alum. If Florence had declared war it was in response to the insubordination of Volterra, one of its subject territories. When Volterra in turn declared war, it was not against Florence, but against the house of the Medici, who held the good people of Florence in thrall.

By the time the Florentine forces arrived, their numbers had been swelled by Milanese mercenaries as well as by many contingents from small, sycophantic, bootlicking towns. And the Papal armies of Rome and Naples were on their way to join them. Antonio's reports to His Holiness, it seemed, had had the opposite effect to that which was intended. As for Antonio himself, I presumed he had left for Rome at the time of the banishment, for I had seen nothing of him since.

At last the day came when, from my outlook on the tower of the palace, I heard dogs barking wildly in the countryside and, a while later, I saw the road from Florence begin to glint in the sun. I shot a blunt arrow tied with ribbons in the direction of the Palazzo della Signoria. Another arrow flew from where mine had dropped. The bells began to toll. Over the past week the farmers and peasants had been coming in from the countryside and, though the floor of every church had been laid with straw beds, there were not enough of them, so the townspeople opened their houses and took in as many of the country people as they could, while the Bishop's Palace began to fill with the white-robed monks from the Camaldolese Abbey on the cliffs. As the bells tolled and the last stragglers rushed into the city to set up their own shelters in the lanes and orchards, one by one the city gates were closed: the gates of San Francesco and San Felice, the old Etruscan gate, the Selci gate. Within the hour, the city on the roof of the world was secure. And alone.

The enemy set up camp in the shallow vale where we used to exercise Antonio's falcon. The soldiers were so jocular and matter-of-fact as they pitched tents and erected paddocks that they might have been preparing for a festival or a joust, except that the structures forming under the hands of the carpenters were siege machines. At night the lantern-shaped tents were illuminated from within by candles and glowed in the valley like faerie mushrooms. It was very still and the occasional shouted command or the jingling of harness carried up to us on the clear air. At dawn, when the sun rose on a day which should have been devoted to cherry-picking, its rays caught the striped tent of the one-eyed Count of Urbino, flagged with the colours of all Italy.

Although the Volterrani were behind ancient, solid walls and the Florentine armies were in tents, there was no doubt who were the vulnerable ones. Watching the siege machines grow stage by stage into towers, we were caught like rabbits in the stare of rearing snakes. But, after having taken our bastion, the army settled down for a siege and to eat our cherries, troubling only once or twice a day to fire mortars at the wall.

The servants, convinced that the Bishop had no hope of return, even if he intended it, gave up cleaning the Palazzo. With the city becoming ever more squalid, there was no incentive to wash floors or polish marble. Our sense of time crumbled. It grew hotter. The makeshift shelters of the peasants became nurseries of disease.

My grandfather was the first in the house to succumb to the fever. When I followed a day later, I welcomed the sickness and hoped for a quick death. In delirium I was haunted by the Count of Urbino. His ugly face had been painted on the targets of the practice ground and I knew it well: nose wickedly hooked, one eye socket empty, the other eye full of malicious arrogance. He battered on the gates calling for me by name. The magnanimous Count of Urbino, patron of scribes, lover of books, friend of Lorenzo – his loathsome face was grim and menacing, his single, hawkish eye searching.

I thought I was looking down on the camps of the ten thousand. It was night; soldiers were laughing; I looked down bitterly on their lights. All Italy was laughing, laughing at the Volterrani. The laughter stopped when the Bishop came. He towered above them, his mitre black and purple and the snakes of Hermes writhing on his crozier. On his chest, hanging from his neck, was a bronze medallion bearing a scene in relief of a charioteer driving a pair of horses. One horse, winged, reared.

The Bishop held up his arms, the crowds fell to their knees and cowered before him. He called my name, demanding that I should come out, but I did not know from whence or to where.

There was a wall. It had neither beginning nor end and I could not see over it. The Bishop was there, as golden as an archangel. He said: 'The principle of perspective is to find the invisible source from which all things flow. All lines draw you to it.' His outline softened and he merged with the wall, disappeared. Antonio hammered on the wall with his fists. 'Blocks of stone,' he gasped. 'We must knock them down.'

Somewhere the sound of a bombard crashing into masonry, the whole earth vibrating.

I was alone with the wall. Was I on the inside or out? Which side was I on?

'Tommaso ... ' a voice called from nowhere and everywhere. The wall began to glow and shimmer. Tentatively I touched it and passed through. On the other side I met the Bishop, normal now, a diminished giant.

'Can you hear me, Tommaso?'

I reached out and touched him. He was warm. He grasped my hand.

'You are back?' I said.

'And at what cost! I had to go to the tent of the Count of Urbino himself and obtain a pass to enter Volterra. I said that I intended to rescue the Captain.' The Captain, being a Florentine, was in much danger being enclosed in Volterra. 'But of course my real concern was for a young urchin.'

He made me drink some foul herbs which he himself had prepared, and while I drank he told me gently that my grandfather had died. 'He left me a letter, asking me to take care of you, to become your guardian. A foolish request – my own death cannot be far away.'

'Do not say so!'

'Perhaps I can have it postponed for a few years.'

'Do you have that power?'

He laughed and shook his head. 'No one has that power. But God would not give me a duty without giving me the chance to fulfil it, would He?'

He told me of the progress of the war, how the noble citizens were defecting to the Florentine camp, how even the members of the Signoria had left by night and thrown themselves on the mercy of the Count, while my cousin had gone in the opposite direction and was now openly with the rebels. We were lost. The city was finished. As the Bishop spoke, another mortar shook the walls.

'Let us escape then,' I said. 'I know a way out down by the cliffs.'

He smiled. 'I am sure you do, but no, we are going to stay. The city is lost but no one has died yet, at least not in battle. To prevent a massacre, we must formally surrender. Charged with that duty by the Count, I have called together all those prepared to accept the only possible, dignified, solution we have left open to us. We meet tonight to begin drawing up the articles. Meanwhile, I must find Captain Malegonella and use the Count's passes to get him out of here. Then I shall be back.'

'You are returning to the Count of Urbino?'

'I shall be safe: he is an honourable man. All will be well so long as we secure the agreement before the wall is breached. As strong as he is, Count Federico will not be able to contain his forces much longer. The contingent here at the Selci gate is Milanese, and they are becoming restless, tired of camp food and cherries. As I have learnt never to trust a Milanese, if you were to tell me that Duke Sforza of Milan is a demon and that all his soldiers are brigands, for once I might agree with you.'

His voice shrank down a tunnel and my mind closed in on me.

There was a wall. It had neither beginning nor end. I leant against it and cried for love of what was beyond the wall. What it was I did not know, whether past or future, this world or the next. Sounds came: the clak-clak-clak of a swung censer. The pungent smoke of incense drifted over me. On my tongue, the host, but I could not swallow. I could not swallow for all the tears I shed.

The bread is the body: the body is the wall.

Someone rushed up the stairs of the Palazzo, his cries echoing those from the streets. *The wall is breached!*

We thought the ten thousand soldiers were going to rush in, but they did not. The disciplined Count of Urbino kept them back, threatening death to any man who disobeyed his orders. With negotiations beginning in earnest, as to how the city might be surrendered without harm to its people, the Bishop was busy every hour of the day. As I recovered, I played listlessly upon my monochord. On one of his rare visits to my room, the Bishop gave me a small, leather-bound book: the *Iliad* of Homer.

'I always meant to teach you Greek, but never had the time. Happily someone has begun to render Homer into Latin.'

At first I was more fascinated by the script than the contents. It was like the Roman chancery script that my cousin Raffaello used, but not so ornate. It sloped and many of the letters linked up; for all its fluidity, however, it was beautifully clear. Over the years I had come to realise that the enormous letters of the Abbey's antiphonals were written in a style known as lettera moderna which was being replaced by a new style called, confusingly, lettera antica. This new style, small, rounded and infinitely pleasing, was used by those men of learning who studied the poets of ancient Rome and Greece. But the script of the *Iliad* was different again, and obviously lent itself to copying at speed.

'Can you read it?' he asked.

'Oh yes, with ease.'

'I mean the text.'

'Ah ... ' I crawled along the first line, translating slowly and out loud. It was at once evident that the book was a tremendous story. The Bishop told me that it was about the siege of Troy by the Greeks, who wanted to rescue their Queen Helen. 'But read it for yourself.' So saying, he left me with it. Compelled by its unfolding – of Achilles against Agamemnon, of the friendship of Achilles and Patroclus, of Achilles in battle with Hector, of the death of Hector and the grief of his widow – the more avid I became, the more fluently I read. What had they suffered, these Trojans, under siege by the Greeks? 'Homer was a Trojan, was he not?' I asked the Bishop the next time I saw him.

'He was a Greek.'

'No! He pities the Trojans.'

'He was a man of great humanity. To call him a Greek is perhaps to limit him unjustly.'

This Latin translation was, the Bishop declared, 'a work of magnitude in itself', made by a youth only a few years older than I was.

'A Florentine,' I said acidly, stung with envy at his accomplishments.

'No, he was born in Montepulciano, a hill town near Siena, which may seem like a pimple to a Volterrano, but still it is not Florence.'

I remained convinced that this youth had enjoyed privileges which I had not, but the Bishop told me that, on the contrary, his father had been murdered in a vendetta, after which the boy, at nine years of age, had been sent to Florence a penniless wretch to work in a shoe shop.

'Since writing this book, however, he has given up cobbling. Certain friends of mine are now supporting his education and it is only a matter of time before he gains a patron, perhaps even Lorenzo himself.'

He was everything I should have been; he had all I had ever dreamt of having, and I hated him for it. His name was Angelo Ambrogini. Thus the first time I heard of the man who was to become my friend and master was as I sat with a copy of his book in my hands, knowing better than he did how the Trojans had suffered.

I arose from my bed and went slowly to the window. It was closed against the stench from the streets.

'What is going to happen to us when the Greeks burst in? Will we be massacred?'

'They are not going to rush in. This very night the agreement will be signed and tomorrow we will wake to find the Count of Urbino in the Palazzo della Signoria.'

'We shall be captives.'

'We shall be liberated.'

I turned, looking scornful.

'Liberated from ourselves and our notions of freedom,' said the Bishop.

'And then?'

'Then of course there will be burdensome tributes to be paid; after that, all will be as it was: Volterra will be subject to Florence again.'

What the Bishop called liberation sounded like slavery to me, but at least we would be alive, unlike the hapless Trojans.

'What about the alum?'

The Bishop smiled briefly, amused as he so often was by the ironies of the Creator as they revealed themselves in the field of mankind. 'Surveyors of the Florentine army have been to the mine to report on its condition. There is alum there, about enough to fetch one hundred florins on the market. But as it would cost over a thousand to extract it, the mine has been closed.'

That evening the Bishop left the palazzo surreptitiously by one of my secret routes, to go to the church by the wall where the documents of surrender were to be signed.

Frustration smouldered in the city. It had a smell, like that of singed hair. Not just the frustration of those imprisoned by the walls, but the frustration of those kept outside. For mercenaries to breach a wall and then be kept at bay by the commander, that was frustration.

At dusk, Andreas the Greek appeared on the streets below. His figure was blurred by the thick glass but I would not open the window and risk admitting the stink, for the city had begun to smell like a hermitage where no one had washed for years. The more I kept my window shut against the sickly odour, however, the more fetid it was becoming in my own room.

Andreas had his arms raised. He cried out: 'Oh people of Volterra, in that day shall this song be sung in the land of Judah; we have a strong city, salvation will God appoint of walls and bulwarks. Open ye the gates, that the righteous nation which keepeth the truth may enter in!'

Those who had gathered indifferently about him grew wrathful. Fired by their anger, he raised his voice higher: 'Trust ye in the Lord for ever: for in the Lord Jehovah is everlasting strength. For he bringeth down them that dwell on high; the lofty city, he layeth it low; he layeth it low, even to the ground; he bringeth it even to the dust!'

The secretary and the chaplain ran out to rescue him from the mob.

Heavy rain started during the night and I did not sleep until Prime, when I dreamt of soldiers marching behind drums. One hundred drummers led the column and step by heavy step the men marched to the beating drums. The drum beats were so low that they seemed like echoes from the depths of the earth. I blinked awake. My heart was thudding like a drum, but the world was silent, more silent than I had ever known it. No sound, no movement anywhere, not even that of an owl or a rat.

What had happened? Were we already in the hands of the Count? If so, it was the quietest victory in all history. Nothing stirred.

I went to the window. Sky and city were devoid of colour; the whole universe was grey. Time passed, but not on sundials; even nature's clocks registered nothing for the sun never came up that morning. It was as if the day had ended at dawn in a twilight. Thunder rolled across the hills and lightning flashed in the distance. Then it began to streak towards us, wrathful light stabbing at Volterra from the west. More rain came. Noah himself could not have known such rain. The desolate tents and box-and-barrel shelters of the displaced peasantry collapsed beneath the deluge. The homeless screamed under the hail of stinging rain. The grey light turned a murky lemon.

The Palazzo seemed deserted as I went towards the stairs. The headless statues began to sway. I froze. I focused all my consciousness on being still. While all inanimate things rocked and wavered, I could rely only on myself to be the absolute, the standard of the perpendicular.

It was a nightmare and I ran through it, down the stairs and out into the street. The city was no longer silent. People were running. A turbid rush of people: peasants, townspeople, neighbours ... Milanese soldiers ...

They were in – the Greeks were in! – riding the streets brandishing swords, cutting down anyone in their path. I saw a baby impaled on a spear. I saw for the first time that which should only be seen in love: how it is that a man enters a woman. I saw a monk with his head cloven by an axe like Saint Peter the Martyr. But though I saw scenes of martyrdom everywhere, I saw no one with his eyes rolled up to heaven, full of adoration of the Lord.

Deranged by my afflicted senses, I took narrow routes through the city without thought of where I was going. Towards the north-west it grew quieter and, led by who knows what mysterious hand, I ran to the monastery of San Francesco. I found him there in a chapel, trembling violently as one with the ague, unshaven and wretched: Antonio.

His eyes were those of the cornered stag; then, upon recognition, he whispered, 'Help me.'

I knew as well as he did that the sackers would justify their actions by the capture of 'rebels', and I hurried him from the monastery by a small door leading to a passage under the walls, out to the road that led to the cliffs. If this area of the city was undefended it was because it was unassailable. We ran through the rain towards the Abbey in the hope that there we might be safe. But as we ran there was a mighty roar and the road disappeared in front of us. The ground dropped; a chapel, two ancient tombs and a stretch of Etruscan wall cascaded into the abyss. I might have gone with them but that Antonio managed to snatch me back from the brink. We laid together face down in the sand far back from the new edge of the cliffs and howled like abandoned children.

I heard later that the Count of Urbino rode into the city and, with his own forces, managed to subdue the Milanese. The city surrendered and rebels were duly hanged, drawn and quartered. But all I knew of it at the time was that, by late afternoon, the rain had stopped and the city seemed quiet. I wanted to go back in but Antonio refused.

'I have no wish to see my own bowels,' he said.

I offered to go alone, to find out what was happening. He looked at me solemnly. 'We need to make a sacrifice.'

'Of what?'

'Of that which we hold most precious, to appease the gods – and to prevent them falling into the hands of any damnable Florentine. You will find my falcon at the San Francesco monastery. Bring her to me.'

So I returned into the city and found it bedecked with Florentine flags and puddled with blood. I went unchallenged through the groups of soldiers who were quietly throwing the dead on to pyres, past where Francesco Caruggi hung upside-down and disembowelled on the Piazza della Signoria; up to the acropolis where many of the tower houses that had survived being gutted by the fire had now fallen to looters. The Bishop's Palace alone stood unharmed.

There was no one there and I left soon afterwards with my monochord. On the acropolis I met Andreas the Greek crying in exhortation: 'Come my people, enter thou into thy chambers, and shut thy doors about thee: hide thyself as it were for a little moment, until the indignation be overpast. For, behold, the Lord cometh out of his place to punish the inhabitants of the earth for their iniquity; the earth shall also disclose her blood and shall no more cover the slain.'

Seeing me, he lowered his arms and fell silent.

'God is on the side of the Florentines, then,' I said bitterly.

'Tommaso, you speak to me across the dead. Find Life. Find immortality.'

'Where? Where in the world is there anything everlasting?'

'Nowhere. You must go beyond the world.'

I returned to the Camaldolese Abbey, collecting Freccia from the monastery on the way. Together Antonio and I bowed to the four quarters of the sky; then, with a simple movement, he twisted his falcon's neck; her proud head fell limply sideways. I stood and, drawing breath, hurled my monochord up to the gods. It turned like a tree seed in the sky before dropping into the chasm. One note echoed its demise. It was re.

SEVEN

THE FIELDS had been churned into dust by the advance and retreat of armies. From the distance, Volterra was reduced to a damaged wall encircling a peak on a mountain ridge, standing out against the sky like a broken tomb. Now I have seen the Alps, I realise that Volterra is not so very high, but during our continual descent it seemed lost in its altitude and removed from the rest of the world. I felt as if I had left myself behind, that the boy who rode alongside the Bishop was a body without a soul. I had neither thought nor emotion, only the dead weight of hopelessness.

Beggars with accusing stares challenged us to give alms. Their faces were familiar, being those of peasants who on market days had hauled their rickety wagons up the winding road to the city. With no produce this year, they prowled the highways demanding charity. The Bishop gave freely until his purse was empty.

In Volterra the war had been caused by Florence; the further we drew away, however, the more I discovered the general opinon to be that the war had been caused by Volterra. The road ascended again, temporarily, as we approached the town of Colle standing on the hill ahead. In the distance we could see San Gimignano, the birthplace of my aunt Lucia. Both towns looked serene, but when we entered Colle it was to find a place which had suffered almost as much from occupation as Volterra had from sack. The Bishop took rooms and advised me to keep my mouth closed, wisely as it happened, for we spent the evening listening to the people of Colle cursing Volterra and all its offspring.

The sack had occured at the very moment when the articles of surrender were being signed. Why? For one simple reason: the Milanese knew that surrender would rob them of their spoils. At the time of their entry, the Bishop was in the camp of the Count of Urbino. He was the first to hear the roar at the wall, and to understand its import. The Count insisted that the Bishop remain in the camp for his safety; when he refused he was promptly arrested, to be released only some days later.

In the absence of the Bishop, and presuming him lost, I went to find Antonio where I had left him, in sanctuary at the Camaldolese Abbey out by the cliffs; what I found there, however, was an abbey which had been brought to the edge of the precipice by the landslip. Abandoning it to its precarious fate, the monks had left Volterra's cultural heart to be inhabited by mice and spiders.

So I lived alone, a feral boy who knew his city as well as any cat did. Sometimes I would come out of a tunnel or underground burial chamber to find food or watch the demolition of buildings on the acropolis. The Bishop's Palace, unharmed by anything that had taken place, was the first to be pulled down. Soon the fallen masonry of Christian builders was joining the rubble of Etruscans and Romans on the ancient and hallowed site, for an order had come from Lorenzo de' Medici that a fortress was to be built, larger than anything in the city, larger even than the Cathedral or the Palazzo della Signoria; garrisoned by Florentines, it would hold the summit of Volterra for evermore.

It was here at the scene of destruction that the Bishop found me. Although he displayed emotion at our reunion, he showed none at the fate of his house. With a wry expression he said, 'What is a house after all but space surrounded by walls? And what do we have left when the walls are gone? – why, the space. Besides,' he added, 'I have two other houses, more properly my own.'

One of these was in the village of Impruneta where, despite his episcopal status, he continued to perform the function of local priest. The other was a town house, and the town it was in was Florence.

We rode slowly across the devastated land, switching flies from our horses with olive branches on which the fruit had withered. If I was riding with a man who said he was taking me to the city I now equated with hell, it was because I loved him, because he was my guardian, and because I did not know what else I could do. Despite these weighty causes, I longed to be riding in the opposite direction, to the sea, a boat, an infinite horizon and oblivion. The Bishop suddenly punctured my silence with a question.

'What do you intend to do with your life?'

'Nothing,' I said, and truthfully, for I had no hope now in the future.

'With God's grace, you have a long life ahead of you. So what will you do with it?'

I shrugged. So far as I was concerned, the question was more what life intended for me.

'Come, let your imagination work a little. Pretend that I have the power to grant wishes. You can be whatever you like. What is it to be?'

I shrugged again.

'You could be a king or a prince.'

'And kill people.'

'A wealthy merchant then, or a banker.'

'And take the quick road to hell.'

'Well then, a man of the Church. And look at the choice: Franciscan, Augustinian, Benedictine, Carmelite, Dominican.'

'No.'

'Why not?'

I could not find the words to explain, but my question was this: how can you give yourself half-heartedly to something at the age of twelve without knowing how you may feel about it by the age of thirty?

The Bishop ran through the orders of society, from the top to the bottom, trying to find within my heart the nature of my special destiny. Not that he needed to find it for himself: he already knew what it was. But he showered me with the seeds of possibility, for me to experience which one it was that fell not on stony ground.

'Would you like to be a happily married man, with a

bouncing brood of children, each one of them a living replica of yourself?'

This was to condemn unborn children to certain misery. 'No.'

'So, let us send you to university and make a scholar of you. Now what of that, Tommaso?'

Though I loved my studies, reading and books, I was conscious of the gulf between me and, say, my cousin Raffaello. 'I would fail.'

'Very well,' said the Bishop sharply. 'You have denied all God's gifts. Therefore I intend to lock you in a room. You are imprisoned there. Shut your eyes and imagine it. Your food comes through a hole in the wall. You see no one and the world is spared your bitter countenance.'

'What is my crime?'

'Failure to serve the rest of mankind. However, I am a merciful God, and you may have whatever objects you desire. So what would you like me to send in to you?'

I imagined myself in the dungeon all too easily. At first I was swept with restlessness and frustration. Then objects appeared in my mind's eye, floating in the air the way painters sometimes depict the instruments of Christ's passion. 'Quills,' I said.

'What was that, Tommaso?'

'Quills, ink, parchment, and books to copy. A desk. A chair. A beautiful oriental rug like yours to drape over my desk. Paper. Vellum. Good light. Is there a window in this prison? – I shall need good light.'

'So, Tommaso, would you be a scribe?'

Since the massacre there had been a single noise in my brain, that of a sustained scream, the wail of a Fury against inexorable fate. I was twelve and had been robbed of happiness. What use was there in wanting to be happy again, since happiness was so easily lost? But now the word *scribe* fell upon my soul and, finding its echo there, gave respite from the scream of despair.

'It is not possible,' I said cautiously.

'Impossible, impossible,' said the Bishop gruffly. 'How we damn ourselves and make God's work so much harder. Not possible? – why, it is inevitable.' The Bishop looked pleased with himself. For how long had he known my dreams?

Thus an inner light began to burn, seeming bright against the dense shadows, shadows composed of one thought, that to fulfil my ambition I must dwell in Florence, the city of Lorenzo de' Medici.

'Oh,' said the Bishop lightly when I had confessed my thoughts, 'Florence is a large city and not like Volterra, where you have only to loiter on the main piazza to see men of importance. Lorenzo may be easily avoided, if you so wish. After all, ninety thousand people live in Florence, and only one of them is Lorenzo.'

'Ninety thousand?' I piped in amazement.

'Is that too large a figure?'

'Ninety thousand ... '

'I am disappointed in you, young man; it seems that, after all my lessons in mathematics, you are still scared of numbers.'

At the town of Colle I had had my first view of the plain. Having always supposed the valleys of the Volterrana to be the low places, I was shocked to discover the flatness of the Val d'Elsa. After crossing the plain, however, we ascended into the hills of Chianti and I could breathe again, but only for a while; for the journey from Volterra to Florence was, overall, one of descent. From the citadel of the clouds I was bound for the plain. The closer we came, the more nauseous I felt, and the Bishop thought it necessary for us to go to his village of Impruneta rather than into the city. We stayed there for a night, but the next day I requested that the journey be completed, for I could suffer the oppression of fate no longer. It was best to meet it.

The nearer we came, the more villages we passed through. From within small houses came the domestic sounds of mothers scolding and children whining. None of those sounds or their makers was happy, but I would have so promptly changed places with them, to be on the inside of a house and family. The vineyards and olive groves were surrounded by walls that obscured any view but then, through the cleft of one broken wall, I suddenly saw it, the long plain of the Arno valley. As we passed the gap, the western battlements of Florence came into view; then appeared a monstrous dome. I had heard about it, of course, but nothing had prepared me for the vision. It swelled above the city, blood red with white veins, dwarfing everything.

Trembling, I slipped from the saddle to the ground. The massive cap to the Cathedral was an affront, an impossibility, ridiculous. My soul stretched. Nothing could have been more unexpected than that dome, and yet ... and yet ...

'What is it, Tommaso? Are you not well?'

I leant through the breach in the wall and, under the very eye of my destiny, spewed up my fear. I do not remember how the Bishop persuaded me back into the saddle; I only remember feeling boneless in the face of the inevitable. This was where all dreams ended, swept away by the gale of reality. There was nothing I could do except follow my guardian.

We began to descend a road which was exceedingly steep and led to the tall, battlemented gate to the city, the barbican. We were inside Florence almost before I knew it. Tall, narrow houses of four or five stories high ran shoulder to shoulder in a terrace down the hill. Ahead, on the opposite bank of the river, I could see the spires and towers of the city like pointing fingers against the sky. The Bishop named them all as if they were saints in a fresco, but I could not take my eyes from the great pap which dominated everything.

The Bishop, proud of his native city, said that I would have to visit all these sites he was pointing out, and that it might take a few days. The idea of a tour was new and inconceivable. I had always imagined Florence to be just like Volterra only bigger. No doubt it had a Palazzo della Signoria, a Baptistry, a Cathedral and a main market square, and I would come across them all in due course. But then we passed a palazzo so enormous that my eyes started from my head.

'Is this the home of Lorenzo?'

'No, no,' the Bishop laughed. 'This is, or was, the home of one who thought himself a king, and met the usual fate of kings in a republic. I am not sure who lives here now, but it is certainly not Lorenzo. It is an abomination, is it not? – a monument to man's hubris. The place should certainly be pulled down.'

Spanning the broad Arno was a bridge, a lively trading area of goldsmiths. Some boys, older than I, stood indolently watching those who passed by. I broke into a sweat under their cold gaze. They were dressed in fashion: brightly coloured hose and jackets with narrow pleats pinched in at the waist by tight belts.

The padded chests of their jackets added to the natural air of arrogance of the Florentine. I noticed their hair in particular: whether curly or straight it looked attended to, smart and well cut. Not only that but it was often brown rather than black, and some of these boys had blue eyes. Somehow I rode on, into the jaws of this foreign place.

At the Piazza della Signoria I faced a town hall three times the size of ours. It rose into the sky to a dizzying height. In the square, preparations were being made for an event, fences erected and triumphal pennants hung. The colours were those of the Count of Urbino. The Bishop seemed discomforted and abruptly changed our direction so that we passed into a road running behind the Palazzo della Signoria. Here my status as dwarf was confirmed by the Palazzo del Podestà; it soared windowless above us, the house of the Chief Magistrate, where criminals were either imprisoned in its dungeons or executed in its courtyard. When the Bishop brought us to a halt outside, I looked at him in fright, wondering for a moment if the locked room he had confined me to had not been imaginary after all. But after we had tied our mounts to the wall rings of the Palazzo, the Bishop led me across the lane at its side, to a small house on the corner. Its front was open to the street and a bench displayed the wares of this shop, which were books.

Vespasiano da Bisticci was a *cartolaio*, a stationer, and his shop near the prison was in a street filled with stationers. Though that was the foundation of his business, he also sold books, and Vespasiano's reputation was such that to many he seemed to be the only bookseller in the city. Firstly, he ran a service of manuscript-copying for which he employed only the finest scribes, and whose work he checked himself; secondly he kept company with the luminaries of that which we call the New Learning who resided in Florence. Since the day when Lorenzo's grandfather, Cosimo de' Medici, had engaged him to create a library of books, princes, rulers and scholars from throughout Italy and beyond had resorted to Vespasiano whenever they required a text.

His shop was in two parts divided by an arch. On one side was the workshop of the cartolaio where parchment, paper, inks and quills were sold, and books were bound. This was where Vespasiano's establishment had its humble roots. On the other side of the arch was the bookshop, furnished as a study, with several desks for the use of customers, and shelves stocked with popular titles such as Plutarch's *Lives* and Lionardo Bruni's *Letters*.

Left to myself, I took a book down. It was a copy of one of Plato's *Dialogues* translated into Latin. Glancing round to see that no one was watching, I sniffed at it. The leather binding, soft and supple, was pungent, but it was the pages that interested me. They smelt nourishing, like new-baked bread. Ever since I can remember, I have greeted books with my nose first. I still do it. My only consolation in this foolishness is that I have met others who do the same and who are not fools.

In the workshop, at a table between stretching frames and binding presses, a wizened man of middle years called Grazia was ruling music staves on to sheets of parchment. He looked up, squinting. 'Who are you?' he snapped.

I explained nervously that I was the ward of Bishop Antonio degli Agli, who was in conversation with Vespasiano regarding my future as a scribe.

'Pah! You are a fool then. Thought so as soon as I saw you sniffing books. Who is this idiot, I wondered, and from what insignificant little town does he come?'

I said nothing.

'But now that I have heard you speak, I do not need to ask. Rough-tongued, the Volterrani, with voices that could saw wood.'

I regarded him truculently.

'Come, come,' said the man. 'Let the past rest. I have no grudge against you.'

My rage deepened into a roaring, silent protest.

'Come and help me draw lines.'

If only to impress him with my capabilities, I sat down with pen and rule to draw staves.

'Not bad,' he said, 'but try to speed up. These are needed urgently for the Count of Urbino.'

At the mention of this name, my pen tore across the sheet and ruined an expensive piece of parchment. The man sucked air through his teeth and told me to go away and be idle. 'After all, if you are to be a scribe, idleness is something you must become accustomed to.' Noting my mystification he smiled maliciously. 'You have not heard have you? I can tell.' He rose up and, walking with a stiff hip, crossed to an open chest from which he drew out a book. 'I have to keep it in here, out of Vespasiano's sight.' He thrust it towards me.

The pictures were but crude, black outlines, without colour. The letters were perfectly regular in form but in execution ragged, as if written with a nib through which the ink flowed poorly. It was a curiosity. I lifted up a page to the light and peered at it. The paper was thin and absorbent; no one could write on such paper. I did not know what to say. In truth, I was frightened of something so unfamiliar.

'It comes from hell,' said the man.

I dropped the book with a yelp and jumped backwards.

His laughter was like the bark of a fox; he picked up the book and tried to touch me with it. I whimpered in terror. 'I am only teasing,' he said. 'It comes from Germany. It is a printed book. Have you not heard about the printing press? Mechanical printing? They have alphabets of letters made of steel which they arrange into words on a forme. This they cover with ink, then with paper, and then they squeeze it all together in something which resembles an olive press.'

'And then?'

'Then they peel the paper off and hang it up to dry, re-ink the forme and slap another sheet of paper on to it.'

'Madonna ... !' My future prospects were withering in the bud.

'As soon as we heard about it, I said to the master, there is only one thing to do: we must obtain a press ourselves. Will he listen? No, he prefers to worry about it. He clutches his head and says, "Grazia, we are ruined." I say it is stupid to spit in the face of fortune. We must have a press built and make some money for our retirement. No, no, no, he says. "I will not end my days being party to this abomination. I was born to make beautiful things, and I intend to die with a clear conscience."'

Leaving the ugly book with the ugly man, I retreated to the bookshop and found the Bishop looking deeply worried. The man who could look on a destroyed house with equanimity turned to me in agitation. 'Apparently a device to copy books has been invented. Soon there will be no further need for scribes.'

'Printed books are ugly,' I said. 'The device is just a novelty and will be out of use long before I am.'

If this astonished the Bishop, it delighted Vespasiano da Bisticci.

'That is my view entirely,' he said, and patted me on the head. 'Nonetheless I do advise you against becoming a professional scribe. Notwithstanding the printing press, there is not much demand for new books these days. Twenty years ago we could not find enough scribes; now, well ... '

I looked questioningly at the Bishop. 'It may be true,' he admitted. He explained to me that, in the span of his own life, he had seen a time when there were few if any books in a household, all books being scriptural and kept in monasteries, or theological and the property of scholars; and he had seen a time when any citizen of standing bought and possessed many books. 'For there was a great change, and it became acceptable to read the works of poets, both ancient and modern. Vespasiano was there, to supply the demand.'

'Ah!' said the bookseller, rolling his eyes in memory of the time of his prosperity. 'Petrarch, Dante, Boccaccio, Virgil, Livy, Juvenal, Pliny. And then, of course, men came to desire rarer, more difficult works. Do you remember the time Poggio Bracciolini came home with the Quintillian, Monsignore? You might have thought he was bringing in gold from old Byzantium, the way he was greeted with cheers and applause.'

The Bishop nodded with a smile. 'Indeed, those were happy days, when each week something new was discovered buried in a monastery and brought back to Florence, to be read again for the first time in centuries.'

'And copies had to be made,' said the bookseller, 'hundreds of copies. At one time I had forty scribes working for me, creating whole libraries for men such as Cosimo de' Medici. Not any longer, Tommaso. I have only one good patron left. You see, today's citizens have inherited their fathers' collections, and now we are fortunate if we make a new discovery once every ten years. It is my belief that the future lies in second-hand books.'

'And Greek translations,' added the Bishop.

The bookseller agreed, but said that there was not enough work from that source to keep one scribe occupied full time. The two men looked down on me sorrowfully.

'Of course,' said Vespasiano, 'the Church always needs new antiphonals, and I doubt if it will countenance printed versions, so perhaps you should become a monk.'

We were interrupted by the arrival of two men. The one who entered first was very tall, muscular and forbidding. In profile he was like a hawk with a veritable beak of a nose, a sickle of a nose, a nose to inspire caricatures. I recognised him at once. Even as he turned towards me I knew that one eye would be missing.

This was astounding. How could the world's most famous condottiere, the Count of Urbino, builder of sublime palaces and conqueror of Volterra, a man due to enter Florence in triumph in the afternoon; how could such a one come in the morning to visit a bookseller? Such things do not happen, at least not in Volterra.

Vespasiano and the Bishop both greeted the Count by bowing low. I stood like a tree about to be felled. Vespasiano pushed me towards the workshop, telling me to fetch the music sheets from Grazia. I went readily.

'Federico da Montefeltro,' I stuttered to the wizened man.

'What of him?'

'He is in the shop.'

'*Santo cielo*!'

I ignored his sarcasm and demanded to know what the Count was doing here. Grazia presumed he was buying books. 'He is a very busy man; not one to let the plaster dry on the wall. Always building cities, or sacking them, wiping out opposing armies and hanging rebels. But in his rare moments of leisure he loves to read, and so we sell him books. Real books. None of this printed fribble. He will not have that. He has to have the best money can buy, with the most beautiful pictures and borders by the best artists. He is our most discerning patron. And, of course, he needs other things, such as music sheets.'

As Grazia wrapped the sheets, I went back to the archway to listen to the conversation of the men.

'What do you make of this Sforza duke, Monsignore?' the Count was saying.

'From the stories one hears,' said the Bishop, 'he makes one wish for the Visconti to return to power in Milan. "Duke" is a title the Sforza have made for themselves. They are self-crowned, and no good can come of that. It is a tyranny, of the kind described by Plato as the worst form of government.'

'Surely to have the Visconti back would be to replace tyranny with tyranny? I would have thought you might have supported the Ambrosian republic.'

'In my heart I would, but it was a weak thing. How long did it last? Three years? With Francesco Sforza as its general, tyranny was inevitable. Just as Plato says.'

'I would rather have Francesco than his son, Galeazzo Maria,' said Vespasiano, 'but then the old devil always seems preferable to the new one.'

'But is not Galeazzo Maria Sforza one of your patrons?' asked the Count.

'He is, and I only wish I could choose my patrons. He is not like you, my Lord. Books to him are mere ornaments. To him the New Learning is a fashion he must adopt, for surely no real man of culture could commit the cruelties that he is known for? He reads the best of the Romans and acts like the worst.'

Their talk continued, of foreign governments, of kings, princes and tyrants. Not once did they mention the tyranny they lived under themselves. Suddenly Grazia hurried through the arch with the music sheets, knocking me out of my hiding place as he passed. I crossed the floor quickly and tried to hide behind the Bishop. The Count watched my every step. His one eye reminded me of Freccia and I encouraged myself by imagining him having his neck twisted. He called his companion, a young captain, and asked him to settle the account; he asked him also for a purse. This he held out to me, on his palm. 'Here, twenty florins.'

Twenty florins! Natural avarice would have had me snatch it, but my cousin Antonio would have me not. He came straight to mind, and forbade it. 'Taking his money,' said the image, 'will only help him ease his conscience. Refuse, refuse. Spit in his eye.'

'Here,' said the Count, 'take the purse. It will help you on your way.' He jingled the coins.

I shook my head and stepped back, away from his outstretched hand. I glanced up at the Bishop: he was clearly disappointed. When the Count pressed the purse on me again, I said, 'Please give it to my guardian.'

The Bishop was irritated. 'What do I need with twenty florins?'

'If no one else wants it,' said Vespasiano, deftly lifting the purse from the hand of the Count, 'then I shall have it.' While everyone stared at him in horror of his presumption, he explained: 'It will pay for the boy's tuition.'

And this was the foundation of my professional life: blood money.

THE SECOND BOOK

A SENSE OF PROPORTION

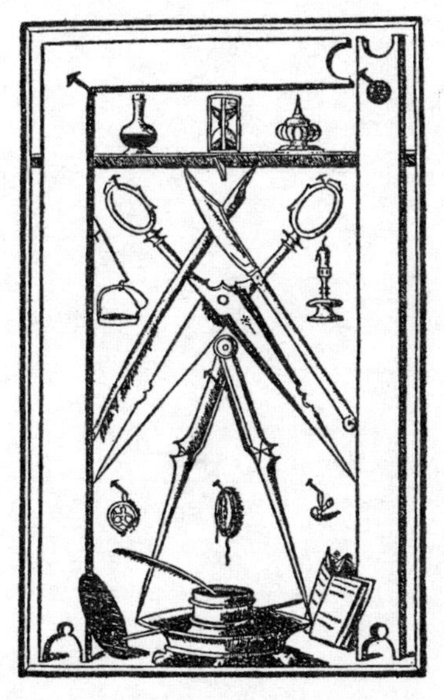

Imitation is a surer way to virtue than reading. Just as harmony has a more powerful effect when actually flowing in the ears than when subsequently reflected, and as a battle stirs us more deeply when watched than when being recounted, so the illustrious deeds of living heroes rouse us more ardently to the pursuit of virtue and fashion us more perfectly for it than do the words of ancient philosophers discussing moral conduct.

Marsilio Ficino

To Desiderio of Rotterdam

Che un miracolo! The sun came out today and the rain ceased. Our Master John Colet preached in the open air, with that vigorous sincerity and enthusiasm which have the Masters of Divinity snorting with indignation. He stood at the cross and proclaimed the Gospel of Christ, to the English and in English, a fresh-faced, stern but handsome graduate of the liberal arts, speaking the truth. 'He is not a divine!' cry his detractors, and they are right. Thanks be to God he was not trained in theology, that he cares little for scholasticism and the niceties of logic, that he cares less how many angels can stand on the head of a pin. What matters, he says, is the condition of the heart. In Italy he would now be under the keen scrutiny of the Dominicans and on his way to excommunication. Here they merely grumble and say that Masters of the Liberal Arts should keep to literature. England is a tolerant place. Long may it remain so.

I know I grumble about Colet as fiercely as any divine, but I love him deeply and consider him, dare I say it, a hero. His courage is an inspiration. Follow him; do not listen to me. If he instructs you to devote yourself to the study of Greek, not so as to read Divine Plato, but in order to translate that ascetic Saint Jerome, so be it. Obey him. I will do what I can to help. The little Greek that I have is, in this land of dearth, comparatively great. Famine has invested my meagre goods with inestimable value. I can charge what I will for my tutorials, especially now that it is rumoured that young Prince Henry desires to learn Greek. To you, Desiderio, I offer all that I have at no charge.

Men such as Colet have brought the New Learning to England. It is the kind of knowledge that has bachelors of arts preaching truth and Italian scribes teaching Greek. It is fresh and invigorating. It brings about rebirth. If the sun can shine in England, perhaps the meadows may fill with flowers after all.

Tommaso dei Maffei
March 14th 1499

EIGHT

THE STREETS of Florence were like gullies which cut men off from any sense of the land. At the end of some you could see hills in the distance, simmering gently in the heat of the rising sun, but nowhere could you see a true horizon, and life without horizons is something which no one should be made to suffer, particularly a Volterrano. Feeling crushed and suffocated, I walked very close to the Bishop. Though he had my permission to take me to see the triumphal entry of the Count of Urbino, I held his hand like a child. The Palazzo della Signoria, built of massive blocks of roughly hewn stone, rose up three tall storeys to a threatening swell of machicolations topped by battlements; up into the sky soared its tower. We entered by a side door, crossed an arcaded courtyard, went up a grand staircase and along vast galleries frescoed with scenes of the history of the city. The place was a very cathedral to civic pride. We went to a grand hall on the upper floor where privileged men were allowed a fine view of the square below. The Bishop greeted several friends, each of whom I regarded sullenly as my enemy.

Having some time before the event, the Bishop took me round the paintings to tell me the history of Florence, and then up the stairs of the tower to the room where Cosimo de' Medici had once been imprisoned. There he told me the story of Lorenzo's grandfather, a citizen who was so popular that the priors had him arrested and exiled to Venice for ten years. Cosimo had returned within twelve months, and from that time on the Medici family, and not the priors, had dominated Florence. I continued to be sullen.

'Cosimo de' Medici' said the Bishop, 'began it all – the New Learning, the new buildings, the art, everything. He was the richest man in the world, and he spent his money on beauty and truth. Do not put the sins of the son upon the grandfather.'

A blare of trumpets sounding, followed by rapping drums and the roar of people, drew us back to the windows overlooking the square which blazed with the colours of the various wards of the city. To one side, at a right-angle to the Palazzo, was a fine loggia, newly built, in which had gathered the Signoria – paunchy, self-satisfied merchants, wearing the robes of state – and the masters of the guilds. Among them stood the proud Gonfaloniere with the lily standard of Florence.

'Which one is Lorenzo?' I asked reluctantly, but the Bishop said he was not among the group, for he held no office of state. The drummers and trumpeters now came into view, striding into the square before mounted knights, and behind the knights came a preposterous chariot, drawn by two white oxen. The chariot had wings, and Federico of Urbino, dressed in a white toga and crowned with a laurel wreath, stood with his arms outstretched as if ready for his apotheosis. Embarrassed on his behalf, I turned to watch two young men, apparently noble, riding out to meet him. The Bishop put his arm round my shoulder and said softly: 'Remember, all men are equal in the eyes of the Lord. Remember, not a sparrow falls. Remember, God is a circle whose centre is everywhere, and circumference nowhere.' The caress of his words stopped my trembling.

Though I could not see the faces of these two young knights, I could feel their power. Dressed in flashing gold brocade, and on high-stepping, white horses caparisoned in red, rode the Medici. Even though I had always known that Lorenzo had a brother, I had ever imagined him alone. Now I suffered not only having a dream realised, but doubly realised.

'Remember the Monad of Intelligent Fire.'

Below me was unfolding a scene more colourful, more beautiful than anything I had ever dreamt of, but I was not free to enjoy it. It was as if, while the Bishop spoke into one ear, my cousin was speaking into the other. 'Remember the screams of the dying; remember the smell of burning flesh; remember how your shoes turned soft in the blood of our people.'

After the Count of Urbino had been escorted into the Palazzo, and thus out of sight, the Bishop knelt on one knee before me, to look me in the face and tell me that he had to go away, first to Impruneta, and then back to Volterra. I clung to him like a leech and begged to go with him. He disengaged my hands and shook me gently. 'I have come all this way to start you on the journey of your life. I have no intention of taking you back in my baggage.'

I would have wailed but for all the important men in the room, gathering to descend to the sala and see the Count being transformed into a Duke.

'Now help me up,' said the Bishop. 'My poor old knees creak.'

I was returned to Vespasiano, to live with the bookseller and to work for him until such time as a master could be found for me. Some of my duties were little different from what they had been before: sweeping, drawing water, removing cobwebs. I even had pigeon droppings to deal with, and was glad to discover that my bird friends could survive at this low altitude. I found other friends in lizards, but my companion elements seemed absent. Some of my duties, however, brought me close to books. There was parchment to be collected from the parchment-makers, to be trimmed and folded into quires; there were goose-feathers to be trimmed into quills and lead plummets to make; there were inks – black, red and blue – their ingredients to be ground on a slab and mixed with gum. Hares' feet, pen-knives and resting sticks, all these things were bought in and displayed in pots. Then there were the books to be dusted, a collection finer than any in private hands; every known text was in that shop, serving as a model for a scribe to copy to order. I was happy in my duties, provided I was left alone; I was even happier to have my bed under the counter, for there alone at night I could read these books by the dim light of a tallow candle. It was then that I entered the world of the ancients and became more familiar with them and their surroundings than my own.

One day, as summer drew on and citizens began their retreat to the hills, I came back from the well to find the shop empty except for Grazia and one customer. Despite being of artisan stock himself, Grazia despised poor men and foreigners. The exalted citizens of Florence he would cluck round as an old hen;

others were likely to be cheated. The long cupboard was open and sheets of parchment were being angrily pulled out while the customer stood helplessly by.

'Parchment,' snapped Grazia, 'what do you mean you want parchment? You will have to be more specific. Is it messale maggiore, messale commune, ragionevole, foglio reale, foglio commune, bolognese maggiore, bolognese mezzano? Which? Hmn?'

'Er, foglio commune,' said the man, obviously chancing his luck.

'Well, how much? Quire, quaderno or ream?'

'Um, ah, quaderno.'

Grazia gave him a quire of bolognese. As soon as the man had been served he fled, leaving Grazia screwing his finger into his temple. 'Neapolitans. They are pazzi – mad, crazy. He only wanted to say that he had been to the bottega of Vespasiano. Still, we made a handsome profit there.'

'It was dishonest!'

'What, taking money from a vain fool? How so?' Grazia ordered me to tidy up the shelves that had become disarrayed. I set to work slowly, practising recognition of the different sizes and qualities of the parchment.

'Messale maggiore,' I muttered, 'messale commune ... '

'Ragionevole,' said a kind voice from behind. 'Foglio reale, foglio commune, bolognese maggiore,' it continued, reciting the names with affection.

He was about eighteen, with lank black hair and brown eyes. He wore the humble cloth of honesty of a university student, and it was patched and threadbare; but though his looks were undistinguished, his voice was very beautiful indeed. It lilted, the voice of one who is a lover of words.

'Where is Vespasiano?' he asked, smiling.

'Out, it seems.'

'And Grazia?'

I looked about. 'He was here but a moment ago.' I seemed to be alone with the shop. 'Can I help you?' I asked cautiously.

'I only came in for the diversion. Do you know, this is the first time I have ever found this place empty? You can usually depend on it for a good conversation.'

'Not today,' I thought. I stared at him, at his ambiguous face. I had seen him here before, in the evenings when the bookshop was full of men who gathered to talk of learned things. Despite his youth, he was ready to correct his elders, and could easily look disdainful or supercilious; therefore I had marked him out as one to be avoided. Now however his eyes were gentle, even friendly.

'I am trying to put these sheets back into order,' I said.

'Let me help.' He sat down beside me and slotted the parchment back on the shelves. 'I have noticed you often,' he said, 'hiding in corners, cloaked in Stygian darkness and looking as vengeful as Medea. Where are you from?'

'Nowhere.'

He blinked at the rebuff but ignored it. 'I understand,' he said.

'What do you understand?'

'I know the terror of being new in the city. I myself was once a shop boy with the face of a Gorgon.' He diverted my attention back to the cupboard and its contents. 'This is Florentine parchment, the best of its kind. See how fine, white and smooth it is? You will not find its like anywhere else. And this is the best paper, Fabriano. Look, do you see?' He held a sheet up to the light from the open door at the back of the workshop. 'There is the watermark.'

Wonderfully, mysteriously, the image of a cardinal's hat shone in the very substance of the paper.

'How is that done?' I asked, genuinely interested.

'Well, as the paper is made ... '

'Angelo!' Grazia barked suddenly, coming up behind us. 'What are you doing, squatting on the floor with that toad from Volterra?'

'Grazia, how wonderful to see you.'

'Is it? Why?'

'The university has closed for the summer.'

'So you thought you would come and waste time here, did you?'

'I knew you would be delighted to see me.'

'Yes, indeed. I am always glad to see a debtor. Have we any chance of payment yet?'

Angelo winced. 'Not today,' he said, 'but I have great hopes.'

'Great hopes! You might be able to live off them: we cannot.

I thought that book of yours was going to earn your fortune.'

'It has been exceedingly well received.'

'But has it won you a patron yet?'

'Not quite, no. Not yet. But it will, I know it will.'

'And I will be the next Gonfaloniere. All that book has brought you is fame. Everyone gasps and says, look, only eighteen and already a genius. But it is our paper you write on, ours until you pay for it.'

Angelo smiled at me. 'I always come here when I am in need of encouragement.' But I was not listening; instead I was remembering a small book telling of Trojan heroes, a translation made by a youth from Montepulciano who had worked in a shoemaker's. I might have lost the book, but it seemed I had found its author.

Though Angelo Ambrogini pretended to be unmoved by Grazia's invective, as soon as a bold 'Ohè!' announced Vespasiano's return, he hurried through to the bookshop. Vespasiano clasped him as if he were his long lost son, patted him on the back and said how happy he was to see him. He made no mention of debts.

In high summer the only people who remained in the city were the shopkeepers and those with nowhere else to go. I could hardly move for the heat and thought I would die from lack of air as a fish drowns out of water. Then, on one of his visits, Angelo asked Vespasiano if he had a copy of the satires of Persius Flaccus.

Vespasiano pulled on his chin thoughtfully, pretending to wonder if he did have a copy, while in reality he was trying to remember who Persius Flaccus was.

'A Latin poet of the second century,' I said, passing by with a heavy bucket of well water. Vespasiano looked amazed; Angelo grinned.

'If you do not have a copy,' he said, 'I believe there is one at the Abbey of Fiesole, but I do not have the energy to walk there in this heat. Vespasiano, support a poor poet with the loan of your horse.'

Vespasiano muttered something about his shop being a foundling hospital for students, but when Angelo further suggested that I accompany him, he agreed. 'I would appreciate a day free from this guilt-inducing wretch,' he said.

I brought the saddle from the back of the shop, but Angelo said it was too narrow for both of us. 'I presume you can ride without one?' he asked. In a flash of my old spirit, I leapt on the back of Vespasiano's mare, and Angelo, with the strong legs of one from the hills, followed. Vespasiano seemed to be on the point of changing his mind about lending us his horse, but Angelo kicked her flanks before he could say anything. 'Vespasiano,' he called back to him as we rode off, 'for the sake of your knowledge and erudition, Aulus Persius Flaccus was a Volterrano.'

We rode through the heat-thrumming city and left it by a northern gate. Almost at once the road began to climb, and I breathed air scented with fennel. I cannot tell you how it felt to see again fruit on trees rather than on market stalls, to hear the drone of heavy bees and the rasping song of the crickets. I began to breathe deeply, to fill both body and spirit with my old companions, the air and the sun.

The road ribboned its way up the hill called Fiesole. We passed a monastery and a lane which, Angelo said, led to the abbey.

'Should we not take it, then?' I asked as we rode past.

'I have already read Flaccus. He is competent enough, but not of the first rank. If I would read satire, it is Horace and none other for me.' Had this been said to one of Vespasiano's scholarly visitors, then the man would have felt stung by this youth's disdain. Realising, however, that Flaccus had been invoked merely as an excuse for this wonderful journey, I smiled – for the first time in months.

'Where then are we going?'

'To the top,' said Angelo, kicking the horse with his heels. As we rode towards the sky, and I began to feel more and more alive, Angelo pierced my heart with the revelation that Fiesole had been one of the twelve cities of ancient Etruria; the Romans built on the plain, to facilitate travel and trade, but the people of the gods built on the high places. Sitting behind me on the horse, he did not realise that I was greeting his history lesson with tears until I began to sob convulsively. He stopped the horse then, and before a view of Florence shimmering below us, he encouraged me in the dissolution of my pent-up grief.

'You have done well,' he said. 'It was six months before I cried, and I was only nine.'

'Perhaps you did not have someone to help,' I managed to say.

In time, when my storm had passed and the rain of tears had left me feeling new born, we rode on to the summit. At the very peak was a monastery, but below it there was a vast hollow in the side of the hill which Angelo told me was a Roman theatre.

'I know,' I said, jumping down from the horse. 'We have one at Volterra.' I ran down the grassy steps to see the view on the far side of the hill. Filled with a sense of renewal, and gratitude, I impulsively bowed to the four quarters of the sky.

'Do not let the monks see you do that,' cautioned Angelo.

'You are an Etruscan yourself, are you not?' I asked.

He said he had no idea. 'Montepulciano is on the route from Florence to Rome, unlike Volterra which is not on the route to anywhere. There is no purity in our blood. I brought you here simply to show you how close Florence is to the heights, for it is often difficult to live on the plain.'

'It makes your buttocks ache, walking on flat ground all the time.'

'Indeed.'

We sat together, bathing in the wind. I wanted him to tell me more about his native town, but he carefully deflected all such questions, telling me instead about his progress at the university, of his redoubtable tutors, of how he could both read and write ancient Greek fluently, and was one of the very few men in Italy who could do so. He was supported by those benefactors which the Bishop had mentioned, but his days as a student were drawing to a close. 'If I were to pray to the gods of the sky, it would be for a patron.'

'Then do it!' I urged him.

He looked uncertain.

'Forget the monks. What do they know? Do it!'

He rose to his feet, facing north. 'No, not that way,' I said, turning him east-north-east. 'This is the direction for Jupiter and Minerva. Pray to them.'

'How shall I pray?'

I made him repeat after me, 'Gods within and gods without, draw the genius from my heart. Grant to me what I desire and hone my talent in your fire. So that I may write to please, grant to me a life of ease!'

'Did you just make up that piece of doggerel?'

I glared at him with the eyes of an offended deity and in a hiss told him to repeat my words. He did so in an embarrassed whisper.

'Say it as if you mean it! Address the wind!'

He tried again, and this time his words went forth with heartfelt conviction. At that moment a monk appeared on the lip of the theatre and called out to him, demanding to know what he was doing. Angelo looked abashed and called back that he, with his young friend, were playing at being Roman actors on a stage.

'Tush!' said the monk. 'If you must act, then act the man.'

Angelo blamed me for the rebuke. 'I knew I should not have done that.'

'You will be pleased enough when the boon arrives.'

'How do you know all this? In what books did you read it?'

'It is what the children of my country know. It is something that you learn when you are six. The older people seem to forget, but the children know the ancient ways.'

'You will have us both burnt,' he said.

Three days later Angelo burst into the shop in a fever of excitement to tell Vespasiano that the day approached when his debts would be cleared.

'I have a patron!'

He was surrounded by a chorus of 'Who is it?' and I jumped on him in delight, asking the same question. He evaded my gaze and, as he told the others of being invited to a palazzo to dine, of meeting a man who was his superior in worldly affairs but his equal in intellect, a man who had praised his *Iliad* as one who had read it with profound understanding, I was already withdrawing.

'Who is it?' I demanded, the shadows of Hades gathering about me again, separating me from my new friend.

He gazed at me as if from a distance. 'Lorenzo de' Medici,' he said.

NINE

Desiderio, I wish I could summon up the ghost of Vespasiano for you. He died just two years ago, at the noble age of seventy-seven, financially ruined and spiritually crushed by the printing press. If you were to name any famous man of quattrocento Florence, Vespasiano would have known him, would have been his friend. Not that he contained his friendships within the territories of the city: several popes and the King of Hungary had been known to visit the bookshop. If I could summon up his ghost, he would tell you himself all you want to know about such heroes of the New Learning as Cosimo de' Medici, Poggio Bracciolini and Ambrogio Traversari. I would repeat here all he told me, but I confess that, as with most boys who keep company with garrulous elders, I hardly listened to his endless prattle. He was so very fond of the past, while I needed to make my own heroes from the material of the present. When he recounted stories about popes, cardinals, kings and abbots, they were of men who had died; I wanted to hear about men who were alive, famous men of my own time such as Angelo Ambrogini. Though Vespasiano admired Angelo well enough, however, the poet was too young and alive to merit entry into Vespasiano's pantheon, too real, too fully human and unpredictable to be the subject of one of his biographies. Vespasiano preferred his heroes to have been pickled by time.

IF THERE is one conversation I do remember vividly it is because it dwelt on dead men who I was keen to hear about: the great scribes. One summer evening, as we walked from the bookshop towards his house on the far bank of the river, Vespasiano deviated from the usual route and led me up a small bump which Florentines called 'the hill'.

'To become a scribe is to join a fellowship of men centuries old. Centuries and centuries. There have been scribes since writing was invented, and they have always been learned men, and most revered. Scribe is a broad term, encompassing everything from secretary to copyist. Now my beloved friends, the ones I want to tell you about, were copyists, but such was their learning and their care that their names will go down in history. Mark my word, they will go down in history.'

We were climbing towards the church of San Miniato. Wide steps had been cut into the hill leading directly up to it. If you stretched your legs, you could cover each step with a pace, but Vespasiano was a dignified, two-pace man and I kept with him.

'"Up to the height and the church whose walls command the city that so discreetly orders things." There, who said that?' he asked, and told me it was Dante before I could answer. Then he launched into a biography of Niccoló Niccoli, a successful merchant who had spent so much money on books that he quickly became ruined. Reduced to having to copy his own books, he designed a script that could be written at speed.

'It is speed that is important these days. The scriptures are still copied in monastic leisure, but the poets are scribbled down by quill-drivers without much time to spare; yet if they would adopt Niccoló's cursive script, they could keep their speed without losing legibility.'

I told him that once I had had a copy of Angelo Ambrogini's *Iliad* which was written in such a script. He told me that the Bishop had written the copy himself and had indeed used Niccoló's script. Learning this, my grief at its loss became acute and I fell into melancholy. Vespasiano cuffed me on the ear. 'Are you listening?' he demanded, and then continued with his story.

When Niccoló died, he left a collection of eight hundred books and some huge debts. Cosimo de' Medici redeemed the debts, took the books, and had a library built at the monastery of San Marco to house them. And that library was a public one. Such examples of civic benevolence, recounted passionately by Vespasiano, were always followed by a postscript of despair about the present state of the world.

'These days we have weasels dressed up as ermine and Everyman parades like a prince. Our exalted citizens would do well to remember the humble origins of their fathers and grandfathers. But do not tell any of them I said so, will you?'

Though he despised men who rose above their station by means of wealth gained through trade, he admired anyone who improved himself by hard work. He spoke lovingly of Poggio Bracciolini, the son of a poor peasant who rose to be Chancellor by striding up that ladder which could, it seemed, carry any man to the top: the New Learning. Poggio had taught himself Latin and, to acquire the books he could not afford, had trained himself as a scribe so that, like Niccoló, he could make his own copies. He too designed a hand, a round, upright, script now called lettera antica, which became the basis for everything that followed, including the fonts of the printing press in Italy.

'Though he was the Chancellor of Florence, he still found time to study, to write histories, and stories in the style of Boccaccio, to make great funeral orations and to go on long expeditions in search of manuscripts. And if that were not enough, he also found time to sire twenty children. Twenty! Fourteen of them by as many mothers. How he kept them all, I do not know. Perhaps he abandoned them to the Foundling Hospital before galloping off to rescue more neglected books in obscure monasteries.'

If Vespasiano was fond of such stars in the ascendant, it was because he was one himself. He was the son of a merchant in the wool trade and had been born in the nearby village of Antella; though the family had money, learning and literature were not encouraged. Unable therefore to pursue a career of study, Vespasiano shocked his father by apprenticing himself to a stationer, this being the only way he could find to put himself into contact with books. Family money helped him become a member of the guild of stationers and, in time, to buy his own bottega; but his learning in Latin, his love of literature, and his association with the circle of Cosimo de' Medici, were all by virtue of his own efforts.

'I wanted knowledge and thought I would find it in books. Perhaps I would have done, if I had ever read as many as I acquired. You must study, Tommaso, every hour that God gives. Study, read, reflect. Do not race from cover to cover just to be able to say, well, I have read that one. You have read nothing if you do not understand it.'

As soon as Vespasiano ran out of breath with which to speak further, I took the opportunity to race to the top and, finding that the run made my legs ache, became dismayed. I bent over to rub my calves and to tell them that never, never were they to become accustomed to the plain. But my legs only showed what was happening to the rest of me: a gradual acclimatisation to my new surroundings and its people.

Vespasiano joined me at last, red in the face and with beads of sweat standing out on his forehead. He crossed to the parapet at the edge of the monastery's forecourt and stood recovering before a spectacular view of the city and of course, the Duomo. The westering sun, which bleached all colour from Florence, burnished the façade of San Miniato behind us, which was striped horizontally with marble bands of cream and green. I gazed up at the façade where there were gargoyles and reliefs of strange figures with their arms outstretched in prayer. Though San Miniato is the oldest church in Florence, it has a powerful sense of the present. Simply to be there restores a man to peace. Below is the city, wearing the crown of the Palazzo della Signoria and the tiara of the Cathedral; and one might believe that these two, church and state, must surely rule the city, but they do not. Beyond the walls are pools of influence, and San Miniato is one of them. It is a place more universal than Florentine, where the city emblems have not been stamped, but which itself has stamped Florence with its own mystic seal. It is a guardian angel in stone, gazing down in forgiveness on those who, quite erroneously, walk abroad claiming the credit for the greatness of their city.

Vespasiano had recovered his breath. 'Somewhere, in amongst the years, I forgot what I wanted. My great desire became divided into many little ones, so that, day by day, my concerns became how to avoid debts, how to win my current case of litigation, how to rise in the guild, how to persuade princes to commission libraries of books from my workshop. And my great desire, which was for knowledge, was covered by a cloud of buzzing, droning, biting ambitions. So I am telling you two things, Tommaso. Listen well. Firstly, avoid business. Trade is a seductive whore with a hidden disease: her gifts are not those which she promises. Secondly, do not do what I have done, which is to put off my studies until tomorrow while I spend today seeing to my affairs. For affairs are like wasps to the pollen of a man's time, a stinging swarm to which there is no end.' He looked out over the plain, full of regret. 'Study, Tommaso. Study, study, study. Be a scribe, but not one who copies blindly, like a man asleep dreaming only of his wages. Know what it is that passes from the nib of your pen in the flow of the ink. Do you know what God is offering you? Nothing less than being paid to read great literature. Make the most of it, boy, make the very utmost of it.'

'Yes, I will, but when may I begin?'

'The man I have in mind for your master is busy copying the works of Cicero for the Duke of Urbino. He will be finished soon.'

'Will he teach me Niccoló's cursive?' I asked.

'He prefers Poggio's round script. Why do you ask?'

I shrugged and said nothing. Vespasiano, not given to understanding anything about a man who actually stood in front of him, surprised me by guessing the reason. 'You would like to make another copy of the *Iliad*? You may do so, at my expense but in your own time. Of course you could use any script, but I suppose that will not do.'

I turned towards the church as, the bell tolling for Compline, the monks came from the cloisters to attend the office. They came uncowled and unceremonious, their noise breaking the spell of tranquillity. I frowned at them. I wanted to run to them and cry, Listen! Listen to this place! They entered the church and left the door open behind them. Within was revealed, in the glint of gold in the shadows, a treasure house of Byzantium. Leaving Vespasiano to his thoughts, I wandered into the church after the monks. They had disappeared. Too nervous to venture any further, I sat by the door and viewed all I could from there. As in any church, frescoes and mosaics enriched the walls, but at the chancel the church was divided into three tiers, three stages, like the very Mystery itself. Even the floor of the body of the church was mysterious, with black and white designs in marble tiling as delicate as lace.

Suddenly came the voices of invisible monks rising in chant. They were hidden because they were in the tier which was below the level of the floor. Their chant came in crescendos and diminuendos of ageless spirituality: the ragged line of noisy individuals had become a perfect choir, singing a chant as old as the church. Carried through time, it had absorbed every drop of devotion on the way until now it was a stream of love that filled the heart to overflowing.

I turned and looked out of the door to a bright, framed picture of the dome. The past made a wonder of the present. When the monks came to the psalm, I was not surprised that they should have chosen my favourite: psalm 18.

> 'Their line is gone out through all the earth,
> and their words to the end of the world. In them
> hath he set a tabernacle for the sun ... '

TEN

THE PEOPLE of the dawn like to greet each other. At the hour of Prime, when Florence was misty and cool, each day the same people passed the shop at the same time: fishwives on their way to market, the devout on their way to prayer, carpenters and masons on their way to the site of the new palazzo being built along the street. No one was too high or too low, too rich, too poor, too old or too young to say good morning to the boy who set the books out on the table in front of Vespasiano's shop. Early risers form a distinct company of their own and the mere fact that you are out of your bed before dawn puts you in a brotherhood which includes monks and street-sweepers. At dawn in Florence I could almost feel a part of the city. Later in the day it was different.

At one end, the street of the stationers led to the Duomo; to reach the river at the other end, one had to pass the back of the overbearing Palazzo della Signoria. It seemed no accident that between these two great symbolic monuments lay the Palazzo del Podestà, next to Vespasiano's shop. As if in sympathy with its occupants in the dungeons, I allowed myself to be imprisoned by the immediate locality and would venture no further.

Opposite the shop was the Badia, an Augustinian abbey. It was a friendly place, open to all at all times. It had a good library and I was often sent there to borrow books for copying. A friar opened its doors one morning as I was displaying a fine copy of St Augustine's *City of God*.

'Ohé, Tommaso!' he called.

'Ohé, Fra Paolo!'

He beckoned me over and looked me up and down. 'Well? What have you seen so far?'

'San Miniato,' I said, glad at last to have some answer to this oft-repeated question.

'San Miniato, eh? At least you have begun with the best. But what else have you seen?'

I looked sheepish.

'Nothing? Now, my son, stop clinging to the shop as if it were your mother's skirts. Go that way, into the heart of the city. Next time I see you, I want to hear about Santa Riparata, Santa Croce, Santo Spirito, San Lorenzo, San Marco.'

'I am very busy with my duties.'

'Tell the truth: you are a coward. This is a beautiful city, and I am a Paduan who says so. Books, my son, are too often used as an escape from the world. Have you not noticed that half the scholars who frequent this street talk to themselves? Where is the intelligence in that? Too much book work and you will lose your wits. Go into the centre, boy, and find some flesh-and-blood friends of your own age.'

'Yes, Frate.'

'Be sure that you do.'

'Yes, Frate.'

He grunted and turned back into the abbey.

If I often lingered in my duty of displaying the books, it was not in the hope of meeting Fra Paolo. At the new palazzo along the street lived the Pazzi family; their house chapel not yet being completed, members of the family went to Mass at the Badia, leaving their palazzo each morning at the same hour in a splendid procession led by Ser Jacopo de' Pazzi dressed in the red robes of the citizen. Servants carried the trailing hems of the ladies' gowns but walking proudly at the rear of the party was an African slave. Slaves were usually tall Circassians; to see one with black skin, bearing the dignity of a chief of his tribe, was exotic beyond compare. Such was my fascination with him that it was some time before I noticed a girl of some eight or nine years who walked beside her nurse and behind her mother. She wore a linen bonnet, tied under her chin, from the back of which confinement spilled a cloud of brown hair; she moved with such a mixture of grace and solemnity that she seemed to me to be innocence personified: a blameless Florentine. Once catching her eye, I challenged her pious expression by making the face of a gargoyle. She responded with a smile so radiant that I lost my balance and stumbled back into the shop as one blinded by light. I longed to repeat the experience but that week the family removed to their country villa at Montughi.

The man whom Vespasiano had in mind to be my master was a priest called Piero Strozzi. He lived in the hamlet of Ripoli and had been sending the text of the Cicero to the bookshop quire by quire, which Vespasiano then checked for errors and passed to me for trimming and collation. On many pages the script only occupied a small area caught in a net of lines; around it, in other described areas, rough sketches had been made of scenes. These pages had to be sent back to Ripoli for an artist called Pipo to work on.

Piero Strozzi's script was one of the most beautiful I had ever seen, the letters so perfect in form that I supposed the scribe to be likewise. I was surprised therefore to discover him to be a lanky old man, stooped with age, who had hairs in his ears and a tendency to cut himself while shaving. He visited the bookshop one day, having been awake all night worrying about a mistake he had made in the last quire and forgotten to correct.

'I know,' said Vespasiano. 'I found it.'

'So I have come all this way for nothing,' moaned the priest.

'Not at all. I have not made the correction, and it would look better in your hand.' Vespasiano cleared his desk for Father Piero, who had brought his own pen, knife and inkhorn. Finding me in the storeroom at the back, Vespasiano spat on his hands and smoothed my hair down then pushed me out to meet the visitor.

'Here is your new apprentice, Father Piero.'

The priest looked up crossly and said that, as Vespasiano well knew, he no longer took apprentices. 'Once you have taught them all you know, what do they do but go out and take all the commissions that would otherwise have come your way? With their youth and superior eyesight, they render the old master superfluous. It was different in the old days, when there was plenty of work, but now, with the press ... '

'Hush, hush, Piero,' said Vespasiano. 'The press is merely a novelty. It will pass.'

Father Piero sighed and began to arrange things neatly on

the desk, fastening the quire to its slope and trimming the nib of his quill.

'If you will not take him as an apprentice, will you take him as a pupil? After all, there is a reward of ten florins, and how many books would you have to copy to earn that?'

I glanced at Vespasiano, wondering where the other ten florins of my blood money had gone. It mattered not; the sum was a fortune to the priest and he agreed he would be dead before he could earn so much. Even so, he wanted no pupil. 'Writing is its own reward but teaching is a very tax on the spirit.' He peered at me curiously, perhaps wondering what such an affluent young man was doing working in a bookshop. Vespasiano gave him a brief outline of my history and, at the mention of Volterra, the stern features of the priest melted with compassion; remarking that the fate of my city was a shameful blot on the history of Florence, he glanced about cautiously to see that no one had heard him other than his friend the bookseller. Vespasiano left me with him, to watch him work.

'I wish,' I said, 'I could write as you do.'

'You will, when you find a good master,' he said.

Did a god pass through the shop then? A little fellow, master of tricks and deceit, with wings on his heels? For I was suddenly inspired to ask if he knew Feliciano, a name I had heard mentioned disparagingly in the bookshop.

'Feliciano?' gasped Father Piero. 'He may be happy with himself, but felicity is the last thing he inspires in others. The man is eccentric. Why, does Vespasiano mean to ... ? No, he could not do that. Feliciano is outlandish. His letters look like mosquitoes squashed on a wall. Does Vespasiano mean to send you to him?' He rinsed his pen violently.

'I think he may be considering it,' I lied, handing him a rag.

The priest straightened and beckoned to the bookseller. 'The work is finished. I must leave now.' An inner struggle played out on his face.

'Ten florins,' said Vespasiano.

'To the devil with your gold.'

Vespasiano went to speak again but the priest held his ears and, saying, 'No! No! No!' he left the bookshop. The following day he returned – on his way, he said, to a convocation in Rome.

'The Archbishop cannot come to us, so we, all seventy of us, must make a fortnight's journey to see him, leaving our parishes neglected for a month or more.'

'It is lamentable that we do not have a man such as Antonio degli Agli for our archbishop,' said Vespasiano, and, having created this opportunity to do so, he mentioned that I was the ward of the Bishop.

'That explains everything,' said Father Piero without looking at me. 'Explains what, Piero?' asked Vespasiano.

'I met Bishop Antonio at a meeting of the Academy last night.'

I rushed at the priest. 'You saw the Bishop last night? How is he? Is he well? Did he mention me?'

'He gave me a very stiff lecture. Apparently if I should dare to keep my talents to myself, they will die on me and I shall be left an empty old husk. If I do not give what I have, he said, everything will be taken from me. Presumably by God Himself. So if I want to remain an active scribe, then I must teach. So said my friend Bishop Antonio. I said to him, Who will I teach? He said to me, No doubt he will manifest himself to you in time. I said to him, a young Volterrano manifested this very morning at Vespasiano's shop. Then the good Bishop began to glorify and honour your talents, talents which apparently are innate at the moment and waiting only to be brought forth by a master. You are ready to learn and eager for truth, he said, but he did not mention that he was your guardian.'

'So,' beamed Vespasiano, 'are you going to do what you have been told?'

'I shall think about it,' said the priest, 'while I am in Rome.'

I asked him then if he would deliver a letter to my family, for they needed to know that I was safe. Having his agreement, I quickly wrote a note to my uncle and aunt, telling them where I was, that I was in good health and that I had great hopes for the future. I did not omit to mention that the bearer of the letter was the finest scribe in all Italy. Piero took the folded letter and opened it up, not to read its contents but to study my script. 'Humph,' was all he said, folding it up again.

'I will send Tommaso to you when you return,' said Vespasiano.

'Humph,' said the priest again, and left with the air of one who would like to kick a wall.

I wanted to know why Piero Strozzi was reluctant to take a pupil; Vespasiano said that Piero had grown so fond of his last apprentice that it broke his heart when the young man left. 'His name was Giovanni, but we called him Velox on account of his speed. Aware of his own talents, and so as not to compete with his master in the same marketplace, he went to Naples, and Piero has never seen him again. Do you know, Velox can copy a full manuscript in a week? Is that not incredible?'

I had heard that the Germans were peeling a hundred pages an hour off their presses. I said nothing.

After the sack, I had helped my cousin to escape Volterra. I cut his beautiful hair off with shears and with a razor I created a tonsure. Then, having dressed him in a white habit I found discarded at the Bishop's Palace, I watched him leave the city disguised as a Camaldolese monk. I had presumed that he had gone to Rome, but in that August I discovered that he was living only steps from Vespasiano's shop, at the Palazzo Pazzi.

I had walked into the courtyard one day to share a meal with the labourers who were paving the ground with stone. The place exuded the odours of new wood and lime-wash. Perhaps because of my association of the house with a small, radiant angel, I enjoyed the sublime architecture of the courtyard with its slender arcade defined by grey pietra serena. It was the noble home of a noble family. Being here only through my acquaintance with the workmen, however, I was surprised to hear my name called from an upper window overlooking the courtyard, and staggered to see Antonio.

'I could hardly return to Rome with a shorn head,' he said, joining me downstairs. 'So I came here, to the house of my friend Francesco.'

'But this is Florence! How could you come here willingly?'

Antonio, however, bore no grudge against the city, only against the Medici. 'Merchant upstarts, usurpers! They have not a drop of noble blood in them, and Lorenzo's marriage to an Orsini of Rome has not altered that.'

I told him that he sounded like his mother and he smiled ruefully. 'Just because I believe that peasants should be fairly rewarded for their labours does not mean that I also believe they should wear a crown or the triple tiara. Each man to his place.' Antonio's views seemed to have modified. 'The world turns upside down when men such as the Medici control everything, and nobles such as the Pazzi are stripped of every honour.'

Glancing round the delicate architecture with its fine escutcheons of a leaping dolphin, I did not see the home of a family which had been cast into ruin.

'Once crusading knights, they are now bankers,' said Antonio, 'and rich, but they have lost their titles and power. My friend Francesco refuses to live here while Lorenzo holds the position which is rightfully his; he lives instead in Rome. His uncle Jacopo runs this house.'

'He has a most handsome wife,' I said.

'He has no wife at all.'

'But I have seen a lady leave here often, to go to church with her daughter.'

'His sister and niece,' said Antonio, unwittingly giving me a rare and precious scrap of information.

'Ah yes,' I said, 'little Maria.'

'The niece? No, Elena.'

I dropped the name like a coin into the purse of my heart. If I was in love, it was not the love which a man knows, but a boy's love for something pure, elusive, and ineffably feminine. Elena.

I told Antonio of the world of books, of the different qualities of leather and parchment and the different colours of inks; of Vespasiano, Grazia and Piero Strozzi; of the many famous people who visited the shop to buy quills. He wanted to know about the world outside the bookshop, so I told him about the Palazzo del Podestà and the prisoners, whose groans and laments you could often hear during the night; and about the Badia and its good monks who practised what they preached. He wanted to know what else I had discovered in Florence. I said that one of the fishwives who went to market each morning had almost a full beard and that, according to the pigeons, the harvest that year promised to be very good.

'But have you seen Lorenzo de' Medici?'

'Once, from the back, during the celebrations held in honour of the Duke of Urbino.'

My first journey into the centre, therefore, was in the company of Antonio. 'For as yet,' he said, 'I have not seen the house of the Medici myself, and I would like to, particularly while they are not in it.'

The city, inflamed by the sun, was deserted. Like all the wealthy families who had left to spend the summer in their villas, the Medici had gone to their house on the nearby hill of Careggi, taking Angelo Ambrogini with them. Since he had entered the Medici household, I had begun to think of Angelo as a friend of one day, as someone who had once taken me to Fiesole and there released me from the cage of misery, as a passing beam of light in my life; but not the brother that, for the short time we had spent together, he had seemed.

Surprised that I had not explored the city and mocking me for my lack of courage, Antonio led me to the Piazza di San Giovanni in front of the Cathedral. Feeling nauseous, I tried to take my mind off my stomach by studying the astonishing bell-tower, built in the French style of pointed arches and pinnacles. Decorated from head to foot in white, green and red marble, it towered above us with as many statues in niches as doves in a dovecot.

'Everything is too big here, Antonio,' I muttered.

'The people were taxed to build this,' he said, 'and it cost ten times the price of all France.'

'But it was for God,' I said, my dizziness increased by such numbers.

'Nonsense – it was so that the bell tower of Florence would be more magnificent than those of Pisa or Siena.'

I followed him into the Baptistry, a small, octagonal building decorated with bands of black and white marble. We found ourselves on a pavement inlaid with the signs of the Zodiac while above our heads was a golden cupola showing the scene of the Last Judgement. I stood looking from ground to vault, from vault to ground, relishing the symbolism of having the planets beneath your feet and doomsday above you. Antonio, meanwhile, was studying the tomb of a pope. 'John the Twenty-third,' he said. 'The anti-pope. Deposed on charges of piracy, murder, rape, sodomy and incest – and they were only the crimes that could be mentioned.'

I looked at the effigy of a kind man, sculpted in the new style of extreme realism. Between this marble effigy and the Byzantine face of Christ in the mosaic above us laid the gulf between the old learning and the new.

'Cosimo de' Medici was his friend,' Antonio continued. 'He probably paid for this piece of aggrandisement, for it was through Pope John that the Medici bank gained the Papal account. After that, their prosperity soared.' He was thoughtful for a moment and then said, as if to himself, 'So all we need to do is to persuade His Holiness to change his banker.'

He led us outside into the blistering sunshine; to find shade, he made for the Cathedral, but I hung back, telling him that I had heard of a church across the river which had some fine painted walls. Ignoring me, he ran up the steps to the arch of the west door; there he turned his back on the church to survey the piazza and its border of grand palazzi. 'Where do you suppose the Medici live? Presumably it must be here, at the centre of things. Look for their emblem: the six balls.'

I looked about the palazzi. They were tall; with their small windows and deeply projecting eaves, they looked arrogant and indifferent. I went to the base of the Cathedral and discovered the cause for feeling so utterly small in its presence: its first string course was above the height of my head. The stature of man had provided the measurement of only the base of this house of God. Antonio, used to the Pantheon and the Colosseum, was unmoved.

Not finding a sign of the six palle, he left the Cathedral to skirt the piazza, keeping to the shade. I followed, wilting. We saw few people, but there was more life on a broad and busy street called the Via Larga. Here, as elsewhere in Florence, new palazzi were reflecting new wealth. In between the palazzi were the tall, squalid apartment houses of the poor which, block by block, were being pulled down to make way for the rich. The street led to the monastery of San Marco and, beyond, to a vista of blue hills. I told Antonio about Fiesole, and it was then that I discovered what the war had done to him, for as I spoke lovingly of the air, the sky and the spirits of ancestors, he listened darkly and rounded off my enthusiasm with a coda: 'Do not be so stupid.'

My Etruscan prince had died, to be replaced by a bitter young man with short feathery hair, dressed as a priest. I followed him sullenly into the Via Larga. Under the lofty new walls of a banker's palazzo, a lane led into a mash of colour, noise and smells. Threading our way through the stalls, the wagons and the donkeys, the dogs and the chickens and the children, we found ourselves in the heart of San Lorenzo market.

ELEVEN

ON THE stalls there were undulating landscapes of tripe, pillars of cheeses, fat sacks of grain, crates of blotched melons. These were common enough in any market, but not the fabrics: wool, linen, brocade, taffeta, silk and velvet; vendors pulled lengths off rolls with the skill of flag throwers. The cloth that billowed luxuriously between their hands looked so much more than the length the customer had asked for; undoubtedly it was far less. By a fountain was a man selling coconut. I watched him smash the whiskery nuts with a mallet and put the fragments, white-side up, to wash and cool in the fountain. Antonio bought me a piece.

'All the way from In-di-aa,' cried the man. 'Followed the route of Han-ni-bal.'

Biting into the white kernel, I was surprised by its texture and unexpected sweetness. I wanted some more, but Antonio said – loudly – that the price was crim-i-nal, and nudged me towards the church. Newly built, its façade was unfinished and rough, like that of the Cathedral. It stood on a raised foundation as if on a plinth.

'Perhaps we shall find some wall paintings here for you,' he said, going up the steps two at a time.

The façade did not prepare me for the interior, so dusky after the bright sunlight that the vision of it came upon me only gradually. I stood with my mouth open, as did Antonio. Here there were no wall paintings; instead were the columns and round arches of ancient Rome, soaring in unbelievable majesty. The walls white, the columns and arches grey pietra serena, the whole lit by the clerestory windows and candles, the church exuded a luminous mist of spirituality surprising in the context of its imperial architecture. Antonio stood speechless, but I began to search for clues, as to how the modules of ancient Rome had been used to create a temple of Christianity. I had learnt enough from the Bishop to guess: following the laws of musical harmony and using the ratios of proportion, the architect had built a church that sang. I could hear the hum of it, beyond the physical range of hearing. The lofty round arches vibrated with their own hymn, and by that sound the whole edifice stood. Behind my back was the roar of the sunny market: in front, a shadowy stillness deep and serene where constellations of votive candles winked in chapels, warm stars in the twilight.

A sacristan appeared and disturbed the sublime peace by loudly bidding us good day. 'Are you visitors to Florence? Where from? Rome? Is this your first time here? Welcome. Let me show you the masterpieces of the great sculptor, Donatello. Let me show you his pulpits. The church itself was built by the great master architect, Brunelleschi, who, as you will know, was the same man who built the dome on the Cathedral. In the sacristy there is more of Donatello's work. We will go there first. Follow me.' The sacristan halted at the crossing and pointed to the floor. 'He is buried here you know, Donatello, in the vault below.'

There was a large marble circle inlaid in the floor, a circle beset by three squares. In the squares were circular grilles, as if the dead below needed air. I peered through one, almost expecting to see the sculptor laid out in the crypt.

'Yes, he died within a year or so of his great friend and patron, Cosimo, and is buried beside him in the family vault.'

Antonio and I glanced at each other. We read the inscription in the marble circle. 'Pater Patriae' – father of his country. Above the inscription was the shield with the six palle. The vault beneath our feet was that of the Medici. Antonio's breathing became laboured.

'We shall see the sacristy first, while it is empty, then I shall show you the pulpits on the way out. A great man, Donatello, somewhat tetchy perhaps, but a great man nonetheless.' The sacristan led the way. I was glad to follow but Antonio remained behind. As the man passed into the sacristy, I turned at a sound, that of Antonio spitting a green globule of phlegm on the memorial of Cosimo de' Medici. Something caught my eye, a movement in the nave. Lurking in the shadows of the aisle, a youth was watching.

'Antonio,' I hissed. 'Come on.'

He ambled towards me.

'Someone saw you,' I whispered.

'Good,' he said without emotion. 'This is their church, with their stamp on it. Look, all around, the palle.'

It was true. We had missed the numerous signs of Medici patronage discreetly carved in pietra serena.

'They have enclosed heaven with their fences, with walls and towers and guards at the barbicans. What should be common land is in the possession of the powerful, and the rest of us can only say our prayers by tenure.'

I sighed in agreement. Now that I knew whose money had paid for it, I too felt robbed of my enjoyment of the beautiful.

'Are you there?' called our guide from within. We entered the sacristy to be shown its architectural and sculptural wonders. Antonio criticized everything boldly, then gave the sacristan some coins to assuage his hurt. 'It is all merely a copy', said Antonio, 'of the antique. In Rome we have the original. Good day.'

'You do not have a Donatello in Rome!' said the sacristan as he counted the coins.

Returning to the body of the church, we found it empty. I hurried towards the doors but Antonio wanted to see the vault again. 'It appeals to me, the Medici vault. If I have any ambition in this life, cousin, it is to add a few more to that crypt. Not many, just two: Lorenzo and his brother.'

'Oh, Madonna ... If someone should hear you!' I tugged at him desperately, pulling him towards the main door. The nave seemed vast, the door a square of livid daylight ahead. As we went towards it, I glanced to the left and the right, expecting an ambush. Someone touched me on the shoulder and I started violently. It was the sacristan, complaining that we had not seen the pulpits. Antonio laughed and, taking my arm, drew me outside. Stunned by the sun, we stood blinking like moles.

They were waiting for us, four of them, two on either side of the door. Palleschi, they were called, followers of the Medici.

They wore the Medici colours as if they were colours of the ward, a sign of tribal, brutal devotion to a party. They stepped forward, smiling, the smile of a jester who has chosen you as the butt of his next cruel joke.

'How dare you lay hands on me!' Antonio protested. 'I am a priest!'

They made ironic obeisance. 'Forgive us, Father,' said one of them, 'but we are concerned for your health. You have a cold, perhaps, a little tightness of the chest?'

'Spitting is natural,' said another, 'but we do not approve of it in church.'

'Perhaps you did not know it was Cosimo's tomb you were spitting on?'

I tried to run but was caught. Last night's wine was stale on their breath. I struggled wildly and managed to spit in the face of one and flatten the codpiece of another before I was gripped by the hair and had my face pushed into the rough wall of San Lorenzo. It smelt of dust.

'Where are you from?'

'Rome.'

This was met by a grunt of derision.

'Rome!' I repeated.

I was pushed harder into the wall. Small pinnacles in the landscape of roughened stone bit into me.

'Where from?' they insisted.

'Who disturbs the peace?' an imperious voice demanded, and at its sound I was immediately released. The crowd that had gathered about us parted deferentially for a young man of about twenty. I knew him at once, from his black, wavy hair, the way he stood, the way everyone fell quiet in his presence. I flinched as he touched my grazed and bleeding face.

Oh cruel fate, to grant a wish too late. For was not this one of those countless dreams I had had of him: I in trouble and Lorenzo to the rescue? My attackers were justifying themselves, telling him what had happened in the church.

'And you dare to mete out punishment in our name? You do us more harm than he does. I would rather see phlegm on a pavement than blood on a man.'

They pleaded with him. 'Giuliano ... ' they whined.

I suddenly began to breathe again: this then was not Lorenzo but his younger brother. I had heard that the two were so close that they had never been heard to argue except once, and that was on the matter of Volterra: Giuliano had begged Lorenzo not to wage war. Giuliano, therefore, was innocent.

My attackers, salvaging what pride they could, swaggered off, leaving me alone with him and his companions.

'There is no cause to look relieved,' he said grimly. 'You have been saved for justice, not mercy, and you may prefer another grazing.'

Finding myself in this subtler, more painful vice, I looked about in desperation for Antonio but he was nowhere to be seen. My next saviour came in the shape of Angelo Ambrogini, who ran up the steps to tell Giuliano that Lorenzo wanted him, that they were due to leave in the hour. He stopped short when he saw me.

'Tommaso! What has happened to your face?'

'Do you know him?' Giuliano demanded.

'Yes, he is a friend of mine; he works for Vespasiano.'

'Then, Angelo, you are a friend of an enemy of our house.'

Informed of the accusation against me, Angelo replied in my defence. 'He is thirteen years old and comes from Volterra, so perhaps he is not your loyal servant, but he is hardly a threat to your safety. If he snarls, it is understandable, and we shall civilize him soon enough.'

Giuliano's eyes rested on me but his gaze was on something else, some thought of the past. Looking remorseful, he sighed then muttered his regret for the fate of my city.

'The blame lies not with you,' I said in a rush, 'but with your brother!'

Instantly severe again, he stooped to look at me directly. He had brown eyes, fathoms deep, and an Etruscan nose. 'Understand this: if you hate my brother, you hate me also.'

I did not believe him and gazed at him beseechingly, but he departed then, going back through the market with his companions. The people stood back to clear a passage but it seemed to be respect rather than deference that moved them. Here was a young man obviously adored. He went through a gate leading to a walled garden at the back of the banker's palazzo we had passed earlier. Glancing up I noticed for the first time the stone shield on the corner, below the eaves. It bore the six balls. The palace of the Medici was not, then, a battlemented castle somewhere in the sky: it was a three storey palazzo on the Via Larga. Less graceful than that of the Palazzo Pazzi, its one distinctive feature was its comparative lack of distinction.

Angelo took me to the fountain and washed the blood off my face. 'Ahi,' he said sympathetically, as the extent of the grazing was revealed. 'You look like Marsyas, flayed alive by Apollo.'

I sat beside him on the fountain steps, wanting to know why the Medici were in Florence rather than in the country. He said that Lorenzo and Giuliano had returned only for the day, to see to affairs of the bank. A question stuck in my throat, about Angelo's welfare in his new home. I both wanted and did not want to know if he was happy, but I could gather the answer easily enough for myself: it was obvious that he was blissfully content, spending the summer with the Medici at their villa at Careggi.

'It is not far from the city, but far enough to catch the breeze. The gardens are like paradise, with dark hedges, cool fountains and graceful statues. We read poetry there in the evenings.'

I noticed that his patched cloth of honesty had been replaced by a linen shirt, a doublet and a fine-fitting pair of hose. Sensitive to my hurt, he said nothing of the friendship that was developing between him and Lorenzo, a friendship so deep that the idea of patron and poet was fast disappearing. But I saw the effects of it in the absence of all care in his face.

He asked me what had happened in the church, and I told him, except that I said that Antonio's spitting was of simple phlegm and not of malice.

'Romans may spit in church, Florentines do not. If I had been Giuliano, I would have pushed your face back into the wall. Simple phlegm! Do you expect me to believe that?'

A man appeared in front of us with a hound at his heels. Under the straw hat he wore against the sun was the brutal face and flattened nose of a stone mason, but the effect was softened by the man's affable expression. Though his skin was coarse and his hair as rough as a horse's, there was a strange sense of familiarity, as if I had seen the same person but moments ago.

Angelo jumped to his feet as the man said, in a high nasal tone, 'There is some enchantment working in the market today.'

He was a caricature of someone else, but I could not think of whom.

'Each time I send someone out to find a straggler, the straggler returns and the hunter is lost ... '

A violent tic abruptly affected my left eye.

' ... so I thought to come and find you myself.'

If he reminded me suddenly of Giuliano, the likeness rested not in the features but in the mannerisms. Blood began to pump in my ears.

'Who is this?' he asked, and as he did so, he touched me. The leprous hand of Lorenzo de' Medici was upon my shoulder! What happened then was like a sudden tempest breaking inside me – brain cracking, emotions thundering, splintered thoughts flashing like streak lightning. (I was told later that what really happened was that I let out a scream of such magnitude that it not only scared Lorenzo de' Medici and set his dog barking, but that Jupiter himself nearly fell out of the sky.) Alarmed, Lorenzo let me go and I fled like one chased by Pan.

Somehow, in blind flight, I found my way straight to the bookshop. I rushed in, nearly knocking the bell off its bracket. As if in answer to my prayers, I found the Bishop there and hurled myself into his arms.

'*Santo cielo*! What has happened? Have you been dragged by a horse?'

I pressed my face into his shoulder. I pressed hard, to blot out both the pain and the impressions of castles in the air crashing to earth, of tyrants walking through markets as carefree as peasants.

'Maso, what is it?'

'Please take me away from Florence. *Please!*'

'Why?'

'Please, oh please!'

'Why? What is it?'

'You said I would not have to meet him,' I cried. 'But I have. And he is ugly!'

TWELVE

FATHER Piero Strozzi was an impatient man. It was not his way to frustrate an aspiring youth by making him spend months and years grinding galls for black ink or infusing chips of brazilwood in his own urine to make red ink. He said I could buy these ingredients as powders for mixing from the stationer or apothecary. Neither did he think it necessary to show me how to sit straight before a desk and keep my hand at right angles to the paper; nor that I should know anything about quill production other than how to trim the nib to the proper angle and keep it sharp. All such disciplines, he said, were the devices of masters who would keep their pupils from doing any work that might overshadow their own. The great scribes – Poggio and Niccoló – had taught themselves. There was no real need for lessons at all, only practice, and prayer.

The decaying church of San Pietro stood alone in a lane running from the village of Ripoli to the Arno, under siege from tall thistles and rough grass creeping in from surrounding wasteland. Once a college of monks, it now housed one scribe and one illuminator. They shared a room devoted to books, its walls covered with shelves and cupboards, its floor taken up by two desks. Piero had designed his own: on a table was a steep writing slope with holes in it to take inkhorns and quills. At its back was a jointed arm to which was fixed a reading stand to hold the book being copied. Various objects hung from hooks: weights to hold down parchment, lead for drawing, rules, compasses, dividers and squares. Thus, within an area of a single pace, the scribe had all his equipment readily to hand.

On my first day with him, which was my fourteenth birthday, he put a pen in my right hand and a knife in my left and set me to copying exemplars of fine scripts; on the next visit I copied short texts; before long I was writing whole paragraphs within the book he was working on.

If I had expected the life of a scribe to be one of peaceful, leisurely study, such ideas were soon blown from my mind. Paid according to the length of the work rather than according to the length of time spent on it, Piero was quick in writing, his hand moving across the parchment with the skill and rapidity of a lacemaker's. I wanted to rest in the forming of letters, to watch them appear from the nib and revel in their beauty, but the priest said that this was work, not a mystical experience. The illuminator chuckled.

Pipo was a fat man with three chins and a barrel belly. He was working on an octavo page, filling its margins with cascades of flowers, garlands of fruit and chains of winged cupids. Quatrefoils and roundels containing little scenes alternated round the border and provided landing places for exotic birds. The top half of the page, as in a window surrounded by dense creeper, was a dock scene: a caravel was being unloaded by a swarm of men, each bare except for a loin cloth. Pipo painted the rigging with a one-haired brush. In the midst of this page of abundant elaboration were three lines of text in Italian.

'Boccaccio,' said Father Piero over my shoulder.

I had never seen anything so wonderful.

'A trap of enchantment. It is the Word that is important. Who would read the words in a book like this? Your eyes never leave the pictures; which is just as well, for the text is nothing but the bawdy tales of a storyteller. Still, it is a commission.'

'By the Pazzi?' I asked, recognising the two bellicose dolphins, back to back with a ship's sail between them, but Piero was not listening. His words having crushed his friend Pipo, he was trying to mollify him, saying that his work was incomparable; he just wished it was gracing a copy of the Gospels. Pipo was a simple man whose feelings were easily bruised. If he was devoted to this ascerbic priest, it was because Piero had rescued him from the debtor's prison, to which he had been consigned through his regular habit of paying two florins for gold leaf and only charging one for the work. Since his release, Pipo had lived at Ripoli, with nothing to do or think about other than the colours and shapes of his figures, or what to plant in the garden of which he had charge.

'He knows everything about the order of nature,' said Piero, 'and nothing of how to order his affairs.'

Whenever Piero left the room to attend affairs to his parish, and I sat back to shake my wrists and free them of tension, Pipo would advise patience. 'He is trying to throw you off like a bucking horse,' he said. 'Sit tight. Hold on. The real lessons will begin as soon as he is convinced that you are in earnest.'

The study faced south and the glare of the sun was diffused by tracing paper tacked over the windows. I measured the windows and sent to Volterra for thin panes of alabaster which we then fitted in place of the paper. 'This is how they diffused the light at the Camaldolese Abbey,' I said, but if Piero was impressed either by my knowledge or my initiative, it had no effect on his tuition. He continued to scold me for sloth and to give nothing in the form of praise or encouragement. Each time I returned to Vespasiano, it was with the growing conviction that life as a stationer's assistant was preferable to that of a scribe; each time I returned to Ripoli, it was with less enthusiasm.

'Patience,' counselled Pipo, and demonstrated the virtue by lifting with tweezers a leaf of gold as fine as a butterfly wing, placing it on to the gesso ground of his painting, and then spending hours burnishing it to a shine of polished metal. Sometimes I helped him in his work, providing him with 'a nutshell of ochre' or 'half a bean of vermillion', as he requested, and thus learnt about pigments and their mixing. If there was an art to letter-forming, however, I was denied all knowledge of it; yet, as time passed, I became increasingly aware that there was an art, and that Piero was practising it in my absence; for it occurred to me that I had never seen him outlining the areas of a page, that I only ever saw the page already prepared with its grids. So I asked him how it was done.

'The day you can tell me what I am doing is the day I will tell you how I am doing it,' said Piero.

The way of the wise is to take short cuts to knowledge. The next time I saw the Bishop, I asked him what Piero could have meant. He thought he knew the answer, and demonstrated it by drawing three lines of equal length – 'One and one and one', he said, 'joined to each other at right-angles, one line up, one across, one down.' Then he drew a diagonal linking the tips of the two verticals, and a circle linking all the points of intersection. Within this he formed a rectangle. 'If you really want to impress Piero, talk about the square root of five.' He cut out the rectangle and gave it to me. 'This is the element of beauty. I think you will find that Piero has it as his foundation.'

I studied my parchment rectangle and measured it with a ruler. The numbers made no sense to me. I showed it to Pipo. 'Aha! the magic rectangle,' he said. 'Now you are getting close.' I asked him why it was magical. He took it from me, folded it in half and tore it in two, thus producing two magic rectangles. Taking one of these halves, he folded and tore that. Now I had four magic rectangles. 'It infinitely reproduces itself,' he said.

'Why is it beautiful?'

'You will find it everywhere in nature.'

'I have never seen anything like this in nature.'

Pipo then explained to me that the numbers which made the rectangle are the numbers of growth, a spiralling progression visible in shells and the seed-heads of flowers.

Piero returned to the study and growled to find me idling. 'I am really not interested in writing letters,' I declared. He looked at me astonished. I picked up a fold of parchment. 'This is what I want to know about: the proportions of the page.'

Geometry is the science of form. My schoolmaster in Volterra, by debasing it to a science of quantity, had stifled my innate love of the subject. By revealing geometry as the science of music, however, Bishop Antonio degli Agli had brought the love back to life. Now, with Father Piero's tuition, I discovered geometry to be the very foundation of the art of the scribe. Where I once had been reduced to inertia by geometric principles, I began to acquire them greedily for the construction of capital letters, happily dividing circles for a C or a G or a Q. Father Piero taught me to rule boxes with diagonals, verticals and horizontals, to turn a compass on intersections and create a net in which to catch a letter. By the winter solstice I had proceeded through the alphabet from A to Z. As yet, I had not been shown how to divide a page, but I was content that such lessons would come in time, for now I was learning according to principle and not by the copying of models.

Models I still copied, however, for the small letters cannot practically be constructed by compasses and straight-edges. I had chosen Poggio Bracciolini's hand as my preferred style and each day I practised writing in it, but Piero began to wean me from copying by the eye.

'All knowledge is within you. If you are measured and harmonious, then will your letters be also. Study Poggio's hand before you work but, while you work, refer only to yourself.'

To become measured and harmonious, I was encouraged to lead a good life, to be studious and disciplined, to go to bed early, rise early and eat only simple, fresh food. But I spoilt the efforts of my master by retaining the indulgent and useless habit of day-dreaming. If I was no longer interested in knights and battles, I now had Poggio Bracciolini for my hero, and imagined him travelling to far-flung places to collect manuscripts, with me as his companion and faithful servant. Together we scaled an Alpine crag to reach a precarious monastery. Poggio diverted the monks with his licentious stories, plying them with more and more wine. Then, while they slept over their cups, he and I crept to the library to take some books, or 'rescue' them as Poggio called it, for the poor antique volumes, kept so safely during the age of the barbarians, were now suffering from the increasing ignorance of their keepers. The books were mouldering – one I picked up, the earliest version of the Bible ever known, crumbled to dust in my hands – and some were full of holes, holes made by beetles and holes made by monks with shears looking for profitable bookmarks amongst the illuminations. And Poggio Bracciolini and I, pirates for Truth, crept away without recording our loans. Back to Florence then, to bring in our finds on triumphal chariots, to the fanfares of all the scholars of Christendom.

Despite such time-wasting, I still made progress, and to celebrate my first anniversary Piero took me to Florence to see proportion in three dimensions.

At Santa Croce is a chapel, built by Brunelleschi and paid for by the Pazzi, which is a rectangle enclosing a circle and two half circles. We stood at its centre while Father Piero lectured on the units of measure. With white stucco walls and pilasters, and round arches of pietra serena, the chapel had that peace which I had discovered in San Lorenzo. This was a place to be listened to rather than looked at. Any noise from the outside became, within the chapel, a soniferous hum; the place was as a shell in which you can hear the sound of the sea. Pipo sneezed, and the echo gave back the sound of a mortal cough. When at last my companions left the chapel, I remained behind for a moment. Alone and standing in the centre I sang one long, high, note. I expected an echo. Instead, the vault of the cupola rang and at once became as if insubstantial: that is to say, my voice did not echo, was not reflected by the cupola, but rather penetrated it, to be received by the vault of heaven itself. I realised then that what both Piero Strozzi and Bishop Antonio degli Agli told me was no mere theory: simple geometry *is* the key to the laws of the universe. There, in the Pazzi chapel, heaven was open.

Feeling transcendent, I rejoined the others outside. If they had heard my experiment, they said nothing of it. Piero said, 'It was designed by the same architect who built the dome on the Cathedral.' This was a lead weight to my soaring spirit. As we left the cloisters of Santa Croce, the great edifice was visible, as it was from almost every part of the city. My cloudy looks betrayed my feelings.

'You do not like our Duomo?'

'It is ... tyrannical.'

'That is too strong a word.'

'I can see what he means, though,' said Pipo. 'It does, as it were, sit on us. Though not oppressively, of course.'

Piero at once changed direction and walked us to the Cathedral. Inside people thronged as in the market place, and the acoustic resonance was such that their voices roared up to the roof and the cupola while the smallest sound was booming. Passing frescoes with only a glance, we went down the aisle between the gigantic pillars and came to a door leading to a narrow stairway. Piero spoke to the sacristan and we began the ascent to the cupola.

Noble aspirations and the goal are forgotten in the rigours of the journey. We climbed the stairs with diminishing thought of what was above and increasing concern for what was below.

'I do believe ... ' Pipo puffed. 'I am ... quite ... content ... to ... admire Brunelleschi's work ... from the ... outside.'

'Save-your-breath,' said the priest. 'Just-follow-me.'

Older than Pipo and I combined, Father Piero had the most energy – a contained, spare energy that allowed him to mount the steps slowly, rhythmically and without exhaustion. Had I been in front, I would have tried to run to the top, and would have been certain to fail; Pipo would have paused at each landing for longer than it took to climb the stair. Piero kept going steadily.

We stopped on a narrow gallery, where the base of the dome met the body of the church, and tried not to look down while Piero told us of how Brunelleschi had overcome apparent impossibilities in building this, the largest dome in the world, exceeding even that of the Pantheon. He spoke of tensions and forces; things which, though I could not see them, I could certainly feel. Pipo, with his back pressed to the wall, muttered prayers. I drew a breath and leant over the rail. The octagonal cupola above us was reflected below by the eight-sided choir.

It was vertigo of course, a momentary loss of one's internal perpendicular, and yet, and yet, something flashed in my mind, the same jarring of time that had happened when I had first seen the Duomo from a distance. This time I was not sick. I merely swayed on my feet. It was all so quick, the vision of blurred figures and blood on the floor below. With a blink of the eye, the spectres disappeared and the octagonal choir was again the clean, geometric, mystical heart of Florence.

'Where do you find the courage to look down there?' asked Pipo, flat against the wall with his arms outstretched. 'Does it not make your head spin?'

'Yes,' I admitted. 'A little.'

'Well, are we rested?' asked Father Piero.

'Oh yes,' said Pipo, in expectation of descent.

'Then up we go.'

'What? Oh no, Piero, please!'

The priest led us through a door in the cupola to the ladders between the inner and outer shells, so that we climbed up the very inside of the great dome. Leaving the marbled church behind, we entered the world of pure construction. Pipo whimpered all the way.

'Look at the bricks,' said Piero, 'laid in a herringbone pattern.' He explained how this innovation had helped the architect to solve the problem of raising such a weight without central support.

Up and up we went in the dark until, at long last, we emerged in the lantern and its gallery, out into the blessed day. Then I shouted, a great yell of freedom and triumph. I stood on the top of the highest place ever built by man, with a view over the valley. Florence was surrounded by little hills and beyond them, to the east, the Appenine mountains; but the city was built on a plain, and therefore had constructed its own high place. The wind whipped us but the air was clear and the vista blue. I ran round the gallery, through the eight slender arches, until I met the others again. Even Pipo looked happy now.

'Oh, it was worth it,' he was saying. 'You will never get me to do it again, but oh, I am glad to have done it once.'

Even Father Piero's usually crabbed expression melted into a broad smile. Opening himself up to the elements, he threw his arms wide and let the wind blow through him.

'On the earth are the animals, in heaven is God. Man stands between the two, partaking of both. But,' he said suddenly, wagging a finger at my own smile, which was betraying an idiot happiness, 'we do not have to build ladders to reach there. This is not a mounting block. This dome is merely the gesture of a man to those who told him, "Impossible – it cannot be done." Everything is possible, that is what this great dome says, all things are possible.'

THIRTEEN

To a poet dressed up as a monk, in bed in his rooms with the shutters closed

Winter in Italy is an antidote to summer: it provides contrast, gives Creation a rest from heat, allows death and rebirth. Here in England it deepens, thickens like soup, creeps into the very marrow of your bones and freezes. It parches the mind until it shrinks to a dried pea. Is it any wonder that you are sick with melancholy? Calling this malady of the spirit a newly minted name such as pusillanimitas will not help.

Just as the bulbs have come up, so has the snow come down. This is a God-forsaken country. If only I could take you to the land of wine and sunshine, you would be cured at once. However, that cannot be; so I must do what I can with what is available to me.

Melancholy – to use its true name – is a common condition of scholars, caused by too much work of the mind and not enough of the hands. From Ficino I have learnt cures; if you are wise, you will follow my prescriptions. I realise that what seems unorthodox even in Florence may well strike a pious Dutchman as positively devilish; but these recipes will work, and a healthy man is a godly man.

First, fill your room with the one hundred candles I have sent and light them all. The banishment of darkness is a fit aim for a Christian, is it not? Next, drink of the fine wine that you will find in the sack, the discovery of which in the cellars of Magdalene College has caused me to review my opinion of the University of Oxford. With the wine take a spoonful of honey. My last prescription, which is to delight the senses with the fragrance of flowers, is out of season, so accept if you will this posy of primroses which I found in the woods; at least they are the right colour.

By these means you will attract the powers of Jove, to dispel those of Saturn, for it is the heavy influence of that planet which is troubling you. And, for the sake of Our Lord, if Colet asks what all this is about, tell him that they are remedies from Ficino's Book of Life. He will accept that authority where he will not accept mine.

If, by the way, he should enquire as to what I am doing in my hermitage of a house, tell him that I am locked in a struggle with the past in order to prepare my soul for the future. I shall emerge presently. Commend me to him and tell him that I am hiding from his whips and scourges. Tell him anything, but do not tell him about my writing. Hide all the manuscript I have sent so far.

May the Muses whisper sweet poetry to your poetic soul.

Tommaso
March 16th 1499

THE ART of Piero Strozzi was founded on the work of Plato. At least once a week the priest disappeared into Florence in the evening without saying where he was going. The most he would admit to when challenged or wheedled was that it was a meeting of his Compagnia. Company of what, I wanted to know.

'Magicians,' said Pipo, quite seriously.

Even at such a gullible age, I did not believe this. Whatever it was, however, had a profound effect on Piero. Whenever he returned, he was like a pie without the crust, soft, peaceful, his irritable nature subdued. Daily he retired to his room to practice exercises of devotion and reflection; sometimes when he chanted alone, I listened at the keyhole and heard hymns addressed not to the Christian company of saints, but to the gods of old; to gods of the river and gods of the wind – most of all, to the god of the sun, Apollo.

Take heart, Desiderio, such things meet with the approval of our own God, of that I am certain. My dear Dutchman, am I really a heretic, to say that Jove is an aspect of the Supreme Lord, our Father, the aspect or quality of Light? And do you really suppose that Our Father would castigate us for seeing Him in all things: the woods, the rivers, the fields, our fellow men? I tell you, Desiderio, the concept of the One, seated somewhere up above in judgement of the many – which includes you and me – is a concept far removed from the truth. That deceit is the lock and key crafted by the Church to keep us in its coffers. The

Church, which can elect as its Holy Father a man so obese that the mere effort of breathing makes him sweat; a man who demands total obedience to canon law from others, and fathers sons for himself; a man who sells the most divine and sacred offices for rich reward and yet pontificates on cardinal sin; a man who raises armies to win new territories, and taxes the poor and landless; this Church, I say, which spawns such a man, demands my allegiance and does not have it.

Desiderio, your misery is understandable, but it is a crime against God. Put it aside. Go for a walk. The next time something smiles at you, whether it be a child or a landscape or – it can happen – an adult human, know who it is who is smiling. Through every part of His Creation He is telling of His love for you. Stop this wilful deafness, and stop threatening me and my philosophy with inquisitions. Such arguments are feeble in the light of Truth.

There was a secret to the art which I had still not discovered, despite all the lessons I had received on proportion, lessons such as the three cardinal virtues of a good hand.

'One is beauty, one is harmony, the last is legibility. These virtues are joined one to another as the hands of the three Graces entwine as they dance. As the three Graces are governed by Venus, so these three virtues are governed by Divine Proportion.

'Without understanding or applying the laws of proportion to your work, you may come close to, but never fully achieve, beauty, harmony and legibility. Proportion is the inner law operating in good work; and if you ever wonder why some scribe's hand appears faultless but does not make your soul sing, it is because he has worked only on the externals and knows nothing of the inner law.'

This was only one discourse of many on the same theme, but still I did not have the secret of the inner law. In my struggle to discover it, I spent much time measuring the heights of capital letters and trying to find the relationship between them and the page. That there was such a relationship was obvious, but I could not see how Piero achieved it.

'You know,' said Pipo, as I sighed with frustration over a

branching tree of calculations, 'God did not make the universe with a ruler. Find the unit, Tommaso.'

I was close to losing my temper. 'It is obvious, the unit is the first capital letter.'

'Wrong,' said Pipo, returning to his work with an infuriating smile.

I went to his desk and pleaded for an answer, or at least a direction in which to find it. Pipo told me it was in front of me, behind me, within me, all around me, here, now; but if I must find knowledge through books, then the place to look was in Plato's *Timaeus*.

I read the book about the shapes of the universe, but, though the answer was indeed within the book, it still eluded me. Father Piero shook his head sadly, saying that I had been very close once but that now, as a result of much thinking and wanting, I was becoming increasingly removed from the answer.

'It is the golden rectangle. The square root of five,' I said, remembering what the Bishop had told me.

Hearing that it was not, I came to the very brink of rage. I was about to tear up everything in sight and hurl desks across the room when I heard a voice clearly within my mind: the unit is the whole.

'It is the page!' I cried.

His face suffused with delight, the priest brought an assortment of parchment sheets from the cupboard and laid them out. 'Paper and parchment come in many sizes ... '

'Messale maggiore, messale commune, ragionevole, foglio reale ... '

'Some of them approximate the golden rectangle, others do not. So we must find our unit of measure by means of what we are presented with, by the whole of it. Now is the time for you to be shown the secret canon known only to the fellowship of true scribes, but first you must take a bath and put on fresh clothes.'

When I asked why, I was told that a young man should look his best when meeting God. I returned within the hour, feeling as pristine and nervous as at first Communion, to find Piero in prayer before a clean sheet of paper. After the amen, he folded the sheet down the middle to make the likeness of two pages in an open book. Taking up his wooden square, he drew in the diagonal across the whole spread. Then he drew a triangle, its base the bottom edge, its apex the top of the fold line. With an economy of movement and precision of line, he turned the square down, across and round to draw a small triangle at an intersection. From this, their starting point always at an intersection resulting from the last figure, he drew horizontal and vertical lines.

Two rectangles emerged, one on each side of the paper. I watched in growing fascination, knowing that these rectangles were proportionate. How does one know? Because your soul sings, like a canary in a cage which has heard the free canary outside the window.

'These are the areas which will contain the text. What is their relation to the areas of the pages?'

I reached for the rule but dropped it when he rapped my knuckles with his square.

'Look, boy, look. There is no need for measuring. Observe the diagonal and remember your geometry.'

'Oh ... '

'Two rectangles of differing size but sharing the same diagonal must be ... ?'

'Of the same proportion!'

'So here, by this canon, we have echoed the proportions of the page without any need of striated rule or scribbles of calculation. The margins are unequal, shallow at the top, deep at the bottom, wider at the sides than in the middle, and that inequality, being proportionate – the ratio here is two to three – satisfies us in a way equality would not. There is much more to learn; from this beginning we can go on to find the size of our initial capital and our line depths, but this is the seed of the matter. This is the secret of the beautiful book: all things on the page must be in proportion to the page itself, including the capital letters, and the lines which determine the height of your script.'

I stood beside him, gazing in wonder as he designed a page with boxes for pictures and text; each one, whatever its size, was related to the others, as they must be, now that I knew the secret behind them. He made me sit in his chair and repeat the exercise several times. Once I had mastered the system, he brought to the desk a book to be copied. 'Say a prayer to Our

Lord before you begin,' he said, 'and then let the pen write, for this copy will be for you to keep, your master-work.' It was Plato's *Symposium*, translated from the Greek to Latin.

'One last word,' said Piero before he left me alone with the work, 'remember our first lessons and be quick. Do not read the text as if to understand it; that will delay you and you will make mistakes. Humble yourself before the Goddess of Beauty, and simply copy.'

The empty page was before me, the proportions drawn faintly in lead. I studied the text on the book rest, considered the empty page. I allowed my mind to empty, then I filled my pen with red, communed again with the space of the page, placed the nib carefully and wrote:

THE SYMPOSIUM OF PLATO, TRANSLATED BY MARSILIO FICINO,
FLORENTINE

I changed the ink to black and began the body of the text:

> Apollodorus. *Concerning the things about which you ask to be informed, I believe that I am not ill-prepared with an answer. For the day before yesterday I was coming from my own home at Phalerum to the city and an acquaintance of mine caught sight of me from behind and called out in mock-official tone:*
> *'Apollodorus of Phalerum, halt.'*
> *I stood still to let him catch me up.*
> *'I have just been looking for you, Apollodorus,' he said, 'that I might ask you about the speeches in praise of love which were delivered by Socrates, Alcibiades, and others, at Agathon's supper.'*

It took twenty days. Sometimes I found the temptation to read the book irresistable, but the arguments of Socrates confounded me and soon I was happy to do as I had been told. At last I ended
with a colophon in which the
last words descended
down the page in
an inverted
triangle
like
so.

Piero and Pipo exchanged opinions on my work as if I were not there.

'It took him twice as long as it took Velox,' said Piero.

'Oh, but it is twice as beautiful.'

'Nonsense. Look at those line ends – ragged and cramped. And he seems to form *g* differently each time it occurs.'

I began to suffer as Pipo did and slumped in the chair. Piero put his hands on my shoulders. 'The capitals are splendid,' he said.

This, the first praise I had ever received from him, shot through me like one of Love's darts. Piero went further and said that graceful writing would come with practice, but that I had fully understood proportion, and that was what was important. 'One thing you already know is that, if there is a slight misalignment at the beginning of a construction, the multiplication of error as we proceed is tremendous. The essence of Creation is perfect; in manifestation, it can lend itself to error, thus it is rare to find something perfect in the material world. However, in the capital of Christendom there are some perfect capital letters.'

He was due to go to Rome for the Jubilee. 'Jubilee! A fine name for tax-gathering. Still, it gives me the opportunity to show you Trajan's Column. Go and pack my bag, Tommaso, and pack your own, too.'

'Am I to come with you? To Rome?'

'Will you leave me behind?' said Pipo.

Piero looked at his friend in surprise and asked him if he wanted to come.

'Of course not! You know I hate Rome.'

We left the following day to join the rest of the clergy journeying south for Jubilee. Pipo came out to watch our departure and Piero recapitulated the various matters to which Pipo would have to attend during our absence. He tried to give him money but Pipo refused, saying that he was going to the city that very day to collect what was owed him by the Pazzi for the Boccaccio. He was happy that, at last, he could support himself financially; he was even happier not to be going to Rome.

FOURTEEN

IT WAS early spring; in a clerical party of twenty, we rode south down the valley of the Arno, through a countryside hazy with trees and the promise of new leaf. Having expected a sanctimonious journey, I was surprised to find myself in ribald company. As the bawdy jokes flew round us like flies, Father Piero withdrew, but I lingered, amazed to hear one of the men referring to the Pope's 'sons'.

'Surely he meant nephews?' I said to Father Piero when I rejoined him at the end of the line.

If Piero looked sad, it was not because of my innocence, but because that innocence was on its way to certain death. 'There is much you must learn; what you will see in Rome will undoubtedly alarm you. I am a priest talking, and you I count as a young man with an innate fount of natural religion. To prepare you for what is coming, I must tell you that the Pope, the highest spiritual authority in the world, is a wicked man: greedy, grasping, ambitious in this life, uncaring of the life to come. Good men bide their time; happily one does not have to follow the Pope to reach Christ. Quite the opposite these days.'

While I was still trying to absorb what he had said, Piero continued to explain that the Pope was of the della Rovere, that his sister had married one of the Riario, and that every high office was now held by a man of one or other of these families.

'Such as the Archbishop of Florence?'

'Precisely. Pietro Riario is the eldest of the Pope's nephews. Fortunately for us he is witty and amiable, and because of that we tolerate him.'

'You speak as if we had some choice.'

'Nothing happens in Florence without Lorenzo's approval.'

'Even Papal appointments?'

'Especially Papal appointments.' Father Piero looked up at

the sky, as if searching for a sign of God. 'There are some who say that "nephew" is a euphemism for "son"; that all those young men with lofty titles are in fact the natural sons of Pope Sixtus, reared by his sister. All I can say is that I do not find the story unbelievable.'

I have heard it from others that there comes a time in the life of a boy when he discovers the fallibility of his parents; then something within him, something that saw his father as God, his mother as the Virgin, dies. I had my moment then, in respect of the Holy Father.

Piero continued, 'Girolamo Riario is the one who concerns me. He is a preening, loutish, conceited ... ' he paused for a better word but found none, ' ... bastard.'

I glanced about anxiously.

'He is the one who would be the Count of Imola.'

Imola is a small town on the road to Bologna which had been sold by Taddeo Manfredi to Duke Galeazzo Maria Sforza of Milan. In itself it was of no value, except of course to the people who lived there. But as it was sited on the border of Tuscany, it was of supreme strategic importance to Florence, particularly at that moment when Lorenzo was busy trying to establish an alliance with Milan and Venice. Lorenzo's aim, I have since discovered, was to form a league of all the major states, including Rome and Naples, with the hope for forging one nation out of Italy which could then defend itself against foreign enemies. So the machinations of the Pope and Sforza, under the guise of a marriage arrangement between Girolamo Riario and the Duke's daughter, Caterina, threatened not only the safety of Florence but the peace of all Italy. The recent news that His Holiness had persuaded Duke Sforza of Milan to part with little Imola caused dismay in Florence; this dismay turned to hope when Sforza demanded forty thousand ducats as the purchase price; it turned to outrage when the Pope demanded the loan of that sum from his banker, Lorenzo de' Medici.

'Lorenzo is being asked to provide the funds to cripple his own alliances; that is, to give the Pope the means to occupy Tuscany. Such supreme arrogance, even in the pontiff, beggars belief.'

In fields that we were passing, peasants were at work preparing the soil for seeds, seeds that would grow into plants and be harvested in the autumn. Steering ploughs dragged by oxen, they moved up and down the furrows with the simplicity of Adam. But when those crops went to market, in towns that had grown up round markets, then the confusion began; for when towns are governed by men who say one thing and do another, who make false contracts, who arrange marriages for political gain, then the life given by God to man is abused and made sophisticate. I looked at the fields and could hear the satisfied hiss of the serpent.

'Has Lorenzo advanced the loan?'

'Of course not. He has refused.'

'What will follow?'

'That is what we are waiting to hear. It must be that Lorenzo has destroyed his relationship with the Pope, but, as this story shows, what one presumes to be the unavoidable consequence often fails to happen. Gone are the days when a man repaid an offence with a straightforward knife in the belly. Now it is a knife in the back, when you least expect it. I can only hope that the obvious outcome may be avoided, for to my thinking it can only be war.'

'Between Rome and Florence?'

'Nothing so simple, no. Venice and Milan would side with Florence, Calabria and Naples with Rome, and soon the whole country would be involved. Oh, Madonna, if only the Pope would keep out of temporal affairs. What does the Vicar of Christ want with land, possessions and forts in the Romagna?'

I could see one of Piero's more irrascible moods building up and did not know what to do about it. In the study he could be easily calmed by being encouraged back to his work; while riding, however, his splenetic temper, provoked by any abuse of power which he happened to think about, was free to rise unchecked. I busied myself diverting his attention to what was beautiful in the landscape around us. However, after a few peevish puffs and one snort of indignation – undoubtedly in response to a thought of His Holiness – he managed to calm himself. 'It is all the Will of the Lord,' he muttered, 'and our just deserts.'

We followed the narrowing Arno south until it veered away towards Arezzo and its source. Continuing on the road to Rome, we entered a burnt and yellow landscape; northern greenery gave way to southern aridity and both light and land became harsh. As we passed Montepulciano, I viewed Angelo Ambrogini's hill town with interest. Angelo was beginning to be referred to as 'Poliziano', a name deriving from that of his birthplace, for it is a habit of Italians either to honour a man with a geographical appellation, or to deride him with it. Thus when I was called 'Volteranno', it had the opposite connotation to 'il Volterrano' – an honour to be bestowed in time upon my cousin Raffaello. Montepulciano rose on its hill – as the Bishop had said, it was to me a mere bump in the landscape – and seemed as indifferent to its famous son as he affected indifference to it.

The source of the Arno is also the source of the Tiber. Meeting this new river at Orvieto, we followed it to Rome. It was to be fourteen days from the beginning of our journey before the Holy City came into view, and by that time I had retreated with Piero to the length of two horses behind our scatological brethren. We entered Rome at the Castel Sant' Angelo, and, as the rest made for the environs of the Vatican, we went our own way into the ancient heart of the city.

Despite all warnings, I still expected Rome to be the most magnificent city I had ever seen; more magnificent, that is, than Florence. Disappointment mingled with disbelief as my horse picked its way through narrow, rank streets. I had anticipated ruins, but not the contemporary ones of the squalid homes of modern Romans. The river of humanity that flowed through these streets was a turbid one, a flood water stirring up a reeking silt. The people – nobles, priests and artisans – shared the streets with pigs, dogs, cats and goats. Markets were spontaneous, occurring wherever there was a man with something to sell. Peasant women from the countryside squatted on the steps of fountains beside baskets of eggs and herbs. Half-naked, dirty children screamed for the attention of neglectful mothers; men without employment diced with novice monks; whores – to my guilty fascination – openly displayed their soiled wares to whoever was passing. In comparison to this, Florence was a theatre of virtue, Volterra a temple of honest work. It was suddenly clear why the Florentines called themselves The New Romans, for they were salvaging all that they could from the ruining estate while the true heirs wallowed in indolence and corruption.

We passed a triumphal arch so buried by the debris of ages that we walked on a level with its uppermost sculptures, enjoying a view of them unknown to the ancient Romans themselves. Then, circling the foot of a hill, we came upon a vista of the past spread out before us: the ruins of basilica and shrine, the broken columns of old palaces and dismembered statues stood in a mire of cow dung and duck ponds.

'This is Rome,' said Piero. 'The rest is merely a foul and barbarous accretion. Let us leave this worrying mixture of opulence and deprivation which is Rome today and ascend the steps of the Capitoline Hill, there to dwell on Rome in her days of glory.'

At the top of the famous hill we came to a small, fragrant garden from which there was a view of the Forum and the huge, broken Colosseum. And there we dwelt on Rome, going over what we knew of her history, trying to arrange it chronologically and thus introduce perspective. Previously I had assumed Romulus, Caesar, Nero and Hadrian to be vaguely contemporaneous. Father Piero stretched them out in a receding line and put them in order of march over the millennial span of the Roman civilisation. He went on to elevate my spirit with the history of Christianity, then chilled my bones with the harrowing tale of barbarian invasions and the subsequent centuries of darkness.

'They are still here,' he said in a wintry voice.

'The huns?'

'All around us, barbarians all. Over the ages, the perpetual fire has been reduced to the flicker of a candle, but remains perpetual for all that. Little candles in the dark, in Paris, Clairvaux, Assisi, each one snuffed out by the night, but not before it has lit another. Now a torch burns in Florence, and I see trails of light running out all over Europe, but I see no light in Rome. None at all.'

The city – ruins, slums and palaces – was unified by the

slanting light of the evening sun which brought the same glow to both beggar and prince.

'The darkness of which I speak is in a man's eyes,' said Father Piero, 'and in his thickened speech: dull eyes and a lazy tongue. If you would know the quick from the dead, Tommaso, look into a man's eyes and listen to his speech. It has nothing to do with learning, wit or wealth. You may see a ploughman in a field aware even of the air he breathes, while all the scholars at their desks know nothing but their own opinions.'

I tried to make my eyes sparkle. Father Piero smiled. 'Fear not – you are one of the quick ones, as quick as the next boy, but it is whether you can carry the quickness into manhood which will determine the matter. The history of the world is a macrocosm of the history of a man. At fifteen you are passing the barbarian stage and approaching your own dark age.'

'What, shall I go blind?' I said flippantly, but Piero was fiercely serious.

'Yes, you will quite possibly be blinded by lust. Most men are. It is at your age of tempest and turbulence that the bark of reason is often blown off course for ever.'

'What should I do?' I asked, serious myself now.

'Look for the light, and, when you find it, stay with it, no matter how the winds buffet. Men suffer every tribulation in search of false treasure. If many never grow out of it, it is because they do not want to.'

'What follows for those who hold to the course?'

'The opportunity to strengthen reason. When that is strong, then comes rebirth.'

'What do you mean?'

'I mean you may attain wisdom again, and when I say again it is because you were wise when you were born. Infants know all but can say nothing. Growing up is a progress into ignorance, but if you attain wisdom, then you may again have true knowledge, and this time have the power of speech with which to express it.'

His words brought to mind the eyes of Bishop Antonio: observant, full of wonder, the eyes of a child in the body of an old man. From then on I was ever able to distinguish between a man of worldly knowledge and a man of true wisdom. And what appealed most about Piero's idea was this, that to become wise depends neither on learning nor on noble birth. Any man may become wise, if the desire is strong enough.

On the piazza at the summit was the museum which the Pope had made of his collection of antiquities. As it was open to all, we went in to view the statues and figurines. I marvelled at so many treasures being accessible to the people.

'Comfits,' said Piero tartly as we left, 'sops to prevent the hungry from screaming. What we require from His Holiness is spiritual nurture; what we are given are such extravagances as this. Do you know, this building was made from a quarry in the valley; that is, from stones of ancient buildings? The man is nothing but a barbarian dressed in a toga.'

'Oh look,' I said quickly, 'what a beautiful sunset!'

As we descended the hill again, Piero enumerated the sights he thought I should see during the coming week, pointing out in particular Trajan's Column and saying that I was to make a study of the inscription at its base.'Tomorrow,' he said, 'I have to attend the Archbishop and no doubt be lectured on my poor tally of sales in indulgences. While I am busy, I think you should visit your family.' He pointed towards the Pantheon. 'They are over there, at Sant' Eustachio.'

I presented myself at the Palazzo Maffei to be told that no one was at home, no one that is except my aunt Lucia, who was indisposed. But a message came to our lodgings later, inviting both Father Piero and myself to dine with the family on the following evening.

This time the palazzo was alive with smells and sounds. From the kitchen wafted the aromas of roasting meats and spices, while in the courtyard garden, where my uncle Gherardo and his wife were receiving their guests, the gentle notes of a consort of lutes tinkled.

It must have been the presence of Father Piero that moved her, but my aunt astonished me by taking hold of my head between her hands and, practically rubbing my nose with hers, cooing like a dove with pleasure. 'Oh Tommaso, Tommaso! We thought you were lost! Holy Mother of God, you cannot imagine what it was like to hear the terrible news about Volterra, and not to know the fate of our son and of you. Oh, Madonna, a mother can die from such worry! We are so proud, Tommaso, so proud.'

I raised an eyebrow.

'Antonio says that he owes his survival to you, that you led him from the city to the safety of the Florentine camp and the Count of Urbino. Those terrible, terrible common people: murdering their betters, causing war. Dear Lord, they deserved everything that happened. We have not been back since, nor shall we go until I am satisfied that the place is safe and no longer riddled with disease.'

I looked for Antonio, but could not see him. 'There would be nowhere for you to go,' I said to her, somewhat cruelly. 'Your house was burnt to the ground, if you will remember.'

'The wretches! The filthy barbarians!'

My uncle urged her to quieten and not to torment herself with such memories. This meeting was the first in which he did not have to stoop to enquire on the progress of my education, for by now I had reached his own height. Eye to eye with him I announced, with no little pride, that I was an apprentice scribe, and that Father Piero Strozzi was my master. 'The best scribe in – ' I began.

'Strozzi!' cried my aunt with delight, impressed by this ancient Florentine name. She smiled winsomely at the priest. 'I am so pleased. After all, being a scribe is often considered a low profession, but I am certain it has much virtue and integrity; as it must, if it attracts one of the Strozzi.'

'I believe your own sons are scribes of the Vatican,' said Father Piero.

'Scribes?' Lucia piped. 'Goodness, no. Secretaries, Father, secretaries.'

I quickly introduced Father Piero to my uncle, who took him to meet his friends: lawyers, doctors and notaries all above the age of sixty. When we were summoned to the hall to dine, Piero took my arm and asked quietly, 'Why does your aunt dislike you?'

'Is it so obvious?'

'I can always see a woman's true face underneath the paint. What is your relationship?'

'She is my father's sister-in-law. Why?'

'I was looking for a reason to excuse the inexcusable.'

'Did you find one?'

The priest smiled. 'If I can see human nature, I am a novice when it comes to understanding it, particularly the feminine kind.'

We took our places at the long table which glinted with silver in the light of many candles. Father Piero was led to the head of the table; left to myself, I was about to retreat to the other end when Raffaello invited me to sit beside him. He was quite the most handsome member of the family: chestnut hair hanging in long curls, ultramarine eyes, courtly manners.

'It is my view,' he said quietly, 'that it is being a secretary which is low, compared to being a scribe. I write letters in an indifferent hand, letters of state and business, church and chancery, whereas you are training in the ancient method, under a true master. And you live in Florence. I long to live in Florence, to study at the university, to be a scholar and scribe, to be a member of the Platonic Academy.'

Now this was not the first time I had heard of the Academy, but it was the first time I had heard it mentioned in such a matter-of-fact way, as if it were of as much substance as the university, yet there was no street in Florence that I knew of where one might find the Platonic Academy. I wanted to ask Raffaello more about it, but he was intent on discussing the art of the scribe.

'All that I know,' he said, 'is that it is an art, and not a craft, an art with principles and laws, but what they might be, I do not know. I do my best, copying fine examples of scripts, but I am aware that I work in ignorance.'

'Copying the external form without knowing the internal secret.'

'Precisely! And do you know that secret?'

'I am being initiated into its mysteries by Father Piero.'

Raffaello blew softly through his lips. 'If ever you would change places with me, cousin ... ' Disconcerted to be envied once again by a wealthy relation, I looked towards Father Piero to try and gain his attention, but he was in the middle of a conversation that he was enjoying.

'It is true,' one man was saying, 'the College of Cardinals is beginning to look like a family gathering of the Riario.'

'No one can obtain a post in the Curia unless he be rich enough to buy his office,' said another who, turning to Ser Gherardo, then asked, 'How much did it cost you to buy your sons their posts in the Camera Apostolica?'

'I must protest!' cried my aunt Lucia. 'Both Raffaello and Antonio have achieved their offices by merit!'

'It cost me five hundred ducats each,' said my uncle flatly.

FIFTEEN

WHERE some men collect bronze figurines, others books, Raffaello collected large stones. Quarried from ruins or bought from masons, each bore a Latin inscription which Raffaello had admired either as a fine example of epigraphy or as an item of historical interest. He took me to the room off the courtyard where he kept them and was delighted to find in me one person in the family who appreciated and understood his enthusiasm.

'Antonio says that my fondness for the past is a denial of present responsibilities. Sometimes,' he admitted, tracing a row of letters with his finger, 'I do wish I could live in the past. In this city today ... well ... '

I sat down next to him and said, 'There is nothing certain in this world, nowhere that is safe and secure or free from harm. But it must always have been like that.'

'A melancholy sentiment for a youth, deriving presumably from bitter experience.'

'Please ask me nothing about Volterra. Two years have passed but the memory has not dulled. Besides, you will have heard all from Antonio. Where is he, by the way?'

Raffaello replied with a question of his own. 'Is it true that he escaped to the Florentine camp?'

'What does Antonio say?' I asked guardedly.

'He never says anything that I believe. Where is he now? – I know not and neither do I care. He is probably at the house of Francesco de' Pazzi, for he seems to prefer that man's company to ours. We rarely see him at home; when we do, it is only to witness a temper as hot as Mount Etna. For all I know, he may not even be in the city. His duties often take him north, but he never deigns to tell us that he is going away, not to be seen again for six months or more.'

'What duties?' I asked lightly.

Raffaello shrugged. 'I do not know. I am only his brother; I only work in the same Camera.'

'There was a rumour in Volterra that he was there as an envoy of His Holiness.'

Raffaello laughed in surprise at this and said, if it were so, then the rumour would have been started by Antonio himself. 'Envoy of the Pope! He is a pen-pusher, as I am, a totter-up of columns in fat ledgers. Envoy, indeed! What else did you hear?'

Thinking it advisable to change the subject, I asked him what the Platonic Academy was, and where I might find it. He told me that it did not exist as a building but as an association of men, drawing its members from all ranks: nobles, poets, merchants, artists – diverse men united by the pursuit of truth. It had at its head a philosopher called Marsilio Ficino.

'You will have heard of the New Learning?'

I nodded.

'With the return of the literature of the ancients, the poetry and the histories, came philosophy. For centuries the works of Plato were lost to western Christendom, but in the east, in Greece and Byzantium, they had been copied continuously, and their lessons absorbed. In the 1430s, the Emperor of Constantinople came to Italy to beg for our help against the Turks. He came with a vast retinue of scholars and theologians to attend a Council, for the Pope had insisted that the eastern and western churches should be reunited before the Latins would help the Greeks in their war. Playing host to such a party of guests nearly exhausted the Papal reserves, and the Council might have foundered except that Cosimo de' Medici offered to accommodate it in Florence at his own expense. Among the Greeks was one called Georgios Gemistos, a man so devoted to ancient pagan philosophy that he was called "Plethon", the new Plato.'

According to Raffaello, Plethon was one of the wisest men in the world and as enigmatic as a magus. Indeed his presence in the city had begun the still popular Florentine fashion for choosing the subject of the Three Magi for their murals; it had also fired the Florentines with an ardour for all things Greek, including Plato. It was at that time that Cosimo de' Medici conceived the idea of having the works of Plato and the Neoplatonists translated into Latin, but it was to be some years before a complete copy of Plato's *Dialogues* was discovered by one of Cosimo's agents abroad and brought back to Florence; and even more years before a translator could be found, for still no Italian could read Greek.

'As the story goes, one day Cosimo's physician complained to him about his son, who was refusing to follow him in his profession. Cosimo had the boy brought to him and, during their conversation, he discovered in him a love of philosophy as great as his own. So Cosimo took direction of the boy's education and, at that early age, the boy dedicated his life to the translation of Plato. That was Marsilio Ficino.'

It was Raffaello's ambition to meet the man and to study with him. 'You see, I want to know about the nature of this universe we inhabit. It is said that at the temple of the Oracle of Delphi was a sign which read "Know Thyself". That which inspired Socrates also inspires me, for I believe, as did both Socrates and Plato, that if we know ourselves then we know God. These men of the Platonic Academy have the key to such knowledge. The keys we have here, in the emblem of the Papacy, unlock nothing these days but corruption. The real key lies in Florence.'

There was another reason for my cousin's yearning to go to Florence: he had a fervid admiration for the poetry of Angelo Poliziano. Though not wishing to increase his envy of me, I told him that the poet was my friend. Raffaello's astonishment was expressed in a flare of anger, but it passed quickly and was followed by a plea for forgiveness. 'Does it not seem strange that, while ostensibly I have everything and you have nothing, in fact the reverse is true?'

'While I am feeling boastful,' I said, 'I believe that the man who became my guardian, Bishop Antonio degli Agli, is a member of the Academy.'

'I know that for a fact,' said Raffaello.

'And Piero Strozzi?' I asked.

'I think we can presume so.'

'Why are they so secretive?'

Raffaello said that one did not have to look far for a good reason. 'Ironically, we should be grateful for our sinful popes of recent years. With their minds intent on their own selfish ends, they have not been in a position to denounce the New Learning, and thus it is through their laxity that the pagan gods have managed to return. Even so, one has to be careful. I do not think that the Academy is secretive; merely cautious.'

'How does one become a member?'

Raffaello laughed. 'Not by being fifteen.'

'Seriously, Raffaello.'

'It is by invitation.'

I wondered if I should ever be invited; Raffaello said that, given my evident good fortune, an invitation was probably awaiting my return to Ripoli.

The inscription at the base of Trajan's Column has provided the model for our capital letters. These letters, created by a chisel, we have recreated with pens, but cannot achieve the perfection of the original. I sat before them on a stool, a notebook on my knees, enjoying increasing wonder at the model and increasing frustration at the copy. I measured the letters and traced them and plucked from the words of the inscription an alphabet. A shadow fell across the page and I looked up to see Antonio.

'I had heard I might find you here,' he said, squatting down beside me and taking my notebook to look at my work. Saying nothing about it, he returned the book to me and stood to gaze at the reliefs that spiralled up the column. Where I saw in them a sculptural work of tremendous power, Antonio saw the subjugation of the Dacians. 'Insolent barbarians, according to the Emperor Trajan,' he said. 'Look there, at that image of free men in chains. What does it remind you of?'

I sat glumly with my head bowed over my book. 'According to Plato,' I said quietly, 'truth is beauty, and beauty is truth. In the *Timaeus* it says, "As being is to becoming, so truth is to belief."'

'And what does that mean?' Antonio demanded, pulling me up from my stool and making me confront the pictures of conquest.

'I think it means that behind all things that move is something which is still.'

'And so frozen letters are to be preferred to living memories?'

'They are not frozen,' I mumbled, 'they are beautiful.'

If the choice was between keeping the memory of horror alive, or replacing it with the contemplation of divine beauty, the latter course was infinitely preferable and much to be desired. Antonio thought otherwise. It was his view that by such intellectual diversions did men avoid responsibility. He clipped my ear. 'Come to me tonight at Francesco de' Pazzi's house. If you do not, I will consider you a traitor to your native land.'

The Palazzo Pazzi in Rome was an old building and neither as graceful nor splendid as that in Florence. Francesco de'Pazzi, a remarkably short man with hair the colour of runny egg, was a bachelor; his house, lacking the softening presence of women, attracted other bachelors, men who loved history, literature and gambling. As dice rolled their discussions ranged from the Catiline conspiracy and the excesses of Nero, to contemporaries: men such as Pietro Riario, the Archbishop of Florence whose banquets rivalled Nero's in ostentation; Duke Sforza of Milan, who had come to power by the sword and maintained his position by the same means; and Lorenzo de' Medici of Florence. Each of these, they agreed, was an offence to humanity. Though Francesco was Lorenzo's brother-in-law, he was the first to declare this opinion. The name that occurred most often that evening, however, was that of Girolamo Riario, the Pope's favourite 'nephew.' I had only been in Rome a week, but already I knew this name to be that of its most powerful citizen. In private, Antonio's friends despised the man.

The next day I awoke to the delivery of a message: 'Tommaso dei Maffei is requested to present himself at the Camera Apostolica. His cousin Raffaello de Gherardo dei Maffei desires to show him the collection of the Great Library.'

Lacking the dignity which a recipient of such an invitation should exhibit, I ran all the way to the Vatican, dodging in and out of groups of sedate priests and unhurried pilgrims. I sped through the famous square and past Saint Peter's: such sights were not for me.

The pikeman at the gate led me through the Vatican precincts to the door marked La Ruota and showed me into a circular office. Though Raffaello and Antonio had not been required to take orders, they were expected to dress as priests and Raffaello looked sombre and distinguished in his clerical garb. Under the curious gaze of others in the chamber, he took me to his desk and showed me what his daily work entailed, the simple, monotonous tasks of a letter-writer; but though the work was dull, the content of the letters required that it be done by a man of complete integrity.

We passed Antonio's desk in the Treasury but he was absent.

'Called away by Girolamo Riario,' said one of his fellows.

Raffaello led me to the gardens, for it was the hour when His Holiness often took the air, and he said, 'What could a good Christian desire more than a glimpse of the Holy Father?'

Francesco della Rovere – Pope Sixtus IV – was a colourful man. He performed his acts of simony with such aplomb that he was all but forgiven them by his subjects. Through his preferment of his nephews he gave a new word to our language: nepotism. The word of course should have been bastardism.

Why, you may ask, did we suffer him? If the sinner was not deposed, firstly it was because all the powerful men of the land were caught in his net of simony and were busy purchasing holy offices for their own relatives; secondly it was because we Italians cannot help but admire style. The Pope's arrogant disregard for law, his refusal to cover up his crimes but rather to present them with a flourish on platters, endeared him to those who value display above everything else. Lastly, and most importantly, he was not the first to abuse the position. Remember, we were only a generation from the time when we had had three popes at once.

No, what worried men was neither his simony nor his 'nepotism' but his absolute lust for territory. Of course our concern should have been for the spiritual health of Christendom, but it was the Pope's temporal ambitions that had our princes in a condition of perpetual unease.

In Rome, in that spring, there was much talk of Imola. If the Romans had been deeply impressed by the Pope's audacity in demanding the loan of forty thousand ducats from Lorenzo, they were equally impressed by the news of Lorenzo's refusal. Raffaello led us through the orchard to the rose garden where, approaching us on the far side of a clipped laurel hedge, was a walking mountain of flesh. While the body of the Pope was the work of a very broad brush, his face had been drawn with a fine nib. Atop an obese neck was an aristocratic head with delicate features and finely scripted eyebrows.

With him were two companions, one of whom, Raffaello told me, was Girolamo Riario. 'The other is a Florentine you might know, Francesco Salviati.'

I shook my head. I had never heard of him.

'He is hoping for preferment, probably the archbishopric of Florence as Pietro Riario is dying, a victim of his own excesses. I thought you might know Salviati, for he is a member of the Academy.'

I stared at the man keenly. He was of middle years and displayed the quickness I was beginning to associate with these mysterious academicians.

'The Florentines will surely rejoice at having one of their own supplant a Riario as Archbishop, and it would be a good way for His Holiness to placate Lorenzo after this Imola affair.'

'The Pope wants peace with Florence?'

'Of course.' Raffaello silenced me: the party was now close.

A stout young man with sensual red lips, a cleft in his chin and hedonistic eyes, Girolamo Riario had the look of one who is not denied his desires. He passed by without sparing us a glance as we bowed in the presence of His Holiness and received a weary blessing. Only Salviati bothered to turn his head and acknowledge Raffaello with a nod.

'Well, what do you think of Sixtus?' Raffaello asked me once they had passed.

When you are with a diplomat your own powers of diplomacy are strengthened. 'He seems ... majestic.'

'Is that what you expected?'

What I had expected, despite all warnings, was the benevolent, patriarchal smile of Saint Peter. 'No, not really.'

Raffaello clapped me on the back. 'Discretion is a great virtue. And Girolamo Riario – what of him?'

'Is it true that he is the son of the Pope?'

Raffaello looked suddenly alarmed. The Vatican was no place to be in the company of one given to asking straightforward questions.

We came to the Great Library and to its keeper, the famous scholar, Platina. If the Pope was a sinner, then he had the sinner's virtue of wishing to appease heaven with good deeds. Surely the greatest thing Sixtus ever did was to re-establish the Vatican Library, and to choose a good man for the work. There was such a lack of affectation in Platina's sturdy face that I warmed to him immediately. He felt like a safe harbour after the sea of arrogance we had just sailed through.

Having been left by Raffaello in Platina's care, I was shown the treasures of the Library, books of immense antiquity and value; but, for all the Early Fathers, the works of the Saints and centuries of Commentary, nothing pleased me so much as the Virgil, a Roman book with Roman paintings. As each of the single desks was occupied by a browsing scholar, I was guided to one of the carrels where printed books were stored and there the splendid Virgil was fastened by a chain to the shelves which bore those abominations of recent invention. I spent hours with the book, studying its pictures to see how men of the distant past had looked and dressed; studying also the letters, for they had been made at the time when script had first become most beautiful. Throughout the Library scholars were rattling chains as they consulted their books and I fell into a reverie, dreaming of a lifetime of scholarship chained to study in marbled tranquility. I woke up at the sound of my name.

'Listen, Maffei, do what you are told.'

'Of course. I am only saying that there will be difficulties.'

Two men were talking in low tones on the other side of the carrel. One of them was Antonio.

'It is to solve such problems that we employ you. Francesco de' Pazzi must persuade his uncle to join us, and it is for you to persuade Francesco.'

'Francesco is already with us. It is the old man who is being difficult and obstructive.'

'I fail to see why, given what we are offering.'

'He has something called a conscience.'

'A pretty name for fear. Find out its price. And if gold does not move him, remind him of our powers to bestow plenary indulgence.'

Antonio laughed cynically, the other strode away, past my carrel. It was Girolamo Riario. I went round to the other side and found Antonio plucking pills of wool from the elbows of his gown and making a little heap of them on the desk. He jumped violently when I touched him.

'Uh, it is you,' he said, relieved. 'What are you doing here?'

I explained and then told him that I had overheard his conversation.

He was unmoved. 'It was nothing important, only my gracious Lord delineating my duties, that is all. His Holiness has been disappointed by his banker, so he wants to change his bank. It is my duty to organise it. That is all.'

'So the Medici are to lose the Pope's custom?'

'Of course. Out of sheer pride and obstinacy they have sacrificed the very jewel of their banking empire. But where Lorenzo has refused to advance us forty thousand ducats, Francesco de' Pazzi is willing. If Francesco's uncle Jacopo is reluctant, it is because he fears repercussions in Florence.'

As well he might. I thought of the Palazzo Pazzi and its inhabitants, of a black slave and a smiling girl, and feared for them. Antonio and I left the Library and walked towards the walls of the palace. On the square below nuns wandered like magpies in search of trinkets of faith and morsels of indulgence. There was a bearded prophet there, his arms raised, his exhortations rising up to us.

'Antonio, is that not Andreas down there?'

'Andreas who?'

'The Greek prophet.'

'So it is, and still ranting.'

As Antonio gazed down indifferently on the scene, his thoughts elsewhere, I studied him. I wondered if he merely wore the robe of a priest or had indeed become one; he assured me he had not. 'I am the oldest son of the family; I will marry soon.'

'Who?' I asked.

He shrugged, insufficiently interested to pursue the conversation any further. 'That is up to my parents. I have more important matters to think about.'

My free cousin seemed diminished here in Rome; an onyx knight become an onyx pawn. 'Antonio,' I said, 'why must you flatter these men?'

'If you think that I am a papal flunkey then my disguise is working. Toadying to the would-be Count of Imola is merely an unpleasant necessity, as is my friendship with Francesco de' Pazzi. Both these men have their own ambitions, and I have mine. I have a vision, Maso, a vision of the end of oppression, a vision of republics rather than principalities. But what can I, a clerk in the Treasury, do to make my vision a reality? I shall tell you ... Have you ever heard the story of Cadmus and the Giants? Cadmus sowed some dragon's teeth and an army of giants grew up and threatened him. So he threw a stone in amongst them, and, each blaming the other, they fought with one another until all were slain. That is the way to rid the world of tyrants.' Antonio's eyes glittered. 'I throw my stones in; I talk to people, now to this man, now to that. And the result? The Pope makes a demand of Lorenzo which is refused, and now the care of the treasury has moved to the Pazzi. Lorenzo is on the brink of ruin. Is this not the best news you have heard for a long time?'

I was disappointed, for I wanted to see Lorenzo stuck with knives and dying slowly, not wandering about in reduced circumstances. Besides, Lorenzo's poverty would affect others. If I had not seen Angelo Ambrogini since he had joined the Medici household, if I felt abandoned by him, I had yet prayed the prayer which brought him success, and I did not want to see it undone.

'Have you been back to Volterra?' I asked.

'Twice. Do not go there, Maso – it will destroy you. They have built a fort on the acropolis, a windowless monstrosity, and the strength of its garrison has turned our city into a prison. Do not mistake me; if I can have Lorenzo cut up and fed to the dogs, I will do it. Meanwhile I am content with this money-letting. When the Pazzi take power in Florence, they will pull that fort down and let the Volterrani go free. The Florentines, too, will be free.'

'If only until the Roman armies arrive, via Imola.'

Antonio laughed at the idea. 'The Pope does not want Florence. All he wants is to remove the threat of the Triple Alliance. It is not so long, you know, since the Papacy nearly lost its power to the Holy Roman Emperor. The Papacy is a weak thing; Sixtus wants to make it strong. Once we replace the Medici with the Pazzi, we shall then have to do something about the Pazzi. But that is the employment of another day.'

Standing on the walls there with him, haunted by images of Volterra, I was troubled to discover no pleasure in Antonio's plans. If I loathed Lorenzo with all my being, I had yet grown fond of several Florentines, and would have preferred them to determine their own future for themselves. I thought of the Bishop, and, wondering what his response to all this would be, my mind jarred. I felt myself dividing in two, the black and the white, the onyx and the alabaster, the light and the dark.

'When you return to Florence,' said Antonio, 'you will deliver letters for me to Jacopo de' Pazzi.'

My unwillingness must have shown, for Antonio said, 'You have only one real loyalty, and that is to your family.' He studied me closely. 'I used to think of you as a brother, but you seem to have grown distant.'

'It was not my intention.'

'It is the company you keep: all these bishops, priests and Platonic philosophers. They are wrapping you up in the wool of dreams. Well, dream on, if that is your pleasure, and leave the rest of the world to suffer its miseries and deprivations. Let me tell you, however, that a true follower of Christ does not build temples; he destroys them.'

'Are you not worried that I shall go back and tell the Medici everything that I have heard?'

'Oh, are we on such familiar terms?'

'Not at all. I have only seen Lorenzo once, and if you had not run off like a coward that day, you would have met him, too. But my guardian and my master are friends of his.'

'You will only tell them what they already know. For what have I told you? That the administration of the Papal treasury is moving to the Pazzi bank. That will not be news to the Medici.'

To leave the Vatican, I went through the basilica, where parties of nuns lined up to weep over the Apostle's relics. I was troubled. This place, the world's centre of prayer, the chapel of pilgrims, the seat of Saint Peter, seemed but the vestibule to an atrium of political intrigue. How did the two things marry?

In the square, Andreas the Greek was accosting passers-by with revelations of their fate. Seeing me, he threw up his hands. 'David!' he called. 'David! The time of battle approaches!'

I shuddered and hurried on, back to Father Piero's rooms, to tell my master everything I had seen and heard. As Antonio had predicted, it was no news at all, and Piero was more interested in Francesco de' Pazzi for another reason. He had seen him that day and stopped to greet him; Francesco was effulgent in his praise for Pipo's Boccaccio and said that, if Piero would care to visit the bank, he could collect the payment. Reliving his astonishment, Piero paced the room flapping his arms.

'That money should have been in the Florentine bank. Francesco said he had it transferred here, knowing I would be in Rome for Jubilee. It is Pipo's money, not mine! It was just an excuse. Bankers. *Bankers!*'

'Hush, Father,' I said, for he was growing very red in the face.

'All he is doing is delaying payment by several weeks. *Usurers!* A pox on them. A *pox!*'

I thought he was about to bleed spontaneously from all pores. I tried to think of a ruse to bring him to his desk and writing instruments, but this did not work; this time he was not merely angry, he was frightened.

'Pipo will be all right,' I said.

'By the time we return, he will have been without any money for six weeks. As a convicted debtor he cannot borrow, so how can he live?'

When we returned to Ripoli, it was to find San Pietro empty. Women from the village were waiting for us in anguish to tell us the news. Pipo had survived for as long as he could on unripe beans from the garden. By the time the villagers realised what was happening and took him food, he was too sick to eat.

Piero seemed to collapse within himself. He went to sit alone in the now overgrown and weedy garden. I wandered listlessly in the study, wondering where the sunlight had gone.

THE THIRD BOOK

THE POET'S SCRIBE

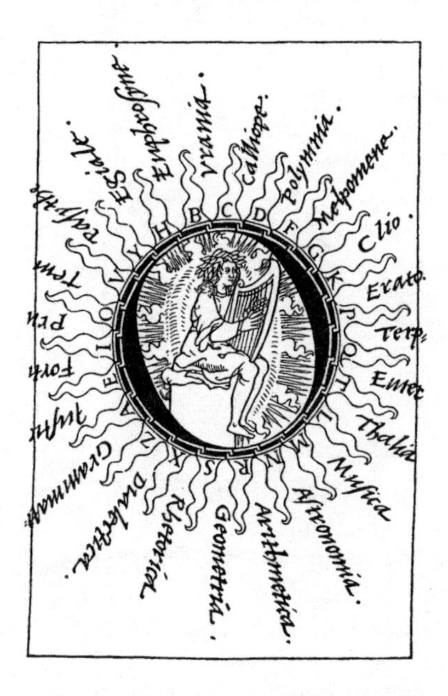

But of beauty, I repeat again that we saw her there shining in company with the celestial forms; and coming to earth we find her here too, shining in clearness through the clearest aperture of sense. For sight is the most piercing of our bodily senses; though not by that is wisdom seen.

Plato

To Desiderio

It seems that a battle is being waged for your soul. I hear that the physician snuffed out my candles and declared the wine to be poisonous. Of course you must do as he says; but whoever it was who prescribed the company of young Thomas is obviously the best physician of all. That you are using the lad as the courier of our letters is an inspiration on your part: his open-hearted cheerfulness is as much a balm to my spirit as to yours. I gather that his visit to Oxford is at the special dispensation of his father, who has forbidden him his wish to study and live here. Is England full of strict, rigid, good men? Desiderio, remain ill for as long as you can, so that we may keep Thomas with us. To indulge your love of punning, let me say that we must have More of him.

He tells me that you are troubled not by melancholy but that you have come to that crisis of the spirit which is inevitable for the Christian who loves the literature of the ancients. Vale! Welcome to our circle. I hear that Colet's remedy is to remonstrate with you, insisting that you give up poetry and literature. Thomas, who has the ability to see into each man's heart, and to view the light and the dark with an equal eye, tells me that Colet himself has not yet given up these things, that he is a secret indulger. This explains everything! I do not know what Colet and Ficino said to each other when they met in Florence. I only know that they met at the time when Ficino himself was suffering this spiritual sickness, and calling upon himself to renounce the pagan philosophies and turn wholeheartedly back to Christ. Perhaps he imparted to John Colet a fear of the soul's struggle in any attempt to reconcile Platonism and Christianity.

How glad I am to be a lesser mortal of small intelligence! In my simplicity I do not see why there cannot be both One and Many, that is, One God and many gods. If the pagans called them 'gods', and the Jews 'thrones' and 'powers', and the Christians 'angels', may they not be the same? In the conversations I overheard between men such as Poliziano, Pico della Mirandola and Ficino, these things are not irreconcilable. It is only when you stand up to make your case before doctors of learning that you court trouble.

It is my belief that Colet is suffering from too much caution, but he knows the situation here better than I. It seems to me that, in Henry VII, we have the protection of a tolerant king, who himself has the benefit of a wise woman for a mother. But we can never be complacent in a world ruled by a church that promotes its doctrines through torture and death. There, I have said it. Burn this letter now, before it burns us, and do as Colet instructs.

Tommaso dei Maffei
March 19th
Oxford

SIXTEEN

PIERO'S lessons came to an end with the words, 'I have given you knowledge which will serve you a lifetime, but I have taught you skills that nobody wants.' Thus I was returned to the world rich in spirit and poor in prospects. Vespasiano allowed me to work in the bookshop in exchange for a bed at night under the counter; in any hour of leisure I occupied myself with ruler and compass, finding bliss in hidden structures and the bringing forth of form. Was I thus escaping the world? – without doubt, but it was an escape into true freedom, if a lonely one. Raffaello had been wrong; no invitation to join the Academy came. I remained a stationer's assistant.

The bookshop was always full of academic luminaries, fascinating both in themselves and in their conversations. As well as professors from the university there were citizens who spent their wealth on rare manuscripts and delighted in being well read. But for every potential customer, there were at least five who did not have the means to buy a book; they were the students and the poets living under patronage. These young men came both to read and in the hope of meeting someone who could advance their careers.

Every notable man passed through that bookshop. On one occasion Marsilio Ficino himself called in with some friends, but I did not know it until after he had left. Vespasiano began to sing his praises as soon as the door closed.

'Which one was Ficino?' I asked Grazia, who was tidying books on the shelves.

He shrugged. 'They all look the same to me in those red gowns.'

The red gown, or lucca, was the robe of the citizen. Vespasiano's shop was thoroughly sanguine with them.

In vain I badgered Vespasiano to find me copying work. Any commissions that came, however, were given to others of more mature talent. He told me to be patient, and to be grateful that, though I had no money, I was rich indeed to be in a position where I could copy any book I wanted and to build my own library. This was good advice and during the nights I began to copy all Marsilio Ficino's translations of Plato's *Dialogues*.

My ambition to be the new Poggio Bracciolini faded. The days of great discoveries had passed and not much had come to light since, thirty years previously, Poggio had found Quintillian's book on education. So it was with much curiosity that we received a book which had been discovered in a monastery in Rome. It was not one of The Great Finds: the *Metaphysics* of Aristotle had never been lost and copies of it abounded. But this copy arrived with the air of a foreign diplomat, that is, full of self-esteem and yet not noted for anything in particular. It had been purchased by a duke of Germany from an agent in Rome; Vespasiano was commissioned to have a copy made of it, which was to be held for safekeeping in Florence until the original had arrived in Germany. When notification of safe arrival had been received, Vespasiano's copy was to be destroyed.

Wanting practical rather than beautiful work, and at little expense, Vespasiano gave the task to me. I asked him why the book was so important.

'To be honest, I do not know. I think the Duke is proud of his acquisition and is creating a commotion where none is due.'

I scrutinised the dowdy, vellum-bound manuscript. There was no other book bound with it; there was nothing hidden in the binding; it had no illuminations; its script was late, demotic Greek. Mystified, I began the copy we were to make of it.

Apart from the distractions of my own making – where I could not work for staring at the long Byzantine beard of Johannes Argyropulous, or the cabbage ears of the poet Luigi Pulci – I was distracted by those interested in what I was doing.

'What is this book?' they would ask, affecting only a passing interest.

'The *Metaphysics* of Aristotle.'

'Is that all?'

'That is all.'
'A lot of mystery attends it.'
'Indeed.'
'Why?'
'It is not my business to know.'

One such was Angelo Poliziano. He came often to the bookshop, where he was usually called upon by other readers to translate something for them from the Greek. We had a copy of Horapollo's work on Egyptian hieroglyphs and Angelo would amuse himself by reading it out loud to anyone who would listen. 'When they wish to indicate a sacred scribe, or a prophet, or an embalmer, or the spleen, or odour, or laughter, or sneezing, or rule, or judge, they draw a dog.'

His audience would protest that he was fooling, but few could prove it as knowledge of Greek was still so rare. So we had to accept Angelo's translations, and cry with laughter, not knowing whether he was teasing us or telling the truth. Regarding Horapollo he insisted vehemently that his translation was literal, that no one could invent such nonsense.

He had a taste for such exotic tracts and loved to sit in a corner and study books which he had no hope of possessing except in his memory, a memory which was phenomenal, at least with regard to languages, literature or history; concerning the time and date of appointments, the route home or the names of his contemporaries, the young man who could recite Homer had no memory at all. Once he was propounding the system of memory that the Bishop had taught me, telling a group of men which had gathered round him how he had only to go into the Cathedral to recall the paradigms of Greek verbs and nouns; Homer's *Iliad*, he said, he stored at San Lorenzo, and Virgil's *Aenead* at San Marco. To visit those places and look at various architectural features was to enjoy recall of those passages which he had associated with each. This stirred his audience tremendously, but one fellow, annoyed at having been referred to as Giuseppe instead of Jacopo, said, 'With all due respect, could you not apply this admirable system to the names of your friends?' As everyone took this opportunity to return to him the mockery he so often bestowed on others Angelo looked stung and ashamed.

This man Jacopo watched the precocious youth's suffering with evident satisfaction. To relieve Angelo, Vespasiano drew Jacopo from the group and brought him to my desk, introducing him as someone I was bound to want to meet. This I doubted.

'This is Jacopo, Tommaso. Jacopo Bracciolini.'

I nearly fell off my stool. Poggio's son! I was as surprised as if I had been introduced to the son of Hercules, for once a man has achieved the status of hero, he leaves the realm of ordinary mortals; and, so far as my imagination was concerned, leaves nothing behind, particularly not sons of the flesh.

'I hear you are following in my father's footsteps,' Jacopo said graciously.

'Oh, no, how could I? But I do admire him above all other scribes.'

Jacopo smiled. 'How easy it is to admire a man you have never known. If it is difficult for me to see that my father had virtues, for others it is equally difficult to believe he had faults. I wonder which view is closer to the truth?'

'Belief in virtue, surely,' said Vespasiano.

'So Ficino would teach us, yes. But myself, I believe we cannot deny what our senses show us. To see only the good in a man is to see but a part of him. Surely we should confront reality and look it squarely in the eye?'

'Ficino says that to dwell on the good is to give power to the good.'

'Well, it is too late for me with regard to my father. Let him be remembered by you as the finest of scribes.'

I found Jacopo's cynicism unsettling.

'Vespasiano tells me you are copying the *Metaphysics*. Let me look, let me see ... ' He leant over my work and scrutinised it. He smelt rancid, as if last night's supper had been cooked in second-rate oil; I realised that, for all his fine education, he probably lived in lodgings. 'Ah yes, beautiful ligatures,' he said, 'and the capitals – simple but sound, yes, very sound. So you read Greek? Admirable.'

'Well, no. I am only copying.'

Jacopo barked in surprise. 'You do not know Greek? You are copying an unknown language?'

'What are letters but shapes, essentially?'

'Well, you are making fine work of your shapes, very fine.'

He was reading the forbidden text, but I could hardly snatch it from under his nose.

'This is a late script, is it not?' he said, brazenly picking up the text and reading it from the beginning.

'I am not supposed to allow ... '

'Come, come Tommaso, are we not friends?'

'I am sorry, Jacopo,' said Vespasiano, returning to us. 'He is right. We are under strict instruction from its owner that it should not be read by anyone but the copyist.'

'And you have chosen a copyist who cannot understand what he reads. You are most observant of your clients' wishes, Vespasiano.'

'On such is my reputation founded.'

Rebuffed, Jacopo Bracciolini bowed abruptly and said farewell.

Vespasiano was distressed to turn a friend away, particularly a friend in need. Unusually, he did not tell me the story of the man, but I gathered it from others: Jacopo had been involved many years before in a plot to overthrow Lorenzo's father, Piero de' Medici. The Signoria had confiscated his inheritance and sent him into exile for a term. Vespasiano, who put the episode down to youthful folly, was keen to help the man rebuild his life, but on this day he turned him away.

A summons came: I was to attend Master Angelo Poliziano at the Palazzo Medici at noon. I walked heavily, reluctantly, up the street of the stationers towards the Cathedral. Passing the Palazzo Pazzi, I stopped to look into its courtyard in the hope of finding a radiant smile but saw nothing but a few statues and a patch of sunlight. Rather than flaunt the increase of wealth that had come to them by virtue of the Papal Treasury, the family seemed to have withdrawn. I was about to walk on when a rose fell to the ground in front of me. Though I looked up at once, all I saw was blank windows. I picked up the flower as a token of encouragement from the gods and carried it with me to the Via Larga.

The Palazzo Medici awaited me impassively. It had three

storeys: the lowest, which housed the bank, was built of large, rusticated boulders; the next was of cut blocks; the third of finely dressed stone. The architecture indicated spiritual progress, of aspiring from the coarse business of everyday life to heavenly refinement. Along the wall of the palazzo fronting the Via Larga was set a stone bench where people coming to and from the bank or the market were free to rest. Here I sat down, too full of apprehension to complete my journey without a pause, too agitated to think of anything other than that there was a cold draught round my ankles, and that it came from a grilled window on a level with the street which must have been that of a storage cellar. Further on, only ten paces away, the gate of the palazzo yawned like a hungry whale waiting for the next little fish to swim in.

The Angelus bell began to ring throughout the city, signifying the hour of my appointment. While everyone paused to lower their heads in prayer, I offered up a silent cry for help to the Virgin and left the rose for the Holy Mother on the stone bench. Wiping my hands down my hose to take off the sweat, I walked on to the gate. There was no porter.

Behind me the city was starting to bustle again as the last notes of the bell died away; in front of me was a vista of tranquility: a courtyard, bounded by a graceful arcade of grey stone with blue friezes which coloured the air and turned midday into poignant twilight. In this misty atmosphere stood a boy, high up on a pedestal, a serene figure of bronze. At first I thought it was David, for his slender foot was on the head of Goliath, but he wore the petasus, the low-crowned, broad-brimmed hat of Hermes the God, and at his heels were the hint of wings. This was no time to stand puzzling over mixed images, but the statue had the power to arrest, and its impact upon a living youth awash with fear was profound. There was no porter at the Palazzo Medici, just a god of the gateway. He looked down on me benignly.

My name was called from above. Angelo was on the gallery of the first floor, beckoning to me. 'Come up. I will meet you at the top of the stairs.'

I went up a stairway peopled by antique busts more rare and exquisite than anything I had ever seen. Angelo led me through large halls to his room and the small study beyond it.

'How quiet it is here,' I said.

'The family is at Careggi. Lorenzo and I returned yesterday, but he has gone to the Palazzo della Signoria, so we have the house to ourselves. Now, this edition of the *Metaphysics*,' he said without further ado. 'How does it begin?'

I admired his directness but could not answer the question. He took a manuscript copy down from the shelf and read the first few lines. 'Is that how it begins in your version?'

I could not be sure until I had seen the page; even then I could not tell. I thought there might be a small difference.

Angelo nurtured a theory – often expounded in Vespasiano's shop – that by noting similarities and variations in texts one could determine relationships between them; relationships which might, in the end, reveal the oldest copy and perhaps the original. 'All the copies of the *Metaphysics* that I have ever seen begin as this one does. If yours is different, it may have a different source, which may well be older.' He seemed as excited by this possibility as most men are by a beautiful woman.

'Is that its mysterious value?'

'A subtle treasure, one that is gold to the learned while to everyone else it would appear as dross.' Inevitably, he asked if he could read the book.

'That is impossible. Vespasiano has it in chains.'

'But the copy you are making, that is free to come and go, surely? You could bring it to me.'

I said that I would like to, if only to please him, but that such an indiscretion, if discovered, would finish my career before it had begun. He appreciated this and nodded thoughtfully. He sat head in hands, rubbing at his nose. Soon he had an idea.

'You could take this edition to the shop; then, as you make your copy, if you note any variant words, you could put a mark in the book. It belongs to Lorenzo but he will not mind. There! That is the solution. Who could complain about that?'

'The German duke?' I asked.

'Apart from him.'

I agreed that the reaction of any Florentine worth his salt would be full praise for initiative. However, the task was beyond me for I could not read Greek.

'Then how can you possibly copy it?' he gasped.

'I know the alphabet. Bishop Agli taught me that much, and I have practised Greek scripts with Father Piero. More than that ... '

Angelo was furious. 'This is intolerable! You must be making all kind of mistakes! What is Vespasiano thinking of?'

'Security,' I muttered.

'What if the original is lost on its way to Germany? The world would be left with your strings of shapes and who knows how many errors!'

This was true. I had no means of checking what I had done, and all scholars being forbidden access to the book, no one else could check it for me. Angelo had another solution, one even more outrageous than the last: I was to move into the Palazzo Medici.

'What?'

'You need to learn Greek, and quickly. You will be drilled in the language every spare moment of the day. If you know the alphabet, all you need is familiarity with the sound and the rudiments of grammar.'

'That is all? Bishop Agli has been working at it for thirty years!'

'He did not have me as his tutor,' said Angelo simply.

'What will Vespasiano say?'

'All he needs to know is that you have been invited here as a guest in Lorenzo's household. Say that it is to repay an old debt owed to your family. You will continue to work on the copy at his shop, and you will keep this edition close to hand, marking it to show any differences.'

There was a sounding note within me, and a low one. How could I live in the house of Lorenzo, under the eaves of the tyrant? The weakness in my stomach made itself felt, my head grew hot and I did not know whether I was going to faint or be sick. 'I cannot,' I muttered.

'It is not a choice, it is a command, and one that should surely please you? Do you want to remain a stationer's assistant for the rest of your life? With knowledge of Greek, you would be assured of work and could name your own price.'

I gazed at him imploringly. Did he not understand? I, a

Volterrano, could never live in the house of the Medici. I bent double in an effort to remain conscious. He touched my head. 'In this house,' he said, 'a man lives not for himself but for something greater than himself. Put aside your fears; they have no foundation.'

Thus my future was determined, not by choice but by command. Now, in long retrospect, I realise that this was the usual style of Medici patronage, in which the embers of talent in a man were fanned to a fire, not for the sake of the man himself (he ran the risk of being burnt up), nor for the gain of the Medicean coffers, but to give the world something of which it had need. It was not a conscious policy of philanthropy; it was a drive, an energy for which the house on the Via Larga was a source. The word 'patron' after all means father, usually taken to mean the patron as a supporter and protector, but in the case of the Medici it meant father as the means of genesis. Anyone patronised by them was caused to work to the point of suffering, but what came forth was too big for any house or city or even nation to contain. And that is why, my friend, we are still talking about it thirty years later.

SEVENTEEN

THOSE months of labour were of an intensity never experienced before or since; I emerged feeling like disembodied intelligence, fine and powerful. In that time I slept four hours a night, to be called from sleep in Greek. I washed in Greek, dressed in Greek, dined in Greek, supped in Greek, conversed in it, sang in it, prayed in it. Within weeks I was dreaming in Greek. I even had nightmares about Lorenzo in Greek.

When Angelo had asked him if I could stay in the house, describing with enthusiasm the plan he had in mind, Lorenzo had listened in silence, sitting back in his chair with his legs crossed at the ankles. His shoes, I noticed, were made of the most supple pig skin with stitching so delicate as to be almost invisible. He gave his approval with the grunt of a man who can deny his friend nothing. All he said was, 'Well, be quick about it. Three months and no more.' To me he said nothing. I might have been a horse on temporary hire, the expense of which was merely being noted reluctantly by the master of the house in his ricordanze.

Poliziano's official position in the household was that of tutor to Lorenzo's son, but as the son was still mastering the art of walking, Angelo had only one student, Lorenzo's brother, Giuliano, and that was in the subject of Greek. While I was whipped into a gallop through the language in the evenings, Giuliano enjoyed sedate instruction in the mornings. Sometimes we would meet in passing, however, and he would always stop to enquire after my progress, taking care to convince me that I was proceeding much better than he. Humility is a necessary virtue in a handsome youth of leisure and Giuliano was well-graced with it. He was a quiet young man who never initiated a joke, but was always ready to respond to the jokes of others – even those at his own expense – with a laugh free and generous. To hear Giuliano's laughter was to be drawn like a beast to the sound of the music of Orpheus.

He had much to laugh at. The Medici household was staffed by Lorenzo's friends, some of them employed on the most slender excuse. Three of them in particular were masters of wit: the chaplain, Matteo Franco; Luigi Pulci, a jug-eared buffoon whom Lorenzo employed as an envoy; and the tutor, Angelo Poliziano. All three were poets; all three were motley fools. Their wit ranged from sardonic banter to horseplay, depending on the mood of the day and the company; but when Lorenzo was present, then they competed in wit of a higher order, making brilliant and funny comment on points of conversation, indulging in wordplay, parrying pun for pun or umpiring battles of synonyms. Lorenzo always did well in these linguistic jousts, the rules of which were so strict that if anyone was stuck, even for the shortest moment, he was hooted derisively out of the game, but Angelo always won. Of the three poets, Angelo was the one with genius; of the three jesters, he was the one with verbal superiority. He so outshone Franco and Pulci that they turned their bile on each other and fought like cats. Sometimes it was difficult to tell where jesting ended and seriousness began.

Lorenzo, ever busy throughout the days, would join his friends in the evenings, ready for his wine and entertainment; this was my cue to retreat to my studies.

You want me to tell you my impressions of Lorenzo at this time. It is impossible. So much has happened since then that I cannot retrieve my impressions, especially as they were so clouded by fear and hatred. If I leave my emotions aside and see him now in my mind's eye, I can say this much: he was a young man, prematurely head of a large and important family. Despite, or perhaps because of, his looks, he had great presence. You always knew when he was in the house: the very sound of the place changed, tuned up to a higher pitch. He resented the demands that the bank made on him for he was not by nature a banker. He also resented the amount of time he had to spend in hosting the visits of important foreigners, or attending meetings of city dignitaries, or in considering solutions to manifold problems that were presented to him by the Florentines. He would have much preferred to be hunting with his brother, playing with his children, composing verse in competition with Poliziano, organising festivities in the city, or pursuing the activities of a normal, lusty twenty-five year old. (That is, a lusty twenty-five year old bachelor; except for those times when you saw him with his children or with his pale and haughty wife, you tended to forget that he was married, and so, it seemed, did he.) And yet, though he chafed at his duties, he performed them conscientiously, and it was evident that he relished his status as first citizen.

His bank survived the loss of the Pope's custom. Indeed, Lorenzo counted it no loss at all, for it had rarely amounted to anything but a burdensome debt which the Pope was never anxious to repay. His only concern was that, having spent years fostering relations with a man he did not like, he now had to mend a breach not of his own making. Then the death of Pietro Riario, Archbishop of Florence, was announced.

Now there had always been an agreement that no ecclesiastical appointment would be made in Florence without the approval of the Florentine Signoria (which is to say, Lorenzo). So when Pope Sixtus stated his preference for Francesco Salviati to be the new Archbishop, and when Lorenzo countered it by stating his preference for Rinaldo Orsini, an innocent layman such as myself might be forgiven for thinking that both were straining to be generous, for Salviati was a Florentine, and Orsini was a Roman. I was therefore confounded when the Signoria rejected Salviati – the man I had seen with the Pope in Rome – until I was reminded that Orsini was Lorenzo's brother-in-law.

Each morning I returned to Vespasiano's shop for a day's work on the *Metaphysics* and there the talk was of nothing else but the archbishopric.

'What have the Signoria against Francesco Salviati? He is a Florentine, and a member of the Academy.' 'Not every member of the Academy is sincere.' 'Ficino does not admit those who only wish to improve their standing. Salviati must have the requisite qualities.' 'Well, whether he has or no, the Signoria do not want him for our Archbishop.' 'The truth is of course that it is Lorenzo who does not want him.' 'That is only part of the truth. The whole truth is that Lorenzo wants the office for his brother-in-law. I do not think he has anything against Salviati personally. How can he – being a fellow Academician?' 'It is but a point of principle. We cannot have the Pope dictating to us.' 'But is it politic at this moment for Lorenzo to wrestle on a point of principle? I say, let us agree to having Salviati and mend our relations with Rome. We could do a lot worse: Sixtus could force another Riario on us.' 'Lorenzo's choice is a Roman. Sixtus should be satisfied with that.' 'There is no love lost between the delle Rovere and the Orsini.'

And so it went on at the shop day after day. At the Palazzo Medici, however, I heard nothing on the matter at all, though I did hear much of the poetry in the *dolce stil novo* and some rather splendid, newly composed carnival songs.

My days, beginning at dawn and going on until midnight, were filled with relentless labour and for the most part I struggled on; but there were times when an uncomfortable thought recurred, the kind of thought that suddenly hobbles the mind and brings it to its knees: was all this exertion simply to provide scholarship with a few alternative words and sentences in one small book, all anonymously and with no offer of a reward? When I was thus brought down, Angelo would only goad me into working harder, assuring me that all mankind would benefit from our work.

In nature and ability both, we were very different, but the differences were complementary rather than opposed. Mentally, he was bright and energetic; I was slow but methodical. Physically he was heavy, lethargic, a phlegmatic man; I was quick, light and airy. I reminded him time after time of things he had to do, while the vocabularies I learnt by rote erased themselves from memory if I missed a day's practice. He created confusion; I tidied up. We worked as well together as two horses drawing a chariot.

With all the Platonic theories of inspiration and divine frenzy, it is easy to think that when something comes by grace it comes without effort on the part of the recipient. I assure you that it does not. I can tell you from first hand knowledge how

Poliziano laboured at his studies. If he was so frequently inspired, it was a reward for the sacrifices he made in working so hard. The Muse loved him; and, through him, I grew to know the Muse. I began to recognise her presence in those times when Angelo lit up as if illuminated from within, when his voice took on a soft assurance which was not his own, when what he composed had a resonance and significance which was as surprising to him as to anyone else.

My expertise in Greek refined in the fire of his tuition; each day more gold could be seen standing apart from the dross. I began to proceed faster and faster with my work on the *Metaphysics*, and consequently to bring ever closer the day of its completion. That day was to spell the end of employment. Worse, it was to spell my divorce from the friend in whose company I was happy. The day drew ever nearer but Angelo said nothing on the matter of my imminent dismissal.

Unbeknown to Vespasiano, I had not only copied the *Metaphysics*, faithfully repeating all its errors, but had also annotated the Medici copy. At the time I felt daring and godlike; afterwards I felt so guilty that I had to go to Confession to gain relief from a heaviness of spirit. Ten paternosters later, however, I felt no better. So I went to Bishop Agli, who was staying at his house in the city. He thought that the penance had been a little harsh for a crime done in the spirit of Poggio Bracciolini and decided that my melancholy was rooted elsewhere. We talked long into the night. Soon the conversation dwelt on Poliziano.

'Perhaps I should not think of him as a friend. After all, he is six years my senior, the translator of Homer, and his own best friend is Lorenzo de' Medici. But I prefer his company to almost anyone else's, save your own, Monsignore.' And Giuliano's, I thought. 'Being with him is like being with poetry itself. He is the high priest of language – I could listen to him for ever. If I am in love with Greek now, the credit is due to him. To hear him speak in Greek is to hear Homer himself.'

The Bishop nodded and said that, having once heard Poliziano recite a whole book of the *Iliad* to a gathering of friends, it was a fair description of the experience. 'I can understand your enthusiasm, but what do you have to offer such a man?'

'He is not very good in matters of this world. He lives in the mind. There he is grace itself, but on earth he blunders about and collides with things. As he guides me through the realm of the intellect, so I guide him through more worldly matters.'

The Bishop thought that anyone could do that. 'Tell me, I have heard from Piero Strozzi that you have an uncanny talent for reading words without taking in their meaning. Piero says that the ability to see letters as only shapes is an advantage to a scribe.'

'Poliziano says that it is a sure way of making mistakes. But as I see it, understanding can be a distraction, at least to the task of copying a book. The mind is a great corrector. For instance, if a letter is missing in a well-known phrase, the mind misses the lacuna and reads the phrase whole and complete. But if you do not know the language, then you just copy it letter for letter. However, this is no recommendation – a good scribe corrects as he goes.'

'Does he? What if he makes the wrong corrections?'

I laughed. 'Angelo blames all the troubles of the world – poverty, wars, famine, everything – on scribal error. You should see him when he finds a mistake! He goes purple with rage and storms as if the perpetrator were in earshot, though more often than not he is long dead.'

'Well that he is,' said the Bishop with a smile. 'I would rather be dead myself than the public target of one of Poliziano's points of correction. He thinks of himself as a poet but to my mind he will one day become a scholar without parallel.'

'Do not tell him so for he hates scholars. He says that the universities are full of such sticks of charcoal that the only chance they will have of illuminating the world will be when someone puts a torch to them, and then they will only create a few sparks and much smoke.'

The Bishop smiled in agreement. 'The schoolmen, yes. They have little in common with our friend. But his lofty aim is the purity of language, whereas the goal of the schoolmen is advancement by logic.'

'He says their Latin is barbaric, and their Greek non-existent.'

'He is right, of course.' The Bishop fell into thought and then asked me if I had written any poetry myself. I confessed to preferring to appreciate the work of others.

'So you have no drive to be a Poet in the true sense of the word, that is, a maker or creator?'

'None. As I have said, I have nothing to recommend me to him.'

'On the contrary ... ' muttered the Bishop. 'It seems to me that you are a born servant, and happy is the man who realises that, happier still if what he serves is the Muse. I should say that you and Poliziano, working as a team, would pull the chariot of knowledge at a breathtaking pace.'

'That is how I see it! But would he see it the same way?'

'Have we not been describing the most intelligent of men? Why do you doubt him? For all we know he could be discussing the matter with Lorenzo at this very moment.'

Lorenzo ... If Angelo no longer required my presence, it was for one reason alone, that Lorenzo had forbidden it. Three months – no longer.

'As one servant of the Muse to another,' said the Bishop, 'my advice is this: leave it all to the Muse herself.'

Thus relieved from the idea that I had to create my own destiny, I agreed to do as the Bishop suggested. Before I took my leave, however, there was something else I wanted to discuss: the Platonic Academy.

'Ah, you have heard of it, have you?'

'I hardly hear of much else in Vespasiano's shop, except the election of the new Archbishop.'

'Who is to be Lorenzo's brother-in-law, I believe.'

The news had been greeted with a rousing cheer in Florence. It was as if Lorenzo and the Pope had been arm-wrestling, and Lorenzo had suddenly won.

'The respective qualities of Orsini and Salviati were not even judged,' the Bishop complained. 'Still, it was a matter of principle at stake, and I am glad Lorenzo won. If relations with Rome are to be restored, they must be restored to what they were, with Lorenzo dictating the terms.'

'You Florentine!'

The Bishop chuckled.

'And you are crafty, too,' I added.

'In what way?'

'You have taken me off the point: the Platonic Academy. Why have you never spoken of it? This gathering of friends which heard the *Iliad* – that was the Academy, was it not? Why are you so evasive?'

'If I am, it is because "the Academy" as you call it, is something I love. One does not lightly discuss that which one loves. Besides, it cannot be conveyed in a few sentences. What is it that you want to know?'

'Only what it is.'

'In the universities, as Angelo points out, knowledge has become debased. Men spend years tuning their intellects to a superb pitch, only to expend all their fine energies debating the reading of "Abimelech" for "Abiathar" in the gospel of Saint Mark, or some such useless theological detail. After centuries of learned disputations, we have forgotten the original questions, questions such as "Who or what is God?" and "Who or what is Man?" and "What is Man's place in Creation, and purpose?" To return to such essentials, we must return to those philosophers who asked the questions, or rather, *the* philosopher: Plato. The Academy, in short, is a private university for men who would know the truth.'

'How does one become a member?'

'I shall give you a clue – it is not by not keeping an elderly Academician from his bed.' The Bishop's eyebrows moved up and down like travelling caterpillars.

'More evasion!'

'By invitation, Tommaso. That is how one comes to the Academy, by invitation.'

'But what kind of man is invited? What are the qualifications required?'

'None but the qualities of the man himself: a good heart and a love of truth.' He leant forward to peer at me and I felt transparent in his gaze. 'You have the second,' he decided.

I swallowed. 'How do I gain the first?'

'By following the second.'

It was on the next day that I completed my work on the *Metaphysics* and presented it to Vespasiano with some ceremony. Then, like a thief in the night, I took the annotated copy to the Palazzo Medici where I found Angelo in his corner-cupboard of a study, a room barely big enough for two. He fell on the book and immediately began work comparing the variant readings of the text.

It did not take him long to discover that what we had to offer the world was only a negative knowledge: Angelo could demonstrate that the German duke's precious manuscript was of later rather than earlier parentage than the Medici edition. And the part I had played in that discovery was a very small part in something which was but an infinitesimal addition to the world's knowledge. We had exhausted ourselves on a task ant-like in importance, yet our work had added to the growing mound of what is really known and not just surmised or thought to be true. The triumph of facts over opinions has been the work of scholar-ants whose individual labours in observing and recording amount to almost nothing, but which collectively are changing the world.

Out of this work came two things of benefit: one, I gained a foundation in Greek; two, Poliziano conceived a science – the genealogy of texts. It was to be years before either of us mastered our new arts, but this was the beginning.

'Well,' I said. 'It is time for me to leave, I suppose.'

'Yes,' he said, without looking up from the book.

'I thank you for the tuition. You have done me great service.'

'Tommaso,' he said, his head still down, 'it is for me to thank you.'

'Well, yes.' Why would he not look at me? 'I shall be away then.'

'Thank you again.'

Suddenly I was speaking: 'There is no chance, I suppose, of a permanent position?' The sentence had scrolled out of my mouth with no by nor leave from me.

He turned then, and he who I thought was being heartless had all his heart written on his face. 'Gesumaria, do you think I want you to go? I want you here, of course I do. You have everything I lack. You are quiet, methodical, reliable – and your strange talent in two-dimensional reading is full of possibilities. And you have a quick and beautiful hand. Yes, you have. This is not empty praise. To have you here, transcribing my scrawls, tidying my desk, reminding me what day it is, of course I want you to stay. I shall feel lost without you. But it is not in my power to engage you.'

'Have you asked him?'

Angelo avoided my eye.

'What did he say?'

'He will not have anyone in the household he cannot trust.'

I gasped. It was as if my every passing thought had been known, if not to the God of the universe, then at least to Lorenzo de' Medici.

'Why?' I said, though I could think of a million reasons.

'Because you ran away from him on the steps of San Lorenzo. And you have barely met his gaze since. That is enough for Lorenzo. He said that if you were a horse, he would have you put down. He was jesting, of course.'

So there was no hope.

I returned to Vespasiano and to my bed under the counter, to days spent binding books and selling parchment, to listening to men of substance and leisure discuss the subjects I loved. I took orders from these men for certain texts to be copied, and they were always careful to stipulate who they wanted, a man famous for the beauty of his hand such as Antonio Sinibaldi, Bartolomeo di San Vito or Piero Strozzi. Having cleared my conscience by persuading them of the virtues of the latter, I would then ask if they might like to have something just as beautiful though considerably cheaper, but they always said no. I waited upon the Muse and her decision, but she was quiet. Often I walked out of the city at night, up to the church of San Miniato where I would raise my arms to the sky and invoke the help of the gods; they too were quiet. At last and in despair I took back the reins of my destiny and, following the advice of Jacopo Bracciolini, I wrote a letter to Jacopo de' Pazzi, asking if he had need of a scribe, a secretary or a clerk in his bank.

EIGHTEEN

By what godly agency was my letter intercepted? – for the reply came not from the Pazzi but the Medici, requesting my presence at the house on the Via Larga. The audience was held in the sala. Upon the soaring walls were three great paintings in gilded frames: Hercules killing the seven-headed hydra, Hercules strangling the Nemean lion, Hercules squeezing the Libyan giant to death. On the large table at which Lorenzo sat was a small bronze of Hercules slaying a centaur. None of these images gave much heart to the suppliant.

The room should have dwarfed Lorenzo but it did not. He looked enormous. Physically he was powerful, his great bull neck only slightly narrower than his broad jaw, but the enormity was not physical. It was subtle, reflected in his strength. His arms folded on the table, he leant forward as if impatient with this interruption to more significant matters. His sentences were short, my replies monosyllabic, but Angelo was there as my advocate.

While Angelo presented the case for my permanent engagement in a display of logic that would have dazzled a schoolman, I sat frozen under Lorenzo's gaze, only daring to glance up for a moment at a time. His rough hair was trimmed bluntly to a level below his ears, a cut which did nothing to make him more attractive but only emphasised the girth of his throat. In profile, he was the epitome of the proud Florentine youth, but full face ... His eyes were narrowly set and on a level with a break in the bridge of his nose; they were more the eyes of a man of fifty who has experienced enough of life to justify a deal of caution and a measure of cynicism. Nothing could deceive those eyes; the more they studied me, the more I undermined Angelo's assurances of my reliability by shifting nervously in my chair as if on trial and guilty. I was scared of this man; if that scared him, then I was doing nothing to change his mind. Becoming convinced of failure, I inwardly gave up. Unexpectedly, this relaxation brought courage: if I had lost, then I had nothing further to lose were I to meet and hold that gaze.

'Tommaso,' said Lorenzo, interrupting Angelo's endless flow of persuasions. His voice, high-pitched and nasal, was at odds with the man. 'You were in Volterra in '72?'

'Yes.'

'Do you hold me responsible for what happened?'

'Yes.' Oh God, I had opened my mouth to say the opposite! 'Yes, I do,' my wayward, independent speech repeated emphatically.

Angelo jumped to his feet in horror. 'What are you saying?'

'Be quiet,' Lorenzo ordered. He looked at me again. 'Have you forgiven me for it?'

'No.' Oh, Madonna ...

'Do you harbour thoughts of revenge?'

'No.' No? Thanks be to God! I started listening to myself, to see what else I had to say.

Lorenzo said: 'There is no one in this house who I do not trust with my life. But you I do not trust.'

'There is no reason why you should, nor any why I should trust you. However, I do not think you will murder me in my bed. As for me, I have as much knowledge of daggers as I have of sewing needles. I am a scribe, Magnifico, but I would not even wield the pen to your harm. Were you to employ me, then to harm you would be to harm myself.'

Who was this sycophant speaking? Was I so desperate that I would do anything for employment, even be charming to a poisonous toad?

'What do you value most above all things, Tommaso?'

'Truth.'

Ha! Now I understood. This was my mouth and my voice, but the speech was Bishop Agli's. He had somehow taken possession of me, to carry me through this moment of crisis. Or so I thought at the time. Years later I realised that the speech had been that of the Muse herself, and that Lorenzo had recognised it as such.

His expression softened. 'Not all of what I have heard about you is bad; some of it is good, very good indeed. Bishop Agli and Piero Strozzi have said some fine things in your praise. But nothing is more convincing than what a man can say about himself. Consider yourself engaged, Tommaso dei Maffei. I will take you into my household: as an equerry.'

'Equerry?' I cried when I was alone with Angelo. 'Is this a joke?'

Angelo was laughing and said that it was, in a way, but one which he found amusing only when it applied to others. 'What more can we expect in this house, where its head is a poet who is confined to councils? If Lorenzo has to spend his days in humdrum affairs, so must the rest of us.'

It seemed that no one in the house was free to follow his talent except Giuliano. And he, said Angelo, took on voluntarily that which the rest approached only with complaint. 'He often goes on missions of diplomacy, or sits in council with Lorenzo; he goes to market with the purchaser; sometimes he helps me catch an errant child, and will even clean up a dirty infant if the nursemaid is busy.'

'Will he help me with the horses?' I wondered.

'Undoubtedly, for the position you have filled is not one that was vacant, but one that Giuliano claimed for himself. Lorenzo wants his brother to spend more time in study and less in the stables.'

The new equerry was told to report to the Medici villa on Careggi in a week's time.

Impruneta is a quiet village on a gentle hill set amidst vineyards. At its centre was Bishop Agli's house, set close to the church which had been built at his own expense. His study was filled with the familiar geometric models, the pyramids, cubes and multi-faceted balls which were the 'solid' shapes, and the honeycomb polyhedra which were the internal structures, each of them representing the essential components of the universe and the shape of the elements.

I told the Bishop about the miraculous audience I had had with Lorenzo, and the equally miraculous employment. He seemed unsurprised, and when I gave him the credit for my saying the right things at the right time, he dismissed the idea and said it had nothing to do with him. He continued to glue sticks of wood together in a construction which, when completed – this was his life's ambition – would include all the polyhedra in one harmonious, spherical whole.

'So,' I said. 'It is good news, is it not?'

'Yes, very good.'

'And I can stay here until I have to go to Careggi?'

'Of course.'

I had confessed long ago my sacrifice of the monochord; now I dared to ask him if we might build another.

'Once sacrificed, forever gone,' he said, but immediately assuaged my sense of loss by drawing from a cupboard a most curious instrument. It was shaped like the letter U with a bar across the top, from which strings were stretched to pegs on the base. He tightened the strings.

'It is what Pythagoras called a heptachord. At least, I hope it is.'

I reached out and ran my hand across the seven strings. The notes sounded from doh to ti and I looked at the Bishop questioningly. Reminding me of my lessons, he asked how I was going to find the last note of the scale, the place where it returns to its beginning. And so I found the top doh on the first string when I halved it.

'A heptachord, or better known as a lyre,' he said, tucking it into the crook of his arm. 'The favourite instrument of the ancients.'

'What can you play on it?'

'The scale.'

'Is that all?'

'Oh, Tommaso, you used to be so satisfied with that. Have you grown up to want more and more sophistication? Plato says that Music is the gift of the gods to Man and was never intended merely as an idle pleasure. Yes, I can only play the scale of Creation, but it is enough.' He plucked the fifth note. 'This is something I forgot to tell you about, Sol, the Sun. The dominant note in the scale. Each note represents a planet ... '

He played through in order: the Moon, Mercury, Venus, Mars, Sun, Jupiter and Saturn.

'... and each is highly significant, but the most important is

Sol. You can hear her harmony, her stillness. She stands apart from the rest. She is the guide for the progression.'

'Why do you call the Sun "she"?'

'All creation is feminine: the creative principle is masculine.'

'Yet I have heard that the sun is Apollo and represents the Creator.'

The Bishop sighed. 'If myths have one fault, it is that the symbols are fluid, now representing this, now that, sometimes entirely opposite things. But then in so doing they truly represent Creation, in which nothing is fixed, nothing is certain. It is all a dream.'

'And the dream is female,' I muttered.

The episcopal eyebrows raised inquiringly and, in a moment of silence, he knew both my heart and my dreams. I blushed and he pushed my shoulder playfully. 'You have grown too fast, have been driven into adulthood. But remember what Our Lord said, "Become as little children ... "'

'"That you may enter the Kingdom of Heaven."'

The Bishop brushed the strings, inviting heaven into the room.

Would that I had spent the whole week engaged in such conversation, but each day I was taken out to the hillside and put to work picking grapes. I could not complain, given that in the next row was the Bishop himself, bent double, going up and down the rows snipping bunches and dropping them into a basket, considering himself no different from anyone else in the village at harvest time. The poets thrive on such scenes and the carefree life of the peasant. I tell you: my back hurt so much that I went to bed every night in agony, to wake up too soon, stiff and groaning at the prospect of another day. Whether he intended it or not – and I suspect that he did – the Bishop put me to this work to thrash the pride out of me. When I went on to Careggi, I felt only for those I left behind, stooped amongst the blistering vines.

Careggi is a hill which begins tamely just beyond Florence and rises into a wild and wooded peak. The villas are on the lower slopes, nestling in groves and behind walls. The hill derives its name from Charitum Ager, so Poliziano told me the day I arrived, meaning the Field of the Graces. I did not notice any graces as I approached on a rough road through a wood and saw the villa ahead, appearing beyond the trees. The closer I came to the place, the more its great projecting eaves loomed. Its smooth walls were interrupted by only a few windows, and they were covered by grilles, so that it seemed to be a prison which I approached. This was the kind of fortress castle I had always expected of the Medici; this is what I had thought to find in Florence. The great wooden doors of the main entrance were firmly closed, but a small adjacent door was ajar. I pushed it open and went in.

The courtyard was cool and quiet. A porter called out to me rudely, mistaking me for a loutish youth from the village. My insistence that I was the new equerry courted his incredulity, but when I gave my name he grunted and said that I had been expected hours ago. 'Master Angelo is in the garden,' he said, and showed me the way to reach it.

That garden was not of this world. Every tree, every shrub, every plant that climbed a wall or trailed from an urn, every blade of grass, had its own spirit, which was a member of a consort playing heavenly music. The very sound of the fountain and the wind in the leaves were a part of this whispering chorus. All time seemed suspended, and to walk down the paths was to dance a slow pavan, or else offend the place. It was in keeping with the spirit of the garden that every word spoken there be poetry. I saw Angelo wandering in the green depths where the garden ended at a steep precipice of the hill. He was reciting an ode to an attentive audience of invisible nymphs, spirits of myrtle, olive and laurel.

I was presented with a choice: I could remain as I was, full of fear and self-considerations, dusty from the journey, polluted by the world, and, in running up to him calling greetings, thus break the spell; or I could enter the theatre as an actor and play the role gracefully. I took the latter course. Saying nothing I joined him in the natural music of the garden and simply walked at his side, listening to his flowing verses.

Sweet words – it is a phrase so often used as to have no meaning, and yet I can think of nothing more apt. Base poetry is that of a man who conveys his opinions in rhyme; the finest poetry is a hymn of praise, and the words have a sweetness to them not of this world; the true poet is one who loves the very taste of words.

These days I often hear Poliziano derided by ignorant men as one who was arrogant and contemptuous of lesser mortals; when I hear such defamations, I wish with all my heart that I could conjure up a vision of that garden and he walking in it, praising Creation, and thus silence them forever.

At the back of the house was one protruding wing, the upper storey of which was an open loggia. Its ceiling was decorated with brightly painted, bacchic vines, while real vines spiralled up the outer pillars of the loggia to clad its roof in green. Lorenzo's mother stood there, a thin-faced woman with oriental eyes, listening to the poetry. Seeing her, Angelo spoke his final verse to her directly then bowed with a courtier's grace.

'Who is that with you, Homericus?'

'The new equerry, Madonna.'

'He has arrived at last, has he? Well, bring him up here.'

We had to return inside the house, mount a flight of stairs and then move through a hall and Lorenzo's own chambers to reach the loggia; with each step my fear increased. I had seen Mona Lucrezia before at the city house and, though I had never met her face to face, I had walked in the substance she created. Her son might rule a city, but Mona Lucrezia ruled him, and all the household. As high were her standards, as firm was her discipline, and nothing was done in the house but that each servant referred to her, either in person, or in his own heart. 'Mona Lucrezia would not approve,' or 'Mona Lucrezia would appreciate that,' were statements which filled the air like dust motes, except that no mote of dust was ever allowed in the house, by order of Mona Lucrezia. And if I am painting the portrait of a figure of terror, let me quickly add the highlight to the shadow: she was a lady who established her authority through love, and for that reason a man such as Angelo, a mere friend of her son, would often and inadvertently call her 'Mother'. She accepted both the title and the role without remark.

She had that kind of face which beguiles but not by obvious beauty. She was about fifty, yet her skin was fine and taut and provided the best of pale grounds in which to set eyes such as hers; eyes which watched the world critically but without comment; eyes which now were meeting mine. She appraised me without a smile.

'Have you brought linen?' she asked, laying aside a book which I noticed was the *Satires* of Juvenal.

'Two sheets.'

'And what will you sleep in when those two sheets are being washed?'

While I struggled to find an answer, she said, 'I thought you were supposed to be intelligent?'

'Mona Lucrezia,' Angelo interposed, 'when I came to this household, I had no sheets at all.'

'Hopeless men,' she said. 'My son is surrounding me with hopeless men. How many shirts do you have, boy?'

'Two.'

'Pairs of hose?'

'Two.'

'Pairs of sleeves?'

'Two.'

'Jackets?'

'Two.'

'And where is your trunk, or should we say ark?'

Though I have met witty women since, I had never met one before that moment. The combination of joke and surprise had me laughing with such innocent pleasure that by this I at last gained her approval.

'It is being delivered this afternoon,' I smiled. 'A farmer from Impruneta ... '

'From where? How did you come here?'

'I walked.'

'From Impruneta?'

'It is but an eight hour walk.'

'And for this I have been kept from my rest, so that the new equerry can amble through the countryside on his own legs? I presume you can ride a horse?'

'I can, Madonna, but I do not have one.'

'Another dependent. Hopeless,' she said and, deciding that I must be hungry and thirsty, told Angelo to take me to the kitchen.

After I had eaten, Angelo showed me to the chamber I was to share with himself and Matteo Franco, in which were three chairs, a Persian rug on the wooden floor, two cassone for the storage of clothes, a ewer and basin on a stand, a heap of rosaries on a shelf beneath a glorious painting of the Annunciation, and one wide bed. An open arch led to an adjoining chamber, one similar in every respect to ours, and which I took to be part of ours, until I was told that Luigi Pulci shared it with the musician Baccio Ugolini.

'Is this not what you expected?'

'Three of us in one bed?' I had not lived like a contadino since I was an infant, brought up on a farm.

'The house has many guests: Lorenzo's sister Nannina and her children and Mona Lucrezia's brother, Giovanni Tornabuoni. So we servants are in rustic accommodation.'

I went to the window. The view was not a grand one of the city but of the wooded hillside above the house. There was another villa further up, much smaller and with one squat, crenellated tower. Its stucco the colour of pale terracotta, it looked out of the trees like a face.

'The others are out hunting and will not return until evening,' said Angelo lying down. 'Time for a rest,' he said with a yawn and closed his eyes. 'You are free to explore, or read, or sleep, or what you will.'

Feeling so ill at ease that resting was out of the question, I went back to the gardens, but whatever spell I had entered earlier seemed to have passed; having toured the knots and mazes of the flower-crowded beds, the secret arbours and the paths that invariably led to statues, I walked round the back of the house through the kitchen gardens and came to the stables. The stalls were empty except for one where a small cob stood haltered and staring at the wall. Its ears turned at my approach and I patted it on the flanks to reassure it. In truth I welcomed my unexpected duty. To see horses running wild, to see them broken to man's will, to see the beast designed for running standing patiently for unknown hours in a stall, is to look upon a wonder of life. The orderliness of the stables, the brightness of the tackle, the smell of leather soap above the other, more pungent smells, spoke of the Medici's respect for their animals.

I kept the horse company for a while, currying her with a comb and gaining her trust. But though she settled, I did not.

Beyond the stables was a gate to the road and I left the villa to wander further up the hill, across the Field of the Graces. The road led to the village but there was also a path following a stream through a small wood. This I took, preferring the anonymity and the shade of the trees. Everything was quiet in the heat of the afternoon, except the insects that trilled everywhere. Though the path was well-trodden, I met no one on it. It began at the Medici villa; it ended at a gate in the boundary wall of the small villa I had seen from my room.

I stood in the low gateway, looking up at the terraces of a formal garden. At the bottom level were vegetable plots and an olive grove; at the next, a rose garden, at the top, peacocks wandering amongst urns spilling with ivy. The house: one little tower, one wing, a small place butting up against the rocky hillside, quieter than quietness itself, and its gardens as alive with spirits as the ones at the Medici villa. If it took no courage to cross the threshold into what was a stranger's property, it is because there was an absence of fear: I passed through the gateway as if drawn. The small peach-coloured, sequestered house welcomed me.

As I approached, step by careful, respectful, step, the peacocks eyed me and walked away carping. There came a beating of wings, doves fluttered over me like white petals, and I stood enraptured, swamped by angels. Suddenly I heard music coming from the house: a seven string lyre. The scale was played three times, then – my breath stopped – there was a melody on the strings, and a voice in accompaniment, singing in a modulated, monotonic chant, a spoken song.

Suddenly I knew whose garden I was in. In my heightened state, I knew also that I was known to the one who was playing. As a horse may panic at shadows, I was taken by an absurd rush of fear and fled the tranquil gardens of Marsilio Ficino.

NINETEEN

FOLLOWING the hour of rest, the garden became a theatre for the youngest members of the Medici family. On the lawns, within the arbours, behind hedges and around the fountain, small children played. Lorenzo's eldest, Lucrezina, was four, Piero was two, Maddalena a toddling one year old uncertain on her feet. To their number were added various small cousins, each of whom seemed to be called either Cosimo or Lucrezia.

Lorenzo's wife and sisters were in an arbour, resting in that manner of which only women are capable; that is, idling in comfort but wearing an expression of distress, as if resting on the orders of a physician. I have seen peasant women give birth in fields like cows, but parturition for a lady seems to require a year's recovery, by which time she is pregnant again. That Mona Clarice was with child was obvious not only by her size, and her expression of woe, but also by the fuss that was made of her cushions by a superfluity of attendants. Unlike her mother-in-law, who enjoyed the company of men, Mona Clarice lived entirely in the world of women, and was unlikely ever to be found with a book on her lap, least of all the *Satires* of Juvenal. This was the first time I had seen her, and I was not introduced. Bovine and self-pitying, what Clarice lacked in beauty she made up for with a natural demeanour of superiority. Without doubt she was an Orsini.

The stamp of that patrician family of Rome was also clearly upon her only son, Piero. Though but two years old, he had already learnt how to use the power of his position and was now in a tantrum which he knew that no one would dare punish. Angelo eventually quietened him with a reminder that Father was due home soon, and that Father would be told. The poet's next contingency was the toddling Maddalena who, lured by roses, had met thorns. As he went to free her, he was taken off course by Piero again: shrieking with outrage, Lorenzo's son was being furiously ducked in a fountain by an older cousin. The children had nurses, but the nurses were attending Clarice. Simmering with annoyance, Angelo rescued his young pupil from drowning while I disentangled Maddalena. Though her long, trailing dress had been caught in a dozen places, she did not cry but only wriggled and stared at the thorns.

'Wose,' she explained as I worked to free her.

'Yes, you have been caught by the rose.'

As I lifted her free, she clutched at the nearest full bloom. The petals fell to nothing, leaving the five bracts. She opened her hand to look at the soft pink things she held and stared at the denuded stamen in sorrow. 'Wose!'

'The rose is gone,' I said, staring at the bracts in wonder of God's geometry. 'Do not cry, little one. It will come again.' But she was not crying; she was now staring fixedly at me, as if my features were as much cause for silent wonder as those of a flower. To my relief, Angelo came and threw her in the air to make her laugh.

'If Clarice was not nearby,' he said quietly, 'I would bellow at them, as Lorenzo does. They are not usually this boisterous; only when I am is near and their father is not.'

At that moment a horn sounded from the wooded hill above the villa.

'Papa!' cried Piero. 'Papa!' He ran on stout, chubby legs towards the courtyard. Angelo went after him, calling, 'Who will come to meet the hunt?' Children ran from all directions. Even Lorenzo's eldest, Lucrezina, who spurned play for the company of the ladies, ran to join us. I had no inclination to go out to meet Lorenzo, but neither did I have any choice. Angelo gave me Maddalena to carry.

Piero, the self-assertive heir presumptive, led the way up the lane, echoing the distant horn with his own vocal fanfares, but when the hounds appeared and surrounded him in a friendly, leaping froth of tails and tongues, he screamed in terror.

The riders emerged from the wood with Lorenzo at their head, cantering towards us and calling greetings as they came. Lorenzo, barely slowing the pace of his horse, leant athletically from the saddle, scooped up his son and rode on towards the house. One of the following riders tried to do the same to Angelo. With a deft turn and a tug, Angelo pulled him from his horse.

'Too heavy a child for you, Luigi!' called another rider.

'Not so much a child as a monster,' said Luigi Pulci, a small man of many years, dusting himself down. He jabbed at Poliziano with a long finger. 'Monstrous child. *Un aborto di natura.*'

In response, Angelo bounded on to Luigi's horse and, pulling one of the Cosimos up with him, rode off in pursuit of Lorenzo. Each one of the children was thus taken home by one of the riders; freed of Maddalena, I was left to walk with Luigi Pulci and the spearmen who were carrying suspended on a pole a blood-soaked boar, its life steaming from its bristly hide.

'Who are you, my little sprout?' Pulci asked.

I gave him my name even though we had met before, both at Vespasiano's and at the house in the city. 'Ah yes, the new groom,' he said, and asked me where I was stabled. I told him with Angelo and Matteo Franco.

'Poverino! – caught between the trilling Scylla and weeping Charybdis!' He told me that my nights would be thoroughly disturbed by Matteo whistling and Angelo sobbing.

'In his sleep?' I asked.

Pulci said that Angelo had bad dreams, as was proper with one of bad conscience. I wanted to know what Angelo's crime might be and was told, gravely, that he copied the work of the ancients and called it his own; unlike Luigi, whose own works were novel and contemporary. 'These young upstarts, they would tell you that the woods are full of nymphs and dryads; I have been there; I have seen with my own eyes: what the woods contain are mushrooms, wolves and wild, bloody boars.'

If I laughed it was because, for all his bile, Luigi Pulci was funny, but his own sad eyes never smiled. The way he wore his cap, with his hair tucked up, made him look bald. It was so thrust down on his head that his ears stuck out. It was only years later, when I once caught sight of him alone and looking thoughtful, that I realised that he was in fact a handsome man;

but he had chosen the part of the fool and presented it so consistently that we never took him for anything else.

Twice Lorenzo's age, he was a friend whom Lorenzo had inherited from his father; a friend of the family, particularly Mona Lucrezia, who was his patron. In another age, he would have been the court buffoon. If he was renowned for his epic farce called the *Morgante Maggiore*, a work continuously in creation, in which he satirised various members of Lorenzo's circle, he would rather have been known for his verses celebrating the joust which Lorenzo had held some years before, but any talent he possessed in serious poetry had been overshadowed by the arrival of Poliziano in the house, and thus was Pulci condemned to comedy.

Just as we arrived at the villa, another horn sounded from the top of the hill. 'That will be Giuliano,' he said, turning at once to go back up the path. He explained how the hunting party had lost Giuliano earlier in the morning when he had galloped off alone in pursuit of a hind.

Angelo and Lorenzo rode out to join us in meeting the lone Acteon who was cantering from the woods, his shirt billowing free and his face begrimed by leaf and bark. When asked where his catch was, Giuliano told a tale of how he had chased a small, white doe through the woods for hours, catching up with her finally in a clearing where, to his astonishment, she had transformed into a beautiful maiden, 'with a white, gossamer gown and long, falling tresses of spun gold. I did not have the heart to kill her.'

Luigi rubbed his hands and guffawed like a merchant who had just struck a bargain. Lorenzo, however, clipped his brother fondly on the head and said that it was unlike him to have concern for a maid. I gazed at Giuliano in awe. He was the very hero, the Lancelot, the Roland of my childish dreams; most of all, the Lorenzo de' Medici.

Meat and wine were being served in the courtyard for the hungry huntsmen, the spearmen and the beaters. Little Piero, demanding the boar's tusks, went to see them being hacked off and ran back holding one with both hands, looking for a cousin Cosimo to charge.

As Lorenzo approached the place where I stood, I suddenly

remembered that I had duties, which as yet no one had explained to me. Thinking that I should be rubbing down sweaty horses, I hurried to the stables, but the horses had already been attended to and were now steaming under blankets. Two stable-boys were moving around, quietly, efficiently, taking bridles and saddles away for cleaning. Someone else was there, running his hand down the leg of a courser, encouraging it to lift its hoof. He cleaned round the frog with a hoofpick. 'Ah,' he muttered. 'Here it is.' Guiliano glanced over his shoulder at me.

'A little pebble,' he said, showing it to me as he straightened up, 'and he was acting as if he had broken his leg. Welcome to the Villa Medici, Tommaso.'

I thanked him. Having stood quietly by him for a while, I ventured to ask him if it were true, what he had said about the hind.

'What, turning into a beautiful maiden? Of course not! I only pursue game, not women.'

'Have you no liking for them?'

'I like them well enough: it is falling in love with them that I cannot abide. Love makes idiots of men, have you not noticed? Besides,' he said, taking up a comb to tackle the knots in the courser's mane, 'I am destined for the Church.'

This was terrible news: Giuliano was born for athletics, jousting, hunting and sport.

'Can you not imagine me as a cardinal, wearing red vestments and white surplice, walking regally in a procession?'

I said I could not.

'No, neither can the Pope. He says I am too young, but between you and me, the real reason is that His Holiness has no fondness for the Medici brothers. I cannot imagine why. Have you ever met a more charming pair than Lorenzo and me?'

I took the comb from him. 'I should be doing this. It is my duty.'

Giuliano said that it was not my duty, it was his, but that I could help him if I liked. 'Find another comb and start on his tail.'

'What is my duty then?' I asked.

'You will find out soon enough.'

It became clear in the next few days, in so far as chaos ever becomes clear. Mona Nannina and her family were to return home to the Palazzo Rucellai in Florence and it was for me to assign to them suitable mounts. Angelo helped and chose six ponies, the cob and the sorrel. All this was straightforward enough, the grooms were told to make the mounts ready, and I arranged for the horses to be returned from Florence by one of the boys riding in escort. Then on the following day Mona Lucrezia decided to go to the baths at Morba. She had an attack of eczema that only the sulphur waters could soothe. 'I shall go on the cob,' she said. The cob was by now in Florence.

'What shall I do?' I cried, smitten already by the household dread of causing Mona Lucrezia any inconvenience or displeasure.

Angelo said that Ficino had a cob and that I should go to his villa to borrow it. If this was not terrifying enough, as I was setting out, Luigi came to say that Giuliano wanted his bay mare and the 'usual' mounts for his page and two servants. Giovanni Tornabuoni, Mona Lucrezia's brother, had just left on the bay to visit a friend at Fiesole, and I had no idea what mounts went with which riders.

Having solved this with the aid of those who did know, I was then about to set off for Ficino's villa when a rider arrived at a gallop from Florence with news for Lorenzo. 'Stay, stay,' said Angelo, holding me back and advising me to see what the outcome might be; sure enough, within minutes Lorenzo was leaping down the stairs calling for the fastest horse in the stable.

'Which is it?' I cried.

'Giuliano's courser,' said Angelo.

I sped off to have the horse saddled, Lorenzo and Angelo both hard on my heels. Lorenzo was shouting with impatience while I fumbled with the buckles of the bridle, helping the grooms saddle up.

'Leave it,' Angelo counselled me urgently. 'Stand back. Let the others do it.'

'Where is that horse?' Lorenzo roared.

We led the courser out; he was on it before we reached the mounting block and riding off in a dust storm with the messenger.

Angelo told me that news had arrived in the city: Francesco Salviati, the man denied the archbishopric of Florence, had been elected by the Pope as the Archbishop of Pisa.

'So?' I asked.

'Pisa is Florentine territory. Sixtus is taunting us again. Now, should you not be fetching that cob?'

'Is it always like this?' I asked in despair.

He assured me that it was often much worse.

I set off on the path to Ficino's villa, hoping not to find the Platonic Academy as before – deserted but for mysterious music – for a door behind which music is being played is not a door to be knocked upon. As I entered through the low gate, however, I saw a gardener, a short man with a face like a walnut under a broad-brimmed hat of straw. He was weeding the flower beds on the second terrace. I asked him if the master was at home, for the Medici had need of his cob.

'You will find it in the stable up there, behind the trees to the side of the house. Do you see?'

'May I simply take it? Should I not ask Master Ficino first?'

'He will only tell you that everything he has belongs to the Medici anyway, so take the cob. He will be needing it in four days' time. Can you have it back by then?'

'Oh, yes, certainly.'

'You are new. Tomorrow, when you are not so new, you will not be so rash in your promises. Do you expect Mona Lucrezia to gallop all the way to the baths?'

'Well, it would not be this cob, but we will have our own back by then.'

The gardener, knocking mud off his hoe, sighed. 'Do not put your faith in uncertainties, boy. How can you possibly know that you will have your cob back? No matter, go on, take my master's.'

I thanked him and ran up to the stable. As I led the beast out, I glanced up at the house; it was quiet and appeared empty, yet I felt again as if I were being watched. The gardener was waiting for me on the path. He asked me if all were well, for I seemed agitated and a little perturbed.

'It is not yet noon of my second day as the Medici equerry, and already I am exhausted.' My voice faltered and my chin trembled with the onset of tears. 'I keep having to perform duties without being instructed in them.'

'Would you like some advice?' he asked kindly, touching my shoulder.

I said that I would, for he seemed wise in the way simple men often do.

'Find out the evening before what the plans are for the morrow. You need to be at least six hours ahead of everybody. And never, never appear flustered before the family. Always look serene, no matter what turmoil you are in.'

'Your advice is good, but some things cannot be planned in advance, such as Lorenzo having to rush to Florence at a moment's notice.'

'You will be surprised at what can be anticipated by an alert mind.'

'You are very philosophical.'

He laughed. 'How could I be otherwise, here in this place?' He smiled at me so affectionately that my agitation dissolved. I thanked him and went to leave but he said, 'Tell me, what has taken Lorenzo to the city so urgently?'

I told him the news as I had heard it, then took the cob away.

That evening we dined early; afterwards the ladies went to the music room and the men to the garden. There was to be a meeting of the Academy and therefore, Angelo told me, I was free. 'So I have left you a piece of prose to translate from Latin into Greek.'

Desiring respite from the house, I set off to walk up the hill, hoping to reach the summit, but no matter how long I walked, the summit always looked as far away; then again, it always looked as close. With the sun going down, expiring like a lover with a broken heart, I abandoned my elusive quarry and decided to return. Emerging from the dark woods, I saw riders approach on the road from Florence and turn into the Villa Medici. One of them was so familiar a figure on his mule that I was certain that it was Bishop degli Agli.

I ran to the villa. In the courtyard I could hear the sound of lutes and voices coming from the music room, and from the garden the deep sound of men in conversation. Luigi Pulci was playing dice against himself at the courtyard well.

'Whoa! Stop now,' he said as I ran in. 'You look like a kitten with the wind up its tail.'

'Is the Academy meeting here tonight? Why not at Ficino's? Why is that? Will you be joining them?'

'Not if I can help it.'

'I thought the Platonic Academy was up there on the hill.'

'Sometimes it is. Sometimes it is here. Sometimes it is somewhere else entirely. You never can tell where it will be next.'

'Are you not a member?'

'For my virtue, heaven has decreed that Luigi Pulci, alone of all men, will be immune to Ficino's mystical verbiage. These philosophers – they deny the evidence of their senses and fill their heads with breezy thoughts about the elevation of the soul. Soul, my foot; it is nothing but a man's pretence to a better part. Come on, play dice with me.'

I played dice half-heartedly, and won. Pulci claimed that we had not been playing for money and gave me an overripe fig as a prize.

'May the bounty of the earth course through you freely.'

'My thanks,' I said.

Matteo Franco, the poet and house chaplain, whistled in his sleep like a pine log on the fire. I only heard Angelo cry twice. Each time Matteo woke him gently and told him he was dreaming again. 'Why cry about the past? Has it not brought you here? Remember the present and rejoice.'

I once asked Matteo what troubled Angelo and he told me that his father had been murdered. 'He was there when it happened. He was only a little boy and stood there frozen as his father was slain. Now the Devil haunts him in his sleep, accusing him of cowardice.'

So if I was not caught between the Scylla and Charybdis that Pulci had described, I was indeed between a singing log and a man who feared to sleep. On the night following the meeting of the Academy, I lay in the bed listening to bats squeaking, crickets whirring and Matteo's resiniferous whistles; from the adjoining room came the sound of Pulci snoring like a bear. As Angelo was also still awake, I asked him what had taken place at the meeting.

'It was ... not the usual kind.'

'What is the usual kind?'

'Sometimes we discuss one of Plato's *Dialogues*, or one of us may play music, or there may be an exercise in contemplation, designed to lift us from our daily concerns and remind us of God's truth. But this evening was devoted entirely to a mundane matter: Ficino wanted to know Lorenzo's intentions with regard to Salviati's election. By what art of astrology or divination he had heard the news, I know not; he has a strange way of knowing things without being told them. As Lorenzo is still in Florence, Giuliano answered for him. It would seem that Lorenzo means to prevent Salviati's entrance to Pisa, quite physically if needs be: he is putting a guard on the road. As Salviati is a member of the Academy, Ficino is quite naturally concerned.'

'Is Lorenzo answerable to Ficino?'

'He rarely does anything without consulting him; but it seems that he means to follow his own counsel in this affair.'

'But what does Lorenzo have against Salviati?'

'Nothing. In truth he is fond of the man, but he cannot allow the Pope to dictate to us. The Pope is deliberately baiting us with someone we like, but the principle remains the same: the election is for Florence, not Rome, to decide.'

'What would Ficino have Lorenzo do?'

'Swallow his pride and accept the nomination.'

'What do you think he should do?'

'I have no opinion on the matter. I find it all so very tedious. But I do think that Lorenzo should follow the counsel of his tutor and master. The last time he acted independently, the result was the sack of Volterra.' With that, Angelo fell into sleep, having consigned me to a wakeful night accompanied by a consort of grunts and rumbles.

TWENTY

IN NOVEMBER of that year, following a tradition that had been instituted by Cosimo de' Medici, there was a Symposium held in honour of Plato's birthday. There were two banquets: one with nine guests only was at Ficino's villa on Careggi; the other, with about forty guests, was at the Palazzo Bandini in the city. Lorenzo had been invited to the dinner in the city, which made me wonder who the select few invited to dine with Ficino might be. I did my best to discover their names but received only evasive answers.

At that time the household was in residence on the Via Larga; thus, in my role as equerry, I went about discovering who required mounts for the evening. It transpired that Lorenzo and Angelo intended to walk to the Palazzo Bandini. 'Will you be walking this evening?' I asked Giuliano.

'What?' he said, 'all the way to Careggi?'

I gasped. Was the younger brother preferred to the elder? 'Are you going to Ficino's? Who are the other eight guests?'

'The nine guests. There are to be nine, the number of the Muses.' A smile on Giuliano's face was a rare thing. His usual countenance was serene, self-composed, reflective more of the man himself than of events going on around him. His smile was reserved for gentle teasing, and I had no doubt that I was now being gently teased. 'I am not one of those privileged to be an invited guest,' he said, his smile broadening.

'So will you be washing the trenchers?'

That smile – he was so pleased with himself, with the shock he was about to deliver me. 'Not quite, but I will be one of the servers.'

'You?'

'It is an immense honour.'

'Serving dinner? You should be at the table, being served!'

'I could be, if I went to Bandini's house, but I would rather hear the conversation at Ficino's, and so I must serve. Have the palfrey saddled, and soon, for I need to arrive early to help with the preparations. Close your mouth, Tommaso, or you will swallow flies.'

'I am astonished. A Medici in service ... '

'Is that an antithesis? How sad if that were true. I have always served at Ficino's table on the sixth of November; Lorenzo used to do so, too, but it is not appropriate now, given his position in Florence. Even so, he will not have the place of honour at Bandini's. The Academy is organised differently to the city, and a man's name counts for nothing, which is as it should be.'

'Who will be the other guests at the villa?'

'You will only have heard of one of them, Bishop Antonio degli Agli. There, does that not give you a marker in your hunt for information? The inner circle of the Academy is not drawn from the rich and notable, but from the meek and mild.'

'Men of good heart and with a sincere love of Truth.'

'Just so.'

'Would that I were one of them,' I confessed.

Where anyone else might have mocked me for saying so, Giuliano nodded gravely. He thought for a while, then said, 'Would you like to serve at Bandini's?'

So it came to pass that my overwhelming impression of the night of the Symposium was of dishes: full dishes to be carried to table, empty dishes to be carried away, dirty dishes to be stacked, taken to the cold well and scrubbed; and two dishes broken, to my humiliation though not by my fault. But of course you do not want to hear about that, so here is what I remember of the Symposium itself, as well as my first impressions of one who was to become the most constant, least wavering of friends.

Forty or more men, conversing in small groups before dinner; short men, tall men, fat men, thin men, men with grey hair, black hair, no hair; men of substance, men of no substance, lawyers, doctors, scholars, poets, priests, artists; dressed sombrely and one of the crowd, Lorenzo de' Medici. But if it was his intention, and that of his host, that he should be merely one of many, it soon failed.

As the guests seated themselves according to a plan drawn up by Francesco Bandini, one place remained vacant. The name at the place was 'His Grace the Archbishop of Pisa, Francesco Salviati.' As news of this reached round the tables, the company grew agitated. This was not the time to be reminded of Lorenzo's political battle with a fellow Academician, or that Salviati would have been present at this gathering had not Lorenzo forbidden him to enter Tuscany. A trick had been played, but by whom?

The host, Francesco Bandini, claiming that the honour of his house had been besmirched, apologised repeatedly to Lorenzo. I noticed, however, that his brother Bernardo was smiling, and the man he was smiling at was Jacopo di Poggio Bracciolini, who was sitting near the empty place. As Francesco Bandini continued to apologise, Lorenzo rose, walked to the empty seat, took the place name and threw it into the fire. He called for a servant and I ran to the call.

'Clear this place. Unfortunately His Grace cannot be with us tonight.'

I took away the place setting and thus brought the event to its close, but now everyone was reminded of Lorenzo's authority, at an occasion where there was supposed to be no superior other than Wisdom, represented in the bust of Plato that stood in a niche lit by candles.

Before the meal began, all turned to face the niche while Francesco Bandini made an invocation to the spirit of the Philosopher and to Wisdom. Heads bowed in as much reverence as one would find in church. Had not all the guests been Christians, and half of them priests of the Church, one would have supposed a new religion here.

One of my fellow servers was a gangly youth of my own age, with a loose mouth through which he breathed noisily. He avoided work as much as he could; while he stood back looking stupid, he watched me as if I were the fool. Eventually I challenged him with a cold stare. He smiled, and so ingenuously that I forgave him everything. In between the courses there were readings from the *Symposium*; along with the other attendants, I listened avidly from the servery, but this youth seemed deaf to it all. 'Are you not interested?' I asked him.

'I might be, if I could understand Latin.'

So at the next reading I translated for him in a whisper: '"Man's original body, having been thus cut in two, each half yearned for the half from which it had been severed."'

'Which means?'

'It means that man was once whole, male and female both, but he became two.'

His one-word response to this is unrepeatable to a monk. I reeled in shock at hearing a word more suited to a scurvy seaman who had hit his thumb with a hammer. I had never met such freedom of opinion, so artlessly expressed. 'How do you come to be here?' I asked once I had recovered. 'Most of us would have paid a ransom for the honour.'

'Not me. I was dragged here against my will. Tonight of all nights – when I had an assignation with little Bionda from Santa Maria Novella.' He sighed like an irritable donkey.

'Your spirit would profit from this, if only you would allow it.'

'Porcheria!' he said.

Though I displayed the righteous indignation proper to an aspiring philosopher, my heart was warming to him. If everyone has a secret word buried in the soul, 'liberty' was his. He simply had a coarse way of expressing it.

'Has your soul elevated yet?' he asked.'You know, lifted. It could happen any time now.'

'Could it?'

'In the service of Philosophy, it is the least we can expect. In return for all this work we will be paid with a quick float in the third heaven and union with the Angelic Mind. Or so I was promised.'

'You run small risk of that,' I said. 'If a man receives what he has given, you are due nothing.'

He pouted. 'I have worked all day, and hard. I am tired.'

'It is less tiring to do what you have been asked to do, less tiring than resisting.'

The time came for the second course, which had a choice of eleven dishes. We formed into a line, each of us holding a steaming plate aloft; then, on the signal, out we proudly went. At least, most of us did. My friend, whose name was Filippino, loped in a rangy gait like a wolf in a parade of high-stepping rouncys. Carrying a dish of anguilla, he placed it carelessly between Lorenzo and Angelo, announcing in a terrifying display of disrespect, 'Here you are, a lovely dish of worms fit for a prince!'

I went rigid with fear but to my surprise both Angelo and Lorenzo and the others near them laughed uproariously.

Father Piero had seen what had happened and did not approve. 'Who's boy is that?' he asked as I served him.

'I only know that he is called Filippino and that he smells of earth and linseed oil.'

'Oh? Then it must be Sandro's lad. So, Tommaso, you have gained entry into the Academy at last, have you?'

'I am merely serving.'

'It is the best way to begin.'

I nodded abstractedly and, as soon as I could, left to find Filippino in the servery. 'How could you dare do that?' I asked.

'I have no fear of Lorenzo. Why, he is almost a brother of mine. As for Angelo Ambrogini, he used to mend my shoes.'

We were interrupted again, this time to replenish the wine. I poured as instructed, that is, to the left of each guest, but I noticed that Filippino was filling glasses with the skilled abandon of a professional vintner. He seemed to be on familiar terms with everybody, and his discourteous behaviour was universally countenanced. If one man failed to find him amusing, it was his master, a short, fair-haired man with keen eyes who obviously regretted having encouraged his apprentice to come. He whispered something to him urgently as Filippino poured his wine.

Filippino crowed, drawing all attention. 'You would not dare!'

His master blushed.

'Who is he?' I asked Angelo as I served his wine.

'The son of his father. Take heart, Lorenzo has agreed to having him locked up with the lunatics.'

'Certainly, I shall arrange it forthwith,' said Lorenzo. 'He has overstepped himself tonight. He needs the bit in his mouth.'

As I returned to the servery bearing some empty platters, a long leg suddenly shot out in front of mine and I fell headlong. Two plates smashed.

'O Dio,' said Filippino lightly.

'Lorenzo is going to have you put away,' I snapped, rising and inspecting my clothes for damage.

'He is always saying that. It is a sign of his affection. Just because his grandfather locked my father up, Lorenzo thinks he has to do the same to me.' As casually as he had made it, he began to clear the wreckage. 'Tell me something: what in your opinion is the nature of Love?'

I stared at him.

'Come, you are as fit to tell me as any of those out there. What is the nature of Love?'

'You are utterly insane,' I said, but he was so persistent that I was forced to consider the question. Instead of answering from my own experience, which I considered too poor a store of knowledge, I tried to remember what I had read in my copy of the *Symposium*. 'Love is a god.'

'*Roba da matti*! What, a tubby little fellow with a blindfold on? The son of Aphrodite, who pierces your heart with arrows? Do you believe that? When was your heart last pierced with arrows?'

I thought of Giuliano, in whose opinion it was a state of blessedness never to have been in love. He kept his virginity not for want of opportunity to lose it, but because he despised the power which love of women exercises over reason. His brother and friends, insulted by his moral uprightness, set every trap for him, but to no avail. And yet Giuliano was present at the Symposium on Love, at Ficino's villa, and therefore there must be two loves, one human and one divine. Such was my reasoning, but to Filippino I gave only the conclusion.

'My master would agree with you,' he said, 'there are two Venuses, the heavenly and the earthly. I know which one has my devotion. With a body like mine, I would be wasted in spiritual pursuits, do you not agree? After all, someone has to father babies. It might as well be me.'

'Who is your master?'

'Sandro di Filipepi, master painter.'

'So that explains the smell!'

'What smell? ... By the way, you are bleeding.' So saying, he promptly wiped the blood from my cheek with my own sleeve. 'It is only a scratch,' he assured me.

Throughout the meal, different men had read the speech of each protagonist in the *Symposium*. It fell to an elderly man called Giorgio Antonio Vespucci to play the part of Socrates; after we had taken out the final, leisurely course of fruit and cheese, he began to read his speech.

'I want you to listen to this,' said Father Piero as I served him. 'This is the key speech.' So when I had placed my dishes, I returned to stand behind my old master and listen.

Socrates was telling his companions at supper of the teaching he had received on Love from a wise woman called Diotima. So far as I could follow it, the argument was that Love is desire. Desire arises from lack: therefore if Love desired goodness, it had it not, and if Love desired beauty, it had it not.

'What do you mean, Diotima? Is Love then ugly and bad?'

'Hush. Must that be foul which is not fair?'

'Of course.'

'And is that which is not wise, ignorant? Do you not see that there is a state of mind half way between wisdom and ignorance?'

'And what may that be?'

'Right opinion, which as you know being incapable of giving a reason, is not knowledge. Clearly such a state of mind cannot be called understanding, because nothing that lacks reason deserves the name; but neither can it be called ignorance; how can one call that mind ignorant which hits upon the truth? Right opinion is a mean between knowledge and ignorance.'

Piero turned to me. 'There. Proportion,' he explained. 'Proportion in all things.'

'What sort of being is he then, Diotima,' continued Vespucci-Socrates.

'He is a great spirit, Socrates, and like all spirits he is intermediate between the divine and the mortal.'

'And what is his power?'

'He interprets between gods and men, conveying and taking across to the gods the prayers and sacrifices of men, and to men the commands and replies of the gods. He is the mediator who spans the chasm which divides them, and therefore in him all is bound together. Through him the arts of the prophet and the priest, their sacrifices, mysteries and charms, and all prophecy and incantation find their way. The wisdom which understands this is spiritual; all other wisdom, such as that of arts and handicrafts, is earthly. Spirits or intermediate powers are many and diverse, and one of them is Love.'

Duty finished, I joined the other servers who were now sitting in the gallery above the hall; legs hanging through the balustrade and chins cupped in hands, we listened intently. Except, of course, for Filippino, who had curled up and seemed to be asleep.

At the point where Socrates' supper was interrupted by the drunken entry of Alcibiades, our supper was interrupted by Bishop Antonio degli Agli, coming in sober.

Everything halted as his friends greeted him warmly.

'Monsignore,' called Bandini. 'What brings you here? Has something happened at Careggi?'

'No, no, all is well. I was called away to attend to someone in my parish. That duty done, I thought I would finish the evening here.'

He was taken to the top table, where Lorenzo himself gave up his seat for the Bishop and moved to share Angelo's bench.

All the speeches done, the guests asked for an Alcibiades, one who would praise not Love, but Socrates. By subtle election, the part fell to Lorenzo.

It was not enough for him simply to read from a book; besides, he had the *Symposium* committed to memory. He and Angelo left the hall. A while later there was a heavy knocking at the gate, accompanied by men shouting; then, as Plato had described that famous late entry, Lorenzo staggered in, leaning on Angelo, lengths of ivy wreathed about his head and apparently very drunk indeed. Vespucci, playing Socrates to Lorenzo's Alcibiades, had to suffer being called an old Silenus with the face of a satyr, a satyr with the power to possess the soul. 'When we hear any other speaker, even a very good one, he produces absolutely no effect on us, or not much, whereas the mere fragments of you and your words, even at second hand, and however imperfectly repeated, amaze and possess the souls of every man, woman and child who comes within hearing of them.'

Lorenzo acted well, with his whole body, so that it seemed that the charming, dissolute Alcibiades, politician and general of the Athenian armies, was indeed amongst us. Everyone in the hall was captivated by the performance. Even Filippino sat up and took notice. 'What is he saying?' he asked, so I translated:

'"Socrates makes me confess that I ought not to live as I do, neglecting the wants of my own soul and busying myself with the concerns of the Athenians; therefore I hold my ears and tear myself away from him. He is the only person who ever made me ashamed, which you might think not to be in my nature, and there is no one else who does the same. For I know that I cannot answer him or say that I ought not to do as he bids, but when I leave his presence, the love of popularity gets the better of me. And therefore I run away and fly from him, and when I see him I am ashamed of what I have confessed to him. Many a time have I wished that he were dead."'

What Alcibiades had said, Lorenzo meant. The hall was hushed in an uncomfortable stillness, for when Lorenzo addressed Socrates in the person of Vespucci everyone knew who he really had in mind.

Alcibiades went on to describe how he had tried and failed to seduce Socrates; then he told of Socrates' powers of endurance on the battlefield: of how he could drink till dawn and stay sober, of how while in thought he was removed from time and once stood for a whole night, caught up in contemplation. 'Many are the marvels which I might narrate in praise of Socrates; most of his ways might be paralleled in another man, but his absolute unlikeness to any other human being is perfectly astonishing.'

Lorenzo coming to an end, Bandini concluded his speech according to the book: 'When Alcibiades had finished, there was a laugh at his outspokenness; for he seemed to be still in love with Socrates.' Bandini cast Lorenzo a knowing look.

Lorenzo accepted the laughter of his friends at his own expense. With a brave smile he returned to his seat.

Bandini called for silence.

'Let us together now remember Plato who, though dead these two thousand years, lives immortally in his words.'

'Plato.'

'Let us remember also Socrates, Plato's teacher, immortal in spirit.'

'Socrates.'

'Let us remember our friends who dine tonight at Careggi and, in thinking of them, be one with them, certain that we are also in their thoughts.'

'The Platonic Academy.'

'Lastly, let us dwell on our very own Socrates.'

All glasses were held high. The rich wine shone like rubies in the light of the sconces.

'Marsilio Ficino.'

Lorenzo looked rueful.

In the house on the Via Larga, I shared Angelo's room but had a truckle bed of my own. After we had bidden each other good night in the dark I asked, 'Is there trouble between Lorenzo and Ficino?'

'Only this matter of Archbishop Salviati. Ficino cannot see Lorenzo's point of view, or that the fight is with the Pope and not with Salviati. Besides, Ficino does not approve of fighting the Pope. Lorenzo has been raised as the philosopher king, but Ficino appears to object to Lorenzo performing the kingly part of his duties and would have him only as a philosopher.'

'Is it a serious quarrel?'

'Not at all. Lorenzo is a stubborn man, but it is in the interests of Florence that he be so and does not allow Sixtus to force an appointment on us without our agreement. Ficino would say so himself. The only problem is that Salviati is a member of the Academy. The situation is unique. Now Ficino says, "Leave it to the gods", whereas Lorenzo says, "I must act." That is the difference between them, and I wish Ficino could see Lorenzo's point of view. A man of inaction, who allows events to take place as they will, is a wise man and a philosopher, but he is not the ruler of a city. I am only glad that the scene with the empty place at table happened at Bandini's and not at Ficino's, but then there would have been no guest at his table capable of such a low trick. I wonder who did it?'

'It was Jacopo di Poggio Bracciolini.'

'Was it? Are you sure?'

I said I thought I was. Oblivious to any significance in the event, or to its being a bead in a lengthening rosary of events, I fell into that blessed state of dreamless sleep which is the reward of all those who serve.

TWENTY ONE

I BECAME devoted to the organisation of the stables and the poet Poliziano. After my storm of exaggerated willingness passed, my duties as equerry became simple, requiring not much more than the keeping of a book, maintaining an awareness of the location of each mount, and the occasional calling for the horse-leech. When Lorenzo was away, the duty became easier still. In those times of leisure, I sought out the company of Filippino Lippi.

He was the apprentice of Sandro di Filipepi, called Botticelli, one of the leading painters of the city. Their bottega was small and crowded, not only with unruly apprentices and visiting patrons, but also with the clutter of a painter's life. Apart from the alchemist's retorts, bubbling cauldrons and grinding stones that provide artists with paint, there were all manner of objects lying about, of the useless kind that would not have survived inspection by Lorenzo's mother, but which here were sanctified by having once had a purpose. Having been transmuted by art into a state of immortal fame, the various rugs, lengths of cloth, vases, urns and peculiar hats were allowed to remain in the shop, as steeped in importance as they were in neglect. Everywhere in confusion were pots of pigments, mortars and pestles, jars of this and that, countless brushes, great rolls of paper bearing designs that had smudged in time, and on every surface was a thick layer of chalk and charcoal dust. Then there were the smells, of pigments and pastes, oils and glues, and the eggs used to make the gesso ground of tempera painting. Sandro Botticelli prided himself on his tidy and well-ordered workshop.

I spent much time there, loving to watch the painters at work, performing the various rites and sacrifices that added up to the great celebration of a Madonna and Child, or an

Adoration of the Magi. Put men together in a workshop and the air soon becomes lively with foolish jokes and bantering insults, but in the midst of the clutter and noise, Sandro worked in peace, so concentrated on what he was doing that he was oblivious to everything else.

The constant output of Madonnas, which Sandro executed to sell as stock while he awaited lucrative commissions, Filippino considered to be wearysome repetition, but I found each Madonna enchanting, even if each did resemble the last. Filippino told me that the model was Simonetta Vespucci, who lived in the nearby palazzo. 'Sandro is in love with her.'

'Is there any hope for him?' I asked.

'Ha! None whatsoever. She is the wife of Marco Vespucci. And when I say that Sandro is in love with her, I mean platonically of course. Every man in Florence is in love with her, platonically. They only have to catch a glimpse of her to begin singing lyrics on Divine Beauty. So that is our livelihood, making images of Simonetta Vespucci.'

'Poor Filippino,' said Sandro, who had overheard. 'He understands nothing of Love.'

'Oh yes I do. I know more about it than you, you anchorite!'

'All you know about is lust.'

'I only wish that our paintings could be a little more, well, masculine,' said Filippino, and told me that if I wanted to see the best paintings in the world, I should cross the river to the church of Santa Maria del Carmine to see the work of Masaccio. 'The men in his paintings have real muscle.'

'All muscle and no movement,' said Sandro. 'Figures should move.'

'Muscle,' repeated Filippino. 'Real legs standing on solid ground. I shall show you; I shall take you there tomorrow; and then we shall call in to the workshop of Andrea del Verrocchio, where they paint soldiers and saints, not Madonnas. Maestro, I have heard that now they are starting to cast in bronze.'

'Tomorrow,' said Sandro, 'we are to begin a new work for Francesco Sassetti.'

'A commission?' barked Filippino. 'Why did you not tell me?'

'So you will have a whole host of men to paint, a panel crowded with figures.'

The subject was to be the Adoration of the Magi.

'Oh no,' Filippino groaned. 'Not another one.'

'I thought you enjoyed Adorations.'

'Madonnas – Adorations. When, oh when, can we do something different?'

'It is natural that, when a man has performed one masterpiece, people want him to repeat it.'

'Do you think they will ever invent a printing press for paintings?'

Sandro spun round on his stool and pointed his brush threateningly at his apprentice. 'Sometimes you are as funny as a knife in the throat.'

Over the following months, I watched the Sassetti Adoration grow from outline to full colour. In Sandro's search for perfection, various designs were abandoned before he was satisfied. In that time, I heard much about the Company of the Magi, one of the lay fraternities of the city. Francesco Sassetti, the manager of the Medici Bank, was one of its members, hence his choice of subject.

The Company of the Magi was centred at San Marco and their festival was Epiphany. Even at Volterra I had heard tales of the Procession of the Magi, when seven hundred horsemen of the brotherhood made their way slowly through the city in heraldic splendour, following the star to Bethlehem, which was at the Baptistry. Finally they converged on the quarter of San Marco, where stood Herod's Palace, made out of wood but with the front cut away so that spectators could see Herod and his harem within. The whole city had been involved in the pageant, each of the quarters competing with the others to be the most splendidly decorated, with flags spanning the streets and colourful rugs draped over balconies. It was held every five years, and it would be fourteen months before the next was due.

'May it come quickly!' said Filippino. 'We need a good spectacle. It has been far too long since the last.'

But the Procession of the Magi never happened again. My desires have become minimal with age, but one thing I still wish to have seen, just once, was one of those great processions.

When all the figures were placed as Sandro wanted them, and he was satisfied with the design, then began the long business of transferring it to a panel. Some of the apprentices worked together at the large table, pricking tiny holes along every line, while others, under Filippino's direction, laboured to prepare the panel of wood with a good gesso ground. Much rubbing down of hardened plaster filled the air with a fine, powdery dust. The ground prepared and the pricking done – it took many days – the paper was fixed to the panel and chalk was dusted through the holes, providing a tracing of the design on the smooth gesso.

As the figures of the Magi emerged, they were revealed as members of the Medici. The heads of Cosimo and his sons Piero and Giovanni appeared as the three kings, while Lorenzo and Giuliano were in their retinue. The Company of the Magi and the Medici were synonymous. From what I had heard, their meetings were much like those of the Academy; indeed membership of one almost implied membership of the other.

'And I am not a member of either,' I complained.

'No,' said Filippino. 'It is forbidden. No member of the Company of Lippi is allowed to be a member of the Magi.'

'Am I in the Company of Lippi?'

'Of course,' he said.

To be a friend of Filippino Lippi was to become one with the youth of Florence. King of the piazza, he was as passionate in games as he was in his art. I exalted in his friendship and spent whatever free hours I had with him, either at the bottega or out in the streets, where anyone over the age of thirty would be, in his opinion, deserving of a practical joke.

It is customary in Florence that when a young man of one of the leading families comes of age, there is a joust held in the Piazza Santa Croce. The next one was to be that of Giuliano de' Medici, but as yet no date had been set. So Filippino, desiring a spectacle, organised one himself on the feast day of Saint Luke, the patron saint of painters: a joust to be held in the Piazza Santa Trinità between the opposing teams of the bottega of Botticelli and that of Andrea Verrocchio. The lances were those long sticks with a padded end which painters use to rest against their work and keep their hands steady. The mounts were those unlucky enough to be chosen for the honour. I was one of them.

The fighting was brutal; though not a drop of blood was spilled that day, many became as bruised as windfall apples. The pads of the sticks dipped in red paint, the object was to mark your opponent. By the time that Filippino came out to meet his peer from Verrocchio's workshop, most of Botticelli's apprentices were in the prisoners' pen. His opponent, a youth called Leonardo, was as popular with the crowd of spectators as Filippino. Therefore my friend not only had to redeem the honour of his bottega, but also to dash his rival's claim to his throne. I feared for the other youth's life. When it came to entering the lists, Filippino leapt on to my shoulders and goaded me with his heels, roaring with such ferocity that I nearly tumbled in fright. Leonardo charged towards us on the back of a youth called Lorenzo di Credi. The next thing I knew, I was lying face down on the Piazza Santa Trinità, Filippino on top of me, dripping with red paint.

Thereafter Filippino devoted himself to the downfall of Leonardo da Vinci. Claiming that Leonardo had cheated at the joust, he prowled the taverns looking for someone willing to murder him in return for a finely executed portrait of Simonetta Vespucci as the Madonna. It was at that time that the bottega of Verrocchio began to go into the ascendancy, and that of Botticelli into decline.

The weather turned cold early that year: a bitter wind eddied round the city and its offspring draughts crept through all doors and curtains to tease candle flames. We shuffled about cloaked in wool and fur, finding the season unconducive to planning an outdoor entertainment, but that was our preoccupation, for it had been announced that it was time for Giuliano's joust. Still no date for the tournament had been fixed, though we knew that it would be within the next few months.

On the eve of the Nativity there was a meeting of the Academy in Ficino's house in the city. When Angelo returned it was in an ill humour. In response to my questions, he said that he had been called upon to recite an elegy he had composed in honour of Lorenzo, and that Lorenzo himself had suggested a more felicitous phrase for the last line. Now, as every poet knows, there are few things quite as painful as helpful suggestions from other poets; when that other poet is both your patron and the very subject of your verse, and when you have only anticipated his pleasure and not his critical comment, then the pain is intense. Angelo sat on his bed, rocking back and forth and growling.

'What else took place?' I asked.

'"I draw life from the fragrance of your leaves" – God in heaven, that is terrible! He has no right! Or if he does have a right, he should have the kindness not to impose it in public. Fragrance of your leaves, indeed!'

I thought the line quite good, given that its subject was laurel, but did not say so. I asked him again, what else took place?

'What? Oh, we determined the date of the joust.'

It was to be on the twenty-eighth day of January. I could not see how we could prepare everything in time.

'From now on, Maso,' said Angelo, his mind turning from fragrant laurel leaves to work ahead, 'we shall be so busy that you will pray for death.'

'But why choose such an early date?'

'It is the most propitious, astrologically.'

'Propitious for what?'

'Tommaso dei Maffei, have I ever told you that you ask too many questions?'

'What do you mean?'

The following day, I joined Giuliano in the stables to review the horses. We inspected each one, discussed its merits, allotted it to one of the squires on my list. A stall had been prepared for the destrier which the Count of Urbino, who had the best breeding stock in Italy, had promised to send.

Pretending to be absorbed by a knot in a rein, Giuliano asked me what had taken place at the meeting of the Academy.

'Why do you ask me?' I laughed. 'I am the last person to know.'

'Surely Angelo tells you everything?'

'As little as possible. But how is it that you do not know yourself?'

'If I have not been invited to the last few meetings, it is because, they tell me, I am the subject of their discussions. They are operating on me, Tommaso.' He looked so doleful that I was flooded with concern, even though I did not know what he was talking about. 'They think I am cold towards women. I have argued with them endlessly. If to lead a philosophic life is to remove oneself from all earthly charms, lusts and passions, then why must I fall in love? And yet they seem to want nothing more than for that to happen. Can you understand it?'

'It makes no sense.'

'None at all. And I have a good idea that they are intending to effect my transformation by means of this joust.'

I could not see how a tournament would make someone fall in love. I thought jousting was no more than a colourful trial of strength; Giuliano said that was so, but there was an additional element, that of chivalry. In ages past, knights had fought to the death, so Venus had been invited to the proceedings to soften the blows. Now to compete in a joust was to contend for the Lady, and Giuliano did not want the prize.

'Since, thanks to Sixtus, there is no hope of my achieving position in the Church, they are going to make a married man of me,' he said. 'That I can stomach, but falling in love ... Be thankful, Tommaso, that you are the master of your own fate and do not have an elder brother deciding things on your behalf.'

It was soon announced that the Queen of Beauty was to be Simonetta Vespucci; thus, as Simonetta was already married, I concluded that Giuliano's fears had no foundation. It seemed true that every man in the city was in love with her. Having seen her portrait so often I was half in love with her myself. Giuliano, however, was not. So I thought him safe from any platonic designs upon his emotions. But then I did not understand the principles and the workings of Courtly Love.

TWENTY TWO

I can see your eyes growing keen, Desiderio. I can hear the arguments rising in your throat. There is only one love, you say, and it is love of Christ. This, of course, is true; but you must admit that for much of the time most of us are overwhelmed by our appetites. What I am describing here is the work of a man who, knowing human nature as well as he did, sought to transform the earthly Venus into the divine; and, when I speak that way, my dear Dutchman, I speak entirely in metaphor.

LORENZO de' Medici ruled the city and his mother ruled the house. From the roof to the cellar, servants moved smartly through the rooms with dust brushes, carpet beaters, waxes and oils. Clothes were brought out from storage; at the order of her mother-in-law, Mona Clarice took up the unfamiliar tasks of cleaning and pressing her husband's silks and brocades. Tailors arrived. Pages and squires were measured for new attire; for Giuliano came the designs of shirts and jackets of linen, velvet and silk embroidered and set with pearls. One jewel-encrusted hat cost more than I have earned in this lifetime.

Under the watchful eye of Mona Lucrezia, men carried barrels of wine, huge cheeses and crates of fruit to the cellars, precious spices to the locked chest for which only she had the key. The great kitchen looked like a butcher's shop: headless deer and boar hung by their back legs from hooks in the wall, while hams, sides of mutton, and all the fowl of the air depended from the beams.

Weary of being repeatedly deflected from my course to help move this or that piece of furniture, I retreated with Matteo Franco to the chapel. He chalked the sign of the plague on the door to keep everyone at bay.

The chapel was a small room, square but for the altar recess, and the entire surface of its walls was covered in one continuous fresco. On the occasions when I had joined members of the family in prayer, I had been utterly distracted from my devotions by the life-size Procession of the Magi. The most arresting image was of a young prince on a white charger caparisoned in red and gold brocade; a prince with a velvet crown, a bloom on his cheeks and long golden curls. This, I was told, was Lorenzo when a boy. Oh fearful metamorphosis, if the dark tyrant grew out of such a gilded child.

Behind 'Lorenzo' rode a crowded procession of more realistic portraits of the Medici and their associates: the Company of the Magi since the time of Cosimo. Each wall had its retinue, and each followed the other, the whole a procession of double significance; for while ostensibly these were the three kings moving towards the Christ child, shown in the Nativity scene above the altar, one of the kings was a portrait of the Emperor of Constantinople, and thus the year of the event was 1439. Then it was that the Emperor visited Florence, bringing in his train knowledge of Platonic Wisdom, the gift of a king to Truth.

The Company of the Magi, formed by citizens of Florence, had existed for many years, but since the time of Cosimo it had changed, from outward pomp and charitable deeds in the community to an inward-dwelling, meditative brotherhood. The discipline, it was said, was as severe as in any monastery; indeed, it was perhaps harsher, for the brothers of the Magi were expected to follow it, whereas these days (Lord forgive us) monks are not. The regularity with which Lorenzo attended the weekly meetings of the Company was impressive. Whatever he was doing, he stopped at the ninth hour on a Tuesday, changed out of the garb of the richest young man in Florence and into the simple robe of one of the Company of the Magi, and left the palazzo on foot, arm in arm with Giuliano, to pray for purity of soul. These meetings inspired him to compose pious verse to be set to music by Baccio Ugolini or Heinrich Isaacs. It was difficult to equate this Lorenzo, who could write lines which sang of the death of Christ as if the singer himself were dying, to the one who had sacked Volterra. 'Oh hard and bad heart, the source of all evil, which does not break at Jesus's death ... '

Could the man who wrote that be the one who had sanctioned the murder of innocents? Perhaps it was for that very reason that the tyrant went each week to a meeting of the Company, to pray and to practise self-flagellation. But if he felt any guilt, he showed no sign of it to me, whom he was happy to ignore.

Though the next great procession of the Magi was a year away, nonetheless there was to be a small, private ceremony on the sixth day of January at San Marco monastery; this was to be preceded by the feast of Caspar on the first, which was Lorenzo's birthday. And so the preparations went on for that joyful month which was to culminate in Giuliano's joust.

Into the tempest of activity ambled Filippino Lippi. He claimed that there had been a long standing arrangement that Sandro Botticelli should paint the portrait of Mona Lucrezia, and he had chosen this moment to come and make preliminary sketches. Mona Lucrezia was indignant.

'This is not the time,' she said dismissively as she walked quickly down the corridor, the household keys clinking in a heavy bunch suspended from her girdle.

'Perhaps there is a more urgent task for us?' Filippino called after her. 'A banner for the joust perhaps?'

I beckoned to him from the chapel; as he entered he threw his arm over his eyes with a groan and complained that the paintings were blinding. When I said that I liked them, I was told that fools should keep their opinions to themselves.

'Look at that hind being chased up the hill there. It is larger than the huntsman. Project it forward to the plane of the foreground and it would be a deal larger than the prince and his horse together. And that rabbit! Have you ever seen one so massive? Monstrous! This melée of figures, they are all the same: these are the faces of a pattern book. And the ears of the horses – pen nibs! How is it that Benozzo Gozzoli lives in this city in complete ignorance of perspective? Has he never seen the Masaccio frescoes? I sometimes think that people look on the holy art of fresco as a cheap alternative to tapestries. Ye gods, it is a wonder that Gozzoli ever worked again after this miscarriage.' He pointed to the altarpiece. 'Now that, that is true Art.'

The quiet scene on a panel of the Virgin and Saint John in

adoration of the infant Jesus was so overpowered by the frescoes that I had never paid it much attention.

'My father's work, you know, another masterpiece from the hand of Fra Filippo Lippi.'

Filippino was as proud of his father as a son could be, and had told me many stories of the colourful life of the painter who had been Sandro Botticelli's own master; what he had omitted to tell me until this moment was that his father had been a friar. I reeled in surprise.

'I must have told you.'

'No one needs to be told that you are a bastard,' said Matteo Franco, 'it is obvious.'

'The son of a friar and a nun, sanctified by love and blessed by the Holy Spirit,' said Filippino benignly. 'A holy bastard, and now quite legal, Cosimo de' Medici be praised.'

'A retrospective legitimacy: you were still born in sin.'

'I would rather be the bastard son of Fra Filippo Lippi than the legitimate heir of Benozzo Gozzoli,' Filippino retorted, squinting again at the frescoes. 'I have divine art in my veins.'

I told him that one of Gozzoli's apprentices had visited the day before, looking for cracks. 'He had heard some were appearing, but we found none. Nor could we discover the source of the rumour.'

Matteo thought it had been a feeble excuse to call upon us. 'Every day some painter makes a visit on a lame pretext. It seems that we need to be reminded of their existence.'

'They have nothing better to do, I presume,' said Filippino. 'We, of course, are hard at work on an Adoration of the Magi for Francesco Sassetti. Gozzoli should call on us, to see how the subject may be properly treated.'

Matteo told him of another visit, made by one of the journeymen from the workshop of Andrea del Verrocchio, who had come to make a copy specifically for a commission.

Filippino swung round. 'Which one?'

'Leonardo.'

'Here? Copying what?'

'Oh, just a little thing, one of the lunettes.'

'Which one?'

'The Annunciation.'

'My father's! Leonardo is copying my father's painting! Who gave him permission? Why was I not consulted?'

Matteo said that, as the painting belonged to the Medici, Filippino's permission was not required.

'To give Leonardo his due, he knows true art when he sees it. If he has to copy designs, he may as well copy the best,' said Filippino.

Matteo scratched his head and said that, as he remembered it, Leonardo's purpose had been to learn from another's mistakes. 'Was that not what he said, Tommaso?'

Matteo was a superb liar; he looked entirely serious. 'I believe those were his words,' I agreed, still smarting at having been called a fool.

Filippino stared at us, open-mouthed and speechless; abruptly he turned, strode out of the chapel and slammed the door behind him.

Matteo looked remorseful. 'Perhaps that was too sharp a point; it is sometimes difficult to remember that Filippino Lippi may have feelings.'

It was becoming painfully obvious that all artists have feelings; each of those who had come to the palazzo in the past few days had worn an expression of rejection, each believing that Lorenzo's silence meant that someone else had been commissioned to help with the joust, when in fact no one had yet been commissioned. There was a banner to be painted, a helmet to be wrought in silver, a triumphal car to be built, and no decision had been made on who should do them. Matteo agreed that time was pressing, that works of art cannot be produced overnight, and that Lorenzo must decide this very day. He left to speak to him about it.

I returned to my desk, which I had moved into the chapel so that Angelo might have his study to himself. The poet was engaged in a major composition, an epic poem to celebrate the joust; consequently he had become an intolerable companion. He wanted the company of no one but himself, no living space but that of his own mind. I was busy with many things, but one of them was transcribing his impassioned scribbles into something legible, and under my hand a great poem was emerging.

The last question I asked him before he became impossible

to speak to was, 'How can you start a poem about an event which is yet to take place?'

'Because, nib-scratcher, the prelude to the joust has taken place, in my imagination if nowhere else. Would you like to hear the first verses, or would you prefer to ask another inane question?'

I chose to hear the verses. I needed no injunction for silence when he was about to recite. He held his scraps of paper in his fist, needing them only in case his memory failed him, which it never did; looking me straight in the eye like a good actor, he began:

'Nel vago tempo di sua verde etate,
spargendo ancor pel volto il primo fiore,
né avendo il bel Iulio ancor provate
le dolce acerbe cure che dà Amore,
viveasi lieto in pace e'n libertate;
talor frenando un gentil corridore,
che gloria fu de' ciciliani armenti,
con esso a correr contendea co' venti ... '

He, the greatest latinist, was writing in Tuscan!

He said that doing so was a crippling experience, that after writing in Latin he now felt like a lame man who had dreamt he had been dancing. But Lorenzo was keen to promote the literary use of Tuscan, our own native language which had been ennobled by Petrarch and Dante.

Now that which so delighted me at the time will mean nothing to you, my friend, who would find Latin easier. But here it is again, in the vernacular of our adopted nation, without the rhyme and wonderful cadence; which is to say, without the very essence and lifeblood of poetry. Here are the bones:

In the comely time of his green youth,
the first flower still blooming on his cheeks,
fair Julio, not having yet felt
the bittersweet cares of Love,
lived content in peace and liberty;
at times bridling a noble steed,
the glory of the Sicilian herds,
he would race in competition with the winds,
now like a leaping leopard,

now turning in tight circles,
now sending a pliant spear whistlling through the air,
often dealing harsh death to the wild game.
So the valiant youth used to live;
with no thought for his fate, dire and bitter,
as yet unaware of tears in the future,
he would mock stricken lovers.

I wanted to know what this fate dire and bitter might be. 'What is to happen to him?' I cried.

Angelo tapped his finger threateningly on the desk, a rapid staccato of barely held patience. I apologised hastily, saying that I had not meant to ask a question. 'Please go on.'

But he shook his head angrily. 'Tommaso dei Maffei, I shall never say another thing to you until you learn to speak in statements.'

Thus the difficult phase began, and I moved into the chapel. In transcribing his work I had, of course, every opportunity for reading the verses, but I wanted to hear them; thus sometimes, late at night, I stood by the open door to Lorenzo's chamber, unseen in the shadows, listening to recitations of the poem about Giuliano. And once I heard more than I should have done: 'May this warm my brother's cold heart, as it melts mine,' said Lorenzo. 'By number, by harmony and by metre, we will make him human, and vulnerable to Love's dart.'

On the day of Filippino's intrusion, I worked late into the night, writing invitations to the feast. As Angelo was out in the city with Lorenzo, I was not disturbed and worked until the candle burnt to its stub. When at last I wearily retired, I started violently to see a long shape lying on Angelo's bed.

'My father used to live here you know,' said Filippino, ignoring my cry of help to the Virgin, 'in this very room. The Palazzo Medici is like a second home to me.'

'You will be expelled from it soon enough, when Angelo returns.'

'He is out with Lorenzo.'

'I know. I think there must be a meeting of the Academy.'

Filippino greeted this with derision, saying that any fool would know that Lorenzo's destination was the house of his mistress. I demanded evidence. 'Listen,' he said, 'when Lorenzo comes out of his wife's chamber, having bidden her goodnight, and meets his friend who is waiting with a lute in each hand, where is he going – to bed, to the Academy, or for a little serenading in the streets?'

'Presumably the last, but that is not what you said.' I filled two cups with wine and handed him one.

'It is January, Maso. Too cold for singing under the stars. And Lucrezia Donati's husband was sent as an ambassador to Venice yesterday.'

'Ah well then, you had relevant information which I did not.'

'Surprising, eh? Considering that you live here and I live in a painter's workshop.'

'It is obviously the place to be if you want all the gossip.'

'Unlike here. I have been haunting these corridors all day and not a single item of interest have I heard.' He drained his cup and held it out to be refilled. Once served, he relaxed against the pillows, ready to tell me a long story about a friar and a nun. Although I was tired, I was too intrigued to deny myself a good tale, and lay down beside him to listen.

Fra Filippo Lippi had been a monk of the Carmelite order; he had trained in painting under Lorenzo Monaco, but had become a true artist by a close study of the work of Masaccio, the spirit of whom, some said, he had absorbed. While chaplain of a monastery in Prato, he had fallen in love with the nun who was modelling for his painting of the Madonna. On the night of the Festival of the Holy Girdle, Fra Filippo carried the girl off to his house; nine months later, Filippino was born. It was two years before the sluggish authorities acted and made Sister Lucrezia return to the convent. Not so sluggishly, Fra Filippo abducted her again. Breaking holy vows was one thing, flouting church authority another: Fra Filippo was brought to trial and tortured on the rack. At this point Cosimo de' Medici intervened and sought help from the Pope. Fra Filippo and Sister Lucrezia were absolved from their vows and allowed to be lawful man and wife.

'It was the end of him,' Filippino complained. 'It cost him his living, and from then on he had to support a family on what he could earn from painting.'

'Was that not enough?'

'Enough? Patrons spend more on frames than on paintings! It is never enough. Besides, my father was incapable of finishing anything on time, which patrons always use as an excuse to pay less. What did one of them say? "I shall take as long to pay you as you have lagged in the work." The only patron who had any patience with him and never penalised him was Cosimo. At least, he never penalised him financially. No, what Cosimo did was to bring him here, to this very room, and provide for his every need, in the hope that it would help him concentrate. But still my father did not complete on time. He was too vital a man, too fond of life, to spend all his time in one room. He kept wandering off. So the day came when even Cosimo lost his patience and locked him in, informing him through the keyhole that he would be let out only when the painting was finished.'

Filippino let the story hang in the air.

'And ... ' I prompted, yawning.

'And so my father tied the sheets together and let himself down from the window.'

I laughed. 'What did Cosimo do?'

'Forgave him, as always. As Cosimo said, you have to forgive the follies of a genius. The Medici loved my father. They love me too – I expect you have noticed that.'

'It has not struck me between the eyes, Pipo.'

'Oh yes, they do. It is just their manner, to turn the shoulder on you in the corridor. You know, when they bark at you to get out from under their feet, that is simply a sign of their affection. The commission for the banner will come tomorrow.'

I wanted to know why he wanted the banner in particular, and not the helmet or the triumphal car, both of which would be more lucrative. He said the banner was the most important thing, for it would bear the symbol of the joust into the piazza.

'The commission is bound to come tomorrow. I know I am being selfish, because the Verrocchio and Pollaiuolo workshops need the work more than we do, but it is not in me to decline such an offer. Those others, they are so ruthlessly realistic that they miss the vision; as when you pull a fly apart to see how it works, but of course, after you have done so, it does not work.

They investigate, we appreciate. In the bottega of Sandro Botticelli, we have vision. Only we are capable of making the banner.'

I refilled our cups and asked him about love, wondering if he had ever met someone with a cold heart who spurned women, and how such a person might be cured, if cured he should be. It was Filippino's opinion that no such man existed, unless he preferred boys. He said that men do not need help to fall in love; that it happens as naturally as the rising of the sun, or the rising of the moon, or the rising of the stars. To illustrate his theory, as well as to educate me in a subject of which I had no direct experience, he mimed his thoughts with obscene gestures which, along with the wine, soon had me laughing until my ribs ached. All the concerns of the day began to whirl in a merry detachment. Filippino was beginning to slur his words; I was relaxing so completely that my limbs felt weighed down, my muscles limp, my eyelids very heavy. It must have been then that the wine-cup fell over sideways.

Filippino prodded me awake. 'Once, you know, my father was captured by pirates. Arabs from Africa they were.'

I started to laugh again. 'Where did this happen, in Prato or Florence?'

'No, stupid. He was in a boat at the time, off Genoa. Anyway ... '

I did not hear the end of the pirate story. Presumably Fra Filippo was either released from captivity or escaped, for he died land-locked at Spoleto.

I returned to consciousness and painful daylight when I heard someone say, 'The sheets! My linen! Ruined!' With thunder and lightning cracking inside my head, I opened my eyes to the apocalyptic vision of Mona Lucrezia standing over us like Nemesis. If I did not know what to say, Filippino did.

'Madonna Lucrezia,' he muttered, smiling like a sleepy cherub. 'You look particularly beautiful this morning.'

The Barbary horse sent by the Count of Urbino arrived, all muscle, pure white. Giuliano walked him round while Lorenzo stood remarking on the horse's form to his friends. When Lorenzo was in a good humour, his face was not so much ugly as strong. His almond-shaped eyes were set unusually close to his eyebrows; eyebrows which, because of the crease at the top of his nose, dipped angrily. That half of his face was almost attractive; it was the flat nose and projecting lower lip that marred him. But as he stood watching his brother riding the Barb, his features were illuminated by affection. If it is rare for brothers to love each other, it is rarer still when one is powerful and the other handsome.

The horse, though a destrier, lacked the usual bulk of a war horse and was elegant, light and swift. 'For,' the Duke of Urbino had said in the letter accompanying his gift, 'it is the lightness of intelligence which wins battles, not the muscle of brute force.'

Lorenzo called out to Giuliano to try now this, now that manoeuvre. In response, Giuliano halted the Barb, laid down flat in the saddle, turned back to front, turned front to back again, then stood up. The horse was untroubled by any of it. Giuliano jumped to the ground and Lorenzo, fastening a long rein to the bridle, set the horse trotting round the courtyard riderless. The rest of us hollered and waved our arms, trying to startle the beast; he flinched a little but his step remained sure. He was unanimously pronounced magnificent. With considerable pride, I accepted from Giuliano the order to stable the Barb.

'Look after him, Tommaso. I do not want anyone to touch him except you.'

I spent the entire morning in the stable grooming Orso. Filippino, who had been discovered loitering in the corridors, was sent to me.

'I have been told that I am your responsibility.'

'In what way?'

'I need feeding. And a comb through my hair would not go amiss.'

'I think it might very well go amiss,' I said, considering his long, tangled locks.

I took him to the kitchen for the midday meal. While we were eating, Leonardo da Vinci and Lorenzo di Credi entered in search of Matteo Franco. They looked wary when they noticed Filippino.

'Ohé,' he said, through a mouthful of fish soup. 'Not working?'

'On the contrary,' said Leonardo. 'We are very busy.'

'Oh? What with? Copying Lippi paintings?'

Leonardo exchanged a sly smile with di Credi. 'Not today. A new commission has just arrived.'

Filippino choked. His face went red and tears came to his eyes. He pretended that a fishbone was the cause. I gave him something to drink. Unbidden, the two apprentices sat down at the table and helped themselves to our food, although Leonardo made a point of avoiding the meat. He was too beautiful for a man: with long, fair hair and perfect features, he was dressed as ever in clothes too fine for his trade. He used to say that if you dressed well, you took more care in your actions. On this day he wore a rose-pink tunic, belted at the waist, and fine woollen hose of dark green. Lorenzo di Credi's admiration of him was obvious; Filippino Lippi's was not. But hatred did not bound fatherless into creation; it cannot exist alone; hatred is the disfigured son of love. How strange, that I could see this so clearly in Filippino, and yet not see it in myself.

The other two started a conversation away from the subject of painting. They had met Jacopo di Poggio Bracciolini in the courtyard, who had arrived at the house to present Lorenzo with his commentary on Petrarch's *Triumph of Fame*.

'Lorenzo is very forgiving,' decided Leonardo, 'if he can receive a work from a man who once tried to kill his father. Perhaps the work is too important to let pass. I have heard it said that Bracciolini has an intellect surpassing that of even Angelo Poliziano.'

I thought this was not possible. The two young painters wanted to know if Angelo was concerned that he might be replaced in Lorenzo's affection.

'By Jacopo Bracciolini?' I laughed. 'He could dedicate thirty works to Lorenzo. He would never take Angelo's place. Nor would anyone else.'

'But it is obvious that he is trying.'

'Too obvious. Why, even his choice of work reveals his desires. He wants fame. May he achieve it. But he will not have that which is due to Angelo.'

Filippino, who had listened to nothing of the conversation, cleared his throat. 'This commission ... ' he said.

'Fate has treated Bracciolini ill,' said Leonardo, ignoring him, 'and he is undeserving of your scorn, Tommaso. Even so, he should be treated with caution.'

'Why?' di Credi wanted to know.

'In the line of his mouth there is a certain weakness.'

'Yes, there is. In the mouth, yes, you are right.'

'The sign of a sycophant – worth noting.'

'Most definitely.'

'This commission ... ' croaked Filippino.

'Is it for the joust?' I asked brightly on his behalf.

'Yes indeed,' said Leonardo. 'Lorenzo came himself to our bottega, late last night, with Poliziano.'

My proud, lupine friend stared into his soup, his appetite quite vanished.

'We have come to take measurements and ... ' Lorenzo di Credi broke off suddenly with a wince and rubbed his leg.

'Measurements?' Filippino asked.

Leonardo looked up at the kitchen ceiling, at all the dead game. An expression of pathos crossed his face, to be quickly displaced by one of indignation. 'Was everything that creepeth upon the surface of the earth made for the Medici to eat?'

'Hush!' said di Credi, flashing a nervous smile at me. Being weak in my allegiance to Lorenzo, and eager not to be seen as a sycophant, I was happy to ignore it. 'Come along,' he nudged Leonardo. 'We have work to do.'

As they rose, Matteo Franco came in to tell Filippino that he must return at once to his bottega. 'Your master needs you.'

'What for?' said Leonardo. 'Has the workshop of laggards something to do?'

'Very much so,' said Matteo, 'and quickly.'

'What is it?' demanded Filippino.

'Go and find out for yourself. Lorenzo called to see Sandro Botticelli last night. If you had been there instead of here, turning Master Angelo's bed into a lake of wine, you would have heard earlier.'

'Heard what? Heard what?' Filippino was hastening to the door. 'It is not – would it be ... ? – is this anything to do with the joust? Oh God be praised! And all the saints in heaven! And Holy Mother Mary! And all the Martyrs! – What are these two doing then?'

'Why, the prize helmet. Verrocchio's silverwork is – '

'The banner! We have the banner? Oh Mercy, oh Justice, oh Love! Oh, you miserable wretches – the helmet. Never mind, praise God for small mercies.' And with a bound of joy he was gone.

When the other two had left, I asked Matteo if, now that the artists had been commissioned, he could tell me what the symbol of the joust was to be? He did not know. It was a closely-guarded secret, but he suspected that it would be the symbol of peace, because of the threat of war.

'What war?' I cried.

Matteo was taken aback. 'Well, *the* war. The one that might happen at any time.'

'Oh, that war.' Ever since the Turks had taken Constantinople thirty years before, Italy had expected an invasion by Muslims. But it was a threat that had been taken more seriously by the generation prior to mine.

'Or,' he continued, 'it will be Love.'

'Oh?' I asked, affecting lack of interest. 'Why so?'

'Because as Giuliano comes of age, his youthful contempt of woman is no longer seemly.'

'How will a symbol help cure that?'

'Do you understand nothing, Tommaso?'

'How can it be otherwise, when no one ever explains anything?' I demanded moodily.

As it happened, the symbol of the joust was neither Peace, nor Love. It was Pallas Athene, known to the Romans as Minerva, the goddess of Wisdom.

TWENTY THREE

WASTREL, joker and tavern-idler, when at work Filippino Lippi was diligent and dedicated. His respect for his master was absolute. At the age of seventeen, he became a journeyman, that seemingly endless stage between being an apprentice and becoming a master. This professional advancement was marked by the Guild of Saint Luke with a humiliating rite of passage: Filippino was kidnapped by other apprentices, stripped naked and painted from head to toe. They left him outside Santa Croce to make his way home through the city alone. Faced with this challenge, Filippino met it in the only way his nature would allow. Not for him a journey made by dark, shadowy lanes, covering himself with the shame of an expelled Adam: no, he walked the main thoroughfares with his arms outstretched, baying with joy. Ladies abroad turned their faces to the wall as this living example of the art of a Phidias of ancient Athens strutted past them.

After the celebrations Filippino settled to his new duties, which included the charge and instruction of all the apprentices. As so often happens, the rebellious apprentice became a rigorous master. Knowing all the tricks himself, he missed none in others and kept his charges on a very tight rein. He worked on paintings alongside Botticelli; he taught the young ones the methods of making and mixing colours; he attended to the customers, showing them the Madonnas in stock, the pattern books and the work in hand. He acted as a bridge between Botticelli and the rest of the world and henceforth no one could approach the master without the permission of the journeyman.

Sandro Botticelli was in need of such a bridge. On his own, he was a distant figure on the opposite bank of the river of imagination. Although he appeared sociable it often happened that, in the middle of a conversation with him, you would suddenly find yourself alone. A strange, abstracted expression would come over his face and he would narrow his eyes as if to intensify their beam. Following his gaze, your own eyes would fall upon his current work, and suddenly you knew you were keeping him from it.

In the presence of Leonardo da Vinci, on the other hand, I often found it to be myself who was the object of scrutiny, and knew that I was being seen as a series of shapes, shadows and planes, a composition called Man. Leonardo was one of those painters to whom what underlaid surfaces was bone and muscle, a physical structure which some of artists, illegally and under the cover of darkness, studied by dissecting dead bodies. In the gaze of Botticelli, however, it was not one's form that was under view, but the mind. In his world there were no skeletons: that which underlaid form was Idea.

About this body, an object which I fondly – and erroneously – think of as myself, Sandro once said to Filippino, 'Why do you think his eyes point in different directions?'

'They do not!' I protested.

'It is only the way the light is catching them,' said Filippino.

Sandro took hold of me by the shoulders and turned me round.

'No, his eyes point in different directions whichever way the light falls. See, one looks out, the other looks within. He is aware of two worlds simultaneously and is not sure which to inhabit.'

Filippino, pretending to peer at me, winked conspiratorially. For the benefit of Sandro he nodded sagely. 'Yes, indeed, I do see what you mean.'

'I do not!' I said, but my point of view on the matter was of no interest to the master, whose both eyes were inward looking, even when studying a subject. Having thus examined my soul, he returned to his work.

'If ever you should want a portrait of yourself,' he said, 'I would be very pleased to do it. It would be a most interesting challenge.'

'Even if I could afford it, I would not indulge such vanity,' I grumbled, though I was flattered to be of interest to the painter.

Fastened to the wall of the shop was a long drop of blue taffeta on which had been drawn a cartoon of Minerva, the design for the banner.

The goddess of Wisdom stood motionless; the only movement was in the play of the elements on her diaphanous under-dress, which rippled in a gentle breeze. Long tendrils of windswept hair flowed from her crown of laurel. And laurel, the shrub which in both its name and its properties says 'Lorenzo', entwined her arms and encircled her breasts. The design on the fabric of her gossamer shift was of three interlocked rings, another of the symbols of the Medici.

Once I had been outraged at the sight of a Medici symbol stamped possessively on beauty. Now I reacted differently. His emblem on Minerva did not say to me, 'By this image it is claimed that Lorenzo has wisdom.' Instead it said, 'By this image, Lorenzo and Giuliano would honour Wisdom and hope for union with her.' Such a different reaction – was it a measure of growth of reason, or loss of independent judgement? Whichever, it was suddenly clear how much I had become a part of the Medici world. If I had not yet forgiven Lorenzo for past deeds, then the hatred, unattended, had fallen quiet, as mud in a pool falls to the bottom when the water is still.

Minerva, in that sublime pose, stood gazing at the sun. With one hand she held a shield with the Gorgon's head upon it; with the other, a levelled lance. In the meadow where she stood, Cupid was bound to the stump of an olive tree with his bows and arrows lying broken at his feet. All around the impotent little god were blazing olive branches. The feet of Minerva stood upon other flames. What fire was this, that caused no pain to Wisdom?

Sandro was painting the scene in sections on silk. When each section had dried, Filippino and the apprentices cut out the images and gave them to Sandro's sister-in-law to stitch carefully to its place on the blue taffeta pennant. Piece by piece, against the background of a green, flower-strewn meadow, a life-sized figure of the goddess manifested, with a complexion as pale as alabaster. Such beauty; the same beauty as in all Sandro's Madonnas.

From the staccato explanations of Sandro, and from what I

could glean from notes tacked about – notes which the artist had taken from conversations with Ficino and Poliziano – piece by piece I gathered the meaning of the image: Cupid represented erotic love, the olive branches peace. Peace – that is, peace of mind – is consumed by the flames of passion, but the fire may be overcome by the greater fire, which is Reason, represented here by the sun. Thus the emblematic meaning was this, that Wisdom manifests when Reason subdues Passion.

Whenever I could snatch a moment from my duties in the house, I ran to the workshop to see how the banner progressed. My levels of enjoyment grew with the work until, one day, I suddenly and unexpectedly transcended mere enjoyment and my relationship with the image became personal and direct.

Wisdom, Wisdom, there you stood, and I saw you for the first time. You, the Lady of so many I knew, and I, the peeper through doors, haunter of the shadowy margins of other people's lives, now fully aspired to be your suitor. But how?

'Through Love,' you said, as soon as the question framed itself. And what is love of wisdom? It is all in the word: Philosophy.

Enraptured, I turned from the picture, for the entry of someone into the bottega had caused such a silence that it shouted. My heart, fully opened by contemplation of Minerva, was defenceless against the vision of another goddess. Venus had appeared in the painter's workshop, a living, breathing, smiling goddess. My own breathing stopped. I glanced at the others. They were similarly suspended, but then their noise erupted again and Sandro hurried forward to greet the visitor. Or, rather, visitors, for the goddess had an escort.

'Ser Marco, Mona Simonetta, welcome to my bottega!'

'We have come to see the banner,' said the man, husband to the lady. A human lady, a neighbour, resident of the Palazzo Vespucci whose walls overshadowed the workshop.

As she stood contemplating her own likeness, a shy blush of pleasure suffused her pale cheeks. She was tall, slender and royal. Her high, round forehead looked like the sun rising at dawn, while her fair, abundant hair was plaited, braided with ribbon and caught up in a luxury of loops and coils. A married woman should by tradition have her hair covered; the unmarried women of Florence kept their hair uncovered but pulled it back into a severe knot. Simonetta Vespucci, not captive to the conventions of our age, did neither. In her abandon of tresses she celebrated female beauty with pagan enthusiasm. She was to dress what Poliziano was to verse, what Botticelli was to painting and Ficino to philosophy: she was the rebirth of the ideals of the antique world.

But why was Simonetta Vespucci more beautiful than other women of similar figure and design? For this reason: when she looked on you, her eyes shone as if it were they which perceived beauty. Thus to meet her gaze was to experience beauty enjoying itself. It was this reciprocity that transformed men. Sandro became jolly and gregarious, the perfect host; Filippino upright, perfectly mannered and clean of speech; the squabble of apprentices orderly, obedient boys. As for me, I became a servant.

Because of the generosity of her eyes, Simonetta drew the admiration not only of men but of women also. Marco Vespucci might have been the subject of bitter envy except for one saving grace: in the presence of his wife, he fell into deep shadow. From the day he married, no one ever noticed him again. He became not the lord of his lady, but the protective escort of beauty.

One moment I was aware of love only as an idea, the next it was coursing through my veins, making body, mind and soul sing with its meaning. Was this it? – the quickening of heart and pulse, and the stripping of veils from the eyes? Was this what made fools of men? I courted idiocy as, in an instant, I passed from a transcendent desire for wisdom to a palpitating adoration of the very human Simonetta. Why, just a glance at her had the invigorating effect of a feast, and took the usual course: one glance leading to two, three and many, until one cannot live and breathe without repeated sight of the beloved.

Thereafter I joined the others to look sadly on Giuliano and his cold dungeon of a heart. It was obvious that, unless he unlocked that heart himself, and soon, he was about to be ripped apart by the power of symbols.

TWENTY FOUR

IT WAS close to Epiphany and cold, but the sun shone in a clear sky as I rode down the Via Larga on a rouncy from the Medici stable. Giuliano was in front on Orso, riding beside his squire, Andrea Cavalcanti. People leant from windows or gathered on the street to see the tournament steed and I basked in the reflected glory. As we passed the monastery of San Marco, the abbot himself came from the garden to greet us. Giuliano leant from the saddle to kiss the ring on his proffered hand.

The abbot proclaimed his joy at seeing Giuliano so well, and remarked knowledgeably on the finer points of Orso, whom he looked forward to seeing at the blessing of the horses at the Cathedral. When the pleasantries were over, his voice took on a more serious tone as he told Giuliano that he had just had news from Rome: Raffaello Riario was to be elevated to cardinal. Giuliano was furious. Not only did it mean that yet another Riario was in high office, but Raffaello had become a cardinal at the age of fifteen, when His Holiness had said that, at twenty-three, Giuliano was too young.

'It was not your youth that concerned him,' said the abbot, 'but your popularity. It would not do for His Holiness to be outshone by one of his cardinals. Think yourself fortunate – the Vatican would be no place for you, my brave, honest young man.'

Giuliano accepted the abbot's condolences graciously but could not hide his anger.

'So,' said the abbot, 'as you are not destined for the Church, we must have you married, Giuliano.'

'You, too?' said Giuliano, wrinkling his nose in disgust. 'I thought I might have relied on you above all men to support chastity. Must even celibates promote marriage?'

'We think of little else. Enjoy your youth, Giuliano,' said the abbot with an indulgent smile.

'I intend to,' said Giuliano grimly.

As we walked on towards the practice ground, he voiced his concern at the growing power of the Riario family in Rome.

'The Pope could never have accepted you. Not only are you a Medici,' said Andrea Cavalcanti, 'but you are allied with the Orsini, known enemies of the Riario.'

Giuliano sighed. 'We cannot continue to let Rome and Florence drift apart; it is too dangerous. Lorenzo must overcome it somehow. No one can resist him when he wants to be charming, not even His Holiness.'

'There are some people around with their noses to the wind.'

'Who?'

'The Pazzi.'

'Oh, them.'

'Francesco wears the title of Treasurer to the Holy See too proudly. When Lorenzo was the Pope's banker, he never went about calling himself by any title.'

'The Pazzi have to compensate for their natural deficiencies, whereas Lorenzo has to play down what he naturally abounds in.'

Andrea laughed briefly but soon grew serious again. 'I hear that Jacopo di Poggio Bracciolini has gone to Rome in his search for a patron.'

'His commentary on Petrarch was execrable, but the Romans are not bright enough to realise that. I hope he finds his patron there.'

'He needs more than patronage; he needs a full-time position. He has lost his inheritance and is massively in debt.'

'Then it is fitting that he should live with swine.'

'Giuliano! You are growing arrogant!'

'Is it arrogance, honestly to admit to Florentine superiority?'

Andrea turned in his saddle and grinned at me. 'Do you ever wonder, Tommaso, why it is that Rome hates us?'

Reaching the practice ground near the city wall, we put Orso through his paces on the long rein. When Giuliano rode him round the field, I stood and watched as if witness to

Bellerophon's first ride on Pegasus. Pegasus, the winged horse, favourite of the Muses, famed by Minerva, given to Bellerophon to conquer the Chimaera: it was a fitting analogy.

Suddenly Giuliano turned Orso and rode him at the palisade used for jousting practice. Where many horses would have followed their instincts and jumped the fence, Orso reared up, as beautiful as a horse of Greek marble. It was the performance of a perfect jousting steed, under the control of a master.

Andrea cantered round the field on the palfrey he had chosen as his mount for the tournament procession and I tried the paces of the rouncy but Giuliano called me to the quintain, there to set up the bag of sand on the pivoting arm. Giuliano and Andrea collected practice lances and cantered off to the opposite ends of the field. I hurried out of the way.

The quintain, a swivelling black effigy of a Turk, stood in the middle of the field. Giuliano galloped towards it, tilting his lance. As it struck the target squarely in the centre, he went flat in the saddle. Orso lost not a step in his pace. The bag swung round and met only air. I ran out to steady its arms for Giuliano's return. He circled and thundered back. Chonk! The lance struck, the quintain spun, the bag flew, Giuliano ducked and again rode harmlessly out of range. Three times he performed the feat without mishap. Boys of the city who were gathering at the perimeter began to cheer excitedly. Giuliano fed on such applause but it unnerved both Andrea and his new mount. The squire decided not to try the quintain.

'So Tommaso, you try it,' Giuliano said. I looked at him aghast as he dismounted. 'Come on, up you go.'

'On Orso? No! Please, I cannot! The Count of Urbino said that no one but you were to ride him.'

'You are my equerry. Of course you can ride him.'

He linked his hands under my bent knee and propelled me up what seemed a vertiginous height. I smiled down foolishly from the saddle, wishing all those boys would be gone. This must be the day, I thought, when the fool is king.

Giuliano was giving me advice but I could barely pay attention. He handed me his helmet and explained that all I had to do was to keep my eye steady on the centre of the target and let nothing interfere with my concentration. All I could think of, however, was that I was wearing his helmet, and that it was a little too big for me. The next thing, he had struck Orso's flank and I was cantering then galloping and the Turk was looming and the helmet was wobbling. I would have done better to follow Andrea's example rather than Giuliano's. Do not entertain fear, Giuliano had said. Impossible! The unwieldy lance clipped the edge of the target, and that was the last thing I knew. When we returned along the Via Larga, I was slumped over the saddle of the rouncy like a sack of grain.

Angelo was delighted to hear of my fall from knighthood. It meant that he had me to himself again, but there was to be a ball on the eve of Epiphany and the house was full of bustling women giving everybody orders; there was no refuge; the chapel was no longer any escape; Mona Lucrezia had even taken away Angelo's key so that he could not lock himself in his study. So we worked all the hours of daylight in aid of the preparations. Having been kept all day from his Muse, by each evening Angelo was like an organ full of air, waiting only for the keys to be pressed for the music to sound. During those hours of the night, when the house was quiet, he composed his long poem for Giuliano, *La Giostra.*

Sometimes the work comprised of poring over Virgil or Petrarch for examples of phrasing. Angelo knew what he wanted to say, and if he could say it by way of an antique allusion, so much the better. To use the words of his idols was his form of worship. Those jealous of him seek out these passages and call it plagiarism. They are mistaken. When Angelo opened his mouth, it was not his voice that issued alone: all who had gone before in the ancient line of poets joined in chorus to sing a song in praise of the golden age of Man.

Sometimes the books were left closed on the desk, and Angelo would sit long and still with his eyes shut, listening to that song. His face became like a landscape where colours change as the clouds pass over the sun. One subtle expression followed another. Now there was a shadow of intensity, now the light of inspiration. I sat waiting with pen poised, ready to take the stanza down, and when it came then I believed in the Muse. She is not a deity who sprang from the imagination of pagans ignorant of the One God; she is a faculty of mind, available to all, but most readily available to those with the ears to hear. Angelo no more composed his poem than I did. He was the voice, I was the pen, some ineffable other was the composer.

The first stanzas dealt with Julio's hunt in the forest. Love awaited him there, to trap the hunter with the image of a haughty doe created out of light air. The doe had a lofty forehead, branching horns, and was white, light and slender. Julio pursued her until he came to a green meadow. There the doe, as one might expect, changed into a lovely nymph.

My own newly sensitised heart quickened its beat. As did Julio's. Cupid drew back his bow and loosed an arrow. It had not begun to hiss in the air before Julio felt it.

'Oh, how he changed! Oh, how the fire
coursed through the youth's very marrow!'

Angelo was dictating fast. My pen dashed out the words; one verse, two verses, three ...

'Pure white is she, and pure white her dress,
though embellished with roses, flowers and grass;
the ringlets of her golden head
fall on a brow humbly proud.
About her the whole forest smiles,
and, as it may, lightens his cares;
in her stance she is both regal and meek,
one glance from her could quell a tempest.'

When he had finished, I was as much spent by my emotion as by my labours. I rested my aching arms on the desk and buried my head in them. He patted me on the back.

'Have I worked you too hard?'

'I know who she is. I have seen her,' I said from within the privacy of my arms.

'Simonetta?'

'In Sandro's bottega.'

Angelo laughed softly. 'And you are in love? Then welcome to the Company of Lovers.'

'It is a large band.'

'It includes everyone except Giuliano. My Julio has been smitten, but not our Giuliano. How can he be, while he refuses to attend any event where she is present?'

'He cannot refuse to attend his own tourney.'

'No, he cannot. But we will have her before his eyes sooner than that. She will be coming to the ball.'

Simonetta was to attend the ball? Suddenly all our wearisome preparations seemed monstrously inadequate.

Dancing is a fine skill which, at that time, I had not. A Burgundian dancing master came regularly to the palazzo, but it was not for me, a servant of a servant, to ask to join the lessons. While Giuliano, Lorenzo, their squires, friends and ladies practised pavane in the sala, I slipped away to Sandro's workshop. Just the thought of going in the direction of Simonetta's home put wings on my heels. Filippino became my dancing master, took me through the intricacies of pavane and balli, and teased me mercilessly all the way.

Sandro was putting the finishing touches to the banner and it was under the aegis of Minerva that I stepped up and down the floor of the shop, hand in hand with Filippino to the music of apprentices who hummed in imitation of lutes and viols. I despaired. I, the master of the farandol, who could jump and thump better than any peasant on May Day, lacked grace, a virtue not easily had since it comes by grace itself.

Later, after we had collapsed in laughter on mattresses at the back of the shop, Filippino showed me some of his drawings. They were studies he had made of the Masaccio frescoes in the chapel of Santa Maria del Carmine. There was great talent in the drawings, but I only had half an eye to them; the other half was kept on the door, at which I hoped a certain vision might materialise again.

'What do you think of this one?' Filippino asked.

'Eh?'

'My study of Saint Peter?'

'Oh, beautiful.'

'Beautiful? That poor adjective has become enfeebled by too much use. Try "powerful". Eh? Powerful? Or "muscular", "masterly", or perhaps, "virile". Yes, virile is the word, if I were to describe my own work, which it seems I must. "Beautiful" is the word of merchants and commissioners and pea-brained patrons. *Bella*, they say, *bella, bella, bella*, like fish blowing bubbles. Surely you, the servant of the Muse, can find some better word?'

'*Bellissimo*,' I sighed. 'It is very beautiful.'

Filippino sniffed and put his work away. 'Thank you for your opinion, Tommaso. As I always say, if you want a fair and intelligent judgement, ask a scholar.'

'Oh, but I am no scholar.'

'And that was no intelligent judgement.'

'Why ask me then?' I snapped.

'Because I thought you were my friend. You come here so often, it must surely be out of friendship? I mean, our being next to the Palazzo Vespucci has nothing to do with it, does it?'

I jumped to my feet. 'If that is what you think ... '

'Sit down. I have no care as to why you come here, I am merely glad that you do.'

And there it was, that affability which made Filippino beloved by all. Contrite, I sat down again. He pulled my hair playfully.

'You look as if you have not slept for a week. Not lovesick are you?'

'Of course not. Angelo keeps me up late, working. And then when I do achieve my bed, I cannot sleep, because he cannot sleep. His mind will not rest. He keeps jumping up to make a note of what has just occurred to him, so we have a candle burning all night, to save having to keep lighting one. And then, if he does sleep, he has nightmares. Something about the final stanza. He screams out, "It is not finished!", but when I ask him what he dreamt of, he does not remember. He seems convinced that he is going to die before he finishes the poem.'

'It is a common fear among artists. I am always having to reassure Sandro about his health when he is in the middle of a work. When he is without work, and more likely to die – from starvation, say – then he has no concerns. There seems to be something in the very act of creation that brings thoughts of death, as if you cannot have one without the other. It happens to me when I am making love.'

'Perhaps you should stop.'

'What, being a normal, healthy man? Do you think it would be better to be like you, lovesick and moping?'

'I am not lovesick.'

'And Simonetta you do not love?'

At the sound of her name the blood rushed to my face and betrayed me. 'Yes, well, a little perhaps. A touch.'

'A touch in love, I thought so. Your heart has been slightly pierced with the merest graze of Cupid's arrow.'

'Pipo, you know about these things. Tell me what to do.'

'I know nothing about these things. Falling in love with a married woman? What should I know about that? All I know is that it is without hope. I will tell you what I know. I shall give you the benefit of my long experience: women are for three things only – making love, having babies and keeping house. Anything else is unnatural. If it is worship that you are interested in, go to church. Simonetta is just an ordinary woman.'

'She is the most beautiful creature in the world.'

'Oh yes, *bellissima*. But stop to think – what constitutes beauty?'

'It is ... perfection of form.'

'It is a pale, round forehead which peeps over her eyebrows like the moon above a cloud.' Filippino cradled his arms, puckered his lips and made popping noises on the face of the imaginary lady.

'It is proportion! Proportion of limb and harmony of feature. Eyes, nose and mouth relate to each other as words in a line of fine poetry.'

'It is blonde hair braided, plaited, looped, and woven, cascading from her head like a tangle of spaghetti.'

'It is clearly something you will never understand.'

'It is something that exists only in your dreams. She is only an ordinary woman.' He tapped me on the head to drive the point home. 'Her forehead is so white, so high, so round, so smooth. Why? Because she has plucked her natural hairline back two inches.'

'Liar!'

'They all do it. Do you think Florentine women were born half bald? They pull out their hair with tweezers. Pluck, pluck, pluck, with little tweezers. It makes my eyes water just to think about it. I would rather chop up onions.'

'You are lying!'

'And then her hair, that cascade of yellow tresses. Yellow? On a Tuscan girl?'

'She is from Genoa.'

'Oh, up in the north? Near Lombardy? Oh well, perhaps it is natural then.'

'Now you are going to tell me that her skin is so white because she puts china clay on it.'

'Ah, there you have me. So far as I can tell, her marble skin is her very own. But it is not natural, is it? I think she must be ill.'

'Oh, do not say so!'

I grew so wistful that Filippino prodded me. 'Are you dreaming of her death bed? Well, stop it. Take Maestro Filippino's advice and contemplate her the way nature made her: thick black hair turned rusty by the sun; eyebrows like laurel hedges, meeting in the middle; and a sallow skin flushed with good health. And then, when you have cured yourself of your desires, come with me to the nunnery at San Frediano Gate. For all your natural philosophy, you have unnatural desires. Let me introduce you to nature in all her glory.'

'Natural – to go with whores?'

'Not whores, nuns.'

'Natural?'

'Very natural.'

'Well, so is death natural, and I do not want that either.'

A call from Sandro allowed me this last word. I left Filippino before he could think of a response. Sandro's desk was covered in bills demanding payment for all manner of items: a year's supply of eggs and six ounces of ultramarine, fifteen sheets of gold leaf, two bracci lengths of blue taffeta and a barrel of apples. In amongst the bills were scraps of poetry, quotations, notes he had taken himself at sermons and lectures.

'Have you anything for me from Angelo?' he asked.

'Yes, this ... ' I drew from my jacket a folded paper enclosing two verses. Sandro was following *La Giostra* stanza by stanza as it emerged.

'Oh, this is good. Good. Better and better. What a tale, eh? – told of our own heroes.' He read the stanzas again and again, and the Muse of the Word began to draw in his mind. What images those verses created for Maestro Sandro Botticelli. What images ...

TWENTY FIVE

ON THE night of the ball, Angelo stayed late at his desk, consulting the works of ancient poets; being his loyal servant, I had to stay with him. I could hear the guests arriving downstairs, and the sounds of conversation and laughter rising from the sala. When the musicians began to play, my patience expired.

'Angelo, the dancing has begun.'

'What of it?'

'Will you not be attending?'

'All in good time.' He pointed to a book. 'Pass me the Virgil. Have you ever considered how short life is? Which is more important, that Angelo Poliziano goes dancing, or that he completes a stanza?'

'Why, the latter of course; but I would have thought that an evening spent dancing would prolong youth and vitality, and much improve your work on the morrow.'

Angelo grunted. 'Pass me the Virgil.'

His reluctance puzzled me. No one was more fond of music than he. After a convivial evening spent with friends and a pitcher of wine, he would be the first to suggest going out into the streets to wake up the city with a song.

'That you can concentrate while I am in such a state of agitation is a great sign of your intellectual prowess, Maestro,' I said.

He frowned at me darkly, then continued to look for a line he remembered in the *Georgics*. I sighed and drummed my fingers on the desk to the rhythm of the farandole which the musicians were playing; it was the one dance in which I was confident. Suddenly Angelo slammed his book shut. 'I cannot work with you hopping about like a cricket.'

I commiserated. 'Shall I leave you then?'
'If you must.'
'Will you not be coming to the ball yourself?'
'Not yet. I may join you later.'

I studied his face, to try and find what it was that he was avoiding, but he kept his eyes averted. I discovered the cause for myself, when I entered the sala dressed in blue hose and a fine pair of red velvet sleeves fastened to my pink doublet – items which had cost me a month's salary merely to rent for one night: it was shyness. It rose up round me like a befogging mist as I beheld the company, who were dressed so exquisitely that my own costume seemed rustic in comparison. All my excited anticipation became at once transmuted into shame and envy. I am not given to shyness; indeed, this was my first and perhaps only experience of it, and with the experience came full knowledge: the emotion is but a perverted sense of self-importance. For the truth was that no one was taking the slightest notice of me. Realising this, and accepting it, I stepped free of the mist.

It was clear that Poliziano, the ascendant star in the heavens of literature, would suffer this same sensation of nonentity, although not for his want of position or talent. He who was at the centre of Lorenzo's affection and utterly at ease with male companions would be nothing but an uncomfortable face to the splendid ladies here in the hall. He was not ugly; but there was a certain disharmony in his proportions that rendered him unattractive to others, at least to those who do not recognise that fine intelligence is a manifestation of the beauty of the soul. It suddenly struck me that Angelo, who could write so sweetly of loving, had probably no experience of being loved except in his imagination. Even his experience of loving was limited: I had once watched him pursue a maiden for weeks, standing dejectedly under her window even in the rain, only for his passion to collapse as soon as he discovered that she had as much understanding of grammar, even in the vernacular, as a horse. Where other men made their amorous choices on the swell of the breast, the nip of the waist or the slenderness of the wrist and ankle, Poliziano's ideal beauty had an ability to scan Latin poetry. Thus his experience of both loving and being loved was one of rejection. And the figures of his imagination were the company he preferred to keep, for, as I knew too well myself, in dreams there is no rejection.

The musicians, led by Baccio Ugolini, played in a consort of viols and lutes. At Giuliano's request they played a slow, flowing dance performed in lines of one dancer behind another. At certain intervals, when the music changed its rhythm, the dancers paused to mime aspects of love such as jealousy or mute adoration. Many of the dancers overacted, rolling their eyes and making clownish grimaces in the attempt to be a convincing nymph or shepherd, but when Giuliano struck a pose of disdain he sent a tremor of admiration through the company. I glanced around the hall to see if an artist was present, for this pose would have inspired anyone with a commission for a David. Walking in the slow procession, now rising on his toes, now descending to the flat of the foot, now bending his knees, now straightening, now alone, now with a lady on each hand, Giuliano moved so freely through the dance that a draught coming in through the windows seemed to be a cheerful zephyr heralding the spring.

I sighed, relinquished my dreams and let them float up with the smoke from the braziers. There was no point in anticipating a dance: I was here merely as a spectator. The musicians changed their instruments to strident shawms and thumping naker drums and began a lively anello. Now Lorenzo led the company, leaping with agility in the step which had so often sent me sprawling in the charcoal dust of Sandro's bottega. Lorenzo had but one challenger to his display of scissor skips and that was his brother. He fixed Giuliano with a fiercely competitive eye as they leapt high to clap their heels together in the air. Lorenzo leapt higher, but Giuliano had more grace. The dance ended in the brothers embracing in laughter, and Lorenzo proclaiming Giuliano the victor.

I wandered round the crowded edge of the dance floor, looking for someone to talk to. Angelo had appeared at last, dressed defiantly in his scholar's gown, and was in earnest conversation with one of his tutors from the university, the elderly Cristoforo Landino. As I approached I heard Angelo questioning his tutor on Dante's *De vulgari eloquentia*, a treatise on the use of the vernacular language in poetry. Landino, despite being the highest authority on the works of Dante, was not in the mood for being impressed by one of his students: he himself was dressed for dancing. 'Hmmm,' he said. 'Hmmmm. Hmmmm. Yes, well, your ideas are most interesting, and the study is obviously of great use to you, my boy, I can see that.' But Landino's gaze lay on a group of unpartnered ladies and his elegantly slippered foot tapped to the music.

Not being in the mood myself for an enthusiastic exposition on the use of the vernacular, I passed Angelo by and went to where the wine was being served. Simonetta's husband, Marco Vespucci, stood alone nibbling sugared almonds and watching the dancing with the happy smile of a man content with life. Simonetta was dancing the saltarello, a dance in which everyone was the companion of all and a partner to none. The swishing lines of dancers moved gently through the pattern, now meeting this person, now moving on to the next. The dance evoked the passage of life itself as a series of significant and insignificant encounters. Inevitably there came a moment when Giuliano met Simonetta. I watched them closely with breath abated. This must be his undoing, this contact with beauty, no matter how brief. But Giuliano kept his eyes lowered, as modest as a maiden. It was only as Simonetta moved on that he spared her a glance, and that was accompanied by a dark frown.

Marco Vespucci offered me some almonds. 'I am sorry,' he said. 'We have met before, but I cannot remember the circumstance.'

'It was in Botticelli's bottega.'

'Ah yes, the wonderful pennant. Are you one of those responsible?'

'No, no. I am only Poliziano's scribe.'

'Only? Fortunate man!'

The husband of Simonetta Vespucci envied me? I laughed at life's irony. 'Why are you not dancing?' I asked him.

'Gout,' he said. 'Besides, I cannot dance, not in these complicated patterns. It is all too esoteric for me. All this subtle geometry ... ' he waved an almond towards the dancers then popped it in his mouth. 'The symbolism is lost on anyone who is not suspended from the ceiling. I have never quite understood what it is all about. Ah, here is Cristoforo Landino. He can explain it better than I.'

With an avuncular smile, Landino was on the trail of a slender niece of Mona Lucrezia. He jumped when Marco Vespucci caught his arm and demanded to know the meaning of the dances. Landino said that they were a marvellous opportunity to meet the ladies.

'No, I mean the patterns they trace on the floor.'

'They engender virtue: nobility in a man and grace in a woman. The slow, stately steps of a pavana, for instance, demand the full, conscious control of one's limbs. The same as in a joust.'

'Yes, but the patterns ... '

'Oh, they are but simple geometry: circles, spirals, squares etcetera.' Landino bowed abruptly and left, but he was too late now to join the dance; the music was ending. Marco Vespucci was left unsatisfied by the explanation. 'These men from the Academy, they keep it all to themselves.'

'What?' I asked, abstracted by the idea of geometry and suddenly realising that the company had taken the form of a pentagram in a circle.

'Their secrets. I know well enough that these dances are significant, but they will not tell me what the significance is. My uncle Giorgio Antonio is a member, and he is as circumspect as the rest.'

We were joined by Marco's cousin, Piero Vespucci. 'Giuliano has been dancing with your wife,' he said bluntly, brushing me aside.

'Well, yes,' said Marco amiably. 'So has everyone else.'

'You are not concerned?'

'There is not a man in Florence I would trust more to have a brief dance with my Simonetta.'

'Oh, Marco ... ' said the other despairingly. 'Florence is awash with talk about your wife and Giuliano de' Medici, and you stand there eating sugared almonds.'

Marco's laughter only thinly disguised his irritation. 'Where do you pick up these horrible gobbets of scandal, cousin?' he said, steering Piero away to a table that, laden with plates of delicacies, was dominated by a hog's head with an apple in its mouth.

There was an interlude in the dancing during which various singers entertained the company, including Lorenzo and Luigi Pulci singing comic songs. Glancing out of one of the tall windows, I noticed Angelo and Giuliano in the garden below and left the hall to join them.

Angelo wanted to know why I was not dancing.

'Corns,' I said.

'Do you have them on your backside also? Is that why you could not keep still on your stool all day?'

'Sssh,' said Giuliano. 'Ladies ... '

I turned. The garden was lit by the stars and the torch light filling the windows above us. It was a cold night but, being hot from the dance, the cool air was agreeable. Four young women, uncovered by cloaks, appeared in the shadows; like shy nocturnal animals they stared at us inquisitively; or, rather, at one of us. Those doe eyes were all drawn in one direction. When Giuliano turned his back on them, they were encouraged to advance towards the fountain.

His voice loud in the still air, Giuliano resumed a conversation he had been having with Angelo about horses. 'Three years have I spent on his training, only to be told today that the gelding was badly done. He remains half a stallion: part docile, part wild, and I shall never be able to trust him. He is what they call a rig.'

'A rig?' I echoed, desperate to be included in the conversation, no matter how inappropriate it was. 'Which one?'

'A horse at our villa at Cafaggiolo. You will not be familiar with him.'

'I thought he looked a bit strong for a gelding,' said Angelo in a strained voice.

Four silent ladies were listening to our every word. Their attention made our speech seem ludicrous. By their presence what would have been an innocent conversation was now ripe with innuendo.

'But he is still a magnificent horse,' said Angelo, coughing.

'Yet of no use. If there was a mare in season on the other side of the hedge, he would be off and no holding him.'

'What are you going to do?' I piped. Then, fearing that the

answer might involve details of further castration, I instantly regretted the question. But the only thing that Giuliano intended to have cut was the horse's throat.

'I have no other choice,' he said sternly.

At the fountain there was a statue by Donatello of Judith quietly murdering Holofernes with just such a slice to the neck. The ladies, or rather – in those thin dresses revealing diaphanous chemises – the nymphs, stood by the stony maid. Every now and then one of them would flash a glance of provocative modesty towards Giuliano. A whisper from one brought forth breathy laughter from the others. I hardly dared look at them, but naturally curiosity found the courage, for at the centre of this tender knot of women was Simonetta. My knees began to tremble uncontrollably.

'God's mercy,' muttered Giuliano, straightening his back and lowering his chin in a magnificent display of scorn. 'Let us go back to the sala.'

Angelo was gazing at Simonetta with the pitiful eyes of a beaten dog. 'Do we have to? We are in no danger; they will not attack us. More is the pity.'

'Women never attack, they lure. They are sneaky hunters, predators of man's virtue. I have had too many on my tracks all evening, and that toothless wife of Francesco Sassetti keeps smiling at me.'

'What a trial it is to be winsome,' said Angelo, transparently unsympathetic. Although my teeth had begun to chatter, I did not want to go back to the dance either.

The windows of the sala were like a golden frieze around the twilight garden, and the distant sound of a girl's voice rising in song above the bowing of viols fell on us like soft rain. Across the golden frieze moved the black shadows of guests. Who was in the real world – those in the glowing sala or we outside in the dark? To be sure, it was not the same world. The whispering garden had become a mystic realm where four nymphs stood by the playing water of the fountain. Three stood as close as the Graces while one detached to step across the grass. She tried the ground with her foot, turned and began to dance alone to the music from the hall.

Simonetta danced alone.

You could almost hear the bones in Giuliano's resistant neck creak as a will greater than his own turned his head. I became so weak that I had to sit down on the plinth of a statue of Marsyas being flayed alive by Apollo. Someone groaned – it must have been Angelo. Both of us were having our dreams fulfilled; neither of us could move; the gods were animating another. As if driven by some supernatural agency, Giuliano went slowly forward and took Simonetta by the hand. Together – the silky sound of cloak and gown as audible as the music – they danced a pavana. It was the dance of heaven itself: Venus and Mars, conjoined in peace, had appeared amongst us.

The spell was broken by an earthly man. Piero Vespucci ran shouting into the garden, caught hold of Simonetta by the wrist and pulled her back towards the house, crying, 'Whore! Whore!'

Giuliano broke Piero's grasp with his own. 'How dare you offend her so?'

'My cousin is a Salome!'

'That is not true!' Giuliano thundered like Zeus in the face of the interfering man. Simonetta tried to run away but Giuliano held her gently as if she were a frightened pony. 'Stay, stay. You will hear your cousin's apology.'

Piero Vespucci looked far from apologising. I stepped forward, throwing my cape back as if clearing access to a dagger, though there was nothing at my hip but a purse, and an empty one at that. This fact was lost on Piero Vespucci in the dark: the gesture was sufficient. Vespucci glanced from Giuliano to me then back again. He snapped forward in a sharp little bow.

'I apologise, Mona Simonetta. I do not understand what has occurred here, but I accept that it was not what I thought. I was mistaken.'

Shivering in fright and with tears spilling from her eyes, Simonetta nodded dumbly.

'I shall tell you what has occurred here,' said Giuliano. 'The host of the joust has had one short dance with the Queen of Beauty. That is all. Do you understand? That is all.'

Vespucci nodded. 'I apologise. I acted in haste. I am sorry.'

He escorted the tearful Simonetta back to the hall.

Giuliano ran his fingers through his hair. 'That was too close a thing. If I had had my dagger ... '

'You would have killed him,' said Angelo simply.

'Only to be killed myself by my brother. The Vespucci are among our best friends and strongest ties. Oh ... ' Giuliano bent forward, breathing heavily, his hands braced against his knees. 'Yes, I would have killed him. And by whose fault? – Women! Now do you see', he asked, straightening up, 'what trouble they cause?'

'I cannot think what possessed him,' said Angelo, remaining convinced that the cause of the trouble lay with Vespucci.

'He is a reptile,' said Giuliano. 'I have always thought so.'

'Then take your revenge in the lists.'

Giuliano began to look cheerful again.

'If you did not kill Vespucci this evening,' said Angelo, 'it is because you wear no dagger. And all that Tommaso has at his belt is a flap of leather as empty as a witch's dug. These are peaceful times – the era of the vendetta and impulsive combat is over. A new age of chivalry dawns. With Lorenzo leading us, we have no further need of impetuous violence.' Angelo's voice was keen and edged with hope. Whatever was at the root of his passion for peace, whatever it was that had held him back when it seemed that we were on the edge of a fight, Giuliano understood. He threw his arm about his companion's shoulders and squeezed him, laughing.

'There will be no blades in the Golden Age then.'

'None. Nothing but the sharp sword of reason.'

'Go on, go back to the hall. And if a pupil may be allowed to advise his tutor, I suggest that you try dancing. You have been at your desk too long, Angelo. You need some exercise.'

'I also need a partner.'

'I shall stay down here for a while longer: that will release a few for you.'

Angelo looked at him curiously.

'I would like to be by myself,' Giuliano explained, 'if that is permitted in my own garden?'

Angelo glanced at me and his look was one of pure triumph. I think it was then I realised that Guiliano's suspicions of a philosophic conspiracy, in which Ficino, Lorenzo and Angelo were contriving to make him fall in love, had some ground in fact. And Guiliano's desire for solitude showed that the conspiracy was beginning to taste success.

'Of course,' he said politely to Giuliano, his expression now one of mock gravity. 'We will leave you to yourself.'

'Before you go, tell me the truth. Was all this pre-arranged?'

Angelo looked innocently bemused.

'You know my meaning: that under-dressed, over-confident Vespucci girl. Did you arrange for her to follow me out here? Or was it you, Tommaso?'

We both protested. 'There is only one who could have arranged such a thing,' said Angelo smugly.

'And who is that?'

'The goddess Venus.'

'Venus!' sneered Giuliano. 'Her wretched son more like. If ever I catch that flighty child, I shall pierce him full of his own arrows.'

'By the look of you, I would say he has none left. You resemble a hedgehog.'

'Or Saint Sebastian,' I said.

Even thirty years later, remembrance of that mindless joke causes me searing pain.

TWENTY SIX

IN FRONT of Santa Croce, the church where the famous men of Florence lie entombed, is a long piazza. Some learned men discern in its shape the place of an ancient Roman arena and say that it has always been a site for circuses. It was to this piazza, the site of the joust, that trundling carts bearing Tuscan soil came with a ceremonious air.

As the preparations, both in the city and in the Palazzo Medici, came to their height, Giuliano, the focus of all attention, spent as much time as he could out on the practice ground.

The aspiring philosopher in me waned, the lad of sixteen waxed, and I was more often in the stables than at my desk. There was plenty of work at both locations. In the stables all the rouncys and palfreys which would be used by Giuliano's escort had to be groomed daily, while Orso was to be fed by my hand and no other's. At my desk there were invitations to be written, stanzas of *La Giostra* to be copied, six times each, and all this on top of the usual task of copying any letter which Lorenzo wished to be circulated. One such, a letter to Lorenzo from Marsilio Ficino, I paused to read. It ended thus:

'Allow me at least to entreat you to give thanks to Almighty God, that in our times he decided to unite, in a citizen of ample fortune, a modest disposition with an illustrious mind. In a young man as a private citizen, he combined prudence with power; in a man of power, restraint with freedom; in a man of affairs, wisdom with eloquence. Great qualities are in you, Lorenzo, without doubt. Lest anyone suspect the vice of flattery, which should be quite alien to a man who is both philosopher and dear friend, I say these great qualities are in you, but do not originate from you. For such wonders are the work of omnipotent God alone. Excellent man, you are the instrument of God, fitted to perform great deeds.'

I had read many of the works of Ficino and considered them words of Truth, but I despaired of his estimation of Lorenzo's character. Flattery indeed. Who was he, this elusive person, so ubiquitous and yet never to be seen? History may record that the prime citizen of Florence in our time was Lorenzo; in truth it was Ficino, the hidden philosopher. The mystery of his reputation transformed my simple desire to meet him into an obsession.

In the time before the joust, Angelo was visiting Ficino at his house in the city nearly every evening. Each completed stanza of *La Giostra* was recited to Ficino before anyone else, even Lorenzo. One evening, I determined that I would accompany my master.

'Did you hear about the butcher who was murdered by a robber with one of his own cleavers? – slit from neck to navel, he was, and strung up from a hook like dead meat.'

'What of it?' said Angelo indifferently.

'It happened near Santa Maria Nuova. Is that not where Ficino lives – near Santa Maria Nuova? If you must go into that district, I insist on escorting you for your safety.'

'There is nothing in me to attract a thief; and nothing in you to repel one.'

There was a rap on the door and I went to usher in the barber. Angelo sat down and had a linen towel tucked round his neck while the barber's assistant emptied a pitcher of steaming water into the basin. I stood by, holding the looking glass, and continuing to plead.

'Please let me come. I have never met Father Marsilio.'

'What are you talking about? You must have done. Why, he is here at least twice a week. If you did not make a point of avoiding our gatherings, for fear of coming too near Lorenzo, then you would know Ficino as well as the rest of us.'

I had seen many of the visitors who dined informally with Lorenzo in his chambers. The arrival of these middle-aged men in the gowns of professors and doctors was usually my opportunity for a visit to Sandro's workshop. Indeed, they provided me with my only chance of leisure. Of course I had studied them, and had decided that Ficino was not amongst them. For not one of these men, be he tall, stooping and grey haired, or short and fair with a face like a walnut, conformed to how I thought the philosopher must look. Though I had once been taken unawares by the arrival of a bishop, I still expected fanfares to herald the visit of one so important.

'What does he look like?' I demanded, but Angelo was under the barber's razor and as he went to speak, the barber caught him by the nose to shave his upper lip. I took advantage of the situation.

'So I can come tonight? Please?'

Angelo glared at me and a negative answer was obvious from his expression.

'*Grazie*!' I said. 'I knew you would say yes. Oh, excellent man, you are so good to me.'

Angelo disappeared under the barber's towels and his reply was muffled and inaudible. I inspected my own face and the silky, squirrel-coloured hairs that grew where other men had beards. When the barber had finished, I handed Angelo the looking glass. He searched for cuts. When he found one, he winced in pain.

Seeing that blood had been drawn, I suggested that the barber be dealt with in the dungeons. Angelo agreed.

'You overwhelm me with your praise,' said the barber gruffly as he packed to leave.

When I had shown him out, Angelo put some salve on his cut and said, 'You are not coming with me tonight. You have not been invited. It is a meeting for a select few and, if the number were to be extended by one, there are dozens more worthy than you to vie for the place. You can meet Ficino another time.'

'How, if I am so insignificant?' I snapped. I went out and slammed the door behind me. My petulance was only feigned: I stood outside, biting my thumbnail and scheming. As soon as an idea occurred, I ran off to put it into action. My goal was the guardaroba downstairs where outdoor clothes were stored.

I handed Angelo his fur-lined cloak, the crimson lucco awarded to him when he was made a citizen of Florence (an accolade of which he was inordinately proud); he wanted to know where his cap was. I told him that he was already wearing it.

'Not this one, turnip, my best one!'

'How should I know, feeble worm that I am? Ahi ... ' I cried as he pinched my ear.

He made me search the guardaroba and I crawled through the small chamber on my hands and knees, calling out from within that the cap was not to be found and was more likely to be in the cassone in his room.

'But it will be crushed!'

Stifled by the smell of camphor, I backed out quickly and said that I would search the nursery, for the day before the children had been dressing up in any clothes they could find.

I ran up the stairs, along the gallery, turned two corners, then stopped to laugh out loud. At that moment, Matteo Franco emerged from the library bearing a ledger. He asked if all was well, for laughing alone is often a sign of lunacy. Matteo being the master of the practical joke, I confided my plan to him. He thought I was playing dangerously; deciding that he ought to supervise this jest, he went to find Angelo. I followed, keeping out of sight.

Coming to our room, Matteo discovered Angelo pulling everything out of the cassone in an ill temper. He told him that he would be late if he did not leave at once, that it was better to arrive naked than not at all.

Luigi Pulci came out from his own room to see what was happening. 'Ah ha!' he said. 'To Ficino's, eh? Off to the God of the Crickets. Chirrup-chirrup-chirrup. What is the theme tonight then? The immortality of the soul? Well, pray commend me to him and tell him that, by the power of logic, I have made an important discovery. It runs like this: all material things are transient; only the immaterial is eternal; the immaterial is that which does not exist; therefore if the soul is immortal it does not exist. Tell him that. I would be glad to have his response.'

'Luigi ... ' warned Matteo.

'Raise your chamber pots! A toast to Plato!'

Angelo brushed past Luigi as if he was not there, although the clash of colour between his scarlet lucco and the crimson of his battered, old, everyday cap somewhat devalued the snub he was making.

'Oh, see how he runs, the man in search of truth!' cried Luigi.

'Will he find it tonight, he who cannot even find his cap?'

I felt sincerely sorry for what I had done; I had not wished for Angelo's humiliation at the tongue of Luigi Pulci. Nevertheless, I did not wish it undone. I came out from behind the door of the opposite chamber. My sudden appearance made Luigi start and he jumped up on a chair in the gallery. 'A nasty little mouse coming out of the walls!' Pulling a face at him as I passed, I ran after Angelo, collecting his cap from where I had hidden it in the chapel. I followed him through the city towards Santa Maria Nuova then, when I thought he must be nearing the end of his journey, I sped up to him breathlessly waving the cap, saying that I had found it on the bust of Homer on the top floor. 'Someone has been playing tricks on you.'

Relieved, he took his red cap off. I placed the black one on his head, making a fuss of setting it right while I artlessly enquired which house was Ficino's. Angelo pointed it out and, thanking me and telling me that I was a good servant, said that I could have the evening to myself. 'I think you will find Filippino on his own tonight.'

'Nevertheless, I shall come with you as far as the door,' I said, leading the way. 'Slit from neck to navel and disembowelled he was, hung upside down from a hook. All his insides had gone. What kind of thief steals a man's guts? And for what reason?'

Angelo thought that it was probably one of my artist friends wanting anatomical reference for his studies.

Ficino's house was tall, narrow and pressed between two grand palazzi; its only distinguishing feature was the wealth of light pouring from its windows: Ficino was obviously not a man to stint in the use of candles. Angelo went to knock on the door, but I insisted on performing this service for him.

'You are making me angry again ... '

'What are you trying to hide?'

'Nothing. What do you mean? Tommaso, be off with you!'

In answer to my knocking, footsteps approached on the far side of the door. It was opened by a young man whose face was thrown into shadow by the light behind him, which made a halo out of his curly chestnut hair. But one could sense if not see the smile of welcome, and hear it in his voice.

'Good evening, Sebastiano,' said Angelo, pushing past me

to enter. I hopped on the threshold like a sparrow. Sebastiano, not being one to close a door in a fellow's face, looked questioningly at Angelo.

'My scribe,' Angelo explained, introducing me reluctantly.

'Come in, be welcome,' said Sebastiano.

With a great show of gratitude, I entered.

'This,' said Angelo to me, 'is Marsilio's cousin. Now he is a true scribe, honest and obedient – unlike some of your profession.'

I looked about curiously. Except in church at Easter, I had never seen so many candles alight at once. Sebastiano led the way up the stairs of the quiet house, ushered us into the study, then left to tell Father Marsilio that Angelo had arrived. Angelo cuffed me wordlessly but painfully on the ear then went to browse among the books. He was obviously at home here. Rubbing my ear, I was swept by a wave of self-consciousness and suddenly alarmed at the prospect of meeting Ficino.

A great fire blazed in the hearth. The room, spartanly furnished, was so well lit that hardly a shadow was present anywhere. It was the place of repose and study for a man of very refined taste. In one corner, on a marble-topped bench, stood a sturdy mortar and pestle. On a shelf above was a row of majolica apothecary jars labelled with the names of common flowers and wayside herbs. An inscription on the wall quoted Hippocrates below a beautifully drawn pentacle, which had a Greek letter at each point of its star. The word it spelt was *hygeia,* 'health'.

Other geometric figures decorated the room: on one shelf were marble carvings of the pyramid, the cube, the tetrahedron and other Pythagorean solids. In a niche, a marble bust of Plato, similar to ones I had seen both at Francesco Bandini's house and in Lorenzo's library.

During what seemed a long wait, I grew more courageous and ventured towards the centre of the room, to a desk and the scene of an abandoned activity. The desk was strewn with charts, tables and almanacs, the ephemerides of an astrologer. I pondered the chart on which were drawn the twelve zodiacal houses of the heavens. Allotted to the houses were the planets in their positions at noon on the twenty-eighth of January: the day of the joust. Hearing someone approaching, I leapt guiltily away. The door opened. Sebastiano looked in, beckoned to Angelo and told him that he was to meet Ficino upstairs.

I was left to see myself out, which I did with a heavy heart. I stood outside the house, looking up at the windows. I had so filled my head with the details of the recent murder on the Via San Rocco that I started violently when a hand touched my shoulder.

'Are you coming to the meeting?' asked Sandro Botticelli.

I shook my head and told him that I was not sufficiently worthy.

He frowned, not understanding me. 'Angelo is already inside,' I said.

'You do not want to wait out here in the cold. We shall be hours.' He suggested I went to his house to keep Filippino company.

I walked – or, rather, ran like a frightened hare – from the district of Santa Maria Nuova to the Palazzo Medici. For once I did not want Filippino's company. There was a weight on my mind that needed easing. I went to the stable, booked out one of the horses in my name and rode off to Impruneta.

TWENTY SEVEN

THE BISHOP was asleep in bed when I was announced; by the time I reached his room he was sitting in his chair by the fire, claiming that he had been sleepless anyway.

'The Academy,' I said, coming straight to the point. 'I want to know why it is that I am not good enough for it. I must be in want of something. What is it? Wealth? Wit? Intelligence? What is it?'

The Bishop laughed. 'Has it occurred to you that it might be years that you lack? The Academy is a weighty affair, and not the place for young lads with a taste for the life of the piazza.'

'Lorenzo has been a member since the day he was born.'

'That is not true. But he has been a member since the Academy was founded. And that rare exception was to a good end, for in Lorenzo we hope for the philosopher king.'

I stirred the logs in the fire.

'The Academy requires the practice of virtue by its members,' the Bishop continued. 'One of the virtues is patience. The more you hammer on the door, Tommaso, the less likely you are to be admitted. Besides,' he added, 'you are knocking on the wrong doors.'

Thinking how impatient Lorenzo had been with regard to Volterra, and not taking in this last remark, I said peevishly, 'Then how may one enter?'

'By invitation. But Tommaso, if you persist with this closed heart against Lorenzo, it will never come.'

'What has that to do with it? Lorenzo's own heart is closed against Ficino.'

'What makes you say so?'

'It was obvious at the Symposium, and there have been other signs since. Ficino writes letters of fulsome praise to Lorenzo, and surely you do not have to flatter someone you are certain of? Clearly their relationship is strained.'

'No more than the relationship of any father with his son. Lorenzo is under Ficino's discipline; sometimes that conflicts with his desires, and then he wishes Ficino dead, but those are the times of passion. When he is obedient to the laws which Ficino expounds, Lorenzo finds himself on the golden path to God, and then he would dwell in the light of virtue for ever. This proves nothing but that Lorenzo is a man subject to the same forces which beset us all. But, being set higher than the rest of us, his roars and his laughter carry further, that is all. Now, shall we forget Lorenzo de' Medici and talk about you?'

I withdrew five paces within myself.

The Bishop leaned forward. 'You have come to the gateway, my son. But it is a gate with no handle, no catch, no knocker; a very subtle gate, and you have to go through it. Look how fate has brought you to this point, look how you have come into the company of men who are on the path. Everything is in support of your passage towards the light. God himself desires it. The only barrier is one that you have erected yourself. Open up that heart of yours and join with life.'

'What do you mean?' I cried. 'Is desire for truth not enough? And if I lack virtue, that does not mean I am bad!'

'But are you good? Tell me the truth – do you not wish Lorenzo dead?'

'No!'

'Do you wish him then to live, to flourish and be happy?'

'No ... '

My answer was left to hang in the air. I bit my lip in silence, then mumbled, 'I thought we were to forget Lorenzo for now. Why are he and the Academy one and the same? Why if I would have one must I accept the other?'

'I told you: the gate is subtle. For each man it has a different appearance. For you it has the shape and form of Lorenzo de' Medici: he is your gateway.'

I jumped to my feet. 'Then perhaps I do not want to join the Academy after all. What is it, anyway?'

'I do not answer questions spat out in petulance.'

'Then I had best leave.' I walked away and, reaching the

door, turned to shoot him a malevolent glance; to my mortification, however, I saw that his eyes were filling with tears. This was worse than anything he could have said. And suddenly, for a moment, I saw myself through those tearfilled eyes. I saw all his hopes in me crushed. I ran to him, threw myself down and bowed my head before his knees, begging his forgiveness. He stroked my hair while I cried.

'It is as if I am two people,' I managed to say at last. 'One moment I am doing everything as I should: my work, my studies, my duties. The next, I am ... '

'Well?'

'Being wilful, I suppose. Sometimes you would not know it to look at me. I might still be doing my work, but inside, all has changed. I am looking at everyone critically and refusing to honour them. And yes, then I shall be out on the piazza at the next opportunity.'

'With Filippino Lippi?'

'Yes.'

'Getting drunk?'

'Sometimes.'

'Gambling?'

'No. It bores me.'

'And women, what about them?'

'I ... well ... No.'

'You are not interested?'

'Oh, yes, um ... yes, I am. It is not that I am not interested. But something holds me back.'

'That something is your armour. Attend to it always, keep it bright. Some men, most men, do not understand what it is. They see it in themselves, they say it is a moral teaching that they have been inculcated with, which is preventing them from enjoying life. They break it down; and thus they lose their only protection from the devil. But if you have that intact, Tommaso, then all will be well. You will be a knight of God.'

I looked him in the eye. 'Please tell me something, Monsignore, I need something explained.'

'What is it?'

'Chivalry, and Courtly Love.'

He asked me if I had read Dante and I confessed to having

only read the *Divine Comedy* and, of that, only the Inferno.

The Bishop smiled. 'Oh yes, the exciting part. Well, proceed to Purgatorio, and then Paradiso. They are not so interesting, I am afraid. The fate of souls in torment is a much more stirring tale than the account of souls ascending to God. But if you do read on, then you will understand Courtly Love.'

'Can you tell me a little now?'

'Dante Alighieri lived about a hundred years ago. He was banished from Florence during the wars of the Whites and the Blacks, two factions of the Guelf party. What an age that was, my son, when houses were embattled, when neighbours fought and murdered each other, when men were banished into exile for merely supporting the wrong party. It lasted right up to our own times; only when Cosimo de' Medici took power did the city begin to settle to its rightful business. But I digress. Where was I? Dante ... Well, he fell in love with a young lady called Beatrice. Love is perhaps the most powerful force we have to contend with. It can and does rob a man of his wits, his will, his happiness, and cause him to languish. Most of us suffer it once or twice, some of us repeatedly. To lose control of your heart is the most wonderful feeling, or so it seems at the time. But Dante was not like other men. When he first met Beatrice, she was a maid too young for marrying and therefore beyond his reach. Then, as soon as she was of age, she was betrothed to another, which put her further from the silent Dante. In such circumstances, a man has three options: one, abduction of the beloved; two, retreat into miserable dreams and fruitless longings; three, to find another object of his love. Dante chose none of these. Instead he followed the code of Chivalry and worshipped his lady from a distance. Then the early death of Beatrice put her beyond his reach for ever. But Dante did not forget her; no, he transmuted his simple love into pure adoration, the kind which requires no return, and in so doing he began the journey of the soul. Poetry provided his guide, in the figure of Virgil, through hell and purgatory. At the summit of Mount Purgatorio, he met Beatrice, who led him to the final stage in Paradiso, where he beheld Our Blessed Virgin Lady herself. So the result of Dante's love was the finest poem in our language, and a close and sure allegory of the path that some of us would follow.'

'So Courtly Love and Platonic Love ... '

'Are one and the same. Or rather, one leads to the other. If you come to Plato at my age, then there is no need for the preliminary stage: the passions are already quiet. But for you, young man, well, those passions require transmutation.'

'Giuliano's joust – it is no ordinary tourney, is it?'

'Giuliano, too, needs transformation.'

'Now this is what I do not understand. You see, Giuliano does not suffer passions. He has no infatuation for any woman but has dedicated himself to the pursuit of virtue.'

The Bishop turned the ring on his finger thoughtfully. 'It is difficult to explain, but the trial of fire is overcome not by avoiding it but by passing through it. There is no way of attaining to Divine Love without first knowing human love. Therefore Giuliano must go through the fire; there is no other way. As it is, what he supposes to be philosophic detachment is, to the rest of us, merely a cold heart in danger of freezing. If Giuliano would succeed in his noble quest, then first his heart must melt.'

'There is no one who could remain cold in the face of Simonetta Vespucci, not even Giuliano.'

The Bishop smiled. 'So you approve of our choice?'

'Oh, I do, and the plan is working. Giuliano became her captive on the night of the ball, though he is denying it of course – so hotly that no one dares contradict him. But he goes out riding every day as if he would sweat out his emotions.'

'Yes, I had heard it was so.' The Bishop chuckled suddenly and rubbed his hands by the fire. 'I am looking forward to this joust.'

TWENTY EIGHT

It was the time when dawn approaches
and the air which was dark becomes misty;
when Icarus inclines his chariot of stars,
and the moon seems to turn pale:
then the Dreams reveal to fair Julio
heaven's destiny, and his sweet fortune;
sweet at the beginning, at the end too bitter,
for lasting sweetness in this world is rare.

LORENZO came into the stables – large, looming, filling the place – and ordered me to saddle his horse. It was the imperious order of a man of power delivered to one who was impotent, a barked command of an emperor to a eunuch. When he departed I was left alone and vengeful. I do not know where I found the thorn – items in a dream need no provenance – but a thorn I had and I put it under the place where the saddle meets the stirrup. I led the horse from its stall to the courtyard and the mounting block. But it was Giuliano who came to mount, not Lorenzo. I tried to speak but the words became a slow, extenuated river of meaningless sound; tried to move but was pinned down by a malignant force; I struggled against the evil that was now bearing down like heavy fog but all my shouts were interior. Until, suddenly – No!

The horse reared. The hooves of the Devil's stallion pounded the air. I saw Giuliano falling to the ground; heard the crack of his head against stone; found him lying motionless in a pool of blood.

The dark chamber seemed an unfamiliar place. For a moment, as I lay with my heart thumping, a larger sense of reality remained with the nightmare, then I dismissed it gratefully.

'Madonna, what a dream!' I said, but there was no reply. Seeing that Angelo's bed was empty, I remembered that he was spending the night with Giuliano at the Cathedral, where the knights of the tourney were keeping vigil. It was the day of the joust.

I leapt from my bed and dressed quickly. It was still dark, but the rim of the sun was trembling just below the horizon; as I ran through the streets towards Sandro's workshop, the sky began to pale in a wash of turquoise. The air had been reborn in the night and, hours earlier than usual, there were people other than market-traders abroad. Citizens of Florence, looking as childlike as their sons and daughters, were making their way to the Piazza Santa Croce to find the best places on the stands.

The city had become a theatre in which everyone had a part to play. Sandro's workshop, boisterous as if it were midday, was filled with a crowd of local men. Mustered to help attach the pennant to the carrier poles, each one of them knew better than the rest how the job should be done. Filippino, his usually giant confidence now colossal, shouted them down. He thundered out orders like a chief mason, and men twice his age were cowed into obedience.

'It is like watching Brunelleschi raise the dome on the Cathedral,' said Sandro approvingly, though he kept well back in the shop. I retreated to join him; as the last rope was attached, however, Filippino commanded me to lend a hand. The capricious journeyman had indeed transformed into a tyrant.

'Imagine what he will be like when he is the master of his own bottega,' said Sandro, enjoying the irony.

We carried the pennant outside and raised it. I craned my neck to see the image of Minerva but was promptly reprimanded by Filippino. Whether the pole carrier or those merely holding stabilising ropes – we each had to pay full attention to what we were doing. As we struggled in our efforts, officials of the tournament arrived, dressed in armour and bearing long white staves. Lorenzo was with them.

Lorenzo the banker, Lorenzo the poet, Lorenzo the brother, Lorenzo the husband and father: each man was different. When

Lorenzo the patron gazed upon art, his face took on an aspect of humility mixed with longing. The man who stood looking up at Minerva was a man who stood at the foot of something greater than himself.

This was my moment. If what the Bishop had said was true, that Lorenzo was my gateway to philosophy, then it was a truth too repulsive for me to find acceptable. What he meant was that I had to learn to love Lorenzo, but, perverted by ignorance, I chose instead to understand that I had to win Lorenzo's affection.

'Is it not wonderful?' I said, approaching him boldly for the first time. 'Truly, a masterpiece!' I continued, pouring oil on oil. My words were so unctuous that I despised myself, while Lorenzo's glance of pure disdain confirmed my self-opinion. Without bothering to reply, he turned to speak to Sandro.

'This is a masterpiece,' he said to the painter, and his words held conviction. 'It is beyond my expectations – and I expected much.'

'I have only painted what others have seen. Between them, Poliziano and Ficino had this vision. I merely held the brush.'

Satisfied to hear his friends praised, Lorenzo ducked his head to enter the shop. He spent some time looking at various studies and half-completed paintings, making intelligent comments. He spoke fondly to Filippino. Neither apprentice nor tyrant now, Filippino met his gaze with that open sense of equality that is purely republican. Lorenzo seemed to appreciate it. Tasting as I was the bitter wormwood of petulance, I wandered out of the shop to stand in a dark cloud of my own gathering. As Lorenzo left, he beckoned to me and said, indifferently, 'At my brother's request you have been allocated a place in our stand at the joust.'

It was obvious that this offer was being made contrary to his own will. I asked if Filippino could come too and was told he could not.

'Then I thank you for your offer but must decline,' I said stiffly. I wanted that place in the stand more than anything, but I could not leave my friend behind.

'As you wish,' said Lorenzo, already thinking about something else.

Sandro had been given a seat of honour, along with Andrea del Verrocchio. Filippino and I had planned to go with some friends, to shin up poles, façades, anything to give us the best vantage point. Having overheard my exchange with Lorenzo, Filippino joined us and said, 'I have been meaning to tell you, Tommaso, but I did not know how to: I have been given a place next to Sandro. Have I not, Maestro?' He shot a glance at Sandro, who was standing at the door.

'What?' said Sandro, puzzled, then, 'Oh, yes. Yes, you have.'

They were lying, of course.

'So you will be joining us, then?' Lorenzo asked me.

I nodded in dumb agreement and looked at Filippino keenly. By his lies, he was forcing me to accept the thing I wanted most. The generosity of his heart was so limitless that any sin he committed, be it a simple lie or one of his more daring fornications, was expunged in the moment, like a drop of water hitting fire.

In the matter of the heart, I believe this lawless painter taught me more than any other Florentine.

The morning was a time of fractured pageantry. Amongst the ordinary and everyday elements of the city, armoured knights and ladies with trailing dresses and long, jagged sleeves, wandered like figments from an old romance. At the Cathedral there was a blessing of the horses. One by one the beasts were led down the nave, their hooves clopping strangely on the marble floor. The slippery nature of the ground made them restive, as did the smoky incense and the holy water sprayed over them with a brush by an acolyte. Only we privileged few with reserved seats had the leisure to enjoy the service in the Cathedral; everyone else spent the hour trying to push their way into the Piazza Santa Croce.

Just before the procession of knights began, we formed our own procession as family and household of the Medici. We crossed the piazza in a stately line to be met with a great cheer from the crowd. Lorenzo, at the head with his wife Clarice, smiled broadly and waved. Mona Clarice, seeming abstracted and miserable, walked with her head down, leaving it to Mona Lucrezia to be the lady of the family. Lucrezia graced the crowds with her rare and magnificent smile. If anyone on that day believed that the Medici were not popular, then that belief was a dogma held fast against all the evidence to the contrary.

But there were a few in that crowd who were so bigoted. They were all there that day, every one of them.

Feeling self-conscious in the midst of the cheering for my patron, I walked close to Luigi Pulci; in a splendid feint of indifference, he was staring up at the sky. That it was a summer's sky was only belied by the fierce pinch of the January air. A gold, pendant sun hung on a ground of sapphire. 'It looks like snow,' said Luigi.

'Snow?' gasped Matteo Franco, in front of us with Angelo. 'You are having trouble with your eyes. Cataracts. Shadows on the retinae. Here, lean on me, blind man.' He held out his arm.

'I would rather go to hell.'

'Where do you think Matteo's bound for, if not hell?' said Angelo.

We came to a sudden halt as Lorenzo stooped to finger the soil which had been brought in from the countryside to be laid on the piazza. More than a convenience for horses's hooves, the layer of earth symbolised the relationship between town and country, burgher and peasant, showing that nothing but paving differentiated one from the other, and when that paving is covered, then even that separation ceases to exist. The peasants had come in from the countryside, the artisans of Florence had laid aside the tools of their trades. As Lorenzo signalled his approval of the soil, up went the cheer, *'Palle! Palle! Palle!'*

I glanced about, trying to catch sight of Filippino. He was easily found: he and other apprentices from the Guild of Saint Luke were at the Judges' Stand, demanding to be allowed to sit on its roof. I brought the scene to Angelo's notice; when we arrived at our seats, he mentioned the matter to Lorenzo. A page was immediately dispatched to instruct the judges to allow the pupils of Sandro Botticelli a place on their roof. 'And the pupils of Andrea del Verrocchio also,' Lorenzo added, in the cause of fairness. The page ran across and delivered his message. It created a new argument. The boy ran back.

'Magnifico, Filippino Lippi refuses to share his vantage point with Leonardo da Vinci.'

'Then send Leonardo to join us here,' said Lorenzo evenly.

Poor Filippino – even at this distance I could see his reaction. Leonardo came, just to spite him, but when he arrived he asked Lorenzo for permission to enter the pavilion enclave where he would have the best view of all; the best view, that is, of the horses. Lorenzo was surprised but agreed and Leonardo was escorted to the place where, as a rule, no one but the contestants and their squires could go.

I saw the results once – pages and pages of notebook with exquisite studies of parts of a horse. One would think that that was all Leonardo saw of the tournament of 1475: parts of a horse. But within any one of his details lay whole worlds. While Botticelli, in his seat of honour near the Queen of Beauty, basked in praise that day, his companion, Andrea del Verrocchio, was long-faced. Even the praise engendered by the helmet and the chariot he had designed did little to douse his growing fears. Masters of guilds do all that they can to deter election of new masters, and some artisans can remain journeymen for their entire lives. But if a master has a journeyman who outshines him, nothing will stop him being plunged into shadow. Verrocchio was fully aware that the sun of his fame was becoming rapidly eclipsed by his journeyman, Leonardo da Vinci.

The Medici family and their retinue settled themselves in their covered stand. Among their guests was the newly appointed Archbishop of Florence, Rinaldo Orsini, brother of Mona Clarice and a living trophy of Lorenzo's recent victory over the Pope. Other guests included men who had contested in Lorenzo's own tournament held six years previously to celebrate his wedding; men such as Lorenzo's brother-in-law Guglielmo de' Pazzi, Jacopo Bracciolini and, to my astonishment, Francesco de' Pazzi. With his whitish-yellow hair so carefully arranged that he looked ridiculous, the man who had publicly proclaimed that he would always live in Rome while the Medici held Florence, sat beside Lorenzo like an old friend. Oh Janus-faced Florentines, one side open, one side closed! Who can ever know their hearts?

To Lorenzo it was nothing but a game of chess. He moved his knightly way across the board, now blocking the diagonal paths of bishops, now meeting rooks in the form of the battlemented fortresses being erected by Girolamo Riario. It was a game of tactic and strategy, and he held no personal animosity for the other pieces on the board. Such an event as this joust provided him with the opportunity to show his essential desire for peace with the bishop, the rook, and the Holy Father.

Other members of the Pazzi family thronged in a first-floor balcony facing our stand across the square. I scanned their faces, looking for a little girl, but of course she had grown. Elena I found at last in the stand next to that of the judges, where the noble young ladies of Florence gathered to inspire the champions of the joust. One glance at her was enough to feel acutely the lowness of my own position. I might be in the Medici stand, but the only men worthy of a lady's note that day were on horseback.

With a sigh, I turned my attention to the far end of the piazza, where the particoloured pavilions of the contestants billowed and snapped in the wind. The horses at the lines were given a final grooming before being armoured and draped with the brilliant livery of the great families of Italy. The clink of harness, the commands shouted by earnest squires, the cymballic crash of dropped armour plates, the whinnies, snickers and snorting of the horses: all held the undivided attention of the children in the square. I leant on the edge of the box and longed with all the passion of a seven year old to be the squire of Giuliano de' Medici, an honour which Renzo and Andrea Cavalcanti were sharing between them. Even to be a squire you need to be wealthy.

Suddenly from a street behind the piazza came the sound of drums. The crowd fell quiet. Now I was a seven year old who would give his soul to be a drummer. Just hearing the weaving rhythms of sticks on taut skin was to imagine clearly those fine young men slowly marching towards the square. And when the sight itself appeared, it matched the imagination exactly. As proud as peacocks the glorious youths with their treasured drums, now raising their arms in dramatic pauses, now rapping a martial beat, stepped into the arena. Shouts quickly built into a roar of excitement as the crowd pushed forward, crushing the barriers. Men-at-arms and stewards moved out across the square to thrust people back. Flags were waving from every balcony and window, and the shinners were climbing, climbing to the most precarious places until every washing-pole in the area was straddled, every roof populated. Now I was a sixteen year old who longed to be with his friends, performing monkey tricks in high places and sending out piercing whistles. As it was I sat quietly with the rest of the companions of the first citizen of Florence.

A brassy fanfare slashed the air. Above the heads of the straining crowd, the waving tassels of a high-held pennant could be seen in a lane, awaiting its moment of entry; but after the drummers came the alfieri, bearing the standards of all the contestants and turning the square into a swelling ocean of colour. More drums followed, with trumpets, sackbuts and shawms. Then, drawn by two white oxen, came Verrocchio's triumphal chariot of ancient, gilded grandeur. On the white and gold car, amidst an escort of nine maids and seven pages, Simonetta sat enthroned.

She seemed ill at ease. She too had kept vigil and the sleepless night had cast a shadow beneath her eyes, but it only served to heighten her beauty. If my heart broke at the sight of her, it was not the only one to do so. In its moment of breaking – and it is not the heart that breaks, but its shell – I felt at one with all those disparate fellows in the same condition. For it is only the shell of the heart that differentiates us one from another: when that breaks, we are one and the same.

Simonetta was dressed in white. In the lap of her fur-lined cloak she carried sprigs of evergreen and winter roses which, as the chariot paraded the square, she cast upon the sacred earth. At last the chariot drew to a halt before the Throne of Beauty and Simonetta stepped down to take her place.

Next into the arena were the champions with their squires. The drumming renewed in intensity like a quickening heart. Then the pennant stirred and moved forward, carried by stewards. And there she was: on her field of shining Alexandrine taffeta, Minerva entered Florence. The crowds were stunned into momentary silence, unfamiliar with the sight of a goddess of the antique world where one would usually see an image of the Virgin. There was some murmuring. Matrons and old ladies studied the face of the Archbishop, to determine his reaction and be assured of the Church's approval of this most pagan apparition. His Grace Rinaldo Orsini assuaged their fears by rising to face the pennant and bless it. This was greeted by a roar from Sandro Botticelli's apprentices atop the Judges's Stand. Their clamour was taken up by the crowd. The Goddess of Wisdom was made welcome.

Fanfares sounded and the trumpeting heralds themselves appeared in their various colours, marching across the square in a line. Behind them, three of the Medici pages, flanked by the Cavalcanti brothers, armoured squires resplendent in blue and silver. Then, at the point of an arrowhead formation of mounted noblemen, Giuliano appeared.

He was Youth, Virtue, Beauty personified. Straight-backed, perfectly at ease on the high-stepping palfrey, he came slowly down the length of the piazza. Knowing him as a man who preferred solitude to public life, I was in awe of him now. Where any lesser man would have betrayed by a blush or a silly grin either embarrassment or pride, Giuliano, pale and composed, rested his eyes on the image of Minerva ahead and simply rode on. By this act, he honoured the occasion and everyone present.

We have a phrase in Italian: *fare bella figura*. Some would say that to cut a fine figure is more important to an Italian than anything else in the universe, save perhaps avoiding damnation. It is possibly true. I notice, for instance, that the English spend more on their furniture than on their clothes, which is why I would rather be in one of their houses than out in their company. Be that as it may, it would be wrong to suppose that Italians are more concerned with appearance than content. A true artist of *la bella figura* is in control of himself to the very marrow of his bones: every element of his body, mind and soul is engaged in fine deportment. In this is Venus, the Goddess of Beauty, served and honoured. On the day of his joust, Giuliano de' Medici cut such a figure that even Leonardo was filled with awe. When such a vision of beauty occurs, then are we removed from the tawdry details of the bodily world and transported to the realm of Ideas, wherein indeed lies the source of *la bella figura*, the true name of which is *virtù*.

The formation of mounted noblemen moved forward behind Giuliano; after them came more pages; then more drummers; then, at the end of the file, a single rider.

My head jerked back. The seat behind me was empty. When had Lorenzo left the stand? Sometime, while our attention was being held hostage by Giuliano, Lorenzo had slipped out to mount a waiting horse, to join the procession at the last moment, all pre-arranged to surprise Florence. He who had processed across the square as the sober head of the Medici family now reappeared as a radiant twenty-five year old and an eager participant of the spectacle. The Florentines became ecstatic.

By now the pennant had reached the church and was being set up. Giuliano's escort duly arrived at the same place, but Giuliano himself turned off his path to approach the Queen of Beauty. He knelt before her. One of her maids presented him with a piece of linen, his Lady's favour. He kissed it, tied it to the shoulder buckle of his breastplate. When he remounted, he suddenly and impulsively turned the horse towards the place where Simonetta's husband was standing. Even though Marco Vespucci was smiling as generously as Saint Joseph, Giuliano felt the need to lean from the saddle, speak to him and touch his arm in friendship.

The first event was a melée: the battle where two teams hurl themselves at each other. This was the hour for the lesser knights to prove themselves; the jousters did not take part. I picked up Lorenzo's son to give him a good view of the thundering hordes. Piero drummed his feet on my legs so excitedly that I was bruised for days after. I was delighted when, with the erection of palisades, the piazza was transformed into lists. The heralds made the customary cries from the four corners. No one was allowed into the arena except the knights and their squires; no advice was to be shouted; the judges' decision would be final.

The first challenge was issued and a knight of Naples came out to meet one from Bologna. The heralds checked their livery and signalled their approval. The King-at-Arms held aloft the white baton and called *Andiamo*! The knights thundered towards each other with lances levelled.

Luigi Pulci, an expert on livery, deciphered the colours and told us the identities of each visored contestant. Like everyone else, we kept score, to make sure that the final decision of the judges was the correct one. On a slate we filled in the points for a shattered lance, a blow to the crest of a helm, or the extra marks for a dehorsing. This last was little Piero's favourite manoeuvre and he squealed with pleasure each time a knight crashed to the ground. For the most part, however, he had to be content with men steadily increasing their scores by splintering their lances on the shields of their opponents. I watched the pavilions impatiently. It seemed as if all the knights in the world had to meet each other first, that whole days were passing, before I saw Orso being led to the mounting place.

The current bout ended, determined at last by a battle on foot. I leant out of the box to be the first to see Giuliano come from the pavilion. My attention was as narrow and as sure as a line of perspective: there was nothing in the world except the entrance to the lists. Even so, I became aware of someone staring at me. I glanced up. On the balcony where the Pazzi family stood was my cousin Antonio, watching me without expression. I met his eye in amazement and waved but he turned his head to watch a knight in red and yellow come out of the pavilion, followed by the one in blue and silver.

TWENTY NINE

At the call, the two knights couched their lances and cantered down the lists. Hooves thudded on the now compacted and bloodied earth; lances struck with the woodland crack of stags in rut. Giuliano's second challenger was Simonetta's brother-in-law, Piero Vespucci, and the outcome would decide the participants in the final contest. On the fourth encounter, Giuliano's lance split.

'It is a break!' yelled some in the crowds. 'A break! A break!' We all thought so, and that therefore Giuliano must have won. But though we had heard the splitting, we could not see it; the judges declared that the lance was not broken and that the contest must continue. Where a broken lance is a gain, a damaged one is a hindrance. Giuliano returned valiantly to the lists with a lance no longer true but difficult to wield. Vespucci fetched him a mighty blow to the shield. Giuliano's body, jarring from the shock, rose from the saddle. For a moment Florence held its breath, then groaned with relief as he regained his seat. The people began to shout, denouncing the judges. Lorenzo jumped up swearing, his fists bunched in anger. 'Are they blind? That lance is broken!'

'Look,' I said, pointing. 'There at the pavilions ... '

Lorenzo peered. 'What is it?'

I had seen was nothing but a quick movement: as Giuliano reached the pavilions and turned for the next encounter, Leonardo passed him and caught hold of the tip of the lance. 'I believe', I said, interpreting what I had seen, 'Leonardo has revealed the split, forced it open with something.'

What ingenuity, what invention! When Giuliano took the lists again, his lance had Leonardo's pen wedged in its yawning jaw. Giuliano, undoubtedly grinning behind his visor, recklessly spurred Orso towards Vespucci. 'Broken lance!' came a shout from the judges. The white baton, thrown by the King-at-Arms, turned in the air and hit the ground between the combatants. The knights veered away from each other. Giuliano had won on points.

The crowd erupted. Student caps and merchant hats mingled in the air like spring blossom gusted by wind. I glanced at the balcony which held the Vespucci family. One or two of the younger ones registered honest disappointment, but the elder members of the family were impassive. None called cheat; indeed, they seemed as impressed as the rest of us to have witnessed a fight won as much by resourcefulness of mind as adroitness of body. Lorenzo, too, was studying their reactions, to satisfy himself that one of his precious allegiances held intact.

The only anger visible was in the face of Piero Vespucci himself. As he removed his helm, his face was clouded with wrath. When, in the following days, a rumour began that Giuliano had cheated, it was not difficult to guess its source. Jealousy can kill a man: it was the death of Piero Vespucci. Potentially one of the finest young men in the city, he killed himself with envy. It would be a few years yet before his body would swing on the rope, but it was at the joust that he died in spirit.

The final contest was between Giuliano and a knight of Milan, a gnarled condottiere who had weathered a generation of battles. None of Giuliano's well-aimed blows had any effect; the knight was like a stubborn old tree which resists all efforts either to hack it down or uproot it. His own thrusts at Giuliano, on the other hand, were bone-shaking even to the spectators. One strike fetched a ringing blow on Giuliano's helmet. The next dashed his shield to the ground, and nearly his arm with it. Giuliano rode on to the end of the palisade where, obviously dazed, he rested for a moment astride Orso.

'His head must feel like the clapper of the Vacca bell,' said Luigi.

I checked the score: Giuliano was many points down. Heralds ran to him, to see if he wanted to concede, but he refused. Leonardo was there, making a rapid sketch of the exhausted barbary. I am certain that, as the heralds left, he muttered something, against the rules. Having recovered, Giuliano rode out to meet the Milanese again; this time he went for the most difficult manoeuvre of all, to catch the coronal tip of the opponent's lance with his own. The Tactic Lethal. If he should miss ... My nightmare came back to me with fearful clarity.

But the lances met tip to tip; the coronals caught each other; the strike was won: Giuliano's score doubled. He turned at the end, came back for another strike.

I blush now to recount what happened next, for fear that you may doubt my sanity. However, here it is, as it happened. One moment I was there, in the stand, watching the lists; the next ... well, in the next moment 'here' was not in the stand. Suddenly I was looking down on the Piazza Santa Croce. I swear it – my body did not move, but I, the real 'I', was above the piazza, looking down. What did I see? It is important to be precise: I saw knights jousting as a bird might see them. (Any painter would have envied me that moment of supreme foreshortening.) I saw the people all about, a convergence of spectators, neatly lined at the barriers, a ragged edge at the back where they spilled into the streets. It is important to say ... I saw men, cantering up and down with levelled lances. Why? Why were grown men trying to dehorse each other? What I knew was this: that whatever the reason might be for this senseless activity, no one had the faintest idea of it, no one that is except one man, and that one man was not there. No one below knew what they were doing, or what the forces were that moved them. The aether in which we terrestrials move is a subtle sea of waves and currents in which many beings dwell and we know them not.

For I was not alone. Seeing the image of Minerva catching the sun, I became aware of the presence of the gods; it seemed that all of them were there, watching. Then I knew that Giuliano could not, was not going to lose. Everything which occurred that day, perhaps every day, begins in the world of the gods. Even apparently chance events, such as the placing of Leonardo at the pavilions, are all arranged. Nothing is by accident. Those words rang in me with the import of divine revelation: *Nothing happens by accident*.

One more thing I must tell you before I rejoin you on earth: in that moment – and it was only a moment in our time – 'here' so far as I was concerned was about one hundred braccie off the ground on a horizontal plane, and 'here' so far as my body was concerned was a vertical standpoint in the Medici box. That supreme realisation of true identity, that a man is his soul and not his body, was before long buried again by daily concerns. But in critical moments the memory of it comes back to me, an angel of annunciation saying, 'Fear not. How can that die which never was mortal?'

I am back in the stand now, dazed and asking Angelo, 'Where is Ficino? Is he here?' In the lists, Giuliano is struggling. Each time he reaches the end of the palisade, he takes off the helmet and gulps air. Then he returns, taking every risk, moving this way and that to deflect his opponent's lance and ensure that it does not break on him. Lorenzo, beside me, is groaning with suspense. I can now see no reason for such excitement. Does Lorenzo believe that the gods will let his brother down? With total certainty of the outcome, I stand back and watch the fight with a cool eye.

At last, when it was least expected, Giuliano switched from defence to attack, and rammed his own lance into the Milanese colours. The condottiere swayed on his saddle then fell in a heap, crashing on the palisade. His squire rushed out to help him to his feet.

Giuliano took off his helmet. His hair was wet and stuck to his brow. 'Swords!' he cried, knowing that his score was too low to win on a fall. The chief judge nodded his assent and the squires ran to the tents to fetch the weapons. They returned, each holding a sword aloft by its point. Andrea Cavalcanti presented Giuliano with his and was given the helmet in exchange. Andrea, astonished, glanced wildly towards Lorenzo. Lorenzo went through a mute agony of gesturing, telling his brother unmistakably that he was an idiot.

'No advice!' shouted a herald. Giuliano was not in the mood for heeding advice anyway. Flexing his sword arm, he took his stance without a helmet. Any civilised man would have expected the Milanese to match him and take off his own helmet, but he did not. When the Codes of Chivalry, conceived in noble France, were passed down to Italy, they must have avoided Milan.

The Milanese made the first thrust. Giuliano dodged backwards and parried angrily. The condottiere thrust again; though more nimble, Giuliano was being forced back towards the broken palisade. Realising the intention of his opponent, which was to put him on treacherous ground, Giuliano steered a different course. The swords clanged together, sparks flying. Each powerful sweep from the Milanese forced Giuliano's blade down. Now they were fighting close to the Throne of Beauty. At one point, as he jumped back from the Milanese, wiping away blood that poured from a cut on his temple, Giuliano caught the anxious eye of Simonetta. Then everything changed. He signalled for a brief respite, took the linen favour from his shoulder and cleaned the blood from his face. When he renewed his stance, his weariness had left him.

Now Giuliano seemed to have control of time, taking as much of it as he required to make his moves. The fight became a dance. Still dodging and parrying, he let the iron-lumbered Milanese stump after him. The captain was one of the old tribe, trying to pulverise that which he could not understand. Moment by moment he seemed to grow heavier, as if a metamorphosis into the mineral state was taking place.

Giuliano, as light as Mercury, flashed before his visored eyes. The sun, sinking behind western roofs, turned Giuliano's silver armour into gold. As the great god Apollo disappeared, Giuliano ceased his dance. Suddenly and without warning he stood his ground. Gripping his sword with both hands and raising it aloft, he brought it down like an axe on the head of the Milanese. The old soldier hit the ground with the fall of a blinded Cyclops.

By Saint George and Saint Michael, in that moment Giuliano killed off within himself something which he no longer desired: the martial, the bestial, the physical, the lower part of man's twofold nature. With the indifference of Odysseus, he turned his back on his groaning opponent.

THIRTY

TRUMPETS blew fanfares to the heavens as the Queen of Beauty placed the prize helmet upon the head of her champion. It was difficult to believe that these two did not belong together; that they were not, as in Plato's theology, two halves of one whole. He dark and majestic, she pale and gracious; even their heights were conducive to a match, her head being on a level with his shoulder, whereas she was taller than her husband by a hand. After the closing speeches, Giuliano lifted Simonetta into the triumphal car and together they rode from the piazza like gods. I know, I know: Italian hearts melt on the mildest breeze; that even swaggering youths with a dagger at the hip will soften in the presence of a baby. But on that day I would defy even a Dutchman not to have been affected by the dream that flowed like gossamer threads from the vision of Giuliano and Simonetta together. As for Angelo Poliziano, he wore the expression of one who sees the world behind this one, and is transfigured.

As the chariot disappeared from view, the event was closed and the ordered ranks of spectators dissolved into the chaos of a departing crowd. Little hunters of mementos escaped their parents and rushed into the arena to collect shards of lance, which was only an excuse to be on the very spot where *he* had been but moments before.

Lorenzo arranged for his ladies to be escorted to the palazzo where a banquet was due to begin in an hour. He himself went to the Judges' Stand; mobbed by boys on the way, he had to stop and answer technically penetrating questions on horses and horsemanship. Matteo Franco and other friends of Lorenzo escorted the Archbishop to the Via Larga, leaving the stand empty but for Angelo, Luigi, Jacopo Bracciolini and myself.

One glance at Angelo and I knew that he was alight with inspiration. I knew I must separate him from the others and take him back to his desk as quickly as possible. But Luigi Pulci reached him first.

'Well, my little Homer, my Virgilino, my very own Dante. If your talents are not remarkable enough, here you sit having witnessed an event you have already described. Did you know', he said to Bracciolini, 'that this young poet has second sight? Is that not wonderful?'

'Very impressive,' said Bracciolini sourly.

'Luigi,' said Angelo, 'my poem is barely begun.'

'Sixty-five perfect stanzas and barely begun? *Sacro cielo!*'

'You know yourself how long an epic can be.'

'My own epic will be as long as my life. I intend to capture all of you for the menagerie of my *Il Morgante*, so that future ages may marvel at you, as they wonder at two-headed snakes, hermaphrodites and other such monstrosities. My epic will be a record of our times.'

'Recorded in an outmoded style,' said Matteo Franco, returning to collect the gloves left behind by the Archbishop. Pulci's foot darted out as quick as a lizard's tongue. Matteo stumbled and fell.

'You milksop!' he shouted. 'You gelding!'

While the two fought with words, words that were all edge and no humour, Angelo took me aside to whisper urgently a list of mnemonic key words. He had twelve stanzas composed in his mind. With the keys I now held, he could safely unlock them from his memory later; meanwhile he was free to enter the scuffle and part the two who, while both friends of his, were not friends of each other.

'Ah, Angelo has woken up,' said Pulci. 'That sleepy look has gone.' Although Pulci mocked Angelo as freely as he mocked others, he had never previously attacked him, but now his tone grew acid. 'Sleep, that is my subject. Call it philosophic abstraction or divine frenzy or what you will. I prefer the good, plain noun sleep. You are a dreamer. Philosophers – pah! You sit in stupors and call your illusions reality. Reality you call an illusion.'

'I have never called myself a philosopher,' said Angelo, taken aback.

'You might as well. After all, you have the audacity to call yourself a poet. You might as well take the title from any subject that your butterfly mind settles on during its eclectic flights. Call yourself a herbalist, physician, historian, grammarian, or even a man, anything where you have read a line or two on the subject. What you are in reality, Angelo Ambrogini of Montepulciano, is a cobbler.'

Angelo's hurt was evident, but he was too recently returned from the Muse for it to cripple him. From his lofty vantage-point, he saw Luigi as a woeful figure, an ageing and desperate man whose own days of fame and glory were fading into the past; so he gripped him by the shoulders and kissed him on the cheek. In almost fifteen hundred years, Christ's only weapon had lost none of its potency.

'Angelo,' said Luigi, collapsing in sudden, surprised abjection. 'I only wish to help. It concerns me to see you wandering about on the hill of Careggi in a dream. Plato hated poets you know, banned them from the Republic.'

'Only because they did not write the truth,' said Angelo, patting him on the back.

'Truth? Truth? What is truth?'

I was eager to hear the answer but at that moment my attention was caught by a young man appearing before the stand. 'Antonio ... ' I said, going towards him.

He smiled handsomely, and clutching the back of my head pulled me close so that my ear was by his mouth. 'How can you be so shallow? My own cousin!' he said, sottovoce and accusingly. 'I saw you here, willing success for the tyrant's brother. Have you forgotten so soon? How long is it since the blood ran in our streets? Three years?' Before I could answer, even if I had had an answer, he was being greeted by Jacopo Bracciolini. Antonio pushed me away playfully. 'My cousin,' he explained. 'And doing very well in his adopted city, by all appearance. Come, Jacopo, Francesco de' Pazzi has sent me to remind you that we are having a celebratory banquet tonight.'

Bracciolini's eyes glittered. 'Celebrating what?'

'Giuliano's triumph of course.'

'Oh yes, of course.'

'Then we return to Rome in the morning.'

Bracciolini vaulted out of the stand to join him.

Antonio peered over my shoulder and nodded to where Angelo was comforting Pulci, the bitter and disappointed clown having been reduced to tears by the conqueror's affectionate kiss. Antonio's voice lowered again, into that other tone. 'Is that him?'

'Who?' I said guardedly.

'The famous Poliziano.'

I nodded.

'Our Raffaello would give his soul to be standing in my place now! Ironic, is it not? – for I am interested in neither poetry nor poets, and yet here I am, in the presence of the great. I shall enjoy transcendent pleasure in telling my brother that I have met his hero but could not be bothered to speak to him. Farewell, cousin of mine.'

'Antonio!' I called as he strode off with Bracciolini. I was amazed and disturbed that he could have been in Florence without letting me know.

Angelo joined me, wanting to know who I had been talking to.

'My cousin,' I said, and offered no further information.

'I did not know that you had relatives in Florence,' he said, stretching. 'Come, there will be no ostentatious suppers for us tonight. There is work to be done. Do you still have those keys?'

I did, and I repeated them to him. Strangely, I felt no sorrow at the news that I was to miss the feast at the Medici palace. The world suddenly seemed a dull place, dull and threatening as before a storm. I wanted to occupy my mind, to take it off Antonio. But the graze of the encounter began to heal quickly as night descended on the piazza and I was reminded of the presence of the gods.

The crowds had dispersed. By the light of torches, men were dismantling the lists, the pavilions and the stands. Boys rode on each other's shoulders, wielding broken lances. As we crossed the square, I watched them with affection, hearing in their cries echoes of my own childhood.

'This is Giuliano's lance!'

'It is not! It is Sanseverino's.'

'No! – Giuliano's! It is! It is!'

Their voices echoed in the stillness. I shivered and pulled my cloak tightly about me. After some time ruminating in silence, I finally found the courage to tell Angelo what had happened to me during the joust. He stopped to listen with full attention, his eyes glowing with recognition of the experience. I demanded an explanation and was told about the flight of the soul when, drawn by love of the Divine, it may temporarily leave the body.

'So it has happened to you, too?' I asked.

'No, not like that, not involuntarily.'

I stood puzzling, wondering which was the better, accidental or pre-determined flight of the soul; wondering how the second was achieved; wondering also if this experience was going to propel me into the Academy over the head of Lorenzo. If it was, Angelo made no mention of it. Instead he was in a playful mood. With his head back and facing the sky, he began to turn slowly in a full circle.

The moon was up and some of the stars and planets could be seen in the inky wash of the sky. The vault began to spin as we turned again and again. Then came a point of stillness, when it seemed as if it were the heavens that turned and not us. We stood together in the centre of a spinning universe and exhilaration took us over. At last, arm in arm and as happy as boys, we wandered giddily home.

'What,' I asked, 'was astrologically significant about today?'

He squeezed my arm. 'You tell me. You are the one who went to heaven.'

'Please, explain. Something has happened today. What is it?'

'A certain conjunction of planets foretells the birth of a new era, when Man once again becomes master of himself, as in ancient times. And look what happened to Giuliano: there came a point when he was no longer subject to chance but was able to take control. That is transformation.'

'Is it a form of magic, an operation?'

'Call it natural magic if you wish. In natural magic, there is no attempt to force change; rather one may see the right time and right place to work in accordance with the laws of nature and thus bring about the Will of God.'

'Is Ficino a magician?'

'Natural philosopher is the better term, particularly in this world where magic is feared.'

And so I asked the question that had occurred during my flight: where was Ficino today? Angelo shrugged and said that presumably he was at his villa on Careggi. 'I have never seen him at a public event and I would certainly not expect to see him at a joust.'

More mystery! 'Yet he created this,' I objected.

'No, he did not create it. He would be the last to claim such a thing. He saw it.'

'What do you mean?' This had to be my last question, because I heard Angelo's breath catch, a good sign of mounting irritation.

'In his mind, or rather, *the* mind, for there is only one mind, shared by all. It was an Idea. Men do not generate ideas, they catch them like fish in the sea of the Mind. Then, if they be fit to do so, they put them into operation.'

We had come to the far end of the square. I turned to give it one last look, and saw Minerva.

'Oh! The banner – what will become of it?'

At once we returned to the church, to collect our goddess and take her back to the palazzo on the Via Larga.

THE FOURTH BOOK

EXILE

... after a little while, darkness was in part brought down having become more dreadful and horrible, sinuously terminated, so that I imagined myself having seen the darkness changed into a certain moist nature, unspeakably disturbed, and giving forth smoke as if from fire, and emitting a certain sound, ineffable, mournful. Then a noise from it was inarticulately sent out, as I supposed the voice of Light.

Hermes Trismegistus

THIRTY ONE

To Desiderio

Thanks be to God, you have recovered, even if that means we have no further excuse for keeping Thomas More from his law studies in London. I was dismayed to find that my new courier was John Colet himself. So, my scribblings have had two readers all along, have they? I must remember never again to trust a Dutch monk of the Brethren of the Common Life. As you may well imagine, my soul was flayed and scourged by Master Colet, but when he had done, the soft light returned to his beautiful eyes and he said, 'So what happened next?'

John tells me that Saint Jerome, the venerable old father he would have you translate, had himself a deep love of ancient, pagan literature. Apparently the saint used to flagellate himself in advance of reading Cicero, putting the penance before the crime, as it were. If it be so, and acceptable in the eyes of God, then the scourging I had last night will probably serve me to the end of my tale. There is so much more to Colet than he would have us know!

He says that, if by writing this account I can leave the past behind me, then it is a worthwhile activity. He therefore urges me to hurry its completion, at which time I can turn my talents to something more useful, such as lessons in Greek for a reluctant Dutchman. Is he not single-minded in his mission? He wants one thing only, which is to restore to Christianity a love of Christ. He says Satan has made the university his own and within its fortress he cuts men off from God. Love of Christ is natural to all men, to peasants and dukes alike, but it has become dormant in the hearts of the people and needs to be called out. The Word of the Lord being in a tongue which is foreign to most, and being interpreted by scholars in such a way that it is fully obscured, it is for men who value truth above learning to devote themselves to the Word and to speak it out. The Bible, he says, must be read literally, and all the work to come is of translation. Did you know that he means to found a school of grammar for small boys – any boys, not just the sons of rich men – with the intention of raising them to this task? Colet speaks and thinks in generations where the rest of us are only concerned with the hour.

He has given me to understand that the cause of your illness was procrastination, and says you would do anything rather than embark on a study of Greek at the grand old age of thirty-six. I told him that if he would trust me – fully – with your education, if he would allow me to teach you as the Muse prompts, to teach you the Greek of Homer and Plato, I would be so inspiring a teacher as to capture your heart and mind for ever. You may imagine his reply, and the tone of it.

Therefore you must needs meet me tomorrow at the usual hour to renew our studies of the Greek of the New Testament. I shall do what I can to pepper and spice it.

I realise tomorrow is Lady Day, the twenty-fifth of March, and that last week I was threatening to die on this date, in spirit if not in body. But who could spend two hours in a small room with a great man and not have such nonsense knocked out of him? The philosophers are right: only the present moment is real, and whether March 25th 1499 is followed by a new century, a new world, or only by March 26th, has no bearing on this moment now.

TO SPEED the conclusion, I must jump a year or so in my account. At the same time, there are things needful of mention, for 1475 was a year of masterpieces. In that year the Pollaiuolo brothers hung their gigantic altarpiece of Saint Sebastian in the church of Santissima Annunziata. The whole city came out to stand amazed before it. The Saint himself, unbloodied and seemingly transcendent of his plight, was rendered flatly and with little detail. This poor Sebastian did not want the attention that his barb-pricked nakedness usually commands. The painters had freed the viewer to look elsewhere in the picture, and our attention was taken by the archers. Bending to load a crossbow, straining to pull a longbow, these were real anatomies showing every stage of loading and firing. All the vile hours which the Pollaiuoli had spent examining the insides of stinking cadavers were here vindicated. The dead were living again.

The authenticity of the figures was complemented by the reality of their background. It was a Tuscan river plain which we all recognised, portrayed in exact detail. This magic had been performed by use of a camera obscura, a black room with a minute aperture in one wall, through which the outside scene entered the room on a beam of light to reveal itself on the opposite wall, there to be traced by the artist.

In the Botticelli workshop such sciences were, to Filippino's frustration, ignored. Filippino argued that the demand of the age was for a realistic portrayal of the flesh, which could only be achieved by true knowledge of the structure and growth of bodies; Sandro denounced him as an Aristotelian. True knowledge, said Botticelli, will never be had by examining the physical world; Filippino denounced his master as a Platonist. Meanwhile they worked together on a commission which had been made by the Vespucci not long after the joust.

It was a panel, destined to become a bed-head, which depicted Venus and Mars. The two reclining figures were Simonetta and Marco Vespucci, though in Marco I could see, as it were, a token of Giuliano, especially in the armour. Mars was naked and asleep. While he slept, two satyrs played with his lance and helmet while another crawled through the empty cuirass. Though one blew a conch shell like a trumpet in the god's ear, Mars did not wake. Venus looked on her lover serenely.

I studied the outline of the painting, mentally applying compass and rule to discover the angles of the strange composition.

'One hundred and twenty degrees,' said Sandro, reading my mind. 'Venus and Mars are in trine.' According to Ficino, in his Commentary on Plato's *Symposium*, in this relation the belligerent qualities of Mars are held in check, overcome by the influence of Venus. 'Man's warlike nature has been subdued by Love. Even the senses, these little satyrs, cannot stir him.'

I gazed upon that picture and saw in it the aspiration of the Academy, the dawning of a new golden age, civilised, cultured, based on the love of God and not on the love of Mammon.

Filippino complained bitterly that, while he was associated with a mystic, he could never become the great painter he was destined to become.

'Do not blame me for your failings,' said Sandro, simply and without malice. It was an accurate shot and the truth of it winded Filippino, who left the shop abruptly and was not seen for days.

Meanwhile in Verrocchio's workshop it was the master and not the journeyman who was melancholy. In response to the blossoming of Leonardo's talent in painting, Verrocchio stoically exchanged the brush for the chisel and took up sculpture. He had immediate success: Lorenzo commissioned another David for the Palazzo de' Medici. This David was not an Hermetic image, such as the one by Donatello which commanded the courtyard. It was a work of sad defeat: if Verrocchio's David, a slender bronze youth, was not a physical portrait of Leonardo, all the same he was Leonardo to those who knew him; and to those who knew Verrocchio, they saw his likeness in the head of Goliath. The youthful apprentice stood sword in hand above the vanquished master. In David's expression was that smile of Leonardo which had in it neither triumph nor vainglory, but equanimity; in Goliath's frown of death was no tyranny, only pain. Verrocchio gave up painting, took up sculpture, and Leonardo left the workshop to become his own master.

Lorenzo de' Medici gave the young man use of a house and garden he owned near the Dominican monastery of San Marco. Leonardo was delighted, for the encircling walls afforded him much privacy and peace. He so arranged it that no one could enter the garden without the permission of Lorenzo, and Lorenzo saw to it that no rivals from the Guild of Saint Luke were admitted. What was happening behind those walls was left to the imagination. Filippino prowled the district, vainly badgering Dominicans and Mediceans alike for information as to what Leonardo was doing. He told me that the continuance of our friendship depended on my gaining him entry.

I applied to Matteo Franco, not for entry but for greater prohibition: on no account was Filippino Lippi to be allowed into the San Marco garden. This I did for his own good, for I had heard from Angelo that Leonardo was working on an Annunciation, similar in composition to the lunette done by Filippino's father, but with a facility of technique which set Leonardo as far apart from his peers as the heavens are removed from the earth. One glimpse of it would, I was certain, be the death of my friend. I spoke not only to the secretaries of Lorenzo, but also to the officers of the Signoria and the monks of San Marco, begging them to ensure that, under no circumstances, should Filippino Lippi be granted access to the garden. And then I prayed to God that our friendship might survive.

What I forgot was how adept Filippino was at climbing convent walls. Alone one night and by candle-light he saw the Annunciation for himself. The rest of the city was asleep. A few people stirred when a lupine howl of grief pierced the silence, but they rolled over, stopped their ears with their fingers and returned to peace.

From what did I seek to protect him? From pain I suppose. But the pain, which by his own volition he accepted, changed him so utterly that in the end I came to envy him for it. The egregious youth became a man overnight. The kindness and generosity which had underlain his outrageousness, shining like beaded light through shutters, now shone forth unimpeded. As he went about the city, Filippino carried, as a wound in the very pit of him, the knowledge that he could never be what he had always presumed he must become. That he should be heir to his father's talent was an assumption as natural as it was false, but Leonardo it was who furthered the work of Fra Filippo. Seeing this, once and irrevocably, Filippino gave up the fight to become a luminary in the starry vault of fame and became instead himself. At once he was graced with what he desired most: the love of his fellow men. Filippino never became the greatest of painters, but he became, and still is, a man beloved by all who know him.

We, who spend our lives searching for the alchemical secret which will transform our dross into gold and make us perfect, will never find what we seek while we avoid the very thing we must confront, which lies not on the library shelf, but within our own being. Filippino achieved this realisation years before I did.

Poliziano preferred to write about transformation scenes rather than undergo them. The first canto of *La Giostra*, consisting of one hundred and twenty-five stanzas, was not yet complete before the poem was in circulation. But, no matter how generous the praise of his friends, Angelo still lacked confidence in his abilities. He fretted. Lorenzo was working on a verse sequence called the *Altercazione*. This poem, instigated by Ficino, was a direct rendering in verse of the teachings of Plato.

'It is useless,' said Angelo late one night, his voice occurring suddenly in the darkness as I was drifting into sleep. 'Useless. My poem is a hymn of failure. Lorenzo confronts his subject directly, while I hide among hints and allusions, evoking sympathetic responses at best, confusing everyone at worst. What I should be doing is what he is doing, writing a tremendous poem about philosophy.'

'Things always seem worse in the dark,' I mumbled.

'You certainly do,' he said irritably. He sighed. 'Lorenzo is looking directly at the sun, while I am only looking at the moon.'

'You were born under Cancer: the moon is your ruling planet, which is why you are a lunatic. You could not write like Lorenzo, no matter how you tried. And why should you? What will profit the world more, two different poems or two similar ones?'

'The difference is stark,' muttered Angelo, but he was consoled.

My words had not been meant as pillows for his head, nor were they the flattery of a servant. I had no doubt that Angelo's was the finer work. It had that indefinable flash of spirit which we call 'genius'. Whatever such a thing is, it comes from the gods as a reward for the man who works for work's sake and for no personal gain. To work hard, spurred ever on by dissatisfaction with what has been achieved, this is the signal the heavens await, and then the flash comes, the inspiration we have named 'the Muse'.

As verses of *La Giostra* began to circulate, passed on by one reader to the next, the translator of Homer became widely known as a poet in his own right. Acclaimed first by his fellow citizens, he soon began to receive letters of praise from abroad. One from Rome had my own family's seal.

'Raffaello dei Maffei of Volterra,' Angelo read aloud and looked at me questioningly.

'My cousin,' I said.

'He has a good Latin style: this is a fine letter.'

In good Latin and fine style, Raffaello assured Poliziano that he had perfected the eight-line stanza and was already, at the age of twenty-two, a source of inspiration to poets much his senior. All Rome was talking about Angelo of Montepulciano.

He glowed with self-satisfaction. I was glad that such moments, though increasingly frequent, were brief. I preferred my master in his periods of self-doubt.

'Does he mention me at all?' I asked.

'Yes. At the end he says, "commend me to your scribe, Tommaso, a cousin of mine."'

'Well,' I said, annoyed by the indefinite article, 'commend me to him when you reply.'

Angelo glanced at me but asked no questions, saying only, 'Sometimes families are best forgotten.'

'It is all very well for an orphan to say so.'

'Am I an orphan?'

So I had always presumed.

'Best forgotten,' he said.

As for Giuliano, there appeared to be no change, except that he disappeared more frequently, often staying out all night. As to where he had been, the answer was invariably 'hunting.' Alone? Yes, alone. He loved the forest at night, where he was anonymous, where he felt himself to be undistinguished from tree or fox. He liked to ride hard, going without food or drink, testing himself to the limit. We all watched him closely for signs of alteration, but he practised piety, sought virtue, and studied as before. Sometimes, however, I caught him in a new attitude, perhaps walking in the garden or standing at the window, looking wistful. When he saw me, he would make a lame excuse for his distraction and immediately raise some matter regarding the horses. He would throw his arms wide in an expansive gesture as he praised the points of a new filly or colt, but I could see that in truth his heart and mind were elsewhere.

Once I tried to draw him out, saying that the discipline of the stables would be much improved if the mares were stalled elsewhere, or if all the stallions were gelded. He agreed energetically and thanked me for supporting his point of view. But I had seen it, that disturbance which will flicker across the face of any lusty male at the mere mention of castration; a tremor as his being recoils from the thought of such pointless torture. Giuliano, I became convinced, had lost his virginity.

THIRTY TWO

It was April, the time of wild asparagus and blossoming bay trees. The lanceate leaves of the olives were silver against a blue Giotto sky; the scented breeze tingled with new life. A company of twenty-six riders, having spent the night at Borgo San Miniato, were now on the road to Pisa. Mindful that it was Lent, Lorenzo encouraged his companions to talk of holy things and to discuss Saint Augustine. Each time one of his friends struck a lute and began to sing of the superlative virtues of Florentine girls as against any other women in the world, Lorenzo joined in the chorus heartily, finding his own disciplines as difficult to follow as everyone else, but then Giuliano would take the same melody in a slower tempo and sing one of Lorenzo's plaintive laude, thus recalling the company to their devotions. And so they covered the distance, alternating between the sacred and the profane, oblivious to the one who dawdled at the rear of the party with a heart like a sticky ball of pitch.

We passed through hamlets and villages where grandmothers sat by the doors of their homes, gossiping as they spun wool from the distaff. In the fields men and women laboured, planting sapling vines or walking the furrows and casting seeds from the fulsome pockets of aprons. All I wanted to do was to race across the fields and scare the birds, to fill the air with the noise of a grinding ratchet.

Towards Potadera, we found the road blocked by a flock of sheep. Matteo Franco went to harry the dull shepherd. The more urgently the sheep were herded, however, the quicker they waddled down the lane, only advancing the obstruction rather than removing it. As it obviously would take some time before our pack mules could pass, the men left the servants to negotiate the obstacle and went to rest in a meadow. While the others tickled fish in a stream, I tethered my horse to a holm oak and set off to walk alone. The thrusting blades of grass and the sun-tracking flowers held the potential for happiness, but my heavy tread flattened them underfoot. After I had passed, the bruised flowers and grasses slowly raised themselves again.

Following the joust, I had gone to the Palazzo Pazzi to find Antonio but was told that he had left for Venice. That was the last I heard of him for a year. Then, in the spring of 1476, while Angelo and I were packing books before leaving for Pisa, a servant came with a message: 'Your cousin, Antonio di Gherardo dei Maffei, wishes to see you. He is in the reception chamber.'

I looked to Angelo and he nodded his assent. 'Leave all this to me,' he said. 'It will be done by the time you return.'

I found Antonio examining a bronze figurine of Hercules in the act of squeezing Antaeus to death.

'Is this an ancient piece?' he asked, as if I had only seen him yesterday.

'No. It was made last year by Antonio Pollaiuolo.'

'Oh? I have just seen his Sebastian in Santissima Annunziata. The Florentines – better than anyone at everything, eh? The New Romans.'

Antonio was secularly dressed in fine clothes and was, as ever, alone. The lone hunter ... For the first time I noticed the similarity between him and Giuliano, in their air of independence and their mutual abhorrence of trivial things. Whatever Antonio's faults, he had no time for life's irrelevancies. I admired both of them for the same thing, but who did I admire the most? The answer was both immediate and alarming.

Before I could dwell on it, however, Antonio delivered his news: my uncle, his father, had died. 'With bad conscience and no hope of heaven,' he said shortly. I wanted to know why he thought so, but Antonio asked if Poliziano were in the house. 'I would like to see him.'

'He is occupied,' I said quickly, remembering Antonio's previous disdain.

He drew a letter from his jacket. 'Here ... this is for the poet, from my sycophantic brother. The fault is all yours, you know.

Since you began sending Raffaello every word that drips from the poet's pen, our house has filled with coxcombs reciting the latest stanza of *La Giostra*.'

Antonio selected an apple from the pyramid of fruit on a majolica plate. He polished it on his jacket and bit into it with a cavernous crunch. 'So,' he said, with his mouth full, 'how is life in the sumptuous house of the Medici?'

'Busy,' I muttered, rearranging the fruit pyramid.

'Can you sleep at night? I could not, not if I lived here.' He ran a hand over the bronze. 'I met a young girl at a tavern yesterday, a pretty little thing with skin as smooth as wax. She offered to pleasure me for five denari. I gave her fifteen in exchange for her story only. Her name is Matea and since the death of her parents she has been cared for by her uncle, a priest. Now the priests of Tuscany, as you will be aware, have become the victims of a new tax imposed by Lorenzo. Her uncle, unable to pay, has been dispossessed and has given up his benefice to become a mendicant friar. Consequently Matea lives at the Unicorn, selling wine and, for an extra five denari, her body.' He put the bronze down on an exquisite table of inlaid marble. 'I could not look a beggar in the eye if I lived here.'

I flushed hotly with unspoken self-justification. But for Lorenzo's wealth Angelo Poliziano would still be sewing shoes and I would be the beggar. But in the cool face of Antonio, I choked on my defences.

Then suddenly his eyes filled with sparkling light and, throwing his arm round my shoulders, he squeezed me until I felt like Antaeus. Never able to match Antonio's rapid changes of mood, I remained sullen.

'Forgive me,' he said. 'I did not mean to disconcert you.' He stroked the velvet of my doublet. 'This is fine cloth. You are obviously doing well and I am glad of it, believe me. Every man needs a patron. We thought you were destined for poverty with your choice of profession and are delighted to have been so mistaken.'

I returned his embrace then and asked him what brought him to Florence. He said that he continued with his duties in the Camera Apostolica and was travelling the countryside about its business, collecting taxes.

'From the clergy?' I asked pointedly.

'That is the legal right of His Holiness and of no other. I am bound for Padua tomorrow. Will you come with me?'

I told him that we were about to leave for Pisa. Antonio suggested that I feigned sickness, or told my masters that I had to go to Rome on family business. 'You need to get away, Maso, to find yourself.'

'I am myself.'

'What, a musty young scribe who has abandoned his family to hide amongst books? I can hardly recognise you. Where is my Tommaso, the boy who could hold his own in a fight, who could turn six somersaults on the spot, who could string bows, flight arrows and catch wild horses? Where is my little cousin who once used to sing like a bird?'

'Perhaps I have changed.'

'Constrained all natural impulses, more likely. How *can* you live here, feeling as you do?'

I glanced anxiously around. 'We cannot talk now.'

'Then meet me tonight, at the tavern on the Piazza Santa Trinità.'

I said I would try. Antonio wedged the apple core in between the wrestling Hercules and Antaeus. 'Be there, dear cousin of mine. If you are not, I shall presume what I must presume.'

'Which is?'

He leaned close to me. 'That you are a true man of the Medici,' he whispered, 'and being so, not one of the Maffei.' He caught me painfully by the ear. 'We want you back in the family, Tommaso.'

I said that the Maffei used to be happy enough to leave me in Volterra when they all went to Rome.

'That was a ... necessary arrangement.'

'Necessary for whom?'

'For my mother. You must have noticed that she cannot abide you. And has it not occurred to you, the reason for her intolerance?'

I shook my head.

'I believe my father hoped you would guess, to avoid the embarrassment of telling you himself. But the time for your knowing is now long overdue, and this must be my first duty as the new head of the family. For many things is Gherardo damned, but most of all for the sin of fornication, which he never confessed. Tommaso, you are my brother – half-brother, natural brother – but not my cousin.'

I stared at him, my mouth open in shock. Then I began to fire questions: Was Gherardo my father? Then who was my mother? Did she die in childbirth? Standing in Lorenzo de' Medici's marble halls, I heard the truth: Antonio's father had sired me on a slave girl. There was nothing unusual in that – there were several men in the Medici family with similar origins; what was unusual was that Gherardo's wife had the strength of character to object, and to refuse outright any suggestion that I might be taken into the family. As for my mother, she had died in childbirth, her life sacrificed to save mine, and no one could even remember her name.

'But now it is my will which Mona Lucia must obey,' said Antonio, 'and she will find it stronger than that of Gherardo, who was enfeebled by guilt. We want you in the family.'

I was so swept by memories which needed reinterpretation in the light of this knowledge that I hardly heard what Antonio said. So he repeated himself more firmly, adding, 'Because you have to realise where your loyalty rests, and it is not with the house of the Medici.'

'Where then does it rest?' I demanded angrily. 'With a family which has denied me? With those who had no respect for my mother? Who treated me like an impoverished cousin, with gifts of discarded clothes and the occasional gold coin?' I shouted, flailing in a tempest of anguish.

Antonio caught my wrists in a strong grip until I had quietened. 'I will leave you with this knowledge. I apologise if it was delivered brutally, but there was no other way. Believe me, had it not been for my father, I would have told you years ago. Do you remember? – when we used to ride on the hills and fly the falcon? You were my little brother, and I could not tell you.'

I went limp in his arms and cried.

'Remember the hills,' he said, cradling me, 'and the free sky. Remember our true inheritance. We shall have it back. You and I together. We can forget about Raffaello and the others: they are content to achieve the small things in life. You and I are different.'

He disengaged me and held my face in his hands. Years of anger were etching his face with bitter lines; the noble youth, the wild Etruscan, was not visible in the man before me, and the light that blazed in his eyes was no longer visionary but fanatical.

I stood back and wiped my face with my sleeve. I wanted him to go, to leave me.

'I am sorry to have missed meeting the great Poliziano,' he said. 'Raffaello will never forgive me. And I sincerely wanted to meet him, to see for myself the squinting eye and the twisted neck.'

'What are you talking about?'

'His deformities. Everyone says that the disciple of beauty is an ugly man.'

'That is not true! And you know it, for you saw him yourself at the joust!' Understanding suddenly, I caught hold of his arm. 'Attack Augustus if you will,' I whispered urgently, 'but leave Virgil alone!'

Antonio looked at me in dark triumph. 'Tonight, then. I have some friends I want you to meet.'

After he left, I stood a long while alone in the chamber. At last I turned, took the apple core from the bronze and threw it out of the window. As I went back to the library, I saw Lorenzo coming along the corridor. The Augustus of our metaphor, he was arm in arm with Giuliano, teasing him, prodding him, asking him if he were in love and, if so, who was she? Giuliano, red with embarrassment, was hotly denying the taunts, and wore the mixed expression of pain and pleasure of one who is being tickled. I bowed low as they passed, to hide the red puffiness of my eyes and the guilt in my heart. What I had said to Antonio – did I mean it? Did I really mean it? As the brothers passed, I felt the touch of a hand on my head, a brushing acknowledgement of my presence by Giuliano.

I tried to think of my cousins as brothers but the thought brought no joy. Instead I felt envious of Lorenzo, for having such a brother as Giuliano, and sorry for Giuliano, for having such a brother as Lorenzo. Once Giuliano had said that I was to think of them as one and the same, that if I hated one then I hated the other. I had never even tried to follow this precept. I would have died for Giuliano, but not for Lorenzo. Perhaps over the years I had blunted my hatred but I retained what I considered to be a healthy resentment, healthy because it kept me from fawning, as so many around Lorenzo fawned, over-anxious for his good opinion. I considered myself independent, and desired to be independent from everything, except perhaps the Academy. And to that, it was said, Lorenzo was my gateway. I was preparing myself for some future time when I could slough off the resentment and meet him afresh, all past deeds forgotten. That was how I anticipated opening the gate, in some peaceful moment when I could talk to him honestly.

I returned to the library and found everything as I had left it; Angelo, bent over an open book in the act of putting it into the chest, had been transported by its words to another realm and another age. I closed the door behind me loudly.

'Ah, here you are,' he said, straightening up and shutting the book. 'That was quick. I thought you were going to be away for some time.'

'I have been away for some time.' I looked into the empty chest with the disapprobation of an officer of the dowry fund. 'It is tomorrow that we leave?'

'Where is your cousin?' Angelo asked, ignoring the sarcasm. I made an excuse on Antonio's behalf. Angelo expressed regret and said he would have liked to have met the brother of Raffaello.

'He only called to deliver this,' I said, handing him the latest letter from Rome.

Angelo tucked it into his jacket and, saying that we had work to do, began to pack the books with vigour. I wanted desperately to speak to him, to share the revelations of the hour, but he did not catch the import of my sighs. He was singing a new song he had composed about the delights of the month of May. Perhaps my fears were best left unspoken, for what could I say that would not lead to Antonio's immediate arrest? Torn by questions of allegiance and loyalty I put myself to work. As to whether I would meet Antonio at the tavern, I pushed that decision aside until later.

At Vespers, the family met as usual in the chapel to pray and sing canticles. I found it difficult to concentrate and my eye roved around the luminous procession of the Gozzoli frescoes. When I missed a response, Angelo nudged me painfully in the ribs. I renewed my efforts to concentrate, but without success. After the prayers, Lorenzo addressed the household regarding the arrangements for the morrow.

'We will make our first stop at Lastra, and someone needs to ride ahead to see that everything is in order for our accommodation. I am sorry, but it will mean that someone must give up the joys of companionship on the road and travel alone. He will have to go this very night.'

My voice was speaking before my mind could present any objections. 'I shall go,' I offered at once. Any other volunteer would have received further commiseration from Lorenzo; all I was given was an expression bordering on a sneer. Lorenzo, who considered me ancillary to his household, an appendage he tolerated merely for Angelo's sake, was pleased to let me go and offered no compensation. But I had my own reward in the avoidance of a decision which I could not make.

I lay on my back amidst the new grass and stared at fluffy white clouds in the sky, wondering how Antonio reacted when I failed to meet him. The haunting image of him oppressed my spirit. I was caught between sneer and sneer, the disdain of my lord on the one hand and that of my cousin – no, my brother – on the other. The laughter of the men at the stream made me feel simultaneously alone and crowded. How long could I inhabit this world of neutrality which I had made for myself? – a place constructed by the effort of not thinking, of not remembering, of having no concerns other than those of the day. A selfish, blinkered world closed to everyone but myself.

I longed to be with Filippino, who required no proof of contract in friendship or brotherhood. I longed to be in the bottega, amongst men at work, telling Filippino my news, that I too was a bastard, and, who knows, perhaps laughing about it.

Angelo was calling my name. Giuliano had caught a trout and was carrying it jauntily, tied with string by its mouth and tail. Angelo rode out to meet me, leading my mare; taking the reins from him, I swung up into the saddle. We rode side by side and I was grateful for his company. Usually when Lorenzo was present I could expect to be alone, for Angelo went to him as iron to a lodestone. Theirs was the friendship of men of opposite nature who find in each other that which they lack. Their mutual admiration was as complete as it was sincere. But now Angelo sacrificed an opportunity to be at Lorenzo's side, for at last he had read the signs of misery in his scribe.

'What troubles you?' he enquired gently.

'Nothing.'

'Is it what happened the night before we left? Is that what has disturbed you?'

I reminded him that I had not been at the palazzo the night before last, but had been on the road to Lastra. When the company had arrived on the following day, I had kept to myself and so was unaware that Ficino had called at the house on the Via Larga, or that he and Lorenzo had had a tempestuous argument.

The news left me speechless. I had long known of the strain between Lorenzo and Ficino, caused by Luigi Pulci, whose attacks on the Academy had become increasingly scurrilous of late. His poems, which amounted to nothing but rhyming invective directed against Ficino, made uncomfortable, embarrassing reading. The wretched man was clearly becoming insane. Ficino had expected Lorenzo's support and asked him to expel Pulci, but Lorenzo had refused, choosing instead to protect his father's old friend.

Lorenzo was famed for his diplomacy, Ficino for his equanimity: no one thought that their argument would become a breach. But it had ended with Lorenzo shouting that Ficino should leave his house, that from then on he would no longer be a member of the Academy.

'"If there is nothing in Platonic Wisdom that allows for a man to protect his friends, even when they err, then I spit upon that philosophy!" – those were his words,' said Angelo.

I was shaken to hear them even in repetition. 'Did he mean it?'

'No.' Angelo looked down the line towards Lorenzo, who was again cheerfully encouraging his companions to be lenten in their attitudes and to forsake their banter for graver, more spiritual topics of conversation. 'He has not slept since and is racked by guilt. When you are a child, you put yourself into the hands of your tutor as wet clay to a potter, and allow yourself to be moulded into something both useful and beautiful. But finally, when the pupil attains manhood, there comes a time when the tutor, if still seeking to manipulate a pliable soul, is rejected. Lorenzo meant none of what he said. I have heard him shout at Pulci with even greater fury, and to threaten to kick the wretch out of Tuscany. But now that he is master both of himself and our country, Lorenzo cannot allow Ficino authority over his actions. That is the cause of the dispute, at least on Lorenzo's side. On Ficino's, he is annoyed by the tax which has been placed on the clergy, for it means he must spend more time on clerical duties and less on his writing. I understand both of them, as I love both of them, and can only pray that the wounds will soon heal.'

He fell quiet then, giving me the opportunity to speak if I so desired, but my problems were now obscured, for the separation of Lorenzo and Ficino was, to me, wonderful news.

'If Lorenzo has left the Academy, will he continue to attend the meetings of the Company of the Magi?'

'No, he has also left the Company, although not because of this trouble with Ficino, but because he fears that his presence will intimidate the new Governor.'

Though I knew well enough how closely guarded was the identity of the Governor of the Magi, I could not resist an innocent enquiry. 'And who is he?'

'It is a secret, as you well know.'

'Angelo of Montepulciano, will you never trust me?'

'Probably not.'

'I once read somewhere in Ficino's writings that trust comes before trustworthiness.'

'Well, perhaps what Marsilio Ficino says no longer has any hold on me.'

I was astonished. How often had I heard Angelo pass all the credit for his poetic inspiration back to Ficino, and to those evenings when, in response to Ficino's playing of the lyre, his soul had taken wing?

'Maestro! You are not leaving too?'

'Wherever Lorenzo goes, there go I.' So saying, Angelo spurred his horse and cantered up the line to join the one who was to him as a god. I stayed at the rear, a detached witness of this party of riders who were bonded together by subtle ties of friendship and family. Giuliano, riding along with four hounds on leashes, led a discussion on Augustine, and turned a disapproving eye on his brother when Lorenzo recalled the saint's famous prayer, 'Lord, make me celibate – but not yet!' I gazed on the swarthy, bull-necked man who had absolute power. Ficino, like Plato before him, had failed to create a philosopher king. Did that mean I was free? Could I now enter the Academy without making my peace with Lorenzo? My heart leapt with hope. Then I fell to wondering how Lorenzo could lightly abandon that which I held so precious.

Yet soon enough I was leaving it myself, on a caprice of fate. Passion is the devil's keenest weapon.

THIRTY THREE

PISA, the great seaport at the mouth of the Arno, was once a powerful maritime republic. After losing a war with Genoa, however, she had declined. Now she was but one of many territories belonging to Florence. The tributes required of her were great, but the cost in pride and dignity were greater still. When the Medici came to power, Pisa had no reason to expect anything of them other than further humiliation, but Cosimo had instituted policies to renew the city's self-esteem by means of patronage and endowments. Pisa, however, viewed the magnanimous gestures of the Medici with suspicion and hostility.

Building on his grandfather's work, Lorenzo had decided to reform the University. He divided the Studio of Florence and transferred the faculties of science and law to the seaport, retaining the humanities in Florence. He acquired houses and farms in the territory and visited them once or twice a year, to make in person what no amount of endowment could obtain, that is, friends. Step by tactful step, he was beginning to succeed.

We followed the Arno through the hills. By the time the river reached Pisa, it had become the main sewer for all Tuscany.

Angelo wrinkled his nose and groaned at the stench of dead fish. My eyes watered and I covered my nose with a piece of linen while others sniffed at plague pomanders to guard against infection. Only Lorenzo, who had been graced at birth with a depressed nose and with no sense of smell, looked untroubled.

'Look a'dat,' said Matteo from within a handful of linen. He pointed to what appeared to be an inflated sack bobbing on the current, but was in fact the bloated corpse of a man. 'What circle of hell are we coming to?'

'We cannot blame Pisa for what Florence has sent down the river,' said Lorenzo.

'What makes you think he was a Florentine?'

Lorenzo shrugged. 'It looks as if he has come a long way.'

'We have come as far but we do not look like him.'

To a man, the party turned to smile at the chaplain, signifying that one of us did.

Lorenzo's intention was to work on the refoundation of the University, but as soon as we arrived it became clear that what the Pisans wished to discuss was their Archbishop. Why had Lorenzo prevented Francesco Salviati from visiting the city? Was it to humiliate Pisa? What right did he have to dictate who should be their Archbishop? Therefore Lorenzo was drawn into a seamless run of meetings and councils and had to abandon his plans. Angelo visited the University alone, to speak to professors on Lorenzo's behalf, and found them intractable and bigoted; Giuliano went hunting, but as it was Lent he could only catch rabbits. Everyone grew irritable.

The city of Pisa being so near the coast, I suffered a mounting frustration as I wrote out countless letters while tasting salt in the air. When Angelo woke up late one morning with a headache and refused to meet any more professors of law, I suggested that, for the sake of his health, we might visit the sea.

We rode the flat road bordering the Arno to the harbour, and at last I saw caravels weighing anchor and moving out with billowing sails towards the horizon. 'Leaving for the lands of spices,' I said wistfully. Angelo thought they were probably going to Naples or Genoa. He was still in a bad mood. At my insistence we rode on until we came to a place where there was a beach. The water was the colour of turquoise streaked with malachite and jade, and it fell on the shore in a froth of waves. Full of bacchic delight, I took off my hose and waded in up to my knees while Angelo stayed behind, calling out about the dangers of jellyfish.

'Coward!' I shouted back, and at once regretted the careless remark. The sight of my master withdrawing like an injured crab brought me out of the sea and back to sit beside him. I tried to coax him out again by asking what was over the horizon straight ahead of us, but this only served to deepen his irritation, for it caused him to realise that there was a patch of ignorance in his all-encompassing knowledge.

'I have no idea,' he grumbled.

I pointed to a great ship sailing past towards the harbour, and wondered what exotic treasures might be in its cargo.

'Slaves probably,' said Angelo, 'and half of them dead.'

Now it was my turn to double up in pain. 'We have no right to call ourselves Christians,' I declared, 'while we deal in human lives.' Tears were springing to my eyes; though I could not see it, Volterra was close, and my mother's blood ran in my veins. Rising, I went to the water's edge to skim stones. Angelo joined me and we competed in silence. At last, after he had won with six bounces, he asked a question which drew my story from me, and I told him that I had discovered myself to be the bastard son of Gherardo dei Maffei and a slave. It was Angelo's considered opinion that I should be pleased, for surely it was preferable to be in the main blood line, and not the withering appendage of a dead offshoot? He asked if it would have made a difference, to have known earlier who my father was, particularly during the time of the troubles in Volterra. My native city, hidden by haze somewhere to the south of us, was something we had not discussed before.

The question was an interesting one. I thought I would have been more likely to have been killed, or banished, and I would not have met the Bishop; indeed, I would not have been there at all, but with the family in Rome.

'Given that your father's wife accepted you.'

'Given that.'

'But as a scion of Gherardo dei Maffei, you would naturally have been pro-Medici.' Now I saw the hook floating in front of me.

'I was anyway.'

This response pulled the angler into the water. 'You supported the Medici?' Angelo gasped.

'Lorenzo was my hero, the secret friend of an only child,' I confessed. Was it the sea air? Was it that we were not in Florence? – my confession became full. 'But I was a Volterrano before I was a Medicean, and my love died when Lorenzo made war on us. I felt betrayed.'

'Lorenzo made an error of judgement.'

I said that it was a painful one which had cost many their lives.

'Do you think I lack understanding?' he asked. 'That I do not know what it is like to see death?' And he told me how he had grown up the oldest son and treasure of a father he had adored, a man of high position in Montepulciano, a supporter of the Medici and all that they stood for, a father who had educated his son in Latin literature and had taught him the rudiments of Greek. Then came an evening in May when they were out walking with Angelo's dog, and the murderers struck.

His chin beginning to tremble, he tried to tell me about the attack but failed.

'O Dio! Would that You had taken me before him!' The winds of the Tyrrhenian sea whipped the cries from his mouth and carried them to heaven. Now I knew the cause of his desire for peace, for a society where no man carries a dagger.

The story came from him in fragments, of walking with relatives one night in May, of chasing his dog and hearing, behind him, his father's scream, of becoming frozen by fear while his dog and his cousin bounded to the rescue, of returning home alone to be asked, 'How is it you live?' By the murder of Bendetto the Ambrogini were plunged into destitution. 'My family burned for revenge. Montepulciano is a barbaric place: a few years later, two cousins of mine avenged my father in a bloody vendetta. Some would say that justice was done thereby but the law thinks differently and my cousins are now outlaws in hiding.'

'Do you have brothers and sisters?' I asked, edging towards the subject he was avoiding.

'One brother and three sisters.'

'And your mother?'

Now his features expressed the emotion to which they were least suited: contempt. This was the face of Poliziano which could make others feel dismissed or rebuffed, the face that sent strangers hastening for cover. People who did not know him thought him arrogant, but it was an aspect unfamiliar to his friends, who knew him better as affable, generous and mild tempered. But to be a friend of Poliziano you had first to prove an interest in things beyond the mundane; if you could not, if you persisted in trying to interest him in details about your wife and children, or profits and losses, then you saw that face with the large nose and down-turned mouth and would feel yourself cast to the pigs.

'I have no mother,' he said, 'for a mother is, by definition, one who loves her children. The woman that bore me threw me out, saying she could not afford to keep me. I was nine years old; my father had not been in his tomb a week when I was on the road to Florence to work for my uncle.'

'Is she still alive?'

'She married again. All bonds are broken. I care not whether she lives, nor where.'

As for the rest of his relations, he was all too aware of them, for they wrote to him regularly, telling him that he had failed in his duties to the family, that what his cousins had done, he should have done himself. A small payment, they said, would suffice to retain the family's health, happiness, and good will.

'They are bleeding me. Everything I am given by Lorenzo finds its way to Montepulciano. It is a slow death; if I had killed my father's murderers, then I could be in hiding now and enjoying a sense of self-righteousness, instead of leading this life of guilt.'

'Vengeance is not in your nature,' I said. 'It was not a role for you.'

'Because I am a coward?' He spat out the word. 'They blame me for my father's death; they say I had no right to survive, as if it were my fault that I was not killed. But there is some justice in their accusations, for I did nothing. I could not move. I could not move.'

'But you were only a child.'

'A child who has grown into a man who is not sure if, were the same thing to happen again, he would not react in the same way. Am I a coward? Yes I am! My very being gives assent to the accusation, and says that it is true.'

'It is a brave man who admits to such a thing.'

He cuffed me lightly, mollified by my logic, and asked me what I would have done in his place. I told him that, to judge from my own experience in Volterra, I would have run like the wind. 'The difference between us,' I said, prodding home my point, 'is that I have not been troubled by it since. A man does what he does, and there is an end to it.'

'And if the same were to happen again? – if, say, you were to see a friend about to be murdered?'

I assured him I would take to my heels, especially if it were he.

'Well, if it were you about to be murdered, I would rush to the aid of the assailants. Then I would know my own strength.' Smiling for the first time that day, he rose, dusted the sand off and said we should return to the house before Lorenzo did. 'There are families of the body, and families of the soul. This blood, flesh, bone – and nose – of mine are from the Ambrogini. My spirit abides with the Medici. They are my true family.' He saw my face clouding over. 'They could be yours, too, if only you would allow it.'

'I am ... not ready yet.'

'You are a divided soul in search of unity. Open up that heart, Tommaso. You are your standing in your own light and casting shadows.'

I burned with indignation. I wanted to shout out in protest at the demands of this life, which would have you sacrifice your very self. When Jesus told the rich man to give up all he had, he was not referring to his material wealth. To give that up is easy in comparison. Everyone was telling me to lay myself at the feet of Lorenzo de' Medici, with all humility, in total surrender, and I could not do so.

THIRTY FOUR

FOR ABOUT twelve hours each day, Lorenzo was engaged with civic receptions, meetings with the Signoria, business at the University and with the Pisan branch of his bank; each day he sacrificed his opportunity to join the hawking and hunting offered to entertain his party. Giuliano assured him that he was missing little other than the company of Pisan worthies who could ruin a good day's ride with shallow conversation and fawning solicitude.

'Your aim is laudable, my brother,' he said. 'Pisa needs this University, to cultivate her torpid mind. Imagine living a life which contains nothing but business affairs, leisure, other people's affairs and leisure, your next pious benefaction to the church and how you may make the size of your gift known to your neighbours. The loftiest thing in Pisa is the campanile, and that leans.'

I went on some of these torturous excursions into the pine forests and, whenever I could, created a diversion which allowed Giuliano to escape his hosts to ride on his own. Angelo, soon as tired of chasing hares as he was of arguing with professors, stayed at the house to write letters to the ladies of the family in Florence. Writing to Mona Clarice and Mona Lucrezia twice a day, he soon ran out of things to tell them. Sometimes he wrote merely to say that nothing of interest had happened since his last letter. At last, and in desperation, he gave the ladies his own news, which was that the local food – mostly fish – had upset his stomach, that boredom was giving him headaches, and that he was about to take to his bed.

When not becoming saddle-sore in pursuit of small mammals, I explored the city with the pages Renzo and Andrea Cavalcanti, seeking out frescoes made by Florentine painters. In the Camposanto, a vast cloister housing the tombs of the noble dead, we found many by Benozzo Gozzoli (for whom, despite the scathing denunciation by the Botticelli workshop, I maintained a great liking). As for the fresco by Sandro, which I knew to have been done the year before the joust, it took much finding and was discovered at last in a dim chapel in the Cathedral. Sandro had returned earlier than expected from Pisa, declaring that the Pisans were incapable of recognising true talent. The painting, which was of the Assumption, had been left incomplete. I gazed on it as one might look upon a featherless baby bird that has fallen dead from its nest, marvelling at its form while yet in sorrow at the waste of a life. I was told that Botticelli, having been compared unfavourably to Gozzoli once too often, had quietly packed up his brushes and pigments and said to his apprentices, 'Let us return to our madre patria, who loves us.'

Despite the many fine works to be seen, life in Pisa was dull. The sensation of an intellectual fast became, in Holy Week, accentuated by a fast of the body. Angelo, who had temporarily recovered from his sickness, began to complain of his health again. Frequently Mona Clarice sent him a consoling letter full of good advice along with either a remedy or a recipe for one. But no simple potion could cure the real illness, which was torpor, leading to mental inertia, loss of memory and the death of inspiration. My god of the logos had become a mortal man, an unhappy, melancholy soul. He moped listlessly, complained and bickered with everyone, even Lorenzo.

The other men also became prone to ill temper. Luigi Pulci was not with us so Matteo Franco, robbed of his butt for witty insults, turned on the harmless musician, Baccio Ugolini, who astonished everyone by silencing his tormentor with one brutal punch to the chaplain's jaw. Lorenzo's personal physician, Stefano della Torre, meted out a potion of valerian to calm us all and help us to sleep. Some blamed the Pisan air and begged for a speedy return to Florence, but I was not convinced by tales of airborne animiculae, invisible to the eye yet potent with malignant force, caused by the position of Saturn in the firmament. I thought instead that what we suffered was the result of Lorenzo's breach with Ficino and the Academy. The unique friendliness and brotherhood of the house seemed to be dissolving.

I sought relief in a book which Angelo had borrowed from one of the professors at the University. The hand was in the style of Poggio and yet distinctly individual. I scoured the book for clues to the scribe's identity but found none. The more I studied the letters, the more I delighted in their perfection: the respective heights of body and stem were in harmony and never varied from line to line. I measured them and formulated their proportions in numbers. Familiar ratios emerged and, as an experiment, I borrowed a lute from Baccio and played the measures that were delighting my eye. The ratios of the script followed Leon Battista Alberti's canon of beauty in architecture, which itself imitated the intervals in the musical octave. No wonder the pages of that book seemed to sing.

Over the years in the Medici household, my hand had developed in response to the needs of dictation; it had become, without my noticing it, careless and irregular. Though it might please an untutored eye, any fellow scribe would have dismissed it: the letters were badly spaced, ill-formed and finished with quick, thin strokes in the place of true serifs; a lazy hand by a scribe whose opinion of himself was greater than was warranted.

Humbled, I spent time refreshing my craft, for something once known is not necessarily known for ever. The way of nature is a way of corruption and decay. Order is a divine force working in the opposite direction, which Man may aid by conscious effort. In exchange for my continuing lessons in Greek, I helped Angelo to improve his writing style and to develop a fair hand, an occupation which, unlike everything else in Pisa, Angelo found good for his health. But it was still my hand that was used to write out copious notes from the books of ancient authors: Ovid's *Fasti*, the Homeric Hymns and Horace's *Odes* in particular. Angelo marked passages descriptive of certain gods which I then had to copy and send to Sandro Botticelli. As usual my master refused to answer any of my questions about this work.

The time of Tenebrae was spent in prayer and private reflection. I copied out an extract from Saint John in my revived formal hand, intending it as an Easter gift for Father Piero Strozzi; if I could finish it before the courier arrived, he might have it by the Sunday.

There was a clatter of hooves in the courtyard, either much earlier than usual or else my sense of time had gone awry. The hour glass had run out of sand – how long ago? I leant out of the window to see the sundial, but a simple glance at the sky was enough. By the clock of the sun itself, it was only mid-afternoon. Puzzled, I went out into the corridor. Angelo was coming towards me, looking pale and distracted.

'Has the courier arrived?' I asked.'Why so early?'

'I do not know. Perhaps he has some urgent message for Lorenzo.'

He looked so wilting that my attention was diverted from my own concerns. 'Are you ill again?' I asked.

'I have in my head a prophet of doom, cudgelling my brain with dire portents. If I am to keep vigil tonight, as Lorenzo desires, then I must go to my bed now.'

In a momentary conflict, duty overcame desire. No doubt Father Piero would be gratified by my present, whatever day he received it. As I helped Angelo to bed, he gave me a list of items he required from the apothecary.

'You should not prescribe for yourself,' I said. 'What if your diagnosis is wrong?'

'Luke chapter four verse twenty-three: Physician, heal thyself.'

'Even so, you could ask the opinion of Doctor Stefano.'

'Please, do not let that man near me ... ' he whispered, holding his arm over his eyes to blot out the light. 'Close the shutters and play some music.'

I darkened the room and took down the lute from the shelf. Baccio had taught me simple lines to play upon the lute, lines which formed the spine round which he would weave harmonies on the lira da braccio, harmonies that came to him in the moment, never to be repeated. The gentle melodies composed by Baccio had a quality which survived my uncertain playing and filled the room with an ethereal contentment. As the notes danced like mayflies it seemed all was well and good and that this is how it always is. The good resides eternally but our transient concerns obscure the peace, and make the peace itself seem to come and go. Plato recommends solemn and calming music as the most wholesome medicine for both spirit and body, a recommendation which Ficino enjoined all his friends to follow. Though I had never met Ficino, though Ficino was no longer a friend of Lorenzo, I played his Orphic music to my master as a remedy much to be preferred to leeches.

Suddenly – and for a moment's duration – I became a part of the Academy, an association of men not only of our time but of all eternity. For though the Academy may be traced in history from the age of Plato to the time of its dissolution by the Emperor Justinian, many think that it existed before Plato, and has continued to exist since its closure in the sixth century. Indeed, many consider that throughout the history of mankind there has been a school dedicated to the union of the soul with God; that sometimes its work is hidden; that sometimes it shows itself in the renown of such masters as Zoroastra, Pythagoras, Socrates, Plato, Plotinus and Proclus. This *catena aurea*, a hidden chain of gold, is often obscured by the brilliance of men such as Aristotle, who use the teachings of their masters to make great strides in beneficial knowledge; but though such philosophers most usefully explain the matters of life, and bring us wondrous new inventions, what are these works when compared to the liberation of the spirit? In the theology of Plato, such men deal with the visible world of creatures and shadows, while real knowledge lies in the intelligible world of Ideas.

The notes vibrated in infinite silence. I listened to the music in the silence, as Baccio had taught me to do. Then I heard something other than music: somewhere in the house there was uproar. I played on, so that Angelo would not hear anything but the music until he slept.

When he did fall asleep, his face calm now and the lines of anxiety gone from his brow, I thought to go and discover what was happening, but the clamour had died away. So I finished my text and wrote a short letter to Father Piero, in which I enclosed some pressed flowers from the Pisan coastline. I folded the letter and tucked it into my jacket.

Angelo had grown agitated in his sleep. Now he lay twisted in the sheet, with strands of his long, straight hair both strewn across the pillow and stuck to his damp face. I felt his forehead. It was hot, but not burning; nevertheless I decided to consult Stefano della Torre.

The doctor's presence in the household was new. Hitherto, with the Medici following all Ficino's recommendations for good health – precepts of diet, exercise and music – they had had scant need for a physician, except for the women at times of birth, and even then a midwife had been preferred. Now we had Stefano della Torre, Paduan-trained and severe. Although his acquaintance with herb-lore had recommended him to Lorenzo, he still believed in blood-letting as the principle cure of almost everything. I rehearsed what I would say to him, so as to make him leave his wretched cups behind and bring his simples instead.

As soon as I entered the gallery, however, I became aware of tension in the atmosphere. On the far side of the house something was amiss. As I approached, the sound of argument grew. Raised voices are common enough in any household, but not these two, raised against each other. I had never heard Lorenzo and Giuliano argue before. I found the other men gathered anxiously outside Lorenzo's chamber; the noise from within was furious.

'Giuliano wants to return to Florence,' Baccio Ugolini explained, 'but Lorenzo will not allow it.'

Giuliano's voice carried from behind the door. 'I am your brother, one half of the Medici!'

'I am the head of this family!'

'I am weary of your orders. Who do you think I am? The shadow at your heel?'

'Oh virtuous brother, let me remind you that virtue lies in obedience!'

'That depends on who you obey.'

'You obey your master, who is me.'

'A man may choose his master.'

'You have no such choice!'

'No? Then let me demonstrate my logic. I am going to her. If you restrain me by force, then I am your slave, not your servant.'

We could almost hear Giuliano's astonishment when Lorenzo told him he was free to go. 'But,' he added cruelly. 'You will have to walk. You are not taking any of my horses.'

'*Your* horses? Did my father leave me nothing?'

'He left you half of everything, including responsibility. The

Medici will be keeping vigil tonight at the Cathedral. You will be there. Exercise this duty and I shall grant you your rights – tomorrow you may go to Florence with my blessing. Indeed, I shall come with you.'

'But she may be dead by tomorrow!'

I turned questioningly to Matteo. He put his hand on my shoulder and whispered in my ear, 'We have just had word: Madonna Simonetta ... '

He clapped his hand over my mouth before I could cry out. I felt grief disembowel me; prevented from making any sound, I stood and listened and wondered at the echo of my grief in Giuliano's voice. That others standing with us were tearful was understandable, but Giuliano? When had he joined our company? At what point had his heart melted in love, and how was it that none of us had known? I had suspected him of having a mistress, yes, but it had never occurred to me that it might be the wife of Marco Vespucci.

'Why are they arguing?' I asked, muffled. 'They should not be arguing. Not about this!'

Stefano della Torre came rapidly down the corridor with two attendants. He had been ordered to Florence by Lorenzo, to offer the benefits of his knowledge and experience to the physicians attending Simonetta, and had heard that Giuliano wanted to accompany him.

'Well, is Giuliano coming?' he asked, drawing on his gloves.

'We are not sure,' said Matteo.

The doctor put his ear to the door as if it were a patient's chest. 'I cannot wait for the outcome of this. Giuliano can catch us up, if he comes. Tell him that we are taking the San Miniato road.' He strode towards the stairs. I ran after him.

'Are your horses ready?' I asked.

'Yes, with no thanks to you. Where have you been?'

Where? – where but transcendent in happiness, oblivious of what was happening in the world. Now shaken and brought back to earth by mortal sorrows, I both remembered Angelo and simultaenously realised that this was not the time to ask the doctor's advice. Instead another frenzy was shaking me, one of the body rather than the soul. Not replying to the doctor's question, I turned and ran on ahead of him, running like a hare which keeps to accustomed routes even in panic. The urge to run filled my being before the motivating idea became obvious; but then it exploded in my mind like a revelation. Now I ran with purpose: if Lorenzo intended to put out an order against the use of the horses by Giuliano, he had not done it yet; he was still in argument.

I rushed into the stables, calling to the grooms, 'Are the horses for Doctor Stefano ready? Good, then bring them out now, and be quick!' Then I ordered one of the grooms to saddle Mercurio and leave him at the fountain beyond the gate. This much was the plan, but not all of it. I hesitated. That moment – it was less time than the heart takes for one beat, but it was an interval in the octave of my life which was to send me off on a tangent. The groom was looking at me expectantly. I told him, 'Saddle Bravura.'

As one can have foresight, so can one have fore-fear. This action of mine was beyond my allotted scope; but then merely by initiating it, I could expect as much punishment as if it were to run its full course. Therefore – the full course it might as well be.

I ran back into the courtyard; meeting the doctor, I told him that his horses were ready. 'And I have had Giuliano's saddled, in case he wants to follow you.'

Such is the force of love that a man may move on the level of the planets, creating events and actions, and everything takes place according to his plans. Thus I could even tell the doctor what I had done, such was my confidence. As I bolted up the stairs, I met Lorenzo's page running down.

'Stop!' I said. 'There is no need for you to go on. I have already given the order.' And like a magician waving a wand, I was gratified to find that I could stop a boy in his tracks, could turn him round and thus change events begun by others.

I ran on, coursing through apparently frozen time. At the top of the stairs, and in accordance with my desire, I met Giuliano; he looked as alert as a hound, ears pricked for the sound of the horn. One glance from me and he knew what to do, part as he was of this communion with the gods. He bounded after me, back down the stairs. We sped past the bewildered page who remained where I had left him on a landing, down to the courtyard and out of the gate. We were mounted and away before anyone realised what we were about.

We did not take the San Miniato road but went by Empoli so as to evade pursuit; not that anyone could have caught us. We had the fastest horses, and Giuliano led us through the dark on a rough road using a sense better even than sight: the instinct of a born hunter. Within the hour we were amongst the hills but our pace barely slackened, until, that is, Giuliano came to a halt near a stream, saying that we must rest the mounts. I jumped about in agitation, wanting to know why we could not change them at a hostelry; but Giuliano was right, we would reach Florence quicker having spent time resting these two winged horses than if we exchanged them for some hard-mouthed nags.

At the second stop, we dismounted at a small chapel, next to which a spring trickled from the hillside to splash into a basin which had been carved in the rock. A statuette of the Virgin stood in a niche above the basin, sanctifying the water. Ghostly in the moonlight, she stood with eyes lowered and hand raised, a reminder of peace to weary travellers. Giuliano led the horses to water, then, when they had done, he plunged his head deep into the basin. Emerging at last, he cupped his hands to drink.

It was too early in the year and the night too fresh for him to cool himself this way. I unlaced my jacket, drew off my shirt and gave it to him to dry himself with. As I did so, something fell to the ground, unnoticed until Giuliano picked it up later. He rubbed his head with the shirt and encouraged me to refresh myself in like manner. I held the back of my neck under the chill fall of pure water and, after the initial shock, was gloriously revived. I joined him where he lay on a bed of fragrant pine-needles to share his hard pillow of a boulder; but Giuliano sat up, beckoned me up too, and dried my hair with my shirt. Then he folded it up, placed it on the boulder and pushed me down towards this makeshift cushion.

'Please,' I said. 'I would rather you have it.'

'I am used to hard pillows.'

'It seems you often stay out all night,' I observed.

'More than I used to,' he said, and smiled cryptically.

'Hunting?'

'No, not hunting.'

He obviously wanted to say more and was awaiting a prompt to do so, but how could I encourage Giuliano de' Medici to divulge his secrets? It was beyond my scope. However, as I have said, my field of activity on this night seemed unusually vast; no longer a servant moving within prescribed limits, I was a free man. So I prompted him. 'What is it, then, that keeps you out at night?'

'My mistress, what else?'

I sat up so abruptly that I nearly hit my head on the sky. 'Giuliano! Who? Is it ... ?'

'No, no, it is not the divine.' He sighed raggedly and lay down to gaze at the stars. 'Do I love Madonna Simonetta? Of course I do. I have done so since my first sight of her, when I was about fifteen years old, as I remember, and she the same age and newly betrothed. That moment spelt the end of my boyhood. But the love of another man's wife, whatever my brother thinks, is a cardinal sin and I have done my best to overcome my desires. No, she is not my mistress. The love of my mortal heart is Fioretta of the Gorini family, and yes, it is also a cardinal sin to love outside marriage. But listen, Maso, I fully intend to marry her, as soon as I dare raise the subject with my brother.' Giuliano sighed again. Fioretta Gorini, he told me, far from being a ravishing beauty, was one of the most quiet, most shy young women, plain in the eyes of many, and the least demanding of attention in all Florence.

I lay back, staring at Venus bright in the sky, wondering what it would be like to be an unattractive girl singled out by one such as Giuliano. I was made giddy by my own imaginings.

'So far as Lorenzo is concerned, my hand in marriage is a political advantage not to be wasted on a small family like the Gorini. He wants me to wed one of the Pazzi, to strengthen the bonds of the two families. I will prevaricate of course, and delay things as long as possible, at least until my son is born.'

Beginning to feel like a nail under the hammer of his revelations, I let out a squawk. Of all the questions I wanted to ask at once, two came to the fore: 'How do you know it is a boy? Which one of the Pazzi?'

'The baby is restless and makes her uncomfortable. This signifies, according to the wisdom of her nurse, a boy.'

'And Lorenzo knows nothing of this?'

'No one knows of it, except Fioretta, her nurse – and you. And why am I telling you? Because I trust you. I could trust the others, of course, but they are too close to Lorenzo and might feel more bounden by their loyalty to him than to me. It would not be fair to tell them. Besides, it would spoil the plot of Angelo's poem, whatever that might turn out to be. As it stands, I am about to be transported into the realm of Venus to learn about true love. I think if I were to reveal the truth of my life and love his Muse would be rendered dumb. But you, you are safe, being anything but close to Lorenzo.'

'No, I am not very close to him,' I replied sardonically.

'Whatever it is that you fear in my brother, you are mistaken.'

'I would say, from what I have heard, that you fear him too.'

'Yes, but wisely. You fear him unwisely.'

I lay back, exhausted. The water trickled peacefully into the basin while owls hooted in the pines which encircled us. Against the starlight the trees stood out in sharp definition, looking down on us like baffled doctors.

'Not so unwisely now,' I thought, and shivered in realisation of what I had done. That sensation of eternal peace I had enjoyed while playing the lute had been broken all too soon by passion. And what of Angelo? I had left him, my master, without a word; and I had left him in need.

'Those platonic conspirators,' Giuliano said, 'who invoked the gods to make me fall in love, succeeded, but not in the way they expected. You see, I was already in love, but because of my belief that love leads men astray, my affections were corrupted – no more than secret lust reined in by guilt. Then, on the night following the joust, and realising the lesson I was being taught, I allowed my love of God to merge with that for my lady; when lover and beloved become as one, that is a moment of bliss. And so, some months later my son was conceived. Which was not, perhaps, the aim of my tutors, but when you invoke the gods, you call upon powers beyond Man's control.' He rose to his feet.

'What is this?' he asked, stooping to pick up the letter which had fallen from my jacket. I took it from him. It was sodden.

'It was nothing,' I said, screwing it up and throwing it away. The youth who had copied a text from Saint John for his beloved old master had been cast into sin by a single, wilful action of disobedience. Father Piero would not want to know me now. 'A thing of the past,' I said.

Giuliano sensed my distress. 'There is no law for lovers,' he assured me, a refrain often heard amongst Lorenzo's friends.

'Yes there is. Lovers may not think so, but oh yes there is. Which of the Pazzi are you to marry, Giuliano?'

He shrugged and said he did not know. It was irrelevant.

Church bells began to ring: close by, further away, distant, all through the land. It was midnight. In hamlets, towns, lonely wayside chapels, bells were ringing. Joy! Joy! While the world celebrated resurrection, Giuliano and I remounted to keep vigil with death.

I glanced at the valley below where a ghostly mist was coiling above the Arno. The land was steeped in mystery. What god moved me tonight, I wondered. Was all this ordained, as much as the first Easter? At the sight of a skeletal dead pine, I thought of Judas, tying a rope, to end the life he had chosen, to pay for the crime which had been divinely ordained.

'To Florence then,' said Giuliano. 'May the spirit of Easter heal and renew Simonetta. Dear God, let her live!'

'And let me live, too,' I thought. Giuliano had nothing to fear from Lorenzo but token wrath, whereas I, I had everything to fear. The initiator of this venture would be its scapegoat.

THIRTY FIVE

ALTHOUGH the bell of the Palazzo della Signoria was the deepest, that of the campanile of Giotto was the loudest. The rest, from Santa Croce in the east to Santa Maria Novella in the west, from San Marco in the north to Santo Spirito in the south, boomed and clanged, their sound reverberating in the tall, narrow streets until all Florence was one joyful tintinnabulation. The fasting was over. The sun rising on Easter Sunday reminded us of the resurrection of Our Lord.

We entered the ringing city like two dusty, unshaven brigands. The streets were running streams of people making their way to Mass, fresh, happy, adding their voices to the babel of bells. We threaded a silent, weary path through them.

'Giuliano,' I said hesitantly as we neared the Palazzo Vespucci. 'How angry will Lorenzo be with me?'

'The worst he will do is to bellow at you at close range.'

'I do not think I could face that.'

'Fear is a strange, irrational thing. When the day comes that you have some authority yourself, you will find it hard to believe that people might be frightened of you, because you will know that you are harmless. Lorenzo, I am telling you, is harmless, and you will come to no harm.'

'Humiliation can hurt more than physical injury.'

'Yes it can, that is true, but know this, Tommaso, you will be the better for it.'

We arrived at the Palazzo Vespucci before Stefano della Torre and his attendants. Making a remark about the tardiness of doctors, Giuliano entered through the gateway. He turned to ask if I would go with him, but I shook my head. I was too distant an admirer to be present at such a scene. 'Then go to Ognissanti and pray for her, Maso, and beseech God in my name also. Tonight, meet me at Ficino's.'

I gasped.

'Have you not always wanted to meet him? Tonight I will introduce you, as my good friend and faithful servant.' So saying, Giuliano entered the palazzo.

The way to Ognissanti led past Sandro's bottega. As usual on a Sunday, Botticelli was at work, for his idea of keeping the sabbath was to work but for no reward. Instead he spent the holy day practising his skills and making studies.

On this day the workshop was dim with sorrow. Dust drifted in on sunbeams to settle on the wooden benches and the broken tiles of the floor. There was a scent in the air, the fragrance of the earth. It was of the pine resin, gum mastic and wax stored on the shelves. Though the precious stones and minerals were locked up in a chest, the dust carried the colours of red porphyry, sinoper, hematite, lapis lazuli and Baghdad indigo.

Filippino, possessing no home other than the bottega, spent his Sundays practising drawing circles freehand in the manner of Giotto. That the master Giotto had been able to perform this feat was legendary, and would have remained a legend but that Leonardo da Vinci had managed to repeat it himself. Now Filippino, like every other painter's apprentice in the city, took every opportunity to stand at arm's length from a wall, turning arcs with chalk, seeking perfection of form, and not finding it.

But on this day I discovered him slumped on a stool with chalk in hand, doing nothing but staring at the floor. Botticelli was standing at the open door at the back of the shop, his arms braced against the lintel, looking out into the yard. Filippino stirred as I entered and, as it were, came back to life. He acknowledged my bedraggled state in one glance and said, 'So you have heard, then.'

'Does she still live?'

He nodded, going to the fire to poke at logs and raise a flame. 'Come, warm yourself.' He took my damp shirt and hung it before the hearth. Sandro returned into the shop and, over cups of hot wine and hunks of dry bread, I told them my story. The more open-mouthed Filippino became in admiration, the more tight-lipped Sandro's disapproval.

'You are a fool to have crossed Lorenzo like that,' he said.

'He will not do anything,' I said, repeating Giuliano's optimism.

Sandro rolled his eyes.

'He may shout at me, but that is all.'

'Oh, he may not have you drawn and quartered, but he may dismiss you, and then where will you be? Is work for scribes so plentiful that you can abuse your patron this way?'

I blanched. 'It had not occurred ... I did not think ... '

'Sandro, enough!' said Filippino. 'Do not frighten him. He will be safe under Giuliano's protection.'

But Sandro said, 'It is Giuliano who will come out of this affair unscathed. If I were Lorenzo and looking for someone to blame, I know who I would choose.'

'Lorenzo is harmless,' I said, as if simple repetition would make it true.

Filippino whistled. 'If Tommaso dei Maffei thinks Lorenzo de' Medici is harmless, times have changed.'

'No, not the times,' said Sandro, irritably. 'It is his mind that has changed, but too late and for the wrong reason. Oh, Tommaso! Why is it now, now that you have every reason to fear, that you become fearless? Think of all those times past, when you flinched even at the name of Lorenzo and for no good cause. It is now that you should be flinching. You are a fool! Still, even fools can be useful,' he said, leading me to the little yard behind the workshop.

'Mona Simonetta ... ' I said.

'We will not speak where only prayers can help. You can pray while I work, for work is my prayer. And there is much to be done, fine work, of the highest order.'

While Sandro moulded me into a pose as if I were a wax maquette, Filippino set up his master's easel. 'Your cousin is still in Florence,' he said.

'He was supposed to go to Padua.'

'Perhaps his orders have been changed. You should visit him and seek his advice.'

The anatomy of the gods is obviously different to that of men. As my limbs were arranged in the pose of Mercury, they began at once to ache. Standing contrapposto was easy enough – I had by now sufficient practice in the jutting hip of the idle Florentine – but then Sandro gave my torso a slight twist and had me holding a stick aloft in the air, for what turned out to be a very long time.

'I do not need his advice,' I said. 'And he is not my cousin after all, but my brother. I am the natural son of his father.'

Sandro, pulling back my head until my gaze followed to where the stick pointed, said, 'So that is what you and Pipo have in common: both bastards. I often wondered ... '

Filippino sought assurance. 'Your father was not a monk, was he?'

'Oh no, that honour is all yours.'

He blew through his lips with relief and settled down to make a brush. With the delicacy of a woman sewing, he arranged miniver hairs into a point, bound them with silk thread and inserted the brush into a goose quill which he stiffened with a twig of maple. Whenever he was agitated, Filippino made brushes, for the intricacy of the operation calmed him. I glanced at him now and again, watching him as he sat fiddling with hairs. Despite the shadow of concern thrown upon us by the Palazzo Vespucci, he was content as ever, and yet he had so little: no home, no possessions, nothing but his attachment to his master. Were he, for whatever quirk of fate, to leave Sandro, he would be utterly rootless. And were we not in the same position? At last the enormity of what I had done dawned on me fully. The action had been based on a fanciful notion of being Giuliano's squire; I was no such thing; I was the servant of Angelo Poliziano, and I had deserted him.

I stood in pose for Sandro for an hour or more, mental torment reflected by agony of body. Filippino, having finished a square-ended brush of hog bristle, went to prepare a meal.

I tried to have a conversation with Sandro. 'What is this work?' I asked. 'Does it have anything to do with the notes I have been sending you from Angelo?'

'Do not speak: I am drawing your mouth.'

There were a series of rapid scratches of charcoal, followed by a frustrated sigh.

'You are Hermes, or Mercury,' he said, 'and you are pointing the wand of Hermes towards the sun, signifying the way of return for the soul. Could you try to look reflective?'

'How?'

'Let your eyes shine. You are in love with God, and gazing towards him rapturously. Let us have some light from you.'

Hermes might be pointing his wand towards God; I was pointing a stick towards the upper storey of the Palazzo Vespucci. The windows of the palazzo were shuttered.

'What ails her?'

'Keep still. It is her lungs, a wasting disease.'

'Can the physicians cure her?'

'Be quiet! She has the best doctors in the world with her, but her cure lies with God.'

'Is this picture for her?'

'No, it is for a new and mysterious commission from Lorenzo. It is to become part of a wooden settle, which, so far as I am concerned, makes it a marriage gift. But for whom? Could it be for Giuliano? Have you heard anything?'

'No, nothing.'

'I told you not to speak! I have been given a year to complete this, but if you keep talking I shall need two.'

I stood for a seeming age with my arm high and pointing upwards. There is a threshold to pain, at which the only desire is to scream for relief. As that cannot be done when Sandro Botticelli has ordered you to keep still, there is but one resort left, which is to pass through a door you had not noticed until it opened before you. To cross its threshold is to step into another realm, where there is no pain, no time, where nothing moves. In that place I saw Simonetta.

She stood in a flower-strewn meadow, dressed in a pale shift which moved lightly about her in the breeze. Her hair was loose, the colour of saffron, the texture of silk, and as light as down. Seeing me, she held up her hand in shy greeting as if I were her annunciating angel. And what I said was this: *These forms are transient; beauty is eternal, and of God.* The scene behind her darkened; a view of a city appeared, and the road leading towards it was a well-trodden one, used by everyone who passes through this life. I raised the wand of Hermes, the snake-entwined caduceus. *Do not take that road,* I said to her. *Go this way!* She began to step cautiously towards the light, the source of which seemed to be myself.

'Bravo – that is it!' I heard someone say. 'The right expression at last!'

The next thing I knew, tears were coursing down my face. Sandro was wrapping me in a blanket, apologising, saying he had taken me beyond endurance. I could say nothing. Everything in me had stopped except the tears. Sandro brought me staggering to the front of the easel. As my head was lolling forward, he held it up by the hair, demanding me to look, to see. I blinked to clear the tears and saw a drawing of a young man with a luminous face. Then my head drooped again. They tried to carry me inside, but I was wilfully heavy, desiring to wait until ...

It came, my release, in a long keening from an upper room in the Palazzo Vespucci. I joined the threnody in a howl, a wail of lamentation.

Sandro shook me roughly. I came back to the world to see Filippino Lippi weeping and Sandro Botticelli with his eyes aflame.

'You know the soul is immortal,' the painter said urgently. 'You have heard it said, now you know that it is true, do you not? What did you see Tommaso? Tell me what you saw, and then tell me why you grieve.'

'We grieve,' said Filippino angrily, 'because we shall never see her again!'

This is the usual retort of Everyman to the Mystic. I stood somewhere between the two, vacillating, torn by the evidence of my senses on the one hand, and on the other that inner knowledge which requires no evidence. I knew in my very essence that there is no death of the soul, yet before my eyes people died and disappeared. And all the knowledge in the world, from the wisest of masters and deepest of hearts, could not stop the grief.

On the twenty-sixth day of April, 1476, Simonetta Vespucci, to all appearances, died. True, a new star was observed that night in the skies. But what is a star to the vision of beauty here on earth? Small exchange. Or so it seemed to me in my youth.

THIRTY SIX

What were the positions of the planets in those Cain and Abel days? Was Saturn or Mars in the constellation of Gemini? Certainly it was not a week to be a brother. My meeting with Antonio was bruising both to soul and body as he physically conveyed his opinion. 'Are you mad?' he shouted, banging me hard against the painted wall of his room in the Palazzo Pazzi. 'You have ruined everything!'

'I tell you, Lorenzo will not be back for a week, and by then he will have forgotten.'

'Forgotten? You are insane!' he cried.

'If not, then I must take the consequences.'

At this, he laughed acidly. '"Consequences" – what a soft word to choose when it means the rack.'

'Lorenzo does not use torture.'

Antonio snorted in derision. 'That is not true.'

'It is true.'

Wearily he rubbed his eyes with his fists. 'Sometimes I wonder whether it would not be best if I just ignored you.'

'Sometimes I wish you would. Besides, you do ignore me.'

'Is it neglect to wait for hours at a tavern for a brother who has no intention of turning up?'

'Antonio, I have explained about that, and I am sorry, but I was sent to Lastra. I do not want to fight ... why do we do it?'

Antonio peeled me off the wall and dabbed the blood gently from my nose. 'It is because I love you. Because I love you, I find your foolishness more galling than gall itself. I want you to be perfect.'

'As you are?'

'Precisely.' His mouth remained severe but his eyes began to twinkle. I punched at him, he parried, we wrestled.

When at last, Antonio having won the scuffle, we lay side by side exhausted on the floor, I asked him why he was still in Florence. Apparently he was waiting for letters to arrive from Rome, after which he had to go to Milan.

'Do you want to come with me?' he asked.

'What, and risk meeting Duke Sforza? No thank you. I would rather stay and risk meeting Lorenzo.'

'Better the devil you know, eh?' he said, helping me up.

'You cannot compare Lorenzo with Sforza.'

'Why not? They are friends.'

'Allies, not friends, and only allies for political reasons.'

'You nursling. If you would learn about the world, you should travel. It would help you to mature, to grow out of these puerile hopes and fancies. True, Sforza is a tyrant, but at least he is an honest one, with no pretence of being anything else. I would rather a tyrant with horns than one with a halo. At least you know where you stand. Come, come with me. Leave the Medici. I will find you a post in the Vatican, something which will allow you to travel.' He seemed urgent in his desire.

I was torn. Despite what I had said, I was truly scared at the prospect of meeting Lorenzo on his return from Pisa. It would be so easy to run away, to set off to Milan with Antonio, but I knew that if I did, I could never return to Florence. After brief reflection, I shook my head. 'Believe me, I dearly wish to come with you, but I intend to remain. Punishment gathers interest like a debt: better to be done with it straight away.'

Antonio gripped me by the arms. 'I will be straight, brother. You are in tremendous danger if you stay here. You asked for my advice and this is it: quit Florence without delay.'

'I can only hope that you are wrong,' I said.

I was escorted from the Palazzo Pazzi by the blackamoor. I asked him if he were happy and he said that he was content to serve his master.

'Would you not rather be free?'

He looked at me then, and his eyes were profound. 'I am free,' he said quietly.

I left the palazzo not knowing where I should go. Vespasiano's bookshop was closed; the moon was rising over the city. Suddenly I remembered ... Ficino's house. Would Giuliano have gone there, or would the death of Simonetta have changed his plans? Either way, it was too late now. I made my way through the streets, avoiding the night patrols, and came at last to Botticelli's workshop and the door to sanctuary.

Over the following days, I earned my meals and a bed of straw by posing for figures: Mercury again, each one of the three Graces, a terrified nymph. I was grateful when Filippino took the most difficult pose, which was of a Zephyr in flight.

'These figures have been taken from numerous sources, but what is the theme of this painting?' I asked, at least once a day, but was ever told to be quiet as my face was whitened with a chalk paste and my cheeks and lips were reddened. Dressed in a gauzy silk chemise and wearing an actor's wig, I sought my reflection in the looking glass; expecting to see a woman, I saw instead a pitiful monstrosity. I erased the red, insisting that no nymph would colour her face.

'You are in pursuit of the nymph,' Sandro said to Filippino. 'You have only one thing on your mind. Look lusty, boy.'

'Lust? Easy. Let me show you.' Filippino arranged himself on the dais. Fixing his gaze on a form within his own imagination, he became lasciviousness personified.

'Bravo!' cried Sandro. 'Do not move!'

It was too much of a temptation not to taunt Filippino as he stood there, not to pucker my lips and blow kisses, expecting him to collapse in laughter. I admit I did try, but I failed. This was art, and art was something, the only thing, which Filippino took seriously. One narrowed glance from him and I stopped my monkey antics and turned away, just in time to see figures at the door. The civic guard entered without announcing themselves, three of them, two guards and the captain, and clearly none of them was in the Guild of Fools.

'Is there a Tommaso dei' Maffei here?' the captain demanded.

'No,' said Filippino straightening up, both unabashed by his nakedness and unafraid of the guard. 'We have none left in stock, have we Maestro?'

Sandro agreed. 'We did have one but he was taken off to Pisa a couple of weeks ago.'

'Has he been here in the last day?' asked the captain as if no one had spoken.

'How could he have been, if he is in Pisa?' said Filippino.

If I stood there trembling, it must have added to my girlishness, for the captain demanded to know what I was doing alone in the company of these men. 'She is my sister,' said Filippino quickly, while my tongue stuck to the roof of my mouth. I nodded demurely, keeping to the shadows.

'When you see Maffei, you are to report at once to the Palazzo della Signoria. Do I make myself plain?'

'What has he done?'

'Just make that report when you see him,' said the captain, indifferent to either Botticelli's reputation or Lippi's irreverence.

When the guard had left, the apprentices mobbed me admiringly, demanding to know what I had done. Sandro and Filippino however, their bravura performance of flippancy over, looked pale and troubled.

'O Dio ... ' I moaned. 'What is happening? Did Lorenzo send them? Is he back?'

Sandro shook his head in disbelief. 'I cannot believe that Lorenzo sent them. No, I cannot believe that.' So saying, he left the shop to obtain more information.

I turned to Filippino. 'Do you have the price of a horse?'

His mouth dropped. 'No, and nothing like it. Anyway, you are not leaving Florence.'

'By heaven, I must!'

'But where would you go?'

'If Antonio has not left yet, I shall go to Milan with him. Otherwise it will have to be Rome.'

He insisted that I do nothing, at least until Sandro had returned. When Sandro finally arrived, he looked relieved but still troubled.

'It was the tamburazione,' he said.

That musical name denotes a box at the Palazzo della Signoria. Into it may be dropped anonymously any accusation a man would like to make against another. It was a feature of republican Florence, designed to make the process of law available to all. It was commonly held that its benefits outweighed the obvious abuses to which it was prone. 'Should a man be wrongly accused,' said ordinary, law-abiding people, 'then he can always prove his innocence in court.' They did not know the damage that can be done to a man by a false accusation, especially when the charge is sodomy.

I laughed in shock. 'Me?'

'Who with?' Filippino asked, his voice bearing, I thought, an interest that was unwarranted, given my innocence.

Botticelli shook his head doubtfully. 'I cannot believe it.'

'So you should not!' I protested.

'Come on, who with?'

'Listen!' I turned on Filippino, outraged. 'It is not true!'

'I know that. But I still want to know who else was named!'

'Leonardo,' Sandro murmured.

This was too much for Filippino. He sat down heavily.

'It is obviously not true,' said Sandro. 'Someone has a grudge against Leonardo, or you, or both of you.'

'Which means that it was not me,' said Filippino. 'I only fulfil one of those conditions, and even I would not do such a thing to Leonardo.'

He and Sandro began to speculate about the rival workshops of Ghirlandaio, Pollaiuolo and Gozzoli. They concluded that no artist would do such a thing, since being found out would result in immediate expulsion from the guild. Interrupting them, I said that I had better go. I needed to find Antonio, if he was still in the city.

Having made my way through the streets wrapped in a woman's cloak, I told the porter at the Palazzo Pazzi that I had an urgent message for Antonio dei Maffei, and that he was to come to the courtyard to see me. To my relief, he was still resident. My disguise was better than I had thought and Antonio was taken aback to discover he had a lady visitor, even more so to find who it really was. Having recovered, he hurried me to his room. No emotion showed on his face as I told him all that had happened. I tried to meet his eye to discover his thoughts, but he evaded my gaze; this, I presumed, was from embarrassment at my dress.

'Well, you certainly look like a sodomite,' he said with disgust. 'I am leaving for Milan as soon as I have one more signature on one more sheet of paper.'

'What paper?'

'That is irrelevant, like all the work I must appear to be doing, but still it has to be done.' Antonio decided that I should ride as his assistant, both of us in clerical robes, and covered by letters from Rome. 'We shall leave at first light tomorrow.'

He said he must find a party for us to travel with, then, as soon as we were out of the city, I would have to double back, skirt the city and take the road to Rome, for he considered it too dangerous for me to go with him to Milan.

'If Sforza's men discovered you, they would make a pie of you and send it back to Lorenzo as a gesture of goodwill. No, you must throw yourself under the protection of the Holy Father. He is the one man in the land immune to Lorenzo's diplomatic strategies. You could not find any safer refuge than the Vatican. I shall write a letter of recommendation to Count Girolamo Riario. He will see you well.'

He thought that, rather than live at the Palazzo Maffei, it would be best if I took rooms elsewhere, for at least until such time as he returned to Rome. 'My mother will have to be told that you know your parentage and I must do that in person.'

When at length we had agreed on what I should do, Antonio stretched. 'By the way,' he said, 'Is it true?'

'What?'

'The accusation?'

'Of course not!'

'You can tell me,' he smiled. 'I am your brother.'

'It is not true!' I cried, stamping my foot petulantly (what is it about costume which affects gestures?)

'I would not think any the less of you. I am Roman, urbane, I understand these things. I mean, Leonardo is very attractive.'

'It is not true of me, and it is certainly not true of him!'

I was about to ask Antonio for the loan of some clothes when a young priest burst into the room crying, 'Aha! Is this our little catamite? I have just heard the news.'

Antonio introduced Stefano da Bagnone, the house chaplain and 'tutor to Ser Jacopo's daughter'. This piece of information Antonio delivered with a wink, but I was more concerned with the accusation that had been made, and my innocence. The odious man began to commiserate with me. 'Poverino! What a miserable business. And your lover arrested and going to trial!'

Certain that the accusation had been made to plunge me rather than Leonardo into trouble, I felt bleak grief and no little guilt for Leonardo's plight. 'He is innocent! I must put a stop to all this. Antonio, if I were to go for trial myself ... '

'They would find Leonardo innocent and release him. You they would castrate.'

Some things are worse than death. Hearing myself whimper, I pulled the wig off. The falling of my own hair into place caught the chaplain's gaze. The decision I had made so daringly, even arrogantly, in Pisa, had released events that were now coming at me in waves and drowning me in fear. I would have given anything to go back a week in time, to make another decision, a simple decision based on duty and obedience, which would keep the world on a steady axis. Now everything felt wrong, chaotic and uncertain, as if under the power of demons. Demons, yes, the wreckers, the breakers of destiny. I had surely been destined to live and do well in Florence? Now I was to be catapulted to Rome, a place I detested, all on an impulsive act. And I had missed my one chance of meeting Ficino; missed it forever. My course in life had irrevocably altered.

'I presume it was Lorenzo de' Medici who made the accusation?' said Stefano da Bagnone, still gazing at my hair.

'One of his men, without doubt, acting on instruction,' said Antonio. 'Does this not have his mark? The first rule of a clever tyrant is to make any act of violence appear to have been made by someone else. After all, he could hardly clap Maso in gaol for saddling a horse, could he? So he manufactures a better reason, and hides behind anonymity. You have to admire him.'

This would have sounded plausible, but for one thing. 'If it was Lorenzo, why did he implicate Leonardo? He is his patron and loves him.'

Antonio and the priest exchanged glances.

'Loves him too much, as I hear it,' said Father Stefano. 'I mean, locking a beautiful youth away behind walls. Is it not just the kind of thing a sultan might do?'

I had already begun to experience adulthood as a process of having veils ripped from your eyes, but the duplicitous world that was being revealed to me now was of shadowy, unnatural sexuality. Antonio saw my expression and bade the priest be quiet. 'Leave it now. You have said enough.'

Father Stefano ran his hand over my head. 'Oh, take no notice of me.'

I spent a sleepless night, kept awake by the belated realisation that Elena was the natural daughter of Ser Jacopo, that the hideous chaplain must spend hours with her every day and yet be indifferent to her beauty, that he was in the next room and that the door between us was not locked. Antonio, however, slept peacefully beside me, leaving me alone with the dark and my torment. As to what other residents there might be in the house, I was as unaware of them as they of me. The hours passed slowly, marked by the bell of the Badia.

The following morning Antonio left me in the chaplain's care while he went to arrange travel. If the constant chatter of Stefano da Bagnone did not drive one to murder, his restlessness might. There was continual movement in him. He was forever touching his nose, rasping the stubble on his chin, running his forefinger across his lips or scratching behind his codpiece.

'So, you have lived in the Palazzo Medici,' he said while I stood at the window. 'Tell me about the Magnificent brothers. Giuliano is a handsome youth, no? Strong in body and mild in temper they say. He is certainly muscular, you can see that at a glance, and his hair – so lustrous and black. Oh, that joust! – what a vision of manly beauty. What is he like in private?'

'I hardly know him.'

'Nobody knows him well, but I hear that you know him better than most. Intimately?'

'What do you mean?'

He looked at me disparagingly. 'You know what I mean. Leonardo was not your first lover, was he?'

'Stop this!'

'Giuliano – now there is a prize. Why deny it? Good heavens, if such fortune were mine, I would be shouting it from the campanile. They say that he has a cold heart, that he has no taste for women. Is it true? Is his taste, then, for boys?'

'Say nothing more!'

'Hush now. I am only curious. Tell me about Lorenzo.'

'Lorenzo is a happily married man with four children.'

'I know that, but what is the truth of him? Where does he sleep in the palace? Does he have his own room or does he sleep with his wife? Forgive me, ha! I cannot bridle my curiosity. Is Lorenzo's room next to Giuliano's?'

Such detail! I demanded to know why he was asking me these things.

'You know why.'

'No, I do not.'

'It is my interest.' He scratched his head and found something of equal interest under his fingernail. This he ate. 'I have long held that you do not know a man until you have seen how he sleeps. For instance, does he toss and turn? Does he lie on his back or on his side? Does he snore? What hour does he retire? What hour does he rise? Does he relieve himself during the night? How often does he bed his wife? Does he bed his mistress in his own house or in hers? These are the questions that interest me.'

'Well, they are of no interest to me.'

His face puckered up as he scratched his chin. 'Antonio tells me that you slept with Angelo Poliziano.'

'We shared a room.'

'And not the bed?'

I spun then and caught him by the throat, an act of aggression that Antonio would surely have appreciated, despite this man being, for some inexplicable reason, his friend. The chaplain's whining apologies transmuted my anger into disgust. I let go of him and turned away.

As the bells of the city began to toll, one by one, with melancholy, I returned to the window and looked down on a funeral procession passing below. The solemn escort was formed of the Company of the Magi; white robed they surrounded the open bier like ghosts. I could see her face clearly, and the mere sight of her cleansed me of the pollution of Stefano da Bagnone. I hung out of the window in grief, feeling such pain as if my heart could bear no more. One glance, one last glance of supernal beauty ...

'Now there is a curious lot,' said Stefano joining me. 'Not like other confraternities is it? I mean, you do not see them abroad engaged in charitable works.'

'You cockroach!' I blazed at him like a hundred suns. 'Take your hand from me. You are disgusting; you are gross! Be gone from me!'

He backed away, whining like a beaten dog. 'I only wanted to know ... It is true, is it? – that the Governor of the Compagnia is Giuliano de' Medici?'

I spun back to the window and leant out again, studying the figures of the procession, trying to recognise the form and gait of the cowled man at its head. And I did recognise him.

'You did not know?' said the chaplain, joining me again. 'That proves it is a secret society, and a political organisation. Lorenzo says that he does not run Florence, that it is the Signoria who are in governance. But where are the Signoria on a Tuesday night? They are at San Marco with the rest of the so-called Magi. And Giuliano de' Medici is their chief.'

He leaned out of the window. 'Who are they burying then? Who are you burying?' he called to those below.

'The lady Simonetta,' someone called back.

While Father Stefano was half way out of the window, I took the opportunity to leave the room and the palazzo, despite Antonio's orders to the contrary. I made my way to Ognissanti along the path by the river. Amongst the swelling throng of mourners, I was unlikely to be noticed by the guard; besides, I had lost care for my own safety. The procession came down the Via Nuova. Consisting of all the members of the Vespucci family, it had the bereaved Marco at its head, and another. His face covered by a pointed hood, the Governor of the Company of the Magi walked at Marco's side.

The bier was carried low so that the people of Florence might gaze upon Simonetta for the last time.

'Look at her,' sobbed an old woman beside me. 'Even lovelier in death. Even lovelier!'

Now that I was close to the cold, alabaster face framed by embroidered linen, I saw only inanimation. Simonetta's beauty had flown with her soul. 'Help me,' I whispered. 'Wherever you are, intercede on my behalf.'

'You would do better to pray to saints,' said a voice in my ear. I turned. Only Filippino could appear at this moment, with a huge black eye and a grazed cheek. In answer to my concerned enquiries, he insisted that an easel had fallen on him. I told him that I was due to leave in an hour, ostensibly for Milan, in fact for Rome.

'Here, I have this for you.' He gave me a bag packed with my clothes and belongings. 'And this ... ' He pushed something into my hand. It was a medallion, cast in bronze, of the Phaedran charioteer, the emblem of the Platonic Academy.

'Where did you get it?' I gasped.

'Giuliano came to the bottega with your bag. The medallion he took from his neck and made me promise to give it to you. He said that you are to keep it as long as you can, to raise money on the strength of it if needs be, but not to sell it at any price. He also said to note its meaning: that the soul is a chariot pulled by two horses. One is a noble steed, the other is a rig. I do not know why I am telling you this: it is all nonsense of course.'

'Do you understand its meaning?'

Looking embarrassed and awkward, he told me that, Platonically speaking, the horses represent the good and bad inherent in each man. 'A good life depends on the skill of the charioteer. Most men spend their lives on an erratic path, pulled about by contrary horses beyond their control. A wise man holds a tight rein. I am only repeating what Giuliano said, you understand.'

'And you think that is nonsense?' I asked.

'Well,' he looked sheepish. 'There may be something in it.'

'I can tell you from my experience over the past week, it is painfully true. I am being dragged to Hades by that black horse.' I contemplated the image. I should have reined in at Pisa. Raising the medallion to my lips, I kissed it. 'Let this be my talisman, to bring me home one day.'

'Poh! Talisman indeed. It is just a graven image!' Filippino seemed glad to have something to scorn. 'Giuliano said more, that you are to be patient, to leave Florence and to bide your time. You will know when to come back. Apparently the stars will tell you. I am telling you all this because I am your friend, and because I promised Giuliano that I would repeat his message faithfully. But I have to add that I would rather drown in a cesspit than have such ideas in my head. I hope you do not mind my saying so.'

'Pipo, how did you get that black eye?'
'I told you, the easel fell on me.'
'Who pushed it?'
'Fear is getting the better of your reason.'
'Tell me the truth!'
He sighed. 'Someone at the tavern began to repeat the slanders about you. So I hit him.'
'And he hit you back.'
'Rather hard. But then he had friends to hold me while he struck.'
I had to be satisfied with that, even though I was convinced that it was still not the truth. According to Antonio, the civic guard only asks once for information. The next time they come, they get what they came for. 'What can I do, to make up for the trouble I have caused?' I asked.
'Go to Rome, keep safe, come home.'
'Farewell then, Filippino di Fra Filippo Lippi.'
'Farewell, *bastardo ordinario*. Write me letters.'
'It would be better for you if I did not,' I said darkly.
He shrugged. 'As you will.' He walked off briskly towards the workshop. One of the apprentices was using the funeral as an excuse to escape from work. Without breaking his pace, Filippino caught hold of him, marched him back to the bottega and pushed him inside. At the door, Filippino glanced over his shoulder at me. There was no smile on his face, only a three-quarter profile of thoughtful, sad, reflection. Then he raised his hand in a dismissive gesture, passed through the doorway and was gone.

THIRTY SEVEN

ALTHOUGH the arms impressed upon its wax seal were those of the Riario, the letter from Rome looked like a papal bull, and had the same effect. The towers of Florence were still visible behind us, glowing serenely in the morning sun, when the messenger caught up with our party and delivered the missive to Antonio. In a moment we had our backs to Milan and had begun to ride south. I asked Antonio why he had to go to Rome suddenly, but nothing in the letter had given him any reason. It seemed that it suited the Vatican – or, rather, Count Girolamo Riario – to have an agent wandering Italy on vague duties. Though Antonio was happy to go where he was sent, and to do what he liked when he arrived, he was annoyed at going from Rome to Florence and back again: it implied lack of forethought on the part of the one who moved him.

Over the following two weeks spent in the saddle, however, Antonio forgot his irritation. He was happiest when travelling, for each day brought him new sights and new acquaintances. One evening we came across a man going to a millstream with a riotous sack in his hands. The sack bulged, heaved and gave out pitiful mewlings. Having paid the man handsomely for his bundle, Antonio presented me with a sackful of piebald kittens. We released them in a wood, where nature would take care of their fate, for Antonio thought that God's will was more cleanly interpreted by nature than by man. 'Most will be eaten by bears or wolves, but, who knows, one might survive.' I wanted to keep one of them, to ensure its survival, but Antonio admonished me for being too tender-hearted, so we let the kittens go. They were cautious in their freedom and were soon bunching together, shivering and terrified.

'Drowning would have been better,' I declared, stricken with grief.

'The world is a cruel place,' Antonio said, pulling me away from the helpless little things.

He talked to everyone we met: pilgrims on the road, peasants, mendicant friars, goatherds, soldiers. Dressed as a priest and having an affable manner and keen interest in what anyone had to say, he made people feel blessed by the attention of a pious man. But he was no Franciscan, content to move as God willed. Antonio dei Maffei had a mission, which was to defeat the power-mongers at their own game. For that reason he rode up and down the peninsula as a servant of Girolamo Riario, using every opportunity to inspire people to renew their self-respect; and, it has to be said, to give more thought to their woes and seek greater reward here on earth.

On arriving in Rome, he arranged for me to stay in rooms near Saint Peter's. We parted near the Palazzo Maffei; Antonio inhaled deeply to prepare himself to confront his mother and said that this was to be the first test of his new authority in the family, that he must not fail. As he was speaking, several friends of his approached and interrupted our conversation with resounding greetings and affectionate embraces. I left him then, to wander away and explore the city. 'Maso!' he called after me. 'I shall see you in a day or two!'

Two days passed without a word from him. To ease the waiting, I went to Trajan's column to renew my studies of the letters inscribed on its base, always hoping that my absence from my lodgings would prompt a message to arrive. Four days passed. I began to keep watch on both the Palazzo Maffei and the Camera Apostolica, hoping to catch sight of Antonio. After a week, I began to avoid my landlord, who was wanting payment for my accommodation.

Late one night I wrote to Filippino to congratulate him, for I had heard news in the city that Botticelli's workshop had won the commission to decorate the walls of the new chapel at Saint Peter's. I signed the letter 'Hermes' in case it was intercepted. Four weeks passed; patience turned to anger, anger to fear. Finally I went to the Camera Apostolica and sought out Raffaello in his office. He looked so astonished at my sudden appearance that at once I shared the emotion. 'You must have heard I was here?' I told him that I had arrived in Rome together with Antonio a month previously.

Raffaello groaned and ran his fingers through his hair. 'What game is he playing now?'

'I have looked everywhere. Something must have happened to him.'

'Antonio is always disappearing. He comes and goes like mist on the Tiber. I cannot tell you how many times I have been left wondering if he is dead, only for him to reappear, perhaps a year later, saying that I was a fool to worry. Well, he has told me that so often that I now agree; I refuse to worry any more.' He looked at me askance. 'So why are you in Rome? And where have you been hiding?'

I had hoped that Antonio would have told Raffaello the story and spared me the necessity. Now I had to tell it myself and face his wrath.

'You have done *what?*'

'It was not my doing!'

'Who was it then, who fled Pisa?'

'Yes, very well, but I waited in Florence prepared to take the punishment. Then came the accusation in the tamburazione. I did not leave voluntarily: Lorenzo sent me into exile.'

Raffaello continued with his own train of thought. 'You deserted Poliziano? Abandoned him? Left your master?' It seemed he was playing the synonym game.

'But I did not, at least, not intentionally!'

I had not seen Raffaello so angry before. His nostrils flared, his lips became thin, his eyes harrowed my soul. 'What have you done? Friends gather at my home for readings of his work, for I am the one in correspondence with the great man and my cousin is his scribe. Now you walk in here, and without a shred of remorse announce that you have forsaken the greatest poet alive! And presumably I shall receive no more verses of the best poem ever written in Tuscan since Dante! – oh, Tommaso, Madonna! Tommaso ... ' Seeing before me a man having difficulty containing his rage, I regarded Raffaello in alarm. The man he idolised was not the man I knew. I agreed that Angelo Poliziano was the best of all living poets, but he was to me, although very dear, as ordinary as the next man. No one can live with another human being and consider him more than human. I was beginning to find Raffaello's hero-worship annoying.

'It is not the life of Angelo Poliziano which is threatened, it is mine. Me, your own brother!'

Raffaello looked up sharply. 'How long have you known?'

'When I left Antonio, he was on his way to the house to prepare the way for me.'

'To live with us? My mother would never allow it.'

'If Antonio says I must live in the house, then she will have to abide by his wishes.'

'Antonio succeed where our father failed? Ha! But he is not here to perform this miracle, is he?'

I did not share Raffaello's certainty that nothing had happened to Antonio. It was as if he had disappeared mid-sentence. When I left him, he was only steps away from the palazzo, and Raffaello said he never arrived. 'Raffaello, I am convinced something has happened to him. Will you not even make enquiries?'

Reluctantly he agreed to do so. We then fell to discussing my future prospects. He found amusing my assertion that Antonio had intended to find me a position through Count Girolamo Riario.

'Is that what he told you? And you believed it? I am sorry to disillusion you, but for the Maffei to obtain a position takes honeyed words, fat purses and much time. I presume you want a lay position? Clerical would be easier, of course, but there would be years of training.' He went on in this manner, making progress in life sound one long, dreary effort. But then Raffaello was a conscientious young man who did everything according to the rules, no matter how arbitrary and obstructive those rules might be. Thus, despite his talents and intelligence, he was destined to achieve little but local fame.

I listened to all his advice and took none. While Raffaello made applications to minor officials, I roamed the city with dual purpose. One was to make enquiries about Antonio, the other was to find employment outside the Vatican. I started picking up odd commissions in unexpected places, for the art of the scribe need not be confined to paper and parchment alone.

In the artisans' quarter I came across a painter working on frescoes in a local church. He needed someone with a good, steady hand to draw the words scrolling out from the mouth of one of his angels. With my combined experience in letter-forming and paint-mixing, I persuaded him that I had been sent from heaven to fulfil his need. Working on a wall among the smells of pigments and binders made me yearn for a reply from Filippino, but nothing came. I began to wonder, to excuse my friend, if in fact he was illiterate. I tried to remember a time when I had seen him read or write, and I could remember no such occasion. It had not occurred to me before, that I had never seen Filippino's handwriting.

On the recommendation of the painter, I was engaged by a mason who gave me regular work, designing epitaphs for monuments. Designing capital letters in Rome! I felt I had come to the summit of my profession in a few easy steps. Soon I was in demand with architects to do the lettering for friezes around halls, or the legends over porticos. It is an art in itself, to have inscriptions conform to architectural limits. You cannot end a frieze with a hyphen or a flourish. The measurements must be exact, the proportions harmonious, the spaces between one letter and the next pleasing. The skills which I had gained from Father Piero Strozzi I employed in Rome to good effect; likewise the skills I had gained from the Bishop, for the difference between mediocre work and great art is the geometry underlying a painting's composition, an harmonious pattern reflecting the simplicity of universal laws. Soon artists were employing me to design for them the geometric composition best suited to the various themes of the Baptism of Christ, the Holy Trinity and the Nativity.

I seemed to be the only person in the family Maffei who was concerned about Antonio, and I knew no rest until I found out what had befallen him. Until I knew for certain whether or not he was dead, I was in a limbo of the emotions, with everything pent up and waiting for the signal to react. Then, on a day during Advent, I was summoned to the Vatican. Certain that the order had come from a petty secretary regarding a mundane position with long hours and small wages, I entered the Vatican halls with an arrogant air, my speech of refusal well rehearsed. In his quest to find me a secure position, Raffaello was often arranging such opportunities, but 'security' is to me a word which evokes images of dungeons and bars. I intended to listen to what this secretary had to say, politely decline, and relish every moment of it. Of course, were he to offer me a position in the library ...

'You are late!' barked a cleric of the Holy City who had been waiting for me. I may have shrugged. I hope I did not; for the door he opened was a tall one of walnut, one of a pair beautifully inlaid with a superb design of cardinals' hats and squirrels. I found myself on the threshold of a great hall of marble and columned aisles, at the end of which, surrounded by attendants, sat a great man in a great chair. Beside him was a girl dressed like a queen.

'You are late,' said Girolamo Riario, the Count of Imola, while the Countess regarded me with a hauteur beyond her years.

I dropped to one knee and made my apologies.

'I expect you know why I have asked you here.'

'Yes,' I said uncertainly, still thinking about a position, only now wondering what it could possibly be.

'It is about your brother Antonio.'

'Oh!'

'You sound surprised.'

'I thought this was regarding a secretarial post.'

'What? No, no. See my office if you need work. No, I simply wish to make your acquaintance, and to apologise.'

I still had my head bowed and was staring at the floor. I became strangely fascinated by a red beetle with black legs that was walking across interlinked rings of pink and green marble.

'You see, so far as I was concerned,' continued Riario, 'it was simply a change of mind. First I wanted him here, then I wanted him there. Antonio is the best of servants. His willingness to go where I send him, at a moment's notice, elevates him above all others. One little puff from me and, whoosh, he is somewhere else, like dandelion seed.' The courtiers laughed. 'Not that I am as capricious as that might have sounded. Look at me, boy.

When there is serious work afoot, I depend entirely on your brother. I had no idea when I sent him to Milan that it would cause his family months of anguish. But then, of course, I presumed he would tell you. There was no reason why he should not.'

'Milan? But if he had to go to Milan after all, why did you call him back here from Florence?'

With a noble and forgiving shake of his head, the Count ignored my impertinence. 'So, are you happy now?

'Oh yes,' I said. I was immeasurably happier. All those months of not knowing were suddenly converted to months of unnecessary anxiety. Raffaello had been right after all.

'And what are your plans in Rome? I hear you are doing very well: your reputation is flourishing. In you the art of calligraphy has been born again, so they say.'

'I am certainly able to earn a living by doing what I enjoy most.'

'Ah, that must be the definition of happiness. I envy you. Are you much occupied?'

'One commission leads to another,' I said.

Riario pulled on his nose, as if thoughtful. 'Would you have time for another, somewhat more ambitious project?'

I looked interested, my thoughts turning at once to the library.

'The new chapel of His Holiness the Pope is about to be decorated. We would like the world to know that Rome can adorn herself as well as Florence, when she wants to.'

Even if it means employing Florentine artists, I thought. I said, 'I believe you have commissioned Sandro Botticelli to do the frescoes?'

'Is he not the best?'

'In my opinion, yes.'

'But then you are a good friend of his journeyman I believe.'

Wondering how he knew so much, I said, 'Filippino Lippi, yes.'

'Son of Fra Filippo.' The Count of Imola smiled then. It was the smile of the diplomat. It said, I know the whole story, I know that in the battle between the Church and the Medici over that dissolute monk, the Church lost and, do you know, I am secretly pleased? It was a man-to-man smile, and I smiled back.

'It would be excellent for friends to work together on our chapel. It is, after all, a holy place, and not an arena for competing rivals. We shall need some inscriptions and I intend to recommend you to His Holiness. Now, is there anything else I can do for you?'

I swayed under the heady caress of this flattery. 'No, I ... I think not.'

'Are you sure? Consider carefully. After all, my powers are wide. Would you not like anything arranged on your behalf?'

'Such as?' I asked cautiously.

'Your relations with Lorenzo are in need of repair, I believe.'

'Lorenzo? But is he not your enemy, my Lord?'

Riario looked offended. 'Lorenzo? My dear Lorenzo? An enemy? Is that what the people say? Good Maffei, a man would be a fool not to have Lorenzo de' Medici as his friend. He and I ... ' he crossed his fingers, ' ... as close as this.' I saw the smirk on the faces of his attendants; I knew the truth; I said I had obviously been misinformed. Riario nodded kindly. 'So, if you wish it, I will petition Lorenzo to pardon you and take you back.'

I gazed at the floor. The beetle had turned back and was retracing its steps towards my feet.

Riario's voice came through the air, soft, warm, persuasive. 'Would you like that, Tommaso?'

To go back? To Giuliano, to Angelo, to the Bishop, to the place of the elusive Academy? Yes, of course, yes. To Lorenzo? I continued staring at the floor.

The gentle voice continued, 'Consider it for a day or two. And you might also consider something else I could offer, such as initiating the process of legitimisation. What we did for Filippino Lippi, we could do for you. After all, we cannot have Mona Lucia locking you out for ever.'

It was difficult to believe that all these bounteous gifts were being offered simply because he had caused me unnecessary worry. I became so bemused at that point that I have no recollection of the audience ending or of being ushered out. I came back to myself in the square where, giddy with excitement, I found myself standing looking stupidly at pigeons. I had met the great Girolamo Riario. Antonio was alive and in Milan. I was on the brink of a tremendous commission, working with my old friends. Among the pigeons I began to laugh at myself for thinking that I had been called to the Vatican to be examined for some minor position.

But I was a fool, then as ever, for I had indeed been examined, had been found wanting, and had been turned down – and all for a task which had not even been mentioned.

THIRTY EIGHT

I SAT with Giuliano's medallion in my hand, running my finger over the relief. It was the work of Verrocchio; if I had been a blind man, then I would have known art by touch. As I ran my finger over the sensuous rises and dips of the relief of two horses, a chariot, and a charioteer, I was indeed a blind man. The sum of my knowledge at that time was but a hazy discernment of the nature of the two horses. It seemed to me then that both my good and bad steeds were pulling together, trotting down the road of life without meeting anything to make the one pull forward and the other pull back. If this were the case, I should have been a happy man, but I was not, and I had a vague feeling that the charioteer – the faculty of reason – was being gently lulled to sleep by the harmonious gait of the senses on one hand, and the notional desire for good on the other.

To remove yourself from all harm and say then that you live in peace is an error. To live in peace is not to protect yourself from exterior threat, but to remove the harm from within. I lived in fact in a void, an avoidance. Indeed, through those days of solitude and prosperity, I was sleep-walking.

I woke up when alarm bells began ringing all over Rome. Everyone hurried to the squares to discover the news: there had been a murder, an act of tyrannicide. Requiem masses were announced in the churches; people were crying as if the loss were their own; great councils were convened to consider the way forward; ecclesiastical Rome tingled with outrage.

My own Tuscan sensibilities tingled, not with loss or outrage, but with sheer excitement. Why was everyone so surprised and upset? Surely it was inevitable that one day a monster like Galeazzo Maria Sforza, Duke of Milan, should be murdered?

Raffaello came to my room that evening.

'I suppose you have heard?'

'You would have to be deaf to have missed that news.'

Raffaello was incredulous, unable to believe that the tyrant had been murdered in a church on Saint Stephen's day and, strangest of all, that his murderers had been devout and pious men. 'Apparently they thought of themselves as agents of God. The people of Milan thought otherwise and slaughtered them.'

'But why? No one could have wanted Sforza in power a day longer than was necessary. I would have expected the murderers to have been carried shoulder-high in gratitude.'

'And yet the liberated slew the liberators.' Raffaello paced up and down. He was disturbed by something as yet unspoken. It was left to me to speculate out loud.

'I wonder if Antonio ... '

'Yes?'

'Well, I wonder where he is.'

'Is that all that you are wondering?'

'What else is there?'

Antonio reappeared in Rome a few days later. He had a kind of quietness about him; the urgency had gone from his manner, and the brightness of his eye had dulled to an opaque gleam. When I had him to myself, I told him of Raffaello's suspicions. 'He thinks you murdered Sforza.'

Antonio laughed shortly. 'Would that I had!'

'But you did not?' A superfluous question, I know, but I wanted to hear his denial.

'What, and arrive in Rome, alive and in the same week? My powers do not extend to the supernatural. But it is wonderful news, is it not? The bringing down of Sforza ... ' He whispered this last as if tasting the words. An image flashed in my mind then, of a satiated cat. This was his look, the repose of satisfaction.

'Did you have anything to do with it?' I asked bluntly.

'I would like to think I played my part, my allotted role. His Holiness the Pope has been praying night and day for the fall of Galeazzo Maria Sforza.'

'Rome wants Milan?'

'You cynic! Rome wants freedom from tyranny for all her people.'

'If you ever taught me anything it was to be cynical.'

Antonio smiled. 'Do you not believe that Rome wants good government in Milan?'

'No, and neither do you. Rome merely wants to add Milan to her subject territories.'

Antonio shook his head. 'What Rome wants is Florence, but, up to now, Florence has had a rather powerful ally.'

'Milan.'

'So, bring down Milan, and ... '

I rubbed my forehead wearily. 'Is this what you have been doing?'

'Girolamo Riario simply gave me a deal of money to donate to certain causes.'

'Only money?'

'What else?'

'I can imagine that, if I were plotting the downfall of a tyrant, but was a pious man and suffering doubt, a word of encouragement would help. And what could be more encouraging than a word from the Pope, and the assurance that, though my life might be in danger, my soul was safe.'

Antonio was delighted with my reasoning and clapped me on the back. 'Welcome to adulthood! You are right in every respect. Look, I even brought Riario's money back, for it was not required. As you say, a word and one holy blessing was all it took.'

'Antonio! Do you want Florence to fall to Rome?'

'I want Florence to fall. I care not to whom. I want Lorenzo de' Medici dead. More than that, I want to be the instrument of his death. And you?' He gazed at me narrowly. 'Tommaso? Do you not want Lorenzo de' Medici dead?'

This was the question that had haunted me for years: now was the time to answer it. I felt breathless, strangled.

'Well?'

'Please, do not ask me that.'

'I know the answer already. If you really desired his death, you could have done it yourself a thousand times. But now, perhaps, you have more cause; the plight of your native city having failed to sway you, you may be more inflamed by your own grievances. The man who exiled you from Florence – do you wish him dead?'

I could not answer.

'The choice is simple: Florence or Rome. Which is it to be?'

All these choices. Did I really have to choose? What difference would it make, if I should choose one or the other? What difference could I make to the world and its history? It was the opinion of Antonio that the future of the world is in the hands of tyrants, and will remain so as long as selfish fools like me abound. 'Do nothing, do not commit yourself, sail with the wind, bend your head, take the knocks and do not complain: that is how to enjoy old age under tyranny. But is that a life worth living? Is it not better to die young in the cause of something worthwhile?'

'Such as the glory of Rome?'

'No! Not Rome. Forget Rome! This is not what I fight for. Rome is but the mallet to crack the nut with. Later, of course, we must dispense with the mallet.'

'So easy in theory.'

'Not so difficult in practice. You have no idea how Popes are elected. Do you really think it is by the Holy Spirit? The Vatican is simple to manipulate once you know how. I, and others of the same spirit, intend to use it against itself. After the war – for a war there will be – we shall set about ensuring the rise of a cardinal who is not one of the della Rovere, or one of the Riario, or one of the Medici. We shall find a good man.'

'And then shall there be heaven on earth,' I said scornfully.

'Perhaps it is a dream, but better by far than this selfish reality you are living, compromised as you are by self-interest and fear. This is our choice: to live under tyranny without complaining, indeed, with some measure of compliance if we would improve our lot, or to fight and die in the cause of freedom. To which course does glory attend?'

I wondered if this noble goal could only be achieved by murder? If so, how can a good pope be born of blood? 'Peace is the difficult path, the path of heroes. And besides,' I added, 'I thought the plan was to ruin the Medici, not to kill them.'

'That is the official policy. But for me, and surely for you too, there is the question of vengeance.'

Vengeance: Antonio's old battle cry. But I had heard it often enough to know now that the sound had changed. There was a weariness to him where once there had been vitality; bluntness where once he had been sharp. Being involved in the Milan conspiracy, however indirectly, he had the blood of Sforza on him. He had killed.

He wanted to know what had passed between me and Count Riario and I told him about the new chapel of Sixtus.

To this Antonio filled his cheeks like a Zephyr and then let the air out in a stream, as if to blow away my arrogance and stupidity.

'It is true,' I said. 'It is not official yet, but I have been led to expect a commission at any time.'

'To do what, pray?'

'The lettering on the friezes. Also, the Count suggested that we start the process of legitimisation.'

Antonio agreed readily to this suggestion, and indeed largely instigated the process himself. Two months later, I was the legitimate son of my father. To celebrate, I was invited to the Palazzo Maffei to dine.

Mona Lucia stared at me in straightforward hostility. After one glance at her, I looked at the other members of the family: four sons and two daughters. The girls kept their eyes lowered but their brothers gazed at me keenly, willing me to keep brave. Not knowing what to say, I took my place in silence. Antonio raised his glass.

'Welcome to our new brother!'

Lucia sat in silence before a dish of uneaten quail. Her grim countenance put me off my own food. I did my best to feel sympathy for her, to see myself as she saw me, which was as a living reminder of her husband's infidelity, but it did not help resolve the conflict.

There was a portrait of Gherardo on the wall. I gazed at it with deep interest, trying to remember any of the conversations I had had with the man who I once presumed to be my uncle. But my thoughts kept turning to my mother. No one has a monopoly on human pain. If Mona Lucia thought she had suffered, what had my own mother undergone?

Half-way through the meal, Lucia suddenly found her voice. In a high, grating tone she began to tell me how well her sons were doing. I agreed that they had all grown and prospered since I had last been to Rome. And, I added boldly, my own mother's son was also doing well. As I was wondering whether to illustrate this point with an example, such as the likelihood of a commission to decorate the Sistine Chapel, I was taken aback by tears streaming down Mona Lucia's face. I glanced round at the others. The girls looked moved, the men aghast, but all were frozen. I found myself rising and going to her, hugging her and saying, 'I do not even know her name.'

'It was unpronouncable. We called her Sylvana,' said Lucia. She gently disengaged herself and rose to her feet to face me. 'A slave girl, Circassian. Gherardo's brother gave her to him as a wedding present. I think it was meant as a jest at my expense, for she was very pretty where I was not.'

'Mother!' cried the eldest girl, rising. 'Stop, you do not have to tell us this.'

'Please allow me the right to speak when I need to. You can see for yourselves that I am no beauty, but I had a good dowry and impeccable ancestry. Despite all temptations, your father was loyal to me for years. Look at you all: Antonio, Raffaello, Mario, Gianbattista, Piera, Caterina – you came one after another – for six years I was either pregnant or confined. Is it any wonder that your father turned to that girl? At least, that was my own father's opinion. "Men must be men, my dear," he said, "and your husband is faithful to you in his heart."'

'Mother,' said Antonio, firmly, 'enough! You can tell the girls about it when you are alone.' One by one, the family was coming to its feet.

'No!' said Lucia resolutely. 'You men need to know these things too; else how will you learn to honour your own wives? Men! You set the rules which only women are to keep. Adultery is a sin says Holy Mother Church, and in the Bible it is the adulterous woman who is stoned, but what of the adulterous man? Men, the rule-makers, bend the rules to suit themselves. Bastards born to the wealthy are made legitimate and become princes; sons of popes rule the land.'

'Mother!' said Antonio sternly.

'No, I will speak! You think that sins may be atoned by the purchase of an indulgence, bastards made legal by a certificate, wrongs put to right by the payment of a fee. You think you can buy your way out of anything. Is there no God above the Holy Father? No Divine Judge of right and wrong? Do you think God is *blind*? Tommaso, your mother was a slave, made captive by Pisan seafarers, wrenched from her village and her own parents, brought to Italy and sold to our family. For the first three years she could neither speak nor hear, our tongue being foreign to her. What did she suffer, working each day from dawn to midnight for no reward? Did she tempt my husband to her bed? Of course not. She submitted, as she had been taught to submit, to his will. And you are the fruit of that sad, sad, girl, who died so that you might be born. And you, Antonio, Raffaello, Mario – what girls have you bedded without thought of their welfare?'

Raffaello and Mario protested; Antonio alone looked guilty. Indeed, he looked penitent. Hearing Lucia speak this way, I heard the son in the mother, but she had discovered him in breach of his own integrity. As for me, I was hearing with new ears Giuliano's self-congratulatory account of the pregnancy of his mistress.

Five young men stood remorsefully before Madonna Lucia Maffei, flagellated by her words. Only Antonio raised his head to meet his mother's eye, and he solemnly promised never to take another woman to his bed but that she be his wife. 'And,' he added, 'as I have no will to marry, let this be my pledge of celibacy.'

'If that is your heart, my son, then take holy orders. Stop this itinerant life and dedicate yourself to God.'

'In time, Mother, in good time, I will.'

I made no such pledge; but, since that time, each random act of lust or love I have tried to commit with anyone other than my wife has been attended by the baleful memory of Lucia, a vision which would quench anyone's fires. A few days later I was invited to live in the palazzo.

'I cannot have my illustrious stepson living in the artisan's quarter,' said Mona Lucia, taking me under the wing of her pride.

THIRTY NINE

IF BEING prosperous consists of living in a home as part of a family and earning a good income through an honest craft, then prosperous I was. I even thought I was happy. But, though my commissions were challenging, interesting and well rewarded, each morning I woke up feeling empty in spirit. I spent much time with Raffaello studying Greek and indulging our mutual appreciation of ancient literature. The time I spent with Antonio was devoted to argument. He alone saw the unhappiness that success was breeding in me and he made his own diagnosis. I was, he said, being untrue to myself. I would have agreed except that his idea of my true self did not accord with mine. And yet, in the end, what you are is determined by the company you keep, and the more I was with Antonio, the more he wore down my instinctive objections to his theories.

In his opinion what good there is in the world goes unrewarded. He had dozens of examples of good men dying of starvation and poverty while evil men flourished. What he thought of God I could never tell because he never discussed the subject. He went to church regularly but more than once I saw him glancing round the congregation critically while everyone else had their heads bowed in prayer. If he lacked belief he did not show it. He would call on the Madonna as loudly as anyone when he was in pain or trouble, and if he was called to play a part in a service or procession he did so with enthusiasm. No one would have thought to examine him for heresy for, if he committed any crime at all against orthodox religion, it was that he gave it little consideration. Once or twice I tried to engage his interest in a conversation on theology or philosophy but soon gave up in the face of blank indifference. His own philosophy, such as it was, seemed to imply that no one has a right to be happy while another is miserable. To my mind this ruled out any possibility of happiness for anyone and, in telling him so, I plunged myself into another fierce argument which I had no hope of winning; no hope because Antonio took everything I said as evidence of my selfish disregard for the rest of humanity. That was the sum of his logic.

So why, you might ask, did I enjoy his company? I have no answer except to say that I found him preferable to any good man who has the social instincts of a sheep. I believed that underneath his cynical surface there was a man better than most, keener on justice, more sensitive to the plight of others. After all, in his disdain of wealth and creature comfort, he had much in common with the disciple, the hermit and the saint. Perhaps I entertained a hope that, once I entered the Academy, I would introduce Antonio to it and therein would he find solace for his tormented soul.

But the longer I was in Rome, the more vague the Academy became in my mind. I had a small box in which I kept items of value, including the medallion. Sometimes I took it out and held it in my hands. Once it had seemed like a magic talisman, and I only needed to hold to find the strength to endure an abysmal exile. But as time passed things were changing, and I might not have noticed except that, every time I took out the medallion, I could measure the difference. Then came a day when, after a particularly brutal argument with Antonio – who, as usual, was accusing me of being a self-satisfied wretch with no consideration of anyone but myself – I went to my treasure to find comfort. I unwrapped it from its cloth and held it in my hand, but what lay there was no talisman now, just a beautifully wrought medallion: its significance had evaporated. It was like a word without a meaning.

Who, after all, was Giuliano de' Medici? Was I not deluding myself to think of him as a friend? Would a friend not have made contact, have done something to help? No, Giuliano de' Medici was merely a rich young man of leisure. I turned the medallion over and wondered what difference the price of its bronze would make to the poor? A new pair of shoes for every orphan; a year's supply of grain for a starving family; a dowry for a girl; the fee for a boy's apprenticeship. All in the price of a medal, a medallion given as a present to an equerry by a young man so wealthy that he could have another struck for himself and not feel the expense of it; it was merely the reward for a passionate escapade, for which the rich young man suffered no punishment, while the equerry went into exile for fear of his life.

With such thoughts attending it, the object was of no more value than the metal it contained. Close by our palazzo was a foundling hospital where abandoned children, many born outside wedlock, were sent. The hospital survived on charitable donations. I put the medallion into the purse on my belt, intending to find out how much I could get for it. Then perhaps Antonio, convinced at last of my inherent worthiness, would let me alone.

That same night I had a dream. I was in the great church of Saint Peter's. On the papal throne sat a man, his face covered by a cowl. That he was the Pope I knew, but, in the strange logic of dreams, at the same time he was also Marsilio Ficino. He listened carefully to a list of grievances made by a queue of supplicants; he listened to the details of the conspiracy to murder Duke Sforza; he listened to the plans for the new republic of Milan; he listened to the fears that Italy, weak now in the north, was about to fall prey to the Turks. He laughed. The people grew angry. The Master took up his lyre, tucked it under his arm and began to play. Each heart, weighed down not only by its burden but by an even heavier weight (which is the desire to keep one's burden), began despite itself to lighten. The Master played on until the misery lifted, from the church, from the city, from the whole world. There was no more misery, no more tyranny, no more poverty.

There are thresholds to dreams; moments when the dreamer knows that he is dreaming and can manipulate the vision. Even while the image of heaven on earth was expanding, a thought occurred like a whispering voice: take the opportunity – lift the cowl – see who he is. The man himself lifted the cowl. I woke up.

I lay there, my heart palpitating. The sight of his face had caused a silent explosion in the soul. Every inner organ was trembling. I knew one thing for certain, that the dream had been no accident, no chance trick of the mind. It had come from the goddess herself, and I did not understand its import. For the face I had looked on, its eyes holding mine with profound love, had been my own.

Antonio called me to stir myself. It took an effort to respond to this banal event, but I succeeded at last and asked him why he was so bright so early.

'What makes you think it is early?' he said, unbarring the shutters and pushing them out so hard that they banged against the walls. Blinding light flooded in. He threw something on to my bed. 'Here, a letter. It was delivered to the office yesterday but I forgot to give it to you.'

I snatched it up eagerly. There was only one person who knew where I was and I gazed at the unknown handwriting in delight. It was the simple, neat script of a man content with himself. 'It is from Filippino Lippi!' I said. Glancing over it quickly, my scanning eye picked up the words *vescovo*, Volterra and *malattia mortale*. I tried to read the letter carefully from the beginning, but my hand was shaking too much. Antonio took it from me.

'Dearest friend, I cannot write of my news while there is other news that you should know. Your beloved mentor, the Bishop, is suffering a mortal disease and has, against all advice of doctors, travelled to Volterra, there to die. Make haste to join him, for he calls for you.'

I was so distracted that I began to dress like a buffoon, putting sleeves on my legs and hose on my arms. 'What is the fastest horse we have?' I demanded.

'Mine,' said Antonio, taking charge of lacing my jacket. 'Are you sure this is the right thing to do?'

I had no doubts.

After Siena, the landscape grew more and more familiar. It was winter and the rolling hills to the left and the right were patched with snow. The road rose inexorably, mounting the long ridge which culminated in Volterra. When I entered the city by a gate in the massive Etruscan walls, it was for the first time in five years. I stared about in astonishment. It was a cold January morning and, at this altitude, it was dreary with low cloud, yet the streets were alive with people going about their business. In the shops artisans were at work, hammering, sawing, tapping wood and grinding alabaster. Wagons of masons rumbled through the lanes on creaking wheels towards the sites of various new palazzi. Noisy geese were herded to market by peasant girls with switches. Everywhere I looked I saw life in a city I had left for dead.

'Lost your way, lad?' asked a passing quarryman; then, recognising me, he asked my name.

I told him cautiously.

'Have no fear, boy, your family is out of exile now. Besides, you were always the odd one out and more like one of us than one of them. You have grown, lad. Still filching melons off grocer's stalls?'

I assured him that I had seen the error of my ways.

'Mai! You have just grown cowardly with age, like the rest of us.' The man laughed and slapped the flank of my horse, starting me on my way. The last time I had seen him, he had been firing brushwood at the Palazzo del Capitano on the night the town murdered Inghirami.

I rode up the steep lane to the acropolis. To the rubble of Etruscan temples and Roman halls had been added that of our own houses. The Palazzo Maffei was now a heap of stone repossessed by grass. At the summit, where the Bishop's Palace had once stood, was a massive fortress housing a Florentine garrison.

'Where does the Bishop reside these days?' I asked one of the soldiers on duty.

'There are no bishops in Volterra. The see is under the Bishop of Florence now. What do you want a bishop for anyway? Are not priests good enough for you?'

'There is a bishop,' said his duty companion, 'staying in the Cathedral cloisters. Calls himself the Bishop of Volterra.'

'Since when?' said the guard.

'Ask at the Cathedral, boy,' the other guard told me.

I returned to the centre, made enquiries at the Cathedral and was directed to a cell in the cloisters. The chamber murmured with doctors and attendants. The old man lay becalmed, unmoved by the breeze of concern, listening to a curate reading from Plato. I slipped in, trying to be inconspicuous, but he glanced up and his black diamond eyes shone intensely. How I loved those eyes, which seemed as candle flames in a dark chapel. How they loved me.

'So, you have come at last,' he said. His voice rasped in his throat. 'Come forward, boy. Where have you been? I have been sending to you for months.'

'But I have had no letters!'

'Letters? I have sent no letters. Where would I send them to, hmmm? You did not think to give me your address. No, I have been sending for you in my prayers, boy.'

I fell to my knees beside his bed. 'Monsignore, I regret everything!' I buried my head in the counterpane. 'And I am so sorry that you ... you ... '

'You pity me? Here,' said the Bishop to his attendants, 'here is a young man whose soul is in mortal danger. He has exiled himself from friend, master and God. And he pities me!' He gasped for breath. 'I ask you, is that generosity of spirit or mere foolishness? I have no need of your concern, Tommaso. I am on my way home. Save your pity for yourself.'

'Father ... ?'

He stretched out a palsied hand. I received it on my head. Its tremulousness was illusory, a mere expression of the physical world of appearances. All the strength of heaven poured through that hand.

'I have sinned,' I said. 'I took your wealth and squandered it on riotous living.'

'Where have you been?'

'In Rome.'

The old man struggled to raise himself but was made to lie back again by a protesting doctor, who glanced at me accusingly. The Bishop ordered everyone from the room but myself.

'Have you really been living riotously?'

'No,' I said, 'I would not have thought so, but now that I see you, I realise ... '

'What do you realise?'

'I thought I was happy, or at least content, but I was not.'

'Of course not,' he said. He laid back and almost at once sleep overcame him. I stayed with him throughout the night; a few hours before dawn, he awoke refreshed and with enough strength to be concerned with worldly matters.

'This affair in Milan ... I have lived as long as this century and seen many things, but murder in church! God knows, these are sacrilegious times.'

'What has happened since? Is there a republic now?'

'Of course not. The people tore the murderers to pieces.'

'This is what I do not understand. The men were acting for the good of the republic.'

'Murder is murder: the taking of life. Have I not had cause to give this lecture before? Well, listen to me now: no mortal man has the right to judge whether another may live or die.'

'Sforza thought he had such a right.'

'And for this he was murdered. Now his murderers too are slain. He who lives by the sword will die by the sword, that is the law.'

'You make it sound simple.'

'And so it is. Those butchers considered themselves brave men acting righteously, but they forgot the commandment: Thou shalt not kill.'

'What of the people who killed them?'

'A mob. And the fate of the mob awaits them.'

The fate of the mob, according to the Bishop, was to live under tyranny, and so the relentless circle was joined.

'But why were they so incensed?' I persisted. 'There was not one in Milan who in his heart did not wish to be rid of Sforza.'

'Perhaps the people had more sense than those foolish young men. Perhaps the people knew that tyranny is to be preferred to anarchy.'

'How can that be?'

The Bishop looked outraged. 'Foolish boy! Have you not read Plato's *Republic* yet? Read it at once, and learn that there is a hierarchy of different forms of government, beginning with government by the wise and ending with mob rule. "Mischief" means being without a head. If you remove the head of the state, mischief is the result. Without her tyrant, Milan is now in far deeper trouble than she has ever been. Under the regency of Sforza's wife, an eleven year old boy rules, a boy whose half-sister, let us not forget, is the child-wife of Girolamo Riario. What can the city hope for now? The people have been freed only to become slaves to a new and worse tyranny. Worse than that, far worse than that, for the Triple Alliance has collapsed. Venice and, even more so, Florence, is now suddenly vulnerable. The peace of all Italy is in danger.'

I sat beside him on the bed, racked with guilt. I knew I had been speaking with Antonio's voice, and I felt awkward and transparent. The Bishop read my face like an open book, but he made no comment on what was written there, except for one curious remark: 'My name, too, is Antonio.'

This simple statement, which had no apparent meaning, tore through all my pretences and left me naked. But he was not interested in hearing any confession; he wanted only my absolution.

'I wish ... ' I began.

'What do you wish?'

'I wish I were as you are.'

'What? Seventy-six years old and dying?'

'No, you know what I mean: wise. You are wise. Why cannot I be wise? I desire wisdom.'

'"Whatsoever ye shall ask in my name, that will I give you."'

'Even wisdom?'

'Especially wisdom. God would rather grant you wisdom than a horse.' The Bishop tried to laugh but caught his breath.

'Sweet man, please do not leave me.'

'Soon enough,' he gasped, 'I shall be closer to you than ever I can be whilst trapped in this worn out body. Do you not know that you are my own self? Whatever possessed you to quit Florence? You were so very nearly in the Academy.'

I pulled up the sheets to his chin and smoothed the linen. His face was yellow and mottled like old vellum. 'Ask Lorenzo,' I said.

'What does he have to do with it?'

'Ask him who put my name in the tamburazione.'

'He would only tell me that it was your cousin.'

I regarded him with horror and for a while could say nothing. 'Antonio did it?' I stammered at last.

'Who else? Who else wanted you out of Florence even more than Lorenzo did? But to what end? That is what I cannot fathom.'

I shook my head fiercely. 'No, it is not true. It cannot be ... '

'You have two Antonios in your life, Tommaso, and one of them is lying. I leave it to you to determine which of us it is.' He fell asleep once more and I sat by his side, considering everything that had happened, trying to think of what might happen next. The next time we conversed, the Bishop asked me my plans, wanting to know whether I would be going to Florence or Rome. I told him neither, that I had decided to stay with him.

'Call my servant,' he said. 'Tell him I want fatted calf for breakfast.'

That day, in accordance with his wishes, we carried Bishop degli Agli to his beloved Impruneta on a litter, there to die. If the village was closer to Florence than I thought I could endure, all fears were overcome by a sense of duty. The Bishop urged me to go into the city, assuring me repeatedly that no harm would come to me, but this I refused to do.

He had much to teach me still. He explained my flight to Rome in terms of the octave, that I had reached the discordant note re in the scale and, instead of overcoming it to attain my goal, which was entry into the Academy, I had been diverted to a new octave. Such is the way of life, he said. It is all deflections and tangents. Only the determined man of faith can reach the goal. He impressed on me the necessity of not only believing in the immortality of the soul but of letting that belief inform all my daily actions. Then he gave a long, gentle sigh and his soul left on a breath.

I sat there for a long while, trying to believe what he had believed, but all that I could see was a corpse, and a remarkably small one at that. Darkness crept in the room. One by one the candles began to sputter and go out. Then suddenly I was taken by anger. 'Where are you now?' I cried. 'You said you would be with me always. Where are you now?' The hollow eyes, the sunken cheeks, the indrawn mouth, the body collapsed in emptiness: nothing.

I arose and left the room, waking the servant who was asleep outside.

'His Grace is dead,' I said, and hardly knew who I was talking about. The following day, I left Impruneta.

FORTY

Desiderio, I admire the clear knowledge you have of your own mind. It seems your decision to leave England has cost you nothing, that you have simply decided to go. How is that? Even as I ask I can hear your answer: 'I follow the will of God'. Then, my dear friend, all I can say is that I would follow it too, if I knew what it was. With what voice does God speak to you? How can you distinguish it from all those other voices which whisper in our hearts?

IT WAS this very question which perplexed me after the death of the Bishop. For a whole day I stood at the gate of Florence, wondering if I should enter or not. But each time an interior voice said, 'Yes, go in,' another said, 'No, go to Rome.' Well, you say, what else may a polytheist expect? It was Lady's Day, the twenty-fifth of March, and the beginning of 1478. The city was bedecked with colour for the celebrations and it would have been easy to walk in and lose myself in the crowds. I desperately wanted to see Filippino and Sandro who, as yet, had not left for Rome. But the desire to see them was fully countered by an opposing desire to avoid certain others. I was nineteen years old, and, so far as I saw it, the next step I took must determine my future.

'Grant me not my will, O Lord,' I prayed, 'but let me follow Yours alone.'

I thought that if I stood still long enough, by divine impulse I would be moved in the right direction. Nothing happened. The day progressed to noon and the Angelus bell rang in the city. Nothing happened. Beside me was a man with no legs, who moved himself about on a plank to which wheels had been attached, but now he squatted immobile at the gate, begging for alms. Next to him, leaning against the city wall, was another man who had an ulcerous leg. To move the hearts and open the purses of citizens, he displayed the festering sore as another might display his pottery. People entering and leaving the gate looked at me askance, to see what it was that I begged for, and with what good cause, but I avoided their gaze and continued to wait for God. I remained there long into the afternoon, but nothing happened. I was a hollow reed waiting for the Master Musician to play his song on me. And still nothing happened.

I stood there for hours, expecting a divine push into the fires of my doom, but it did not come. By the evening I had tired, and the inner dialogue of a soul with a deaf God became a vague soliloquy of other thoughts, of what it might take to heal that leg, of how the man on wheels had lost half his body, of whether it might rain, and of the gnawing of a stomach on a fast.

My thoughts were pierced by a voice.

'What are you doing, young man? You were here this morning. Who are you waiting for?'

I looked up into the face of a captain on horseback, leaving the city with a small party of armed men. They were not Florentines.

'Where are you bound?' I asked and, even as he was telling me, I was untying my horse's rein from the wall-ring and mounting. 'I am bound for Rome, too. I was just waiting for a safe party to travel with.'

'Well, you have found it,' said the captain. 'Safe, but not comfortable, mind. We travel fast and take little rest.'

This suited me and I followed the road to Rome in the train of ten soldiers. The captain, Giovanni Battista da Montesecco, had been on a visit to Florence to meet Lorenzo de' Medici. More than that I could not discover from the sergeants and men-at-arms who were my companions. To sleep at night, the party did not stop at wayside inns or monasteries but set up camp beside the road, for the captain was both a rigorous enforcer of military discipline and a man with a morbid fear of bedbugs. Therefore we camped in the open. It was March and it was cold. I spent the first night without sleep and, at the point where my toes began to feel dead, I crept from the tent and went to the fire.

Another man was there, Montesecco himself, clicking through the beads of his rosary. 'Can you not sleep?' he asked kindly. 'Is the ground too hard for you?' He asked me my name and occupation, wondering if I were a student.

'No, I am a scribe.'

'I thought so – knew it was something scholarly. Desk work is bad for you, lad. You should turn in your quill for a sword and get some muscle on you. Look at you – scrawny – if you do not mind my saying so.'

I told him that I had a sword, but he continued: 'Defenceless and skinny, what use would you be in an emergency?'

'What kind of emergency?'

'Any kind. Life is full of emergencies. Do you know what an emergency is? It is something which emerges when you least expect it. Like a bedbug. Or a snake.' He studied the ground about him cautiously. 'Just because I am a soldier does not mean that I am illiterate. I may not be a scholar like the Duke of Urbino, but I do know my words and their meanings.'

I gazed at the bright stars, trying to identify the constellations. As I watched, one star came shooting to earth. There is great peace in the countryside at night with the fire crackling protectively and the bejewelled velvet sky above. If only a man could do without sleep, sitting out all night has much to recommend it. For one thing, it allows a scribe and an army commander to speak on equal terms, as if differences in rank belong only to the day.

My companion's face was caught in part by the orange glow of the fire while the rest of him merged with the shadows. 'Men were born to stride the earth, to hunt, to quarry, to farm and to fight,' he said. 'Not to sit in the gloom like owls, hunched over books. Let the women stay at home and do the learning, if needs be we must learn: they are quick and bright enough. Too quick and bright by half, some of them. Are you married? No. Well I am, and I tell you, if I did not keep her pent up indoors with her sewing, she would be out ruling the world. Most of them would. A virtuous woman is a quiet one, do you not agree? Only once let a woman speak and you have trouble. I offer Caterina Sforza as my instance.'

Caterina Sforza, the natural daughter of the murdered Duke of Milan, was the Countess of Imola and wife of Girolamo Riario. She it was who had sat passively at her husband's side during my audience at the Vatican.

'How old is she?' wondered Montesecco. 'Sixteen? And she has Rome in the palm of her hand. That is to say, she has the Pope in the palm of her hand, which amounts to the same thing. She is in his company so much you would think he was the one she had married.'

Realising what he had said, he crossed himself hastily and called on Our Lord for forgiveness. This done, he picked up his train of thought.

'She rarely leaves the old man's side. Now Sixtus – was there ever a man like him for single-mindedness? Look at him now. Prey to the whims of a capricious flirt. And she is ambitious, Madonna, she is ambitious.'

'In what way?'

'Never you mind. Do you think I am indiscreet? Well, you are wrong. I have just chosen her for my instance. All I am saying is that women must be locked up at home with their needlework, or else they will be telling us what to do. The Greeks knew all about women.'

If he expected some reply, he had none.

'Everyone these days is intoxicated with the Greeks,' he continued. 'They read books about them. But what did the Greeks themselves do? Did they spend their lives reading books? No, they wrestled in gymnasia, held games, fought Trojans and vanquished Gorgons. You would not catch an ancient Greek reading a history book.'

'Perhaps not,' I said, 'but you might find a few writing them. Thucydides for example, and Herodotus.'

'Yes, yes, that is all very well and clever, but my point is that these men wrote about wars in which they had fought themselves. Even your Socrates was a soldier, was he not?'

'It is true, he was.'

'Well then, point proved. Not a bad *disputatio* for a soldier, eh?'

'No. It was very good,' I agreed, trying to remember if Herodotus had fought in wars. Certainly Xenophon had led an army.

'We milites are not all brawn, as some people think. We have our mental faculties intact.'

Montesecco then asked me my story, which I gave cautiously

in a shortened version. He was interested to learn that I had been present at the sack of Volterra, for he had been there himself, in charge of one of the Papal companies. 'In support of Florence,' he said incredulously. 'How things change! You would not find Rome siding with Florence these days ... ' He broke off, looking thoughtful. 'At least, I do not think you would. You can never tell. "You must not allow your personal feelings to have sway, Giovanni," – that is what Count Riario is always telling me. "Do not let your emotions intrude." Quite right, of course. First rule of a soldier.'

'You sound doubtful,' I observed.

He sighed heavily, the sigh of a dog who feels much but can tell you nothing. He stabbed at the embers. I kept quiet, for he was a garrulous man and it was only a matter of time before his sense of discretion crumbled under the urge to speak.

'I met Lorenzo de' Medici in Florence,' he said. 'First time I have seen the man. The way he is spoken of in Rome, I expected a hunchbacked, diabolic monster.'

'And?'

'Have you ever met him?'

'Once or twice.'

'You know for yourself then.' His voice dropping to an undertone, he seemed to be withdrawing into himself, to be in fact speaking to himself. 'One of the most noble men I have ever met. Charm, grace, wit; yes, well, they all have that ... '

'What makes Lorenzo different, then?' I asked.

Montesecco was quiet for a while, then said, 'It is a good question.'

Before I could prompt him further, he suddenly asked, 'Do you believe in fate?'

'Sometimes. It depends. I believe in fate when things go wrong; in my own capabilities when they go right.'

Montesecco smiled and nodded. 'Honestly said and true enough. But do you believe in destiny?'

'What is the difference?'

'Fate is what happens to you: destiny is what you may fulfil. Fate like death is inevitable, but you can choose your destiny.'

'Choose your destiny? Of course you cannot.'

'Oh, but you can. Every now and then you have a sign of

what lies ahead, and then you can choose whether to go towards it or not.'

'I suspect that if you turned away from it, you would meet it just the same.'

'Do you?' Montesecco was intrigued by this idea and became abstracted by his thoughts. I stared into the embers, equally thoughtful.

Thus two men sat by the fire, considering their destiny; for all their copious thoughts, neither had an idea that it was one which they were to share. Over their heads the stars began to fade, and in the woods a lonely bird heralded the dawn with a song.

FORTY ONE

As March turned into April and the spring sunshine brought the flowers into bloom, the mood throughout the peninsula was one of reconciliation. The drama in Milan had so alarmed the various despots and tyrants of Italy that they now desired peace, both with their subjects and with each other. According to a persistent rumour, Count Girolamo Riario was keen to forge an alliance with Lorenzo; to this end he invited Lorenzo to Rome. But Lorenzo, the one ruler who had always worked for peaceful co-operation between the states, refused the invitation.

Having been elected into the College of Cardinals, Riario's young brother, Raffaello, was deputed to tour the cities of the north, carrying news of the Pope's good will abroad. Although his ultimate destination was Perugia, no one doubted that the whole purpose of the journey was the visit to Florence. Antonio was appointed as the Cardinal's secretary early in March. When I arrived in Rome, he was making arrangements for his departure with the Cardinal's entourage.

My brother Raffaello was annoyed. He resented Antonio's new appointment, if only because Antonio openly despised the role; to Raffaello, Antonio's way of making it seem that any prestige he gained was unlooked for, was a transparent falsehood. But the true root of his annoyance was envy that Antonio should once again be on his way to Florence, for it remained Raffaello's fervent hope to meet Poliziano. Antonio goaded Raffaello mercilessly, saying that he had already met the dwarf and had no intention of repeating the experience. I practised the art of remaining expressionless while Antonio attacked that which I still held precious. Knives cannot stab water. But Raffaello always retaliated, and in doing so was inevitably wounded. He brooded angrily.

He was mollified by the arrival of a letter from Poliziano. Though it was a brief missive, accusing him gently of flattery and praising him for his fine style, it restored his spirits. It was more, however, than an empty acknowledgement, for it contained another letter. Poliziano had seen fit to add Raffaello's name to the circulation list of certain letters of Father Marsilio Ficino.

This I was eager to read, and Raffaello was about to pass it to me when Antonio snatched it away.

'I forbid you any philosophy. It has a bad effect upon you.' Antonio began to read the letter, and then to laugh. 'On further consideration, perhaps you should read it, and see for yourself what nonsense it contains. Here ... All about beauty. Beauty! He should be in Rome telling us about beauty, not in his Tuscan villa.'

He pushed it towards me. I read it through quickly and, agreeing that it was nonsense, tossed it aside. Antonio was obviously relieved. Raffaello, his anger now curdled by deep hurt, picked it up, smoothed out its creases and laid it on his desk.

Letters from Ficino are to be read alone, in peace and silence, for to understand them fully you must take them line by line, and not move from one paragraph to another until images arise like the sun in the dawn of understanding. Having a strong notion that the letter was meant for me rather than for my brother, in the middle of the night I arose stealthily, took it from Raffaello's desk and went to the church of San' Eustachio; there, by the flickering light of a votive candle, I sat and read.

It was about Virtue. In order to love Virtue, said Ficino, it is better to see it than to read about it.

'Picture a man endowed with the most vigorous and acute faculties, a strong body, good health, a handsome form, well-proportioned limbs and a noble stature. Picture this man moving with alacrity and skill, speaking elegantly, singing sweetly, laughing graciously: you will love no one, you will admire no one, if you do not love and admire such a man, as soon as you see him.'

An image arose; more than an image, a subtle reality, for suddenly I saw Giuliano in all his detail: his black hair, his nut-brown eyes; the sonority of his voice; the touch of a velvet sleeve as he threw his arm companionably round my shoulders. And then the non-physical details: his gentleness, his concern for others, his humility.

Ficino said that outward manifestations of beauty and virtue are shadows of true beauty and true virtue, which reside in the soul. Thus the form of the body represents the form of the soul.

'In truth, just as Virtue herself, when perceived by the eye, would instantly draw each man to her own self by the graciousness of her aspect, so, without doubt, will vice, if clearly perceived, immediately terrify everyone with its deformity.'

Was this a remark about Lorenzo? I stared fixedly at the candle. The aureole trembled but the centre of the light was perfect stillness. If only the light would burn me up, its purifying fire ridding me of all my dross, leaving my heart flame – refined gold. The end of the letter I almost dared not read, in case the taut string of my emotions should snap.

'Come then, friends! Let us always hold before our eye the divine idea and very form of Virtue. She will at once draw us to herself by the grace of her splendour, unceasingly delight us with the sweetness of order and harmony, and completely fill us with an abundance of good things.'

All strength ebbed. The letter fell from my hand, followed by the candle. The light was out before it hit the floor. The silence of the church was filled with the echoes of my grief; the tears washed where the fire had failed to burn, and when at last the grief subsided, I felt empty and clean.

Dawn light was seeping through the windows. Out of the darkness of night began to emerge the figures of the church: Christ the Infant, Christ the Baptised, Christ the Saviour, Holy Mother Mary, Saint John, Saint Ambrose of Milan, Saint Augustine, Saint Sebastian, angels everywhere; and, in the triumphant dome of the apse, the hand from Heaven: God Himself. All the powers, that is, whom I had forgotten.

When I returned to my room I took the medallion from my purse, polished it and replaced it in the purse, to carry with me always in memory of Virtue. Even without it I could not have forgotten Ficino's words. Phrases or whole sentences would come to mind when I least expected them. One day, for instance, I was walking towards Saint Peter's when I saw several familiar figures standing together in the square. One was the dwarfish Francesco de' Pazzi, the Treasurer, as he was fond of telling everyone, of the Apostolic See. He was a man of Lorenzo's age, that is, about twenty-five, and he had that kind of arrogance peculiar to men in their early twenties, when they are old enough to realise their own worth, and too young to recognise the worth of others. With Pazzi was Jacopo di Poggio Bracciolini, looking healthier than when I had last seen him, fuller in the face and more self-assured. Perhaps like me he was finding patrons more easily in Rome. The person these two had met was Count Girolamo Riario.

As I knew each of these men, and, indeed, even owed my legitimacy to one of them, I felt it judicious to approach them, to bow before them and pleasantly to bid them good day before passing on; in short, it would be worth my while to draw their attention to myself. Sycophantic, perhaps, but such things are vital when you live under patronage.

I approached, trying to wipe all this preparedness from my mind so that, when I came to them, my actions might appear spontaneous. Then suddenly I heard an interior voice, resonant with authority: *Vice, if clearly perceived, will terrify everyone with its deformity*.

I halted in my tracks, for vice I did indeed clearly perceive. So clear was the perception, and so stark the voice, that I turned and hurried away. Which is not to say that, in seeing this particular group of men, I saw vice. I was not a prophet. No, I saw the vice within myself. I saw how my lust for the approval of influential men was deforming my soul. If I fled in terror, it was not from others.

Philosophy, it seems to me, is the process of unravelling the twisted tangle of lies and deceits we practise against our very selves. Therefore it appears that the search for truth is painful, but what suffers is the false person, who has wrapped himself dragon-like round our treasure. Challenge the dragon on your own if you can, but it is a perilous affair and may lead you deep into the mire of self-deception. It is better by far to find a master, a guide for the way, as Virgil was to Dante on his spiritual journey. Marsilio Ficino was our guide, even for those of us who had never met him, such was the power of his wisdom. It was no accident that he had written a letter to Angelo Poliziano, which was then passed on to Raffaello, and to me. Of course he did not initiate this sequence of events himself; however, being a friend of the gods, he was their messenger; thus, on the very day, at the very hour, when I was about to offer my services to Count Girolamo Riario, I was repelled and deflected from my course by a terrifying vision of my own vice. I fled across Saint Peter's Square, holding my ears, thinking I had lost my mind, when what I was doing was following Truth.

A few days later, Raffaello and I watched the departure of the entourage of a cardinal who was a mere sixteen years old. Giuliano de' Medici's application for the cardinalate had been rejected on the grounds of his extreme youth; as I watched this callow boy, the Cardinal Riaro, riding proudly by, I watched with the contemptuous eye of a Florentine. Antonio, riding among the crowd of attendants, raised his hand to us. Beside him was a man I recognised as the army captain with whom I had travelled to Rome, Gianbattista Montesecco.

I sighed heavily. 'Do you believe that this is a mission for peace?' I asked Raffaello.

'Without doubt.'

'How can you be so sure?'

'There has been news from abroad: the Turks are gathering their forces. In the twenty years since they took Constantinople, we have been expecting this moment, and now here it is. Our dear Mother Church may be spotted with age, but no one wants to see her turned into a mosque, not even Lorenzo de' Medici.'

I had not heard the news from Turkey. It put everything into such a dramatic perspective that my concerns were reduced in scale.

'It is vital for us to unite against the common enemy,' said Raffaello, 'but standing in the way of unity is Lorenzo's pride.'

'Which is hardly likely to be softened by a visit from a puerile cardinal.'

'That is true, certainly, but Lorenzo must yield, for the sake of the nation – for the sake of all Christendom.'

We were in Raffaello's study when, about a week later, another letter came from Poliziano. We had spread before us a map of the heavens, some tables showing the positions of the planets, and Raffaello's horoscope. He had Mercury in the house of his ascendant; I wanted desperately to know what the heavens showed for me but, as I had no knowledge of the hour of my birth, my own chart was an almost empty square.

'Whatever hour you were born, we are certain at least of the date, and look, here is Jupiter, a heavy planet, in your sign.'

'What does that signify?'

'Wisdom and right action ... ' Raffaello stopped to take the letter brought to him by a servant. I saw the seal as he broke it, the lily of the Medici.

As he scanned its contents, excitement grew like a hectic on his cheeks. 'Angelo Poliziano invites me to Florence, to study with him!' He thrust the letter towards me. The major part of its contents were three ballads on the subject of a young girl in Prato who sang like a nightingale and had caught the poet's heart; there were many metaphors about bird netting; this was the letter of a man who was distractedly in love; the invitation to study with him was a footnote.

'Will you go?' I asked acidly.

'Of course! As soon as I can arrange it with the Camera Apostolica.'

I looked out of the window. My heart was leaden, borne down by regret for the act which had exiled me from Florence, by contrition for squandered opportunities and a misspent life. Raffaello, my tortoise brother, was about to walk steadily past an exhausted hare.

'What troubles you?' he asked gently.

I shook my head.

He laid his hand on my shoulder. 'Having Jupiter in your sign makes this a propitious time for you, when wisdom may overcome passion. Tommaso, come with me to Florence.'

'No!' I cried, and was surprised at my own vehemence.

'I have watched you for nigh on a year, growing as wan as

a shadow at sunset, a listless exile. Admit it: your heart is in Florence.'

'I belong here! I have work which is enjoyable, well received and well paid. I have a home and a family. What is there for me in Florence except imprisonment and death?'

'Do you not have friends there?'

I stood with my head against the cool wall. 'I have friends here.'

He questioned this and told me to name them. I could think of none.

'Can you not see that this is the perfect opportunity for your return? Poliziano is unlikely to welcome me with one hand while he knifes you with the other. And besides, next week there is a party travelling from Rome to Tuscany to meet the Cardinal on his way from Pisa.'

The party was to be led by Archbishop Francesco Salviati. Still prevented by Lorenzo from entering the territory of Pisa, he had not travelled with the Cardinal. Now, with Lorenzo's permission, he was to join the Romans in Florence.

'He wishes to meet Lorenzo face to face, to attempt reconciliation. They were once friends, you know. I believe that Lorenzo has no personal complaint against Salviati; it is merely that, in Lorenzo's contest with the Pope, Salviati happens to be the pawn, or rather the bishop. Now, under the aegis of the Cardinal's visit, they will meet again and perhaps restore their friendship. Even Francesco de' Pazzi is going, such is Rome's desire for peace. Cynicism is a poisonous thing, Maso. You must trust me when I say that the Pope sincerely desires concord. If we fail now, within the year we shall all be bowing to the east with our buttocks in the air.'

'If we are still alive, that is.'

'Precisely. So you will come with me? If there is any risk, it is mine for the taking, for Poliziano might be offended that I have brought you without consulting him first. But I am prepared to hazard it. Are you?'

Thus I returned to Florence in the splendid entourage of Archbishop Salviati, which included many dignitaries of the Church, several legates and members of the Pazzi family. Under a silken and tasselled canopy, the Archbishop rode sedately north, stopping in every town to bless its inhabitants and receive their supplications. People melted before him, as if he were the sun upon snow, bowed their heads in all humility, mumbling prayers and begging forgiveness for sins. The splendid pageant of atonement progressed through Tuscany, following the other papal deputation that had taken this road but a few weeks earlier, leaving the humble people certain that redemption was at hand.

As we approached the walls of Florence, the party turned east, heading for the Pazzi villa at Montughi, there to meet the Cardinal. Raffaello and I left them to enter Florence alone.

It was a soft morning in April. The towers and the palazzi, washed by rain during the night, stood clean and fresh. Was it because I had grown, had reached a man's full height, and the monsters of childhood had diminished, that the dome on the Cathedral looked beautiful? I was entering heaven, and could only hope that I did not have to die to make that entry.

If to me the word 'security' means dungeons and bars, to Angelo Poliziano it meant a house of his own, something for which he had often petitioned Lorenzo. Now he had it, a narrow, three-storey dwelling on the Via di Fossi, and with it the benefice of San Paolo, a small church near Santa Maria Novella. For another man, this might have been the foundation for personal wealth; for Angelo it was the means to pay off his importuning relatives without having to ask Lorenzo for money. Raffaello and I took rooms in the same district, on the Via Nuova and therefore close to the Palazzo Vespucci and the bottega of Sandro Botticelli. I found the bottega empty except for one apprentice deputed to keep shop.

'Where is your master?' I asked him.

'In the Church of Ognissanti, working on a fresco.'

'Is Filippino Lippi still with him?'

'He is still,' sighed the apprentice miserably.

It was a colourful walk to Ognissanti through the quarter of the wool-dyers, where leagues of fabric were stretched out to dry in the sun. I entered the church to find the screen of the choir obscured by scaffolding. Apprentices were either holding bowls of paint for the master, or were at a bench grinding pigments in a mortar, a practice of patience not to be exceeded in any other trade. Just to watch them made my wrists and elbows ache.

A fresco painter has no time to spare. He must cover the area of wet plaster he is working on quickly before it dries; therefore I did not interrupt but stood back to watch Sandro and Filippino, my eyes feeding on the ambrosia of their beloved forms, the stocky master with blue eyes, the long-limbed journeyman with untidy hair. They themselves were oblivious of anything other than their painstaking work. Sandro, standing, filling in the hand of a bearded saint, completed first. Filippino, kneeling, remained engaged in his work on the draperies of the saint's robe.

'Augustine?' I asked, as Sandro climbed down from the scaffolding.

Looking at me narrowly, his face suddenly opened in an expansive smile. 'Yes,' he said quietly, not wanting to disturb Filippino. He ruffled my hair in welcome. 'Yes, it is Augustine, best of saints. Do you like it?'

'What I can see of it, yes. What is that book open on the shelf?'

'Euclid.'

'May I have a closer look?'

'Please ... ' Sandro gestured me towards the scaffolding. I climbed up and stood beside Filippino. In his state of concentration, he was aware of the presence beside him, but not its identity. He did not glance up but kept working quickly on the yellow folds at the feet of the saint. He breathed through his mouth as he hunched over his work. The scaffolding was the perfect height for the areas being painted by Sandro, but too high for Filippino to work comfortably. Doubled up, he laboured in silence except for occasional instructions delivered curtly to his attendant. 'Giallorino. Orpiment – careful, do not put your fingers in the bowl! How often must I tell you? Madonna, do you want to die a quick death?'

I watched the pigments soak into the plaster and grow pale. To feel the wall drink the paint from the brush was for him the ultimate satisfaction, as for me it was to see wet ink form a letter. This was the art: the point of contact between the artist and the surface. The medium, whether it be ink or paint, is that which runs between the two, and when all three are in harmony, as in a triangle, then the chord is struck.

As he neared the end of his area of fresh plaster, I studied the open book of 'Euclid' on the shelf behind the saint's shoulder. I could tell the anguish that it had caused, and which painter it was that had suffered.

Filippino inhaled loudly. '*Bastante,*' he groaned and began to move with care, rising slowly and straightening his back.

I looked down at Sandro. 'Is this a book which Augustine is supposed to have copied in his own hand?'

'Why do you ask?'

'Would a saint not have a fair hand? This is nothing but an illegible scrawl trying to pass itself off as Greek.'

Rubbing the cramp from his legs, Filippino growled.

'It is a splendid painting,' I said, 'but I am afraid that this careless detail ruins it.'

Filippino, having difficultly focusing his eyes after his close work, peered at me. Then, as recognition dawned, he leapt on me and squeezed me until, as if I were a pair of bellows, all breath had gone. We wrestled on the plank, sending one apprentice and the bowl of orpiment flying.

'Come down you two!' thundered Sandro, pulling the apprentice away from the venomous pigment and sending another for sand.

Filippino and I, like devils to hell, made ungainly jumps to the floor, all arms and legs and shouting.

'Tommaso is returned!' he cried to Sandro. 'Tommaso is back! Did I not say he would come?'

To my confusion, I noticed that there were tears in his eyes. Then, suddenly, the rusting portcullis over my heart flew up and its doors were open. Arm in arm, banging against each other, we marched noisily off to the tavern on the Via Nuova, leaving others to clear up after us.

THE FIFTH BOOK

THE OPENING OF THE WAY

For he that beholds must be akin to that which he beholds, and must, before he comes to this vision, be transformed into its likeness.

Plotinus

FORTY TWO

BETWEEN the Via Nuova and the Via di Fossi was a narrow alley, and it led from our lodgings to the house of Angelo Poliziano. Each morning Raffaello walked down the alley to study Roman and Greek literature with his tutor; each morning he suggested that I should go with him; each morning I refused.

'The longer you leave it, the worse it will be. What stops you from coming with me to meet him?'

'Pride, I suppose.'

'And what do you have to be proud of?'

The answer, of course, was nothing, but I would not know what to say, and I was proud of my power of speech. Whether Angelo was angry or forgiving, I would not be able to control my expression, and I was proud of my dignity. Oh, perhaps it was not pride, but cowardice. 'Tell me Raffaello, what is his mood? Is he still angry with me?'

'He is still, although now his wrath has subtly transformed into exasperation, that you are so close and will not trouble to visit him. A vexation heightened by frustration that he has found no replacement for you. Is he still angry? At the very mention of your name the pupils of his eyes contract and his cheeks redden with irritable heat.'

I brightened a little to discover that I had not been replaced.

'He has had many assistants, each dismissed within the month. He says that you spoilt him, that he will never be satisfied with anyone else.'

I considered this in amazement, and found it to be not so much praise for myself as a sorry reflection on my competitors, for I had no illusion that I was the greatest of scribes. What I had that others lacked was perhaps a certain *simpatia* with

Angelo. I thought about him much, and missed him badly, but until I had forgiven myself for deserting him, I could not hope for his forgiveness. So I stayed away.

One evening, when Raffaello was dining with his tutor and his tutor's patron at the Palazzo Medici, I went with Filippino to the tavern. He was in a celebratory mood. The bottega had plenty of work, the contract to decorate the Vatican chapel was being drawn up at last, and the mysterious *Realm of Venus* was completed.

'You remember it,' he said. 'You posed for Mercury, though we have changed him since, replacing your image with one less likely to provoke the wrath of the Medici. Everyone who has seen it says that it is the best painting of our time, better than anything done by Verrocchio, the Pollaiuoli, or the Ghirlandaii.'

'Or by Leonardo?'

'Who can tell?' said Filippino casually. 'Leonardo has not brought any work to fruition, not since the time when ... ' He left the sentence hanging, but he meant since the time when Leonardo was imprisoned. Lorenzo had obtained the artist's release, and all charges against him were dropped, but perhaps the event had its use in serving to remind Leonardo always of the transience of life, of health and freedom. 'Our painting,' Filippino continued, 'is a Mystery. No one understands it. It has become our entertainment to refuse to divulge its secrets until we have first heard the interpretations of our visitors. "Ah, aha! Yes," one will say. "The Virgin Mary, three angels, and – Mary Magdalene? And who is this fellow here, grasping devotedly this young lady saint?" That is a common version. Then there are those with pretensions to learning. They say, "It is a classical scene. From Claudian? Am I right? These are the three Hours and this is Fortuna. And this youth, to judge by his wand, is Mercury. And of course up there is Eros. But who is this god grasping the nymph? And why are there flowers coming out of her mouth?"'

'This sounds the strangest composition.'

'Oh, it is a complete enigma. I tell you, it is embarrassing having to explain your own work. But our landlord is often on hand to give an exposition on our behalf.'

'Your landlord?'

'Yes, our new landlord, a wonderful man, full of knowledge. Each day in the bottega while we were working on the panel, he gave us a singing commentary on antique themes, illustrating the Platonic idea of the return of the soul to the Divine. Creation on the one hand, Grace on the other, Venus bridging them, Mercury pointing the way back to God. You can imagine what I thought of it all, but I have been converted. It has a magic, this painting. It works on you. You will not hear me mocking Plato these days.'

This amazed me more than anything and I longed to see the panel. 'Who is this landlord of yours?'

'Oh, an exceptional man. Do you remember that noisy weaver who moved into the workshop next door? Well, we complained about him, and the landlord, who is as well versed in the law as he is in medicine and all the arts, said that the weaver was doing nothing illegal; for the law states that a man can do as he pleases on his own property. Then, after some thought, he said, "Of course, that applies to you as well." Wisdom of Solomon! On his suggestion we heaved a boulder up on to the roof and rested it on the party wall, in such a way that, should it fall from the vibration of the looms, it would fall on the weaver. Then we left the bottega, in case chance interfered with science. The weaver tried to continue, despite the overhanging threat, but his workers refused and abandoned him. In the end, the weaver left and took a shop in another district. We have fletchers as neighbours now, as quiet as their feathers, God be praised.'

'A most admirable landlord,' I said suspiciously.

'Yes indeed. Benito!' he shouted across the crowded tavern. 'Where is that pasta we ordered?'

The tavern keeper pushed his way towards us, wiping his hands on a greasy apron. He was large and pugnacious; only Filippino Lippi could have challenged the man so audaciously.

'My Lord,' Benito raised his hands in mock dismay. 'Have you been forgotten? What can I say?'

'You could try an apology.'

'I am sorry. I am so sorry. *Mi dispiace molt-issimo*. Marietta! Where are you, woman? The Master awaits his supper!'

Filippino accepted the title of Master with such ease that any sarcasm intended by the tavern keeper was lost. It was obvious from the friendly smiles of our audience in this play that, so far as everyone else was concerned, Filippino was a master, a master painter.

The pasta arrived, cooling rapidly in a thick earthenware bowl, and was banged down on our oak bench without ceremony.

'Just as I remember it,' I said.

'It never changes. The menu of our host is more immutable than any law. Life is so full of change that it gives a man wonderful security to know that, notwithstanding an invasion of the Turks, an epidemic of plague or the sudden fall of the house of the Medici, Benito's pasta will always be the same.'

'I like to think so,' smiled Benito.

'Be assured, good man, it is so.'

Filippino had changed; in the place of brash over-confidence was a quiet acceptance of things as they are.

'You seem to have discovered some foundation in your life.'

'How can a bastard ever have foundation?' he mumbled through a mouthful of food.

'By resting on his own abilities.'

'Well then, you must share the same foundation.'

'I am built on sand, shifting sand, that holds no form.'

When I told him that I felt this, despite having been declared legitimate, and sponsored by no less a man than Count Girolamo Riario, Filippino looked at me anxiously. I asked him what his concern was.

'Nothing,' he said, and continued eating.

'Come on, what is it?'

'I would just rather be sponsored by the Medici, that is all.'

'Well, you were,' I said sourly. 'I might have preferred it too, but I did not have the choice.'

'How much did it cost you?'

'Nothing.'

'It cost the Medici one hundred florins on my behalf; for you it is free. I wonder why?'

'Perhaps because of my inherent charm and good grace?'

'I do not trust Riario, or Salviati, or any of these Roman

ambassadors in Florence today.'

'You Florentine.'

'You Roman!'

'Would that I had the choice.'

He asked me if I intended to stay in Florence and I told him that it depended on my summoning the courage to face Lorenzo; that and the more practical difficulty of finding work.

'Well, I know someone who is looking for a scribe, a man who has much influence with the Medici. He has been looking for a good penman for nearly two years without success.'

'Who?' I asked.

'Our landlord.'

'This superlative landlord ... ' I said, with difficulty as Benito's pasta was beginning to stick to my teeth. 'Who is it?'

Filippino grinned like a satyr. 'The new Prior of San Paolo: Dom Angelo Poliziano.'

When Raffaello returned from his supper at the Palazzo Medici, he brought with him several stanzas of *La Giostra*. The poem had continued into two more cantos, but still the plot had not come to the joust.

'Did you see ... ' I asked, with my face working to hide my emotions, 'Was Giuliano there?'

'He was, and also Lorenzo.'

'How is he? Giuliano, I mean.'

'Even more handsome than I had been led to expect; more modest than I could have hoped for. He is a superb man, an embodiment of *virtù* and a model for us all.'

'Unlike Lorenzo.'

'The roughness of Lorenzo's features is compensated by his pleasant nature. He is generous, intelligent – altogether charming.'

'Charming? I never noticed charm in him.'

'Perhaps he never graced you with it. I was all but overpowered by his good will.'

My lip curled at this. 'Have you forgotten Volterra, so soon?'

'You sound like Antonio.'

'At least Antonio was never overpowered by anyone's charm.'

Raffaello sighed. 'I am tired. I need my bed. God keep you this night, brother. And, by His grace, may reason dawn on you with the morning.'

The following day being the sabbath, I went to the bottega and found, as I had hoped, Sandro and Filippino at work. But the *Realm of Venus* was not there. It had been sent away to the joiner who was making the settle for which the painting would provide the back. Filippino, however, showed me a mass of studies for the composition.

There were nine figures in all. They had been sketched both individually and in groups innumerable times. One group showed the Zephyr of the west wind about to ravish Chloris, the spirit of the earth. For this correct identification, I earned a slap on the back from Sandro and a whistle of appreciation from Filippino.

'You forget whose scribe I used to be,' I said.

'Have you been to see him yet?' asked Sandro.

'I do not understand this third figure. Is it Flora?'

'Yes, but in this scheme she is a metamorphosis of Chloris. When the west wind breathes on the earth, flowers are begotten. Flora is the spring; she is also the goddess of Florence. As Athens had Athena, so Florence has Flora.'

'I thought we had adopted Athena-Minerva.'

'She is the goddess of the Platonic Academy. Now do not digress: you know how shifting these symbols are, each one embodying all manner of things and each one becoming another. Let Flora stand as the goddess of our city which, you will agree, is indeed flowering.'

'Transformed earth,' I said.

'Clothed and ornamented by every fine art.'

The next study showed what I might well have taken to be the Virgin Mary, with her hand raised before the angel of annunciation. But if that were the case, then the viewer himself was the angel. Besides, a winged child attended this lady: Eros. Therefore was she Venus.

'The heavenly Venus,' said Sandro, 'Goddess of Love, love being the means of transformation, the prime mover.'

'But she looks like the Virgin Mary.'

This earned me another whistle of approval. 'Everyone else

says she looks like Simonetta Vespucci,' said Filippino.

'She is the Divine Woman, call her what you will,' said Sandro.

The next group held me transfixed. I have seen many images of the Three Graces, mostly clumsy ones on medals and ancient reliefs. Nothing I had seen resembled these three. Their hands clasped, they formed an eternal knot, of such outstanding beauty that I could think of no way to express my astonishment and delight. This pleased Sandro more than anything I could have said: for any artist the ultimate praise comes not in words. Fully content to see me dumbfounded, he insisted that, of course, this was but the result of much hard effort; to prove it he drew out twenty earlier studies so that I could see how far he had come from his first attempt to portray the Graces.

'How did you do it? How did you travel from this to this? The end is a mighty leap from the beginning.'

'Do you want me to say it was inspiration?'

'Was it not?'

Filippino grunted. 'If inspiration is drawing and re-drawing until you and everyone else around you is half-mad with it, then yes, this is the result of inspiration, which is why it is often and aptly called "divine frenzy".'

'Nonsense,' said Sandro, 'inspiration flashes in a moment, so brief that one sees only the idea which it leaves behind. In this case, it was the idea to raise these arms and lower those. Would that one could see where such ideas come from.'

I thought that the the whole scheme was an inspiration in itself and wanted to know if it was Poliziano's. They told me that, although Angelo had supplied all the narrative details from literature to inform the design, the scheme behind it had been made by Ficino.

Sandro explained: 'Here, on the right, is creation. The soul comes down to earth, in the form of the Zephyr. Then, through love, represented by Venus, and by grace, it returns to the Creator. That is Mercury's role, to point the way. This is not just the course of a lifetime, but can happen within a lifetime. The man who, in himself, returns to the source, will, when he returns to creation, add something significant, a flowering. It is a metaphor of our age, if you wish: as Florence has been the location of certain men seeking God within themselves, so has she flowered. One man returns to God, and the whole world is the beneficiary.'

'And that one man is Ficino?'

'Yes. There is more to it still. There is the music ... '

'Stop, Sandro,' said Filippino. 'He is already reeling. Leave the music for another day.'

'What music?' I insisted.

'In the composition. But Filippino is right. I have told you too much at once, and you not a member of the Academy. You would not understand. Not unless you had been taught the octave on a monochord.'

'But – I have!'

Sandro looked amazed and said, if that were so, then I could see the music of the painting myself, without his help. I protested that to do so I needed to see the complete work.

'Of course you do,' Sandro agreed. 'The joiner will be finished next week, and then you may see it – at the Palazzo Medici.'

I sank, defeated. I went to speak but Filippino interrupted quickly, wagging a finger at me. 'Ah! Do not say it ... '

'What?'

'You were about to say, "Well then, I shall never see it."'

I admitted it sheepishly.

'What are we to do with him, Sandro?'

Sandro thought it would be best to knock me unconscious and to deliver me to Lorenzo in a sack.

'It might help,' I said.

The following evening, when Raffaello returned from his lessons, he found me with a lyre I had borrowed from Leonardo. Borrowed via a third party, I might add, for I was too embarrassed to meet Leonardo face to face. Though he had been declared innocent, he was bitter that the accusation had been made in the first place and did not want to be reminded of it by me. Raffaello picked up the lyre, turned it about, asked what one was supposed to do with it.

'Listen to it,' I said. 'Listen.'

I played the tonic note, the first string. Then I plucked the third and first strings simultaneously; then the fourth and first, the fifth and first, the sixth and first.

'A dull tune – or are you just learning?'

'Listen ... ' I played the sequence again. 'Now, listen to this.' I played the first and second strings together. Raffaello winced. I played the first and seventh. He winced again.

'It is painful, discordant,' he complained.

'Listen again ... Is it really painful? Is it not rather mournful, the sound of restless longing?'

'It is a discordant note: there are two in the scale. I know that.'

'Yes, but have you listened to it? Is it not like a soul yearning, or like a gate to another world, mysterious? Do you not think that the Orphic hymns sung at Delphi might have sounded like this?'

'Perhaps. But what are you trying to do?'

'Nothing. I am just listening. It is what the lyre is for. Seven strings, and the first one halved, for the eight notes of the octave. Only on this can you really hear it.' I laid aside the beautiful instrument which Leonardo had made himself. I took a deep breath. 'Raffaello, when you visit Poliziano tomorrow ... '

He laughed shortly. 'Oh, trust you to be too late! I will not be going to the Maestro's house in the morning. Nor will you. We have been invited to the Villa Pazzi at Montughi, for it is tomorrow that the Cardinal is due to arrive.'

FORTY THREE

THE PAZZI villa, lying between the hills of Careggi and Fiesole, was only a short ride from the city. It was the month of lime greens and deep blues, of euphorbia and grape hyacinths; the wind from the west was fragrant with spring and blew the nut blossom from the trees: the Feast of the Ascension approached, along with May Day and all the hope of renewal.

An old battlemented farmhouse had been transformed into a place of leisure with an antique air, the walls covered in fresh white stucco, the windows framed by architraves of grey pietra serena, the roof newly tiled in terracotta. It stood in the midst of vineyards and olive groves, with a formal garden which copied that of the Medici at Careggi in nearly all its detail. On this day it housed a party of men from Rome well known for their animosity towards the Medici, but they were here to make peace. Perhaps this was the beginning of a rearrangement of power: Rome and Florence would join with at least one other state – Naples, Venice or Milan – to form a new alliance so powerful and strong that the peace of Italy would be assured. No Turk would dare to land on our shores. In such an alliance, the army commanders of Italy could join together and no longer waste themselves in petty wars against each other.

The Turks were not the only threat. The French, with their claim to the kingdom of Naples, were an equal if less alarming danger, but Lorenzo held them in check by his friendship with King Louis. The real enemy lay to the east and was a bronze-skinned man with an infidel faith and a scimitar with which to impose it. There was talk of a new crusade, to counter Turkish ambitions and retake Jerusalem, but it was less a crusade to win back the Holy Land than a high ideal to embolden the flagging spirits of Europe. Perhaps now, at the Villa Pazzi, the idea could begin to move towards realisation. With Lorenzo and the Pope together, the unimaginable could become possible.

The villa's courtyard looked like a forum, with men passing to and fro in groups. Having stabled our horses, we went to join the bustle in this strange market place. There were bankers and bishops, priests and laymen, two jesters, a dwarf, a multitude of servants and one black slave. Entering the garden, we found a tent pitched there, accommodating, we were told, Captain Gianbattista Montesecco. Antonio was close by, talking earnestly with that obnoxious priest, Stefano da Bagnone.

'Speak to Francesco, Stefano, I beg you. I must have a place in this, I must!' Antonio pleaded.

'We would do better to approach the Captain.' The priest coiled a strand of hair round and round his finger. He had done this so often that his thin locks hung in rats' tails. 'Ah! More of the family Maffei,' he said, seeing us. Raffaello greeted his brother with vacuous expressions of reunion but Antonio was not listening. He stood regarding me in silence, his eyes restoring that special connection between us. Stefano da Bagnone considered us both and misinterpreted this silent communion. 'Brotherly love!' he said, raising his hands unctuously. 'How wonderful!' Raffaello, midway through an excited account of his studies, looked bemused, but he soon regained the saddle of his topic and cantered on through his eulogy of ancient literature.

Antonio fixed his brother with a withering gaze. 'When you have finished,' he said abruptly, 'I would like to continue my conversation with Father Stefano – in private.'

In the mellow evening air there was a banquet under an arbour of vines. I was at the age when just the scent of May excited the blood; thus, when the company turned to dancing, I joined in with the other two sons of Gherardo dei Maffei. The musicians were adept and could play a pavana as well as a saltarello, moving from the stateliness and nobility of lutes to the raucous beat of naker drums, bagpipes and shawms. Raffaello, with his sinoper hair and indigo eyes, had no shortage of partners, but he was a shy and ungainly dancer. Antonio, on the other hand, was self-assured, particularly in the rustic dances, in which the company greeted the season with the pretence of being happy peasants. But Antonio had learnt his steps in the villages of the Volterrano, and not from some dancing master of Burgundy; the banging of his heels on the ground added a rough excitement to the music. Knowing these steps too, I jumped into the circle with him and together we gave the Pazzi family and their friends a bucolic display of the joys of music, of spring, and of life. The naker players caught our mood and doubled the tempo. As we turned, stamping in exhilaration, a crescent moon appeared like a pale gold sickle in the sky, attended by the sparkling diamond which is Venus. All the guests were now clapping in time to the drums, encouraging us. Then, on a signal from old Jacopo de' Pazzi, who had evidently had quite enough of this display of youthfulness, the naker drums rolled and the dance ended.

We were greeted with cheers and presented with beakers spilling with wine. 'You surprise me,' declared Francesco de' Pazzi, looking up at Antonio with admiration. 'One day you are a noble youth, another day a priest, and now, on this day, a true swain. My Protean friend, I honour you.' Laughing, he clapped him heartily on the back, and asked to be reminded who I might be. And then, as I was being presented to our host, I noticed her.

She stood in the midst of cousins, haughty young ladies playing the game of indifference towards their suitors. She had grown, of course, and her unruly hair was now held in the captivity of braids, but her face retained the wonder of a nine-year-old who looks on the world and its events as something which other people experience. She was an onlooker, and content to be so. Catching my gaze, she failed to recognise me; I reminded her by pulling the face of a gargoyle and was rewarded by laughter which sounded like a fountain.

Not having the courage nor the right to present myself to these ladies, I went to the loggia to rest. The musicians were now playing 'Ben venga Maggio', a song greeting May.

> 'Welcome spring, which would have men fall in love
> and you, ladies, arrayed with your lovers
> who by roses and flowers are made beautiful by May.'

If I had any doubts that it was one of Angelo's songs, they were dispelled when I heard his name buried in the lyrics, flying in as the 'angel of love' to honour the ladies and the season. Even in his songs, he too was an onlooker and not a participant. The melody, surely one of Baccio's, dipped and soared; the voices of the musicians produced seductive harmonies; I looked on couples with a mixture of wonder and envy, my heart beginning to feel as if it were dough being kneaded by a deft baker.

'Yield, beauties, to your lovers
surrender, hearts, with passion.
Do not make war in May.'

When I dared to look back at the array of ladies, she had left their ranks. A plunging sense of loss was replaced by hope as I caught sight of her standing alone by a banquet table, hope which soared when an African voice said in my ear, 'My mistress wishes to dance.' I walked towards her as one who no longer has control of his life. The volition which moved my limbs was not my own. With Venus twinkling like a diamond in the velvet sky above, I surrendered myself to the goddess, bowed before my lady and led her to the dance. If I then danced as I had never danced before, it was because of an endowment of grace and sureness of foot which was supernatural.

I had suffered all the fantasies and lusts natural to a youth. Now something unexpected was growing in me like the sun on dawn's horizon. My heart filled my chest and ached. Every sensation became exquisite. If this was love, and I had no doubt that it was, no wonder men hungered for it!

I danced; I excelled; no one leapt higher than I – but the impetus for this excellence came from her. And in her eye was such a return of admiration that I could have been Giuliano de' Medici himself.

Among the guests was Guglielmo de' Pazzi, husband of Lorenzo's sister. Much was being said of another marriage to unite the two families, that of a niece of Jacopo de' Pazzi to a certain young man of the Medici. To my relief I discovered that the bride-to-be was not Elena but the young woman who, on that night, was the dancing partner of the Cardinal. I studied her curiously and, as critical as a prospective mother-in-law, found her lacking in all good qualities. She, as many others there, had lightened her hair and plucked it back from her brow by two inches in a wretched attempt to look like Simonetta Vespucci. I pitied her as I pitied the men who were attracted by such things; I pitied Giuliano, but I knew that, in all selfishness, I had no intention of making him aware of another daughter of the family, one with brown hair and soft eyes, who was radiant with internal beauty.

If I did not sleep when I reached my bed, it was not because I had heard that Lorenzo and Giuliano were to visit on the morrow. This was not the sleeplessness of anxiety; it was desired; I did not want to waste my time in unconsciousness when I could spend it dwelling on the sensation of love which coursed through my body. I wanted to be awake for ever, in a drowsy, luxurious slumber, resting, floating, sinking in the warmth of my own heart. Oh, sweet, tingling joy! I spent the night not dreaming of her, but in close contact with her, knowing that wherever she was, abed in whichever room in the villa, she was also dwelling on me: two hearts awake and reaching for each other.

In the morning, I leapt from my bed as refreshed as if I had slept a full six hours. I leaned impatiently out of the window, rebuking the sun for its tardiness.

'Get up, get up, you sluggard,' I said to the pale horizon.

'Who, me?' mumbled Raffaello sleepily.

'No, the sun.'

It began to bulge and pulse on the rim of the hills, swelling like a ball regaining shape after having been flattened. It was blood red. Then, as it emerged, there was a sign, chilling to behold – a fissure in the sun's face, a jagged blue scar.

'Raffaello!' I cried. 'The sun has cracked!'

He came blearily from the bed and looked out. 'It is just a cloud, you cretin!'

It was true. As the sun rose, it became its whole self again. Blinded by too much sun-gazing, I groped my way to my clothes. Raffaello had returned to his bed.

'Cretin,' he repeated as I stumbled about. 'What is the matter with you today?'

There was no matter, only a fine substance of anticipation. It was spring. I felt alive. I was happy. 'Is it because Lorenzo is coming?' Raffaello asked. Turning, I knocked into the wash stand and sent the ewer flying.

The garden whispered the secrets of dawn. My shoes grew soaked by the dew, but, ah, I thought, the discomfort is in the wet shoes, not in the dew itself. So I took my shoes off and knew the pleasure of wet grass under bare feet. Shoes! Boots and pattens! They cut men off from nature. I padded about, a man reborn to original sensations. Wild roses held me spellbound. I stood before them so quietly that rabbits, which had been scared off by my approach, cautiously returned. Communing with them, I realised how it was that both Saint Francis and Orpheus had attracted the beasts. I was feeding one with succulent leaves when it was scared away by the first sounds from the villa – a barked order to a servant, a conversation in the kitchen, logs being chopped. I put my sodden shoes back on and went exploring below the windows of the ladies' quarter. Where was she? Why was she not responding to my silent calls? Did she need a physical voice? Would she come to the window if I stood below and sang?

The family and their guests were a long time rising. When at last men emerged to stroll in the garden, rumours began to fly. Launched by Stefano da Bagnone, they revolved on the Archbishop of Pisa and with whom he had spent the night. Whoever it had been, it was not a young lady, nor an old one, nor even one of middle years. Was it Gianni, or Rico, or Carlo the slave? Whoever it was, he was under ten years old. I considered these slanders unbefitting of ambassadors of peace.

Suddenly the gate-bell was being rung by the porter, warning of riders approaching on the road from Florence. Lorenzo, always an early riser, arrived before old Jacopo de' Pazzi had even emerged from his bedchamber. I ran to the front of the villa to watch the party come in. My poor, vulnerable heart was prepared to burst at the sight of Giuliano, but there were only three in the party, and no attendants. Typically disarming, Lorenzo had come to meet Cardinal Raffaello Riario accompanied only by his son and his closest companion. Little Piero was squeezed behind the pommel of his father's saddle, while Angelo Poliziano rode beside them.

If Eros is often shown with a blindfold on, it is not because he himself is blinded; blindness is what he causes. Were there signs that morning of what was afoot? There were, and I saw them, but I did not realise their significance. If the consternation of the Pazzi at the absence of Giuliano was greater than perhaps is usual in a host, I did not notice it. All I saw was what I wanted to see: ambassadors of Rome and Florence greeting each other warmly like old friends.

As Lorenzo offered Giuliano's apologies, explaining that his brother was unwell, I hid from his view behind a hedge formed of the bodies of Gianbattista Montesecco, Stefano da Bagnone and Jacopo Bracciolini. Their muttered consternation echoed my own; when Bracciolini exhibited apparent grief at the absence of Giuliano, Montesecco put his arm round him comfortingly.

'God's blood!' Bracciolini muttered, shrugging off Montesecco's arm.

'Guard your tongue, blasphemer! If anything, it is God's will,' said the Captain. Bracciolini glared at him and moved away, trembling with rage. Stefano da Bagnone followed him.

Montesecco stood alone, snorting like a frustrated stallion. I pulled on his sleeve.

'Do you remember me? We met on the road to Rome.'

He stared at me uncomprehendingly, as if he were in the midst of battle and had been approached by a kitten wishing to be stroked. 'Yes, of course I remember,' he snapped, 'I recognised you last night, when you were dancing like a woodcutter. What are you doing here?'

'I am with my brothers.'

His eyes widened a little. 'Of course, the Maffei ... Are you ... ?' He began to gaze at me as if unsure whether he could see me or not.

'Am I what?' I asked.

He scratched his head. His hair was tousled and uncombed, his chin unshaven. 'Nothing,' he said. 'Forgive me. It is too early to think. Are you ... that is, did you come with Antonio or Raffaello?'

'With Raffaello,' said Antonio, joining us. 'He was in Salviati's party.'

Love has this curious virtue of being limitless and gracing everyone you meet. Even though Antonio was evidently angry about something, I looked on him as my beloved brother. 'Good morning, slugabed!' I said cheerfully. Ball lightning struck me then, full in the face. Montesecco picked me up. 'Why blame the boy?' he said to Antonio. 'It is not his fault.'

Antonio ignored him. He stood rubbing his fist and gazing towards Lorenzo with the eyes of the Medusa. For a moment, dazed as I was, I was scared as to what he might do, but he did nothing. He merely stood there looking like a gathering storm while Lorenzo walked past surrounded by his hosts. Amidst a crowd who were doffing caps and bowing, Antonio stood erect with his cap firmly on his head.

'Avert the eyes, avert the eyes,' Montesecco whispered urgently, placing himself between Antonio and the object of his hatred.

As the hosts and guests disappeared into the house, Montesecco turned abruptly on Antonio and pushed him towards Stefano da Bagnone and Jacopo Bracciolini. I joined Raffaello and asked him if I were bleeding.

'Yes, at the mouth,' he said, handing me a piece of linen abstractedly as he stared in the direction of his brother and friends. 'Why are they so agitated?'

'Everyone seems strangely upset by Giuliano's absence,' I said irritably, for in my opinion I was the only one with the right to such an emotion. 'Antonio is in a very rage about it. Ahi ... I seem to have bitten the inside of my cheek.'

'What is going on here?' he muttered, considering Antonio with an expression of profound distrust.

'Oh Raffaello, what balm is there for the inside of a mouth?' I asked, my only concern being whether unsightly bruises were forming.

'You do realise that Antonio seeks revenge for Volterra?'

'So what will he do? Murder Lorenzo at breakfast? You said yourself this is an embassy of peace.'

'And so it is, but Antonio's intentions are his own.' Distracted by his thoughts, Raffaello led me absently towards the fountain, filled a cup with water and handed it to me. 'We must hope and pray that he does nothing. Given Antonio's ever-lengthening history of impotence, we have some cause for such hope. What did he actually do at Volterra? Nothing. What did he do in Milan? Nothing.'

'How do you know?' I rinsed my mouth, spat and rinsed again.

'By knowing Antonio. That he left the city before the murder of Sforza does not tell me he was innocent, only that he was scared. I know him, I grew up with him. He was always inspiring others to wickedness, but never himself.'

I felt tenderly inside my mouth. 'He seems potent to me, often enough. I sometimes wonder if I am his brother or his quintain.'

Despite my burning desire to see Elena, I avoided the breakfast being given for the Medici. Later, when I was standing again with Raffaello, a servant approached with the request that my brother attend Dom Angelo Poliziano. I barely heard what was said, for at last my eyes had found her. She was with other ladies gathering round a lutenist. I felt Raffaello's hand tug on my sleeve, and followed him like a puppy, oblivious to everything but the girl whose eyes were now engaged with mine.

Angelo did not share Lorenzo's ability to converse easily with all men. Unable to find a good conversation on matters linguistic or antique with anyone except Jacopo Bracciolini, whom he had still not forgiven for slighting him in Vespasiano's bookshop, he stood alone, waiting for Raffaello.

'At last, an intelligent man ... ' he began, and then, noticing me: 'Madonna! Come away,' he said sharply, glancing over his shoulder to where Lorenzo stood in a knot of conversation. 'Quickly! This is not the place for our reunion.' He pushed me towards a long hedge of laurel that was hollow in the centre. '*Per amor del cielo*! Are you witless? What if Lorenzo were to see you?'

'What if he were?'

'Then he would be constrained to be polite to you while in company. And that would count against you heavily later.' He ushered Raffaello and me into the corridor within the laurel hedge. 'After all, there is a certain outstanding debt of yours that he wishes to have settled.'

'I have spent two years in exile. Does that not count?'

'It might satisfy the law but it would not satisfy Lorenzo.'

'I thought they were one and the same.'

Raffaello intervened. 'Angelo, my brother lacks humility. What he is really saying is, could you forgive him? And can you not intercede with Lorenzo on his behalf?'

Angelo stared at me coolly. 'Is that what you are saying?'

I nodded. 'I cannot find the words to express my regret,' I muttered. 'The words do not exist or, if they do, they do not have the sincerity of what is in here.' I slapped myself hard on the chest.

'I invested so much in you, not only my time and tuition, but also my affection, and you deserted me.'

'I know, I know.' I hung my head in shame. He lifted my chin to study my eyes. His anger and hurt were evident, but I held his gaze and awaited his judgement.

What is it to be, Angelo? I thought. Love or hate? Forgiveness or retaliation? Will you, who have given me so much, give even more now? I watched him hover over the decision for a moment of agonising length. Suddenly he gripped me painfully by the hair. 'You little wretch,' he hissed, spitefully bunching his fist in my already bruised face. 'You disease of a friend!'

Raffaello, unfamiliar with this particular form of Poliziano's affection, started in alarm. But I told him, 'That is how they say "I love you" in Montepulciano.' Then I crowed in joy, sending birds flapping from the hedge.

FORTY FOUR

WALKING the length of the hedge, we emerged at last in an olive grove. The old trees were green with new moss; the grass was spangled with daisies and forget-me-nots; a shallow stream was flanked by purple irises. The poet stood and breathed in deeply, as if the scent of the grove was food for his god. 'Nature,' he said to Raffaello, 'is the true cathedral. Cities are but dungheaps of deceit. When you have had enough of the rank stench of politics, resort here, to Mother Nature.'

The sun was dappling shyly through the trees. Each time it glanced on my face, it brushed the lyre of my soul. Being at the side of this man recreated a music I had not heard for two years; my happiness would have been unbounded, but for a nagging concern.

'Where is Giuliano?' I asked, feigning nonchalance.

The answer was not immediate. 'He fell from his horse yesterday and injured his leg.'

Giuliano? Fall from a horse? I was angered to be told a lie.

Angelo, uncomfortable herald of the official statement, deflected the conversation. 'So, where to now, Tommaso?'

My future having been so long obscured by the past, by the obstacle which was Angelo in one form, Lorenzo in another, I was bemused to think that the way ahead might now be clearing. This was a question I could not answer. I shrugged. He was quiet. I said: 'I suppose you have someone in my place?'

He remained silent and, avoiding my gaze, simply nodded.

'I have been doing very well in Rome.'

'So I hear.'

'Does Lorenzo have spies everywhere?'

'No, only in the major cities.'

'Everything is known to him, then?'

'I wonder ... ' Angelo looked pensively towards Raffaello. 'What are these noble lords and dignitaries doing here? Do you believe it is an embassy for reconciliation?'

'Yes I do,' said Raffaello. 'His Holiness is sincere in his wish to restore his friendship with Lorenzo.'

Angelo looked doubtful.

'It is true,' I said. 'The very air is balmy with peace. Can you not feel it?' After all, I thought, this visit has brought you and me together again.

Angelo remained unconvinced. 'What I cannot understand is why all the men I loathe seem to be friends of each other: Salviati, Bracciolini, Bagnone, Francesco de' Pazzi.'

'Perhaps they have a dislike of you in common,' I suggested.

He made a grunting laugh, happy to be insulted in a way he had not enjoyed for a long time. 'It is one of the burdens of fame,' he said to Raffaello, 'that it brings you as many enemies as friends. And even the friends become suspect.'

'In what way?'

'I do not mean one's true friends, I mean the new ones, those who suddenly attach themselves to you and persist in treating you as special and extraordinary. Their fawning devotion ... '

I saw Raffaello flinch, but Angelo, not having my brother in mind, continued unabated. 'The worst of it is, I was once the same towards those I admired, and now I see how fatuous admiration is. Admirare ... etymologically it speaks of mirrors and reflections. There is nothing true in it; it is all illusion and self-deception. To admire another is to think little of yourself. One needs to appreciate one's own worth. By all means respect others, but avoid admiration.'

'What about a woman's admiration?' I asked tentatively.

Angelo's mouth turned down at the corners. 'Women and mirrors come together in my opinion.' Obviously his nightingale in Prato had escaped his nets and he was in no mood to hear any confession of my heart; I held my tongue.

'Take my current scribe, for instance,' Angelo said, regaining his track. 'A good, capable lad, but his respect for me is becoming stifling. The more he fawns, the more abominable my temper. What I need is someone who can give back my rudeness in equal measure and keep my opinion of myself from becoming overblown.'

'Oh, where would you find such a one?' I asked.

'Where indeed? I am sorry to hear about your prosperity. With all the fame and fortune Rome has to offer you, presumably there is nothing to tempt you back here.'

'Nothing in the way of financial benefit or creature comfort, no. But then I find no happiness in such things. If you must know, the more richly I am rewarded for my work, the more I despise my patrons. They are so easily pleased! Having done little to earn their praises, I find success empty. The truth is, prosperity has found me in a time of drifting ... '

'Two years.'

'Almost to the day.'

'It is time to stop.'

'Drifting? Yes, indeed. I want nothing but to rise each day, as I once did, with the prospect of hard work ahead, hard work devoted to a great ideal. I once served the Muse. I would serve her again.'

Angelo brightened. 'You will stay in Florence then?'

'Will she have me?'

'I think she might.'

'But first I need to see Lorenzo,' I said, with more breath than voice.

Angelo nodded and said that Sunday would provide the opportunity, when Lorenzo had invited the Cardinal to Florence as his guest. Apparently His Eminence had a rare taste in treasures and fine objects of art and wanted to see everything in the Medici collections. So on Sunday he was to come to the palazzo, there to change into his vestments before officiating at High Mass in the Cathedral. 'Come with his party and, when they leave, stay behind.'

'Will Lorenzo be angry with me?'

'Undoubtedly,' Angelo smiled. 'Magnificently angry. Prepare to meet thundering Zeus face to face.'

'You have lost none of your powers of encouragement,' I groaned.

The Sunday before Ascension Day in 1478 fell on the twenty-sixth of April and the second anniversary of the death of Simonetta. I entered the city thinking of her, for her departure from this life had signalled my own from Florence. Was it my imagination or did the city seem a changed place without her? From what I had seen of Lorenzo from a distance, and from the conversations I had had with Angelo, both men seemed not so much older as less young. The springtime of their youth had flown with the soul of Simonetta.

The grand entourage of Cardinal Raffaello Riario consisted of Archbishop Francesco Salviati, various members of the Pazzi family, Jacopo Bracciolini, and, amongst a vast attendance of clerics, Antonio dei Maffei and Stefano da Bagnone. At the rear of the procession came Gianbattista Montesecco, leading thirty mounted crossbowmen and fifty infantry who had arrived that morning from Imola. This force was for the protection of the Cardinal on his journey south to Perugia later in the day.

The Florentines stood twelve deep on the Via Larga, curious to see both the youngest cardinal of the Church and the man whom Lorenzo had so successfully prevented from taking up his archbishopric in Pisa. With Francesco Salviati being invited as a guest to the Palazzo Medici, it seemed that a new chapter in the political life of Florence was about to begin.

Arriving at the palazzo, the leading members of the party were welcomed by Lorenzo alone, for Giuliano was still unwell. This news created another spasm of agitation among the Romans. They were ushered in to begin a tour of the statues, the paintings, the jewels, the armour, the furniture and the frescoes. Montesecco sent his troops to await him at the Santa Croce gate while the rest of us were entertained in the courtyard of the palazzo. Leaving my companions to their wine and cakes, I went up the grey stone stairs to the chapel, to discover that the Magi were still in procession on the walls.

'One day,' I thought, 'I shall bring her here and point everything out to her: the leopard, the massive hind, the enormous rabbit, the three kings. She will love this.' Such dreams I indulged whenever I was by myself. But now in the chapel, and against the backdrop of Gozzoli's unrealistic scenes, a cool draught of reason made my dreams shiver and retreat. What, after all, did I have to offer? I might be a Maffei, a name which could have some appeal to the Pazzi, but I was a natural son who lived off his wits. And if I was about to return to the employment of Angelo Poliziano, then I could bid farewell to a good income. I sighed listlessly, wondering perhaps if the object of my love was as unobtainable as Beatrice.

I was lost in such considerations for longer than I thought; by the time I left the chapel, the tour of treasures had finished and the banquet in the sala had begun. I went to the stables to reacquaint myself with my old friends. Orso was not there, but there was a superb Jennet in his place. That it was Giuliano's, I had no doubt. I smoothed his flanks and made friendly noises as I edged forward to his head. He twisted against the restraining leash, his eye showing white.

'Hush, hush, a friend,' I said softly. When he could see me, he calmed down and I stood stroking him.

At the voices of two men approaching, I withdrew into the shadows. They looked into the stables and called out for Giuliano. Recognising them as attendants of Francesco de' Pazzi, I came out of hiding.

'Have you seen Giuliano de' Medici?' they asked.

'No. Is he not at the breakfast?'

They glanced at each other.

'What troubles you?' I asked, for they looked nervous.

'If we do not find him, well, I will not be the one to tell Francesco,' said one.

'Nor I!' said the other. 'I have never seen him in such a humour. It seems that the whole day is to be spoiled. Can you think of anywhere Giuliano might be?'

'Have you tried his room?'

'Which is it?' they asked eagerly.

For fear of being caught wandering through the palazzo with two strangers, I pretended not to know. 'You must ask one of the servants,' I said.

They left, frustrated, and I returned to the stallion. 'Where is Giuliano, if he is not at the breakfast, eh? Where is your master?'

The stallion nuzzled my hand. Giuliano was everywhere here, in the smell of hay and leather and horse, in the sound of doves in the loft, in the glint of harness and a pair of spurs hanging on the wall. Why was he avoiding the Cardinal? Had that been a question asked of any other man, the obvious answer would have been that he was jealous of him, but in Giuliano such an emotion was inconceivable.

Guests began to appear in the garden, wandering in convivial groups. Lorenzo was there, with his hand affectionately on the shoulder of Archbishop Salviati, who was now dressed in full vestments. Francesco de' Pazzi and Gianbattista Montesecco were head to head, engaged in an argument as furious as it was sottovoce. Leaving the stable unnoticed, I made my way through the gathering crowd, keeping as far as I could from Lorenzo. As I passed Francesco de' Pazzi, he was saying something about the Cathedral which made Montesecco stamp his foot and shake his head in absolute refusal.

'Will you ruin everything?' Pazzi muttered.

The Captain's expression was two parts annoyance to three parts anguish. Noticing me, he beckoned. 'Where is your brother Antonio? Find him. Bring him here.'

I found Antonio with Stefano da Bagnone. They went to Montesecco together, making it very clear that I was not welcome to join them. Well used to Antonio's conspiratorial airs, I left him peevishly.

Angelo joined me and asked the cause of my thunderous expression.

'It is nothing, only that my brother needs to treat everything as a great secret which I am not allowed to share.'

'What secret?'

'I have no idea. In all likelihood, there is none. But it seems that for some reason Montesecco is refusing to go to the Cathedral.'

As if to prove me a liar and idle gossip, at that moment the procession began to form up and Montesecco took his place in it. Angelo glanced at me and I shrugged.

The courtyard was small and the procession was large. A coil of people began to wind round itself as more and more came from the palazzo to join the line. Lorenzo with his wife and mother, the Archbishop and several attendants, many of the Pazzi family, Jacopo Bracciolini, Lorenzo's friends, members of the noblest families of Florence, members of the Signoria, the manager of the bank and the Cavalcanti brothers. Lorenzo's cousins were there, and his sisters with their husbands. Francesco Bandini, the host of the Platonic Symposium, was also there, with his brother Bernardo. A friend of Lorenzo's, Francesco Nori, haggled with the Cardinal's secretary over the order of assembly. As this comedy of social priorities was performed, I caught the laughing eye of one short man with golden hair and a familiar, open-air face, but could not remember his name. Indeed, it would be easier to say who was not there on that bright morn, as I only noted two absences: Luigi Pulci and Giuliano.

Raffaello had a place beside Angelo; I joined the line at its tail. Lovesick, listless, and – in the absence of Giuliano – suffering a waning interest, I walked in the procession with my head down. As we crossed the square to enter the Duomo by the great west door, we came to a sudden and unexpected halt. I was not the only sleepwalker to cannon into the man in front of him. Something had interrupted the procession. The man in front of me for some reason took fright, but then the word came down the line: Archbishop Salviati had been stopped with a message that his mother was grievously ill. Even as we heard about it at the end of the line, we could see the figure of the Archbishop making his way rapidly across the square with a small retinue of attendants.

The Cathedral was already filled with those who had come to hear the Cardinal say Mass, but the nave was clear for the entry of the procession. The Cardinal and his attendant priests moved towards the great octagonal choir and the high altar; the rest of us found places where we could on the outside of its wooden rails. The altar was raised on steps and visible to all, but the canons and dignitaries seated within the choir were not clearly to be seen. I was surprised, as ever, to find Lorenzo standing amongst men and not in the place of honour, but still I avoided him and chose instead the company of Francesco de' Pazzi and Bernardo Bandini.

As the two men talked, I relished the numbers of the architecture, flowering octagons in the sacred end of the church; squares, double squares and golden rectangles in the nave.

I have since heard a piece of music, composed at the time of the Cathedral's building, which renders the sacred geometry audible; but then, just by looking, I could hear it for myself.

Bernardo Bandini had obviously been eating garlic the night before and his breath was alliaceous. 'Where is Giuliano?' he asked Francesco and discreetly I covered my nose with my hand.

'Well, do you see him?' Francesco demanded, for Bandini was the taller of the two.

'No. Lorenzo is over there, by the old sacristy, with that poet of his and other friends, but not Giuliano.'

'They said he would be here!' said Francesco, then, glancing at me, he explained, 'I promised the Cardinal faithfully that I would arrange a meeting, but as yet we have had no sight of Giuliano. What can I tell His Eminence? We are to leave for Perugia directly after Mass. I dare not let him down! Have you any idea where Giuliano could be?'

'No, none. I have been looking for him too.'

'But, Maffei, you know the Palazzo Medici, surely? Did you not live there once?'

'Yes, for a while.'

'Come then, let us return and persuade Giuliano to join us. However ill he is, he must come. We shall carry him if needs be. Lead us to his room.'

The palazzo would be all but empty now, and, Holy Mary, Mother of God, I saw no harm in accompanying Francesco de' Pazzi there. Lord, forgive me my blindness: stupidity was my only crime, but it was enough.

FORTY FIVE

IT SEEMED an age before Giuliano's door opened after we had knocked. He stood there alone, taking in all three of us at a glance. Though his eyes widened a little when he saw me, no smile came to his face. Curtly, he asked the men what they needed.

'Giuliano, you promised that you would be at the Cathedral to meet the Cardinal.'

'I can barely walk.'

'If you will not come for the Cardinal's sake, then think of the ladies of Florence. It would seem that every one of them is in the Cathedral this morning. To see Cardinal Riario? To hear Mass? Of course not. Giuliano, have pity on them. Do not disappoint them.'

'My reputation would crumble to dust if I were to be seen on crutches.'

'How little you know about women. If there is one thing they prefer to a hero, it is a wounded hero.'

Giuliano coloured. 'This noble knight fell from his horse.'

'So? It happens to the best of us. Do come. You will not need crutches, for Bernardo and I shall help you. If I may be serious, Giuliano,' said Pazzi, lowering his voice confidentially, 'it is vital that you meet the Cardinal, and we shall be leaving for Perugia directly after Mass.'

'Why is it vital?'

'You are closer to his own age than Lorenzo, and, until recently, you had a shared ambition. He is grieved to have won his office at your expense and wishes to do whatever he can to alleviate your disappointment. In short, though you may not become a Cardinal, you could become a Cardinal's friend.'

I believe that this would have quickened the anger of most men, but the pretty sentiment found a receptive soul in Giuliano and he noticeably relaxed. 'I would not have it thought that I am deliberately avoiding him,' he said.

Pazzi said that departure could be postponed for an hour while Giuliano and the Cardinal met in the sacristy. Giuliano sighed in agreement, but said that first he must dress.

'Be quick,' said Pazzi. 'Mass will have begun by now.'

'Wait for me downstairs. Not you, Tommaso. I need your help.' Giuliano drew me into his room and shut the door firmly on the other two. He winced as he took a step and put his arm out for my support.

'Is it very painful?'

'Not as painful as finding a weasel like Francesco de' Pazzi at your door. Lorenzo somehow manages to be gracious to him, but then he could be pleasant to the Devil himself if circumstances required it.' With a grunt he sat down on the window seat. 'Fetch me my jacket, there, on the chest.'

'This one?'

'No, the one in blue velvet.'

On the wall above his bed hung the banner of Minerva from the joust. Her eyes seemed to follow me about the room as if she had a message to convey, but my years in Rome had dulled my communion with the gods. Instead of hearing her warnings, I fell to thinking of Simonetta.

'It is exactly two years since she died,' I said as I gazed up at her image.

'Ah, you remember? I am gratified that somebody does. Then you will understand what has kept me in my room, even at the risk of appearing to be too jealous to face Cardinal Raffaello Riario.'

'Everyone knows that you have hurt your leg.'

'I have not hurt my leg. It hurts me. Fall from my horse? Me? How could you believe such a thing?'

'Then ... ?'

'It is gout. The disease of the father is visited upon the sons. Lorenzo has it too.'

My face fell. Gout had brought his father to an early death.

'Do not be concerned,' Giuliano said. 'There are cures. As soon as this rabble has departed, I am going to the sulphur baths in the Volterrana.'

But I knew him too well: for all his display of indifference he could not conceal one overriding fear, that of becoming a premature invalid. He would rather die than become dependent on others.

As I laced up his jacket he said that he was eager to hear about all that had happened to me and asked if I would return to the palazzo with him after Mass.

'Will I be safe?'

'With me? I think so.'

I smiled. 'That is not what I meant.'

'I shall arrange for you and Lorenzo to meet, and I shall be present. Will that help?'

In all my anticipations of the inevitable meeting with Lorenzo, I had never been imaginative enough to picture Giuliano in the scene. Suddenly reconciliation seemed possible. I beamed in gratitude.

He wanted to know where the medallion was and I showed it to him in my purse.

'But you do not wear it?'

'Well, I ... I am not worthy. Not yet.'

'What are you talking about? Did you not realise that, with this gift, I was inviting you into the Academy?'

'What?'

'We can discuss it later.' He stood up and arranged his cloak around his shoulders.

'Your sword ... ' I said.

'Leave it.'

'You should wear it.'

'I have enough of a burden with this leg. Wear it for me if you will.'

I took up his sword belt and buckled it round my waist. Then I helped him towards the stairs.

'I have heard rumours that a marriage is being arranged for you,' I said.

'I am pledged but not yet betrothed. I have constantly prevaricated, but cannot put it off much longer. The wedding presents are already arriving. That will be the next major festa in this city.'

'And your mistress, did she have ... ?'

'A son, as I told you she would. And,' he added, 'you are still the only one in this house to know. You are my secret will, Tommaso. If anything should happen to me, I want him raised in our family. I will take him in myself when I am married, but if anything should happen ... '

I told him that nothing would happen, that all the portents boded well. Giuliano rolled his eyes and wondered that I had not grown out of studying entrails and the flights of birds. I laughed and said that I merely felt it in the air. But Giuliano had a better guide to the mood of the gods in Marsilio Ficino. Whatever was in the stars was apparently making the philosopher anxious.

'Will he be at the Cathedral?'

'Yes, of course. The whole city is there.' Giuliano sighed deeply. 'What would I not give to be riding in the woods of the Mugello today!'

'Giuliano, describe Ficino to me.'

He looked at me uncomprehendingly. 'Why do you ask? Are you saying that you have never met him? But you must have! He is so often here, or at our villa on Careggi. Why, he was even here this morning, at the breakfast.'

Pazzi and Bandini coming impatiently up the stairs to find us stopped further conversation. I was left to assume that any rift between Lorenzo and Ficino must have healed. The two men took Giuliano from me and, of no more use, I walked behind them down the Via Larga with Giuliano's servants, gazing upon Giuliano's back, allowing the reality of him to replace the memory. I smiled to see his head jerk back as Bernardo Bandini laughed close to his face. As Francesco de' Pazzi helped Giuliano along, he patted him frequently and squeezed his waist. At the time I took it as a specious act of friendship, but of course he was feeling through the cloak for the sword, and it was on me.

We entered the Cathedral by the north door and joined the congregation milling in the ambulatory. Giuliano scanned the faces around him.

'Where is Lorenzo?' he asked softly.

'Over on the far side of the choir,' said Francesco, moving forward to lead Giuliano to his brother. Giuliano resisted.

'Not now, it is too late. Let us stay here.'

'Come on,' Bandini cajoled him. 'You should be with Lorenzo.'

Giuliano shook his head.

'At least he should be told that you are here,' insisted Francesco.

'True,' Giuliano agreed. He turned to me and asked me to deliver the message to his brother. I looked at him wildly. He smiled, the open, generous smile of a man to whom all things in this world are easy, even delivering messages to Lorenzo de' Medici.

Swallowing my apprehension, I bowed abruptly. 'Very well, I shall do as you ask.' I left him to move through the congregation surrounding the eight-sided choir beneath the great dome. From the balcony above the north sacristy came the music of an organ proclaiming belief. It was a musical setting by the Flemish master Josquin des Prez, based entirely on only five notes of the octave. As the voices of the choir arose, the top notes danced in the cupola and wove harmonies that dissolved my heart; but my limbs grew heavy as I continued to push my way through the crowd towards a goal I dreaded.

> *'Et resurrexit tertia die secundum Scripturas; et ascendit in coelum; sedet ad dexteram Patris; et iterum venturus est cum gloria judicare vivos et mortuous ... '*

As I reached the old sacristy on the south side of the choir, the homilies were beginning. Lorenzo was not as easy to find as I had expected. You may presume that he stood head and shoulders above the crowd but he did not. However, as a landscape grows more familiar the closer you approach your native city, so, as I began to recognise more and more faces, I knew I was nearing Lorenzo; then, when at last I saw Angelo, I knew I had found him. I came up to them from behind, shouldering my way between two cowled priests. As Lorenzo was standing on Angelo's right, I went to Angelo's left, and it was to Angelo that I delivered my message.

'Tell Lorenzo that Giuliano is here, on the north side, with Francesco de' Pazzi and Bernardo Bandini.'

Angelo passed on the message. Lorenzo peered round him at me. I stared into that terrible face like a rabbit. His eyes narrowed, his chin jutted forward, his lower lip hid the upper.

He said nothing but looked furious and, oddly, alarmed. Then he returned his attention to the altar.

Angelo gazed on me with some amusement. I rubbed my face with the back of my hand.

'Have you got something in your eye?'

'A tic.'

'You should keep away from sheep.'

'Not that kind of tick,' I said. 'A tic. The kind which makes your eyelid twitter.' The kind which occurs when one is being studied by Lorenzo de' Medici.

'To twitter is a verb relating to the sound made by birds.'

'You know what I mean. Why do you always have to be so pedantic?'

'You know I detest being called a pedant.'

'Then do not be one. My eyelid is twittering, I tell you.'

The Medici steward, Francesco Nori, standing in front of us with Andrea Cavalcanti, turned with a frown.

'Be quiet, Tommaso,' Angelo hissed.

'Ssh,' said Nori.

Andrea Cavalcanti glanced at us both affectionately, then, catching Lorenzo's reproving eye, he turned back quickly towards the altar.

Obediently quiet, Angelo and I stood side by side as the ceremony moved towards communion. I absorbed it all, swelling with the cadences of the music, with the pungent cloud of incense, with the awareness of being here, in Florence, in the very heart of the city, under the mighty dome of the tabernacle of its spirit. The angel of communion went through the church and the crowd of restless individuals melted into a silent, expectant unity.

Then it was as if both past and future dropped away. There was only the now, the limitless, eternal moment of peace. The Cardinal kneeling at the altar raised the chalice above his head. The sacristy bell rang. All heads bowed in reverence to the supreme moment. I was so entranced, so deeply still, that I could not move, not even to bow my head. I remained gazing at the altar. Then ...

It is impossible to write of what happens in the present moment, for in that omnipotent condition all things occur simultaneously, whereas, in writing, things must proceed in some kind of sequence. Let this then be the succession: first the future, then the past, then the present. For what I heard, from the opposite side of the choir, had not yet happened. What I heard from the past was every hint, every clue I had failed to recognise at the time, shouting at me. What I heard in the present was that inner voice of the Goddess, impelling me to turn, to spin on my heel, to throw myself against the priests behind me. Do you see? Writing of such events can make no sense, for writing is of necessity a transcription of temporal things, and some things are beyond the realm of time.

Here it is then, as it happened: the sacristy bell rang, all heads bowed. I spun round. One of the priests behind Lorenzo was reaching to catch him by the hair, to pull his head back and plunge a dagger into his throat. Even as I turned, I was lunging at him. Even before I turned, I knew it was my brother Antonio.

Thus, when it comes to the moment of action, there is no time to think: the choice is made by the heart and not the mind. To my own amazement I found myself saving the tyrant from my brother's knife. There was nothing else I could have done. I was born and raised for that one action.

As I carried Antonio with me in my lunge to the floor, I felt or heard his knife cut Lorenzo. I rolled away and leapt to my feet, drawing Giuliano's sword but – oh Madonna! – not for the protection of Giuliano. As Stefano da Bagnone fought with Lorenzo, Antonio met me sword in one hand, dagger in the other. He came at me furiously. Our swords rang as they met, echoed by other swords in other fights starting all around us. Our contest was short: Antonio was, as ever, the better swordsman, and in his rage he now had the strength of Hercules. As I turned from a vain thrust, he knocked the sword from my hand with a mighty blow upwards. I shouted for help. Antonio stabbed forward. I dodged back wildly.

'Maso!' Angelo called, and my sword was coming back through the air to my hand. In one movement I caught it, swung it with a power and skill hitherto unknown to me, and disarmed Antonio. But he kicked out wildly. His boot caught the side of my knee and sent me to the floor; once again I lost the sword.

Antonio was on me before I could rise. I struggled to hold off his dagger but it inched down towards me, Antonio pressing all his weight against my outstretched arms. The dagger's tip was red with Lorenzo's blood. Now it sought my flesh with cruel indifference. I began to weigh the pain of death against the effort of keeping alive. The thought that it might be less painful to die threatened to enfeeble me. The strength in my arm began to ebb. My elbow had only to bend ...

Antonio's maddened eyes never left mine. As I stared into them, I could not see my brother but only the evil that possessed him. Out loud I commended my soul to God. My arm buckled. Then there was no more pressure. For a moment I thought I was enjoying the absolute, final knowledge of that sweetness of death which certain philosophers promise. Then I realised that Antonio was gone. With a powerful kick to the ribs, Andrea Cavalcanti had sent him sprawling. Andrea now stood astride me, alert, protective, his sword gripped in both hands as he awaited Antonio's return. But Antonio did not return. He rolled away, jumped up and fled after the vanquished Stefano da Bagnone, leaving the Cathedral by the south door.

The church was now a scene of broiling uncertainty, for most people had no idea what was happening. Screams echoed down the nave. '*Aiuto*! The dome! The dome! It is falling on us!' The crowd began to stampede towards the doors.

Andrea helped me to my feet. Lorenzo was alive, though blood poured from a gaping wound in his neck. While his companions, swords in hands, were nervously glancing this way and that, wondering where the next blow might come from, Angelo alone had the presence of mind to think of finding refuge. Suddenly he called out, 'To the north sacristy! Quickly!'

Francesco Nori led the way, vaulting over the railings of the choir. The rest of us followed. The priests and canons within the choir were in uproar. Only one stood still: the boy Cardinal. He was transfixed by shock and his face was turning to the colour of candle wax, a pallor which, I have heard, has never left him since.

Francesco Nori was the first person through the gate leading to the sacristy. As Lorenzo followed, he met Nori staggering backwards with Bandini's knife up to its hilt in his chest. Bandini, his face contorted with rage, struggled to retrieve his dagger. Lorenzo threw himself at him, but Angelo charged into Lorenzo with his shoulder and deflected him powerfully towards the sacristy. Lorenzo roared, wanting to fight Bandini, but Angelo was pushing him, pulling him, shouting at him with a blazing authority that carried even above the demonic roaring which had filled the church. He bullied Lorenzo into safety and left it to others to deal with Bandini. All this I saw, but something else had caught my eye. Behind the altar Giuliano's servants were cowering in terror. Careless now for my own safety, I vaulted out of the choir on the west side where the Cavalcanti brothers were chasing past in pursuit of Bandini. Skidding on a pool of blood, I fell.

I scrabbled to my feet, glancing about for attackers, but saw only the one who had been attacked. It was in his blood I had slipped, blood which streamed across the marble floor. Many people running through it had left bloody tracks. All around feet were running, a whirlpool of which he was the still centre. He lay face down, arms outstretched. Black hair, blue velvet jacket, torn, stained with dark blood, ripped by a frenzy of knives.

Suddenly the whole floor tipped. Lightning travelled up my spine to strike my brain, sending all thoughts into collision and annihilation.

Then I – my soul – was looking down on the octagon of the choir, as if from the gallery of the cupola. All was still and utterly peaceful. I watched the people below, running in tumult, but their sound was a dull echo as if heard under water. I smiled at their ignorance, for not one of them knew how still it was, in truth, in reality. Nothing was happening to be scared of, nothing but the release of a soul. And I saw him go. If that blinding light that does not burn, that prismatic, multi-faceted light in which every object sparkles, being of the same light, all being the one thing, the monad of intelligent fire, if that light dancing in my eyes marked his passage, then I saw him go.

Angelo's voice is shouting my name. My eyes blink open, to see him beckoning wildly from the sacristy. I walk towards him as composed as a saint in a massacre. He runs out and hauls me to safety. He does not see the body.

The still breathing Nori is laid on a table in the centre of the sacristy. Andrea and Renzo Cavalcanti rush in, the last to arrive, Renzo's arm slashed like a fashionable sleeve. Angelo and others push on the heavy bronze doors to close them. The weight of the doors, their slowness in closing, is a nightmare for Angelo, but, as if I have been bequeathed my hero's sprezzatura, his nonchalance, I stand there coolly watching. Having finally locked the doors, Angelo leans against them and slowly collapses to the floor. His moment of heroism is over.

I sat down beside him and could feel him trembling convulsively. I watched everyone talking at once and knowing nothing. Some were tending the dying Nori. Andrea was trying to revive his brother, who had fainted. A faithful page was sucking at the wound on Lorenzo's neck, in case the dagger had been poisoned. Lorenzo seemed oblivious to it.

'Who were they?' he demanded. 'Does anyone know?'

'The one outside was Bernardo Bandini.'

'But who were those priests?'

'Lorenzo, keep still, you need bandaging. The blood ... '

'Still? How can I keep still, pent up in here? What are we doing saving ourselves? Our duty is to the city. Those men, those Romans, they are our enemy, every one of them. Florence is in mortal danger! Open those doors!' Then he noticed me and, remembering the message I had delivered, his eyes filled with horror.

FORTY SIX

I STARED at the blood on my hands and clothes, wiping at it, trying to clean it off. Men outside were shouting frantically for Lorenzo to come out before the enemy gathered strength. Lorenzo directed one of his attendants to a ladder to find out if these men were the friends they claimed to be. When the young man reached the organ loft, which opened on to the gallery above the sacristy door, he was there too long; when he called down, 'It is true, they are our men,' his voice was too bright. He came down the ladder wearing a smile like a scar on a chalk face. Without doubt he had seen what I had seen. Avoiding Lorenzo, he helped open the doors.

'Is Giuliano with you?' Lorenzo demanded of the men outside, while he gazed at me. 'Is he safe?'

'You must go at once to your house, Lorenzo. The city is under attack. The Pazzi are calling Florence to insurrection.'

They escorted Lorenzo from the sacristy, in a phalanx so tight that he was kept from the sight of his murdered brother. Soon only Angelo and I remained.

'Shall we bring him in here?' came a solemn request from one of the Medici supporters.

'Yes,' said Angelo, not taking his eyes from mine. 'That would be best. To bring him in here.'

The corpse that was borne in was unrecognisable as Giuliano, for the knives had killed beauty and left us with meat. For the second time in his life, Angelo looked upon the raw viscera of someone he had loved. He clutched at me like a fainting child. His need was my salvation, his madness my sanity. To escort him safely to the palazzo became my duty and I applied myself to it, keeping him conscious with an inspiriting flow of words.

The city was in uproar. The bell of the Palazzo della Signoria tolled in alarm. Everyone ran for arms, even priests, women and old men. It was less than an hour since I had last passed this way to the Palazzo Medici; in that time a world had ended.

As we entered the palazzo, we were separated by Lorenzo's men. Angelo was helped upstairs; I was dragged struggling to one of the store rooms in the cellar.

'What have I done?' I shouted to the guard.

'Lorenzo's orders!' was the reply as I was pushed roughly back from the door so that it could be closed and the key turned. I yelled and hammered on the door, but to no avail. At last I turned in defeat, breathless with fury and gasping for air. Had I saved his life for this?

The noise from the street was deafening. By standing on a chest I could look through an iron grille to see pandemonium. It seemed worse, standing there gazing out passively, than if I had been running in its midst. Any call for help I might make through my grille would have been futile. Soldiers of the city militia were trying to instil order but their horses were rearing out of control in the murderous welter of the mob.

How does news travel in such chaos? How did the people know so soon the names of their quarry? Yet as I stood at that window, I heard that Archbishop Francesco Salviati was about to be hanged at the Palazzo della Signoria, and I saw the impaled heads of Salviati's men brought hither by men who, like cats, expected praise for their gruesome offerings. 'Pazzi!,' brayed the mob, seeking other members of the family. 'Salviati!'

'Bracciolini!'

'Maffei!'

My fury was doused by chill realisation. I trembled violently until my teeth chattered. Raffaello was out there, bearing our name, while I was already caught and penned like an animal awaiting slaughter.

A sudden blare of trumpets pierced the cacophony, sounding from a balcony on the upper floor of the palazzo. The tumult reduced to a murmur as Lorenzo began to address his city. Though stretched by pain and grief, his voice was clear. Having reported what had happened, and given his thanks for the people's support of his house, he then rebuked them.

'We know the names of the murderers and their accomplices. Some we have captured, and their execution will be immediate. As for those still to be found, a list of names will be posted on church doors in all wards. However, I implore you, leave the fate of these men to justice. As you love me, do not take the law into your own hands. No one has more reason than I to wish the death of these men, but I will be satisfied if they are arrested, confessed and executed according to law. For obedience to the law is the mark of civilisation; neglect of the law is the mark of barbarism.

'Therefore resist all desire for vengeance. Reserve your strength and prepare yourselves quietly to defend the city, for I have had tidings from our borders, that foreign armies approach Tuscany. The Pazzi have been used as puppets by an enemy who is common to us all. It is not the Pazzi attacking us, but Rome herself.' There was a stunned silence. 'Our defences are strong,' Lorenzo continued, 'but our trials are only beginning. Therefore, beloved Florentines, be steadfast and obey authority, for only order may vanquish chaos. This is the New Rome. Do not let the barbarians in!'

I lay exhausted in a cellar filled with wine barrels and great jars of olive oil, staring blindly up at the window. Every now and then memory came like a dagger to the heart, followed by a shuddering, dry sob. But that was all. I heard others crying, within and without the palace, their grief and outrage directed at heaven in a high-pitched keening. But I had no argument with God, only with men. Numbed by shock, I lay there witless until, in the evening, the door was opened. Several guards entered, followed by Angelo bearing a tray. Seeing him, I raised myself up wearily.

He had brought me some food. I stared at this preposterous gesture of hospitality, and, as I did so, noticed that beside salvers and a dish of broth, there was an inkwell on the tray, and a quill. Angelo sat down and took the lids off the salvers to reveal baked fish and roasted meat. Who had been in the kitchen, cooking meals, on such a day as this?

Trying without success to encourage me to eat, he told me that Raffaello had been found, that he was alive and that Lorenzo had sent out word of his innocence, saying that he was not to be harmed. 'We have tried to persuade him to come here, but he has refused and has taken sanctuary.'

I was surprised by this and wanted to know if there was any news of Antonio.

'No sign of him, gone to earth. Here, eat ... '

I shook my head. Angelo lifted the broth so that my nose caught the scent of meat, beans and pepper. I took the bowl then and drank a little. I demanded to know why I was locked up, whether it was for my safety or my imprisonment.

'Lorenzo needs to satisfy himself that you had no part in this affair.'

'But I saved his life!'

'And by that action, saved your own, or he would never have been convinced that you were not instrumental in Giuliano's death.'

I cried out then, in torment at the accusation.

'It was, after all, you who brought him to the Cathedral,' said Angelo, opening a notebook and dipping the quill in the inkwell.

'Is this an interrogation?' I snapped.

'I need to gather details to try and make sense of this day's confusion. Someone must do it.'

Reminded of Gianbattista Montesecco and his admiration for Greek historians, I asked if the captain was incriminated in the affair.

'Even now he is being questioned at the Palazzo della Signoria. He was one of the conspirators, yes, but it seems either that his courage failed or his piety triumphed. Certainly he refused to commit murder in a holy place; I believe also that he had not the heart to kill Lorenzo. From what we know, the murderers had planned the deed at the Villa Pazzi, but were thwarted when Lorenzo arrived without Giuliano. Then they planned to do it here, but again Giuliano was absent. Each time Montesecco insisted that they must wait until they had the brothers together. In the end, the Cathedral provided the only opportunity, and at that point Montesecco withdrew. Your brother took his place.'

I wanted to know where he was getting his information from and was astonished to learn that he had spent the afternoon at the Palazzo della Signoria. If Angelo was the coward he considered himself to be, how had he ventured out in the midst of riots?

'I only returned this hour. As you know, I have no stomach for interrogation, but Montesecco has been confessing freely. However, when the inquisitors turned to discover what part His Holiness has played in all this, the Captain began to need encouragement. It was then that I left.'

I gazed at him in wonder at the difference between this Angelo and the one I had almost carried to the palazzo.

'All we know here in the house is what we are being told by report. Lorenzo must have accurate details, presented in a coherent form. So that is my task ... and yours.' He tapped the quill in the inkwell then passed it to me with the notebook. Giving me no time to prepare myself, he began rapid dictation of his account of what had taken place.

'When Archbishop Salviati suddenly left the procession, it was not to visit his mother but to take control of the Palazzo della Signoria. This was planned to coincide with the murder of the Medici. The Archbishop went with Jacopo Bracciolini and a band of retainers to the Gonfaloniere, saying that he had an urgent message from the Pope, but the Gonfaloniere became suspicious and called the guard. Salviati panicked and fled. The Gonfaloniere knocked Jacopo Bracciolini down with his fists and consigned him to the guard. He then ran with the Signoria to take refuge in the bell tower, where with a kitchen spit, which fear and anger had put into his hands, he defended himself and the others from the attackers. Lorenzo's men, arriving at the Palazzo della Signoria, cut Salviati's men to pieces, but the Archbishop and Jacopo Bracciolini were saved for the rope.' Angelo paused and, while I caught up with him, ate of the meat I had left.

'Jacopo de' Pazzi, seeing that his attempt on Lorenzo's life had failed, went to the Piazza with relatives and called the people to arms. Nobody listened to his calls of "People and Liberty!" So many stones were hurled at him that he took flight and is yet to be discovered. His nephew Francesco was found in bed at the Palazzo Pazzi, naked and bleeding. He it was who killed Giuliano, stabbing him so frenziedly that he caught himself in the thigh.'

Angelo spoke with detachment of that which, only hours before, had threatened his sanity.

'Francesco de' Pazzi was thrown out naked from a high window of the Palazzo della Signoria on a halter. When the Archbishop was thrown out after him, he bit into the corpse of Francesco. The tighter the halter became round the Archbishop's neck, the fiercer the clamp of his teeth. Clearly he was trying to tell us where the blame should lie.'

'Angelo, have you been at the executions also, to gather these details?' I asked. 'Then you are either a brave man, or a fool. After your actions this morning, I must presume the former.'

'Someone has to make the record. It may as well be a poet with a sense of history. Besides,' he admitted wryly, 'being active keeps me sensible. And as for being brave, I can only remember being foolish this morning. I believe I have you to thank for bringing me home?'

'You were brave before you were foolish. Who was it who stood by Lorenzo, alert, keeping his nerve? A coward would have dashed for his own safety and not have worried about anyone else. But you went into action.'

'Action? – a fine name for my doing nothing but yell at the top of my voice.'

'The best kind – it hurt no one and saved us all.'

'I would rather have been taking off heads with mighty strikes of my sword. Brave indeed! Enough of this flattery.' He took back his notebook and pen. 'Now, tell me all you know: who was at the Villa Pazzi and what was said? And how was it that Giuliano was brought to the Cathedral?'

The memory was painful, but it was the pain of cauterisation: I felt the better for recalling all that had happened. As we talked, the mob re-emerged on the street outside, and Angelo crossed to the window. 'Terrible crimes are being committed this day in the name of vengeance. There is looting, arson, and only with difficulty have we succeeded in keeping the Palazzo Pazzi from being sacked. Who knows how many private vendettas are being pursued, under the cloak of turmoil? Nearly all the Pazzi have been slain, before we could determine which of them was innocent and which guilty.'

'What of the women of the family?' I asked, my mouth dry.

Angelo said that they had been taken to the nunnery at San Frediano. 'Why do you ask?'

I shook my head, saying that I was merely curious. I only wanted for her safety: nothing else could I want now. I sat with my head in my arms. If I was mortified by the idea of Elena in a nun's rough habit, her lovely hair shorn as she became a bride of Christ, I was doubly mortified by my revulsion at the thought.

Angelo wrote up his notes into a full account, recording events with a clear dedication to fact. These days he is famed as both poet and historian. In truth, he was a poet first. The historian was not born until April 26th, 1478, when he discovered that by becoming a detached observer he could transcend the pain and grief that a poet, with a poet's love of his subject, could not have borne. The writing of *La Giostra* ended on that day, an unfinished epic in praise of a youth to whom it now stands as an enduring memorial. From the last words of the final stanza to the first words of the renowned *Account of the Conspiracy of the Pazzi* there was but a moment's interval, and, in that little space, Giuliano died.

When poets become historians, it is a change which marks the ending of the golden age and the beginning of the silver.

FORTY SEVEN

ON THE second night in my prison, a torch was set in the sconce in the wall. It was not sufficient, however, to keep the rats in their holes, and I still could not sleep. As I moved about to stretch my limbs, I came upon a door leading to another room, so I took the burning torch from the wall and went to explore. The room, lit by another grilled window at street level, was full of furniture, mostly chairs kept in store until the next banquet. They were covered in dust sheets and thus old memories were evoked, of a childhood spent in a bishop's palace. I lifted each sheet only to discover more chairs, but then I came to something else and pulled the sheet off in excitement.

There it stood, smelling of fresh wood and polish, innocent of all that had happened: a newly-made settle, a marriage gift, with Botticelli's panel forming its back. I held up the torch to view it as best I could.

Desiderio, imagine a painting. It is large and its figures are almost life-sized. It is not a holy scene, nor is it a portrait, but is of a theme hitherto unknown to our age. It is painted in the delicate strokes of tempera upon a wooden panel, and apart from two significant touches of red its colours are muted shades of blue, white and grey, sharply contrasted by dark green. I shall draw the compositional lines for you another day; for now let your mind wander in arcs to see a serpentine row of eight figures moving in a grove of orange trees. Beyond the trees one may glimpse the pale shades of a receding landscape, enough to tell us that our grove is on a hill in Tuscany.

In the centre stands a magnanimous lady, dressed in a white chemise and draped in a red cloak. She is at once both Venus and the Virgin, haloed by the dawn light which gleams through the meeting boughs of orange trees behind her; orange trees, but their fruit reminds us of golden apples. Beneath her feet lie flowers such as violets and pinks which symbolise marriage, flowers common in the spring, dotting meadows and the lawns of gardens. Above Our Lady's gentle head, at the apex of the main arc of the composition, flies blind Cupid. He is aiming his arrow at the three Graces, who move hand-entwined in a dance to the left of Venus. I will return to them, but now must tell you of the group which, as we view the painting, stands to the right of the Goddess.

Zephyr, the generative power, is swooping on an alarmed nymph. She is Chloris, the spirit of the earth. Pallid and unadorned she stumbles forwards, but blue Zephyr has caught her; roses stream from her mouth, spill on to the chemise of the young maiden beside her, and merge with the other flowers which adorn Flora's billowing shift. Flora is at once elegant and abandoned as she steps barefoot across the grass, casting to the earth the rose heads which she carries in the lap of her dress.

The three Graces are dressed in flimsy gauze through which their plump beauty is visible. Before you click your tongue against your teeth, my dear, celibate Dutchman, let me hasten to say that there is nothing erotic in this picture, not even Eros himself. Here is the nakedness and beauty of sublime innocence. Botticelli never painted to stimulate physical appetites nor, it has to be said, did Filippino. The effect of a painting upon the viewer is the surest indication of the heart of the artist. Even Chloris is only fleeing from her husband-to-be and not from a deity bent on rape. This realm of Venus is inviting but not devouring; at the same time it is pure without being ascetic. It often seems that we spend our lives either indulging or abstaining, but there is a middle way, where the soul may dwell in harmony in the body, the temple of the spirit. This Via Media, as recommended by Plato, is a world which is measured, where Nature flourishes under the discipline of the Creator. Ficino had a motto which formed a frieze around the walls of his study; it best expresses that which I am struggling to explain: ALL THINGS FLOW FROM GOODNESS TO GOODNESS. REJOICE IN THE PRESENT. SET NO VALUE ON PROPERTY. SEEK NO HONOURS. AVOID EXCESS. REJOICE IN THE PRESENT.

To the left of the Graces stands Mercury. He, like Venus, is cloaked in red. With his back turned to the rest of the company, he is gazing upwards to where his dragon-entwined caduceus points through a line of cloud. But what manner of cloud is it that obscures trees?

With Mercury I began at last to penetrate the mystery, to leave the painting's surface and to enter a deeper plane. Of course I looked for myself in the god, the figure for which I had posed, and there was a faint resemblance, though not enough for anyone to be reminded of me. I had been idealised, turned into a form of perfect beauty. Indeed, the only aspect of it that I recognised as mine was the liquidity of the eyes: Mercury seemed to be on the verge of tears as he gazed towards heaven in wonder. But he was not me. Where then was I in this picture? Was I the one whom both Venus and Flora gazed at, the tenth figure, the one outside the painting?

My thoughts returned to the enigmatic Graces. One gazed towards Mercury, as if she were prepared to break the dance, to leave the trinity and to move towards her heart's desire. That she was the target for Cupid's aim made certain her fate, and yet she was restrained by her sisters. If that fiery arrow were to pierce her heart, and she unable to break free of the trinity, her pain would be profound indeed.

Something in her gaze, in her very human gaze, the gaze of a woman longing for a man who is intent on other things, captivated me. If I was to find an answer, it was here, in the line of vision between her eyes towards Mercury, and his towards the Divine. I studied then all the eyes. Chloris and Zephyr gazed at each other, Venus and Flora looked at me, Cupid was blindfolded, two Graces looked towards each other, the third at Mercury, and Mercury at the Beyond. The rhythm of eyes, the rhythm of feet, stepping as if in a dance, the rhythm of colour, the rhythm of hands. Everything was speaking to me, and I was deaf.

But then I remembered something I had heard. Perhaps Angelo had told me, or was it Bishop Agli? – fixed meaning is dogma. Platonic symbols should never be defined, and Platonic philosophers may freely interpret things one way today and another tomorrow. Symbols are as little mirrors hanging from the boughs of the tree of knowledge. We can choose whichever we like, and in it we will see what we need to know. Realising that, my mind relinquished both what it knew and what it wished to know, and looked into the painting as into a glass.

How many hours passed? I do not know. For a while I was plunged into darkness when the torch expired but I continued my reflections, for now the image was imprinted on my mind and could be recalled in all its detail. As dawn seeped through the window it joined with the painted dawn in a quiet suffusion of light; the painting became visible again and then, with the first ray of the sun, the meaning struck. I was no figure in the picture, nor was I the viewer. If I was anything, it was the grove. To be clearer, the grove was a depiction of the mind, in which the gods move and dance. Each figure here was an aspect of myself. I knew them all. The mind is the theatre of the gods, and the play is one of astounding beauty. It is this: through generation the earth is peopled and made abundant, but at the end we return to the Divine, to rest there, perhaps to stay there, but it is from the Divine that generation comes. This great picture, perhaps the greatest I shall ever see, showed in its chorus of figures the whole story of Man, a story of love, beauty, generation, contemplation, return – and rebirth – all as one rhythmic, breathing flow of love.

It had been painted as a marriage gift for Giuliano. Grief, who had been lurking in the shadows of my heart, took this thought as her signal to move on to the stage. I might have fallen to the old crone's power except that suddenly I heard a note – one clear, pure note. It caught my attention as a tinkling bell diverts a child from whatever emotion is playing. The note sounded again; after an interval, it was followed by another; and then another; note after note, played on the lyre of Orpheus himself, sounding like harmonics on sympathetic strings, here and yet not here, distant, angelic. Doh – Zephyr, re – Chloris, me – Flora, fa – Venus/Eros, sol, la, ti – the Graces, and then doh again – Mercury. The music of the painting was a simple octave.

Life is an instrument played by the gods and suddenly I could hear my own song. Themes, motifs and refrains became obvious. Past joys and past sorrows sang contralto and bass. Suddenly it was clear that everything – each action, decision, coincidence, meeting – all events are but single notes in a polyphonic hymn of praise, which is the life of a man.

And yet what do we dwell on, but anxieties and fears, the discordant notes? They too have their place in harmony, but we exaggerate them, consider them the whole song. The fear I suffered then, imprisoned in the house of an angry, wounded Lorenzo, was but fear experienced by something which is greater than fear.

For I am the field of the Graces, I am the father of Venus, I am He to whom all returns, I am the ground of love. I am Love itself.

That, in the end, was the secret the painting had to tell.

What became of it? Finally it became a marriage gift to Lorenzo's cousin, but on the way to its new home it passed through the workshop of Sandro Botticelli once more, and to the bridal flowers in the meadow were added those that are short lived and signify death. But to him who knows, to him who has glimpsed beyond the clouds, death is merely an interval between notes of an eternal music.

A little after sunrise I was taken from my prison and escorted to Lorenzo's chamber. He stood facing the window, unmistakable in outline against the light, against the great dome of Brunelleschi: Lorenzo and his Florence.

I remained by the door. I had never previously been into his chamber. On one wall was a large painting of a battle scene, all rearing horses and lances in deep perspective, and yet bloodless, quiet – no doubt a work of the disciple of the vanishing point.

'The Battle of San Romano,' Lorenzo said, turning.

'Paolo Uccello?'

He nodded indifferently. 'My grandfather commissioned it when Giuliano and I were boys. At that time battles seemed wonderful to us. But they become more serious as we grow older, or is it that we take them more seriously? The Battle of San Romano – it was famous in its day. Who remembers it now? And is it possible that one day the Siege of Volterra will likewise be forgotten?'

'It already has been, by those who were not there at the time.'

'And what of those who were there?'

'If they remember, it is because they practise remembrance. Vengeance like a fire needs constant stoking, and memory is its fuel.'

'Then it is as kindling that you have been to me all these years. I do not know why I agreed to have a Volterrano in my house, unless it was to assuage my guilt.'

'You? You suffer guilt?'

'What man of sense and reason would not? Yet, given the same circumstances, I would probably make the same decisions. You must see it from my point of view, Tommaso. There is nothing new in Rome's designs on Florence. Had I allowed your city's insurrection, war would have resulted, a larger war than that which did occur. If it had seemed possible that Volterra would triumph, Rome would have taken your side against us, and what you are witnessing in these streets today might have occurred six years ago, when I was new to this role and inexperienced. The outcome would have been the certain enslavement of Florence.'

His reason filtered into my thoughts; then he reminded me of the obvious fact that all the Volterrani had chosen to forget: he had not ordered the sacking; quite the opposite. 'I put the Milanese under the direct command of the Duke of Urbino, but even he could not control them. I have yet to hear, however, anyone blame Milan.'

With that graceful hospitality which so many others had remarked upon, Lorenzo ushered me to a chair and poured two glasses of wine.

'If you have always known of Rome's ambitions, why were you not suspicious when the Cardinal's entourage arrived?' I asked.

'I was suspicious. Ficino had been warning me, as much from his own knowledge as from the portents of the stars. Indeed, he gave me a list of the names of the conspirators, for they had tried to involve him. But I also knew they would only attack when they found Giuliano and me together. I never thought they were so impious as to strike in the Cathedral. But they were ... they were.' He stroked the bandage at his neck.

'Several of them were Academicians ... '

'This is what I do not understand! How can it be?'

Lorenzo sighed. 'It is beyond my comprehension. Either they were good men turned bad, or they were never good in the first place. Of course, there is another possibility: that I am indeed a tyrant, and that men such as Jacopo de' Pazzi were sincere in their desire to liberate Florence from my yoke. Am I a tyrant? Certain members of the Academy think so. If Ficino is among them, he alone has good reason, for if there is one person I fail to be diplomatic with, it is he. Here I am, his philosopher king, Dion to his Plato, fencing off one crisis after another, trying to find time to create new systems of good government, and he says, forget the world, ascend with me to the higher realms. Is it any wonder that sometimes I explode in frustration and wrath? How did Alcibiades put it? "Socrates makes me confess that I ought not to live as I do, neglecting the wants of my own soul and busying myself with the concerns of the Athenians; therefore I hold my ears and tear myself from him."'

'Surely Ficino understands that?'

'Yes, but he cannot condone. It is the old, old dilemma between the active life and the contemplative life. If my soul craves the latter, it is the former which attracts my nature. This philosophy of unity tears me in two. The most I can do is compromise and try to control my temper more effectively.'

'So there is no real breach between you and Ficino?'

'None. The little there was healed some time ago, after Luigi Pulci married. I loved Pulci, as I might love a hound that had once belonged to my father. He reminded me of a secure time, when my father was alive. His biting retorts amused me. When you are a man of position, it is well to have at least one person in your company who is not impressed. I had two: Luigi and Giuliano. But then Luigi's attacks on the Academy went beyond caustic humour and began to injure those I love. So I found a wife for him, to sweeten his gall with honey, and dispatched him to a life of nuptial bliss.'

As for Ficino, who had kept Lorenzo company throughout the night, he was 'the one man in the world who has the cure for bereavement.' The full nature of this cure Lorenzo did not specify, but said that Ficino had played upon the lyre, and had read to him from those dialogues of Plato which recount the last days of Socrates. As Lorenzo spoke, I heard in his voice an echo of the same elation that I had known while contemplating Sandro's painting. Perhaps it was that unity of experience which enabled us now to sit leaning towards each other as if we were old friends and eager to converse.

Ficino's philosophy had so exalted Lorenzo's spirit that, he said, he almost envied Giuliano for making the mysterious journey ahead of him. His words took me back to that moment in the Cathedral, and a scintillation of light. I had told no one of it; indeed there were few to whom I would confess such things. Now I could add Lorenzo to their number, knowing that he would listen seriously, as he did. He made me repeat the account three times, encouraging me to attempt description of the ineffable. But what words can describe the joy that dissolves a heart in a radiance of tears?

'Tell me,' he said quietly. 'Where is he now?'

'Here,' I answered at once. 'He promised me that, when you and I should meet again, he would be with us. And he is.'

Lorenzo met my gaze with the sincerity of a heart stripped of all pretences; our first tentative meeting in the field of trust. 'When Giuliano and I were boys, Ficino often used to say that we were as one soul in two bodies. At the time, I took it for a rhetorical flourish aimed to please, but it was true. I know that now. But why did God choose my body to house the united soul, and not Giuliano's? Does He have no preference for beauty?'

'It takes more than good looks, or even good character, to rule a city; Giuliano knew that as well as Our Lord.'

'One thing is certain, that corpse we are to entomb is not my brother, nor ever was.'

I was crying; I was also laughing. One expects rainbows in such conditions. Instead there was silence, in which I heard the words yet to be spoken, and space, in which I saw a goddess in a meadow, regarding me, urging me on with that expectant, female gaze which stirs a man to courage.

'Lorenzo,' I asked, in little above a whisper. 'Is it possible for you to forgive me for what I did at Pisa?'

'Of course,' he said, and laughed at my surprise – for this was not the answer I had expected. Then he added, 'What I find difficult to forgive is the voluntary exile which followed. What was it that you feared?'

'Oh, many things – execution, torture. What I did not expect was my name in the tamburazione.'

'And you believe I did that?' Lorenzo's obvious astonishment proved his innocence. I was left with the question: who, then, had been my accuser?

'We shall never know,' he said. 'The strength of that little box is also its failing.'

The arrival of a message from the Signoria, who required his immediate presence, brought our conversation to an end. Lorenzo rose. 'If a soothsayer had foretold that my life was to be saved by another, I would never have imagined it would be you.'

I smiled diffidently. 'Nor I! But then, at the moment of choice, there was no choice to make. I was merely an instrument in the hand of God.'

'Would that you could have been in two places at once.'

'It was Giuliano himself who sent me to you, wearing his sword.'

Not looking at me, Lorenzo said, 'The man who attacked me, your brother Antonio. Where might I find him?'

'If I knew, do you think I would tell you? How could I?' Even if, as I now believed, it had been Antonio who had accused me of sodomy, I could not have betrayed him to Lorenzo. He was my brother.

Lorenzo gazed at me narrowly. 'If you said as much to a Sforza or a Riario, you would be opening the door to your torture chamber.'

'Ah, but I am saying it to a Medici.' And as I spoke, I saw Lorenzo for the first time. Neither the hero of my boyish dreams, nor a tyrant, he was il Magnifico, and aptly named. I had seen enough of the world by now to be able to recognise at last a true man of virtue. One might expect to be able to recognise such a man at once, only first it is necessary to have some measure of virtue oneself.

Lorenzo's voice softened. 'You have another brother in the city: Raffaello. He is in sanctuary, but he would be more secure here.'

'I wish to find him. Will you release me?'

'You are in mortal danger, being a Maffei.'

'Grant me a suit of blue and silver. I will be safe in your colours.'

He considered it, and agreed. 'If the city is quiet tomorrow, you may go, but, for mercy's sake, be careful.' He accompanied me to the door. 'Ask Andrea Cavalcanti for the clothes, and God go with you.'

'One more thing ... ' I said, and tentatively held out the medallion.

He took the bronze from me. 'How do you have this? He would never say what had become of it. Once I even accused him of having a mistress and of giving it to her.'

'He gave it to me when I fled the city. He said it would bring me back. Please, it should be buried with him.'

But Lorenzo told me to keep it, that it was mine; and he placed the chain over my head and settled the bronze disc on my heart. In that moment any sense of two separate people disappeared; I gazed into the eyes that were my own; love displaced fear. The gate opened.

But there was yet more to be said, and I was hesitant. 'There is something else ... The night we rode from Pisa, he entrusted me with a secret. Why, I know not, except perhaps that it was safe with me. Giuliano did have a mistress.' These five words sent various emotions in waves across Lorenzo's face.

'A lady of the Gorini family,' I hurried on. 'Lorenzo, there is a son.'

Lorenzo's composure, already shaken, was destroyed by this last mortar of information. His face contorted and there was an inward moan like the first rumblings of an earthquake; then, bursting from him in a roar, came the tumultuous anguish of overwhelming relief, as that of a soul freed from torment on Judgement Day. The knowledge that Giuliano had left to the world some mortal part of himself crippled Lorenzo with excruciating joy.

To Tommaso dei Maffei, Florentine abiding in Oxford, greetings

If I have not written sooner, it is because melancholy attends me in Paris, and no one here is sufficiently acquainted with 'natural wisdom' to fill my room with burning candles and sweet-scented flowers. I have begun my earnest study of Greek under a real Greek from Sparta. (You know that he is a real Greek by the size of the fee he charges.) It is better to learn, even if somewhat late, than not to know those things which it is imperative to have at one's command. Now that I have stopped sipping and begun to drink, I perceive that Latin learning, rich as it is, is defective and incomplete without Greek. For we have but a few small streams and muddy puddles, while they have pure springs and rivers of gold. I see that it is madness even to touch the branch of theology which deals chiefly with the mysteries unless one is equipped with Greek.

It is my delight to set foot on the path into which Jerome summons me, so help me God. As you once said, so have I discovered: Jerome's works have been partly corrupted by half-learned persons, and partly mutilated by practitioners of your own noble craft, amongst whom you stand proud as an intelligent man (or would do, but for your unorthodox interest in pagan deities).

Do you think Colet will be pleased with me? Do not attempt to find out. Say nothing of my designs. I look forward too much to telling him myself, in person, when I return to England. But that can only be when the work is complete, and not before. Ah, Colet. When I remember him, I seem to hear Plato himself. And what has nature ever fashioned more gentle, sweet or happy than the character of Thomas More? But I must not whip myself with memories.

Send me your book, Tommaso, as soon as it is done. Farewell my beloved Maffei.

Desiderio Erasmus, in Paris, March 1500

FORTY EIGHT

THE HEAVENS wept. For a week it rained, heavily and without respite: rain falling, dripping, running in streams and turning the streets to mud. Searching in vain for both Antonio and Raffaello, I drifted like a sodden wraith. On the fourth day, I joined a crowd gathering in the courtyard of the Palazzo del Podestà. Squeezing in among those who were sheltering in the loggia, I came to rest between a butcher and a joiner. The two men continued their conversation as if I were not there.

'My wife says that it is because they have buried him in consecrated ground,' said the butcher, peering at the leaden sky. 'Now it is not my custom to take notice of what my good woman says, but I agree it was a peculiar thing to do, to give that wicked man a decent Christian burial.'

They were discussing Ser Jacopo de' Pazzi, who had been caught and hanged a week before, for it was at the moment of his burial that the rain had begun. This particular capture was now a favourite story of the Florentines. Ser Jacopo, having been discovered in the village of Castagno by two young boys, had confounded them by falling to his knees and begging them to kill him, crying that he did not want the shame of a public execution. He offered them six florins to do the deed. The boys were not as simple-minded as he supposed, and, being peasants, they knew how to kill a chicken, and how merely to stun one. Thus they brought him alive to Florence, added the city's reward to their six florins, and stayed to watch as Pazzi was duly hanged.

The butcher and joiner recounted the story between them, as men going over the last play they had seen while waiting for the next one to begin. Today's performance was to be a novelty in a week of hangings.

'This one will be the best of all,' said the butcher, 'for they are taking off his head rather than breaking his neck.'

'Why is that?' asked the joiner.

'Because the old dog deserves the honour.'

'But why?'

'I am not sure.'

I had read the confession of Gianbattista Montesecco; indeed, I had made a copy of it for Angelo. 'It is because he was drawn into the conspiracy by his loyalty to the Pope,' I said. 'But, having no wish for the death of the Medici, he consistently prevaricated. Then, at the last moment, he withdrew.'

'Thanks be to God,' said the butcher, 'for he might have succeeded where those two priests failed.'

'He confessed quite freely, without the candle and the rope, and his confession shows without doubt who was behind this affair.'

'The Pope ... ' whispered the joiner.

'To be more accurate, the Pope's nephew, Girolamo Riario,' I said. 'But His Holiness out-Pilated Pontius in the matter.'

The joiner crossed himself.

'To think,' said the butcher, 'if the plot had succeeded, this would be a papal state by now.'

The joiner crossed himself again.

I said, 'Lorenzo has no desire to kill Montesecco, but the law must be satisfied. The best Lorenzo can do is to give the man the honour of the axe.' I looked towards the upper gallery of the courtyard from where a dozen or more corpses hung on their ropes like plumb-bobs. The most fresh was Bernardo Bandini, who had been captured and hanged the day before. With his head lolling on his chest and his hands bound together before him, he hung in an unconvincing attitude of repentance.

'How many more are there to be found?' I asked.

The butcher shrugged. 'So far as I know, only the two priests. They are thought to be in sanctuary in one of the city churches.'

'Which one?'

'If I knew that, would I be standing here?'

'Oh, I think you would,' said the joiner. 'You said yourself you would not miss a beheading for all the rewards of heaven.'

'So only two left,' I muttered.

'So far as I know,' said the butcher, 'but then they are adding new names to the list of conspirators every day. After each confession, the list grows. The latest is Piero Vespucci.'

'Vespucci?' I gasped, not having heard this news. So far as I knew, the young man had had no part in the affair, but then I remembered his hatred of Giuliano. I asked what he had done, and the butcher told me that, alone of all Florence, Vespucci had rushed to join Jacopo de' Pazzi when the old man was charging through the streets calling the city to freedom. 'My wife says that he harbours a grudge against the Medici because of an adulterous affair between Giuliano and Simonetta, but it would be a foolish man who repeats what she says. I told her, Woman, there was no affair, it was all show. The Medici are frolicsome, in love as in all things, and make merry with life. To be honest, I admire them for it, for there is much that I would prefer to take a lot less seriously. Such as marriage.'

'And dying,' said the joiner gloomily.

'In my opinion,' the butcher carried on, 'all that happened was that Piero Vespucci, believing that the Pazzi were indeed on the verge of power, mistook a freak gust for a change of wind and reset his sails in error.'

A solemn bell began to toll the hour of execution. All gossip in the crowd ceased. We watched the door at the head of the open stairway. At last Montesecco, haggard and unshaven, came out with his hands bound. He stopped on the stairs and looked down on the courtyard and the block. His guard pushed him forward, causing him to stumble, but he regained his balance and came down the stairs with a dignified tread.

Remembering my conversation with him on the road to Rome, I stood the astonished witness to his destiny as he approached his executioner in torrential rain. An accompanying priest, who had been muttering consolation for some time, now increased the speed of his prayers as if there was something of which he had urgently to convince the soldier. Montesecco appeared not to be listening. He glanced up at the crowd but his eyes were opaque and saw no one. A roll on the drums. His sentence proclaimed. His soul commended to God. He knelt down, rested his neck on the hollow of the block, and turned his head from side to side to make it comfortable. Then he was still.

I stared through the rain. I had a view of the crown of his head: he was balding. While the butcher studied the executioner with professional interest, the joiner gripped my arm and held on to me like a woman.

A series of raps on drums, beating out the last seconds of a life. The axe raised aloft; the drumming stopped. All breath was held. Then down like a hawk in an arc of silver came the axe, riving the bone to jam into wood. The balding head jumped forward.

The butcher nodded appreciatively. 'Excellent. Excellent. Clean through the spine.'

The joiner's grip loosened.

'Whoa!' said the butcher, catching his friend under the arms. 'It is always thus. I cannot think why he comes.'

As the crowd dispersed, I found Filippino and Leonardo sitting together at the back of the loggia. They had notebooks on their knees, and now that their view was unimpeded they had returned to sketching. Filippino greeted me with an open smile and enquiring gaze.

'No success?' he asked, referring to my quest.

'None.' I cocked my head to look at his studies of hanging corpses. Botticelli had been commissioned to paint the wretched scene in a fresco on the wall above the gate of the Custom House. Filippino held his work at arm's length and regarded it through narrowed eyes. On Leonardo's notebook the corpse of Bandini was being deftly outlined in ink.

'Have you been commissioned too?' I asked him.

'No, I have not. When there is a need to make studies of the dead, Botticelli is the obvious man for the task. I am merely showing Filippino how to use a pen.' He turned then upon his fellow painter a smile so generous that it creased his face and disarmed his own words. His solar eyes shone with affection.

Filippino sniffed and continued with his own sketch. I watched them both working, captivated by their skill. In their hands the line was the gold of the goldsmith, the wood of the carver: a material of random nature brought under man's control.

Finishing the sketch of Bandini, Leonardo annotated it in cryptic handwriting. 'What language is that?' I asked, intrigued.

'Back-Latin,' said Filippino before Leonardo could reply. 'As he thinks, so he writes. He has all knowledge, but it comes out backwards. Pity him.'

'It is intentional,' said Leonardo, 'to prevent minivers such as you from stealing my ideas.' Again the Apollonian smile, dispelling all rancour. Bearing no malice in his heart, Leonardo could speak as he pleased.

His attention turned to a horse which the scent of blood was making restive. His gaze was a beam of such intensity that I wondered the horse did not ignite and burn to ash. Suddenly my own attention was caught. I looked now at the horse, now at its linear counterpart growing on the paper; my pulse began to slow down, my breathing to stop – the usual reaction when one is in the presence of divinity. I looked again at the horse, and saw Horse as if for the first time: power, glory, majesty, contained in the form of Horse, an invention of the Creator. I gazed in awe.

Leonardo, who no amount of noise ever disturbed, was unsettled by my profound silence. 'What is it?' he asked.

'Look at that horse ... '

'I am.'

'No, I mean really look at it, see it for what it is: the handiwork of God. We are all so impressed with each other's skills, and yet what are we but breathing sculptures of the Creator? How feeble are Man's achievements when compared to those of God!'

Leonardo grimaced. 'I thought it was my art which had you enraptured.'

'What does your drawing amount to when compared to the horse itself?'

Filippino was delighted by this exchange.

'Thank you,' Leonardo said.

'Oh, do not mistake me. Your work is very good.'

'I agree,' said Filippino. 'I am always telling him so, but he needs constant reassurance.'

'Thank you,' said Leonardo again, with a face like Cararra marble.

I was breathing again, quickly now. 'But compared to the horse itself, it is only a series of lines on paper.'

Filippino howled like a wolf in season.

'Look at that horse!' I persisted. 'Can you not see it? It is moving, breathing, pulsing with life. God is the one true artist! And there is no point in your crowing, Pipo. I include you in this.'

'You think God is better at making corpses than I am?' said Filippino.

'Do not confuse me.'

'I will make a corpse of you if you say more.'

'Tommaso,' said Leonardo. 'You have enjoyed a moment of true seeing, but my vision is always thus, which is why I am a painter. I implore you, keep this dangerous knowledge to yourself, for I make my living by selling paintings to the blind. If everyone saw the beauty around them, which God bestows quite freely, I could not sell them anything. Equally, if every man woke up to the knowledge which is innate within him, he would need no books. So if you do not betray me, I shall not betray you. Is that agreed?'

His apparently light-hearted logic revealed a great deal to me and won him the argument.

'It is a wonderful drawing,' I said. 'After all, if it had not been for your horse, I would not have seen the real one. So this must be the purpose of art and of learning both, to awaken us to that which we cannot see for ourselves.'

Leonardo reflected briefly on my deduction and pronounced it correct.

'Holy Mother of God!' said Filippino. 'Return us to the old times, when painters did not have to think.'

It was Ascension Day when the tolling bells called the people to a funeral. Under the lashing rain and pewter sky, the procession left the Palazzo Medici. It was only a few steps to San Lorenzo and the family tomb, but such a short journey would have deprived Florence of a ceremony to mark this end. Thus the procession made its way through the city, led by the resplendent Company of the Magi. And unrehearsed and unanimously every young man of Florence came out to join it. The silent throng grew until it seemed that there were more in the line than in the watching crowd. The youth of Florence, their backs straightened as if by an invisible hand, walked in double file to the beat of a melancholy drum. They walked proud, indifferent to the rain, to honour the one who was the best of us, he who, of us all, represented man at his highest in grace, nobility, humanity – in that indefinable quality, *virtù*.

The priests leading the procession, walking between the mounted escort of the Company of the Magi, were ignoring the Pope's recent decree that Giuliano de' Medici was excommunicant; in contravention of the Bull, they buried him with due ceremony and according to the Holy Sacrament.

The church of San Lorenzo filled with mourners whose rain-drenched clothes dripped on to the marble floor. The cold dampness compounded our grief. The sun should have shone for Giuliano. He would have preferred that to all the tears.

The rain continued to fall on the city and to swell the Arno. I darted from doorway to awning to loggia, sheltering wherever people gathered, hoping always to discover the whereabouts of Raffaello or Antonio. Whenever I was near the Palazzo del Podestà, I went to Vespasiano's bookshop, for there the talk was of the legality of the Pope's threat to excommunicate all Florentines if we did not give Lorenzo up to 'justice'.

I entered the sanctum of parchment and ink, inhaling the familiar scents of my craft, while myself smelling like a wet dog. Many learned men were gathered there, Angelo among them. They were discussing the Donations of Constantine, the ancient document from which the popes had derived the doctrine of infallibility. Angelo was telling the company how Lorenzo Valla had proved that the document was a forgery, and of a much more recent date than the Emperor Constantine. Some of the men, who preferred to believe everything that was written in faded documents, and did not want to have their faith shaken by scholars, grumbled and objected. Angelo grew vociferous. With the fiery confidence of youth, he denounced their 'superstitious cast of mind' and declared in ringing tones that if all men, by their very nature, were sinful, that must include the Pope, who was a man. 'The very concept of papal infallibility rests on a document written in the language and script of the eighth century. This was proved by Valla over thirty years ago, and still we act as if it were true!'

He was close to losing his temper, but, encouraged by friends from the University, he calmed himself with a deep breath and began to explain, patiently and as if to idiots, the linguistic details of Valla's argument.

I stood by the door, looking out on the rain. Everyone in Florence was sharing in this discussion, at their own level. For most it was more straightforward: the Pope had given his blessing to the attack on the Medici; now he claimed that Lorenzo had murdered the conspirators. To the Florentines, in their simplicity, the contrary was true: it was Giuliano de' Medici who had been murdered; the rest had been executed. Pope Sixtus, however, enjoying a conviction of infallibility which no scholarly opinion could damage, had all Florentines living in Rome imprisoned. If he did not have them massacred it was due only to Lorenzo's wisdom in having kept the boy Cardinal hostage.

Angelo joined me. 'I have had word of Raffaello. He is in sanctuary with the Friars Observant.'

I leapt towards the street but he pulled me back. 'Lorenzo says that we are to respect his sanctuary and leave him alone, so that he may come to trust us again.'

'Antonio must be in sanctuary too,' I said. 'But where? I have searched every church and monastery in the city: Santa Croce, Santo Spirito, San Marco – all of them. Nothing. Not a sign.'

Angelo nodded towards the Badia on the far side of the street. 'Have you tried there?'

'Of course. But is it not rather close to the Palazzo del Podestà and the Palazzo della Signoria?' It seemed an unlikely place to hide, but Angelo's doubtful expression made me ask, 'What is it? What do you know?'

'The monks are subdued.'

'All monks are subdued, as are all priests, clerics and nuns. And is it any wonder, with their most fallible patriarch threatening them with excommunication? Everyone is subdued.'

'Even so ... ' said Angelo. 'Brother Paolo comes here each day, as if he would drench himself with reason, and seems most dispirited.' As he spoke, that same monk ran towards us through the rain, looking so haggard that I barely recognised him.

'Brother Paolo, good morning!' I said, as I used to do habitually in the days when I had worked in the bookshop. He looked at me.

'It is I, Tommaso.'

He looked bemused, so I added the family name, 'dei Maffei.' Brother Paolo flinched then, as if at a devil, and pushed past into the bookshop. Vespasiano greeted him affectionately and drew him into the group continuing to discuss the legitimacy of the Pope's actions. Leaving him there, Vespasiano came to the doorway and clapped me upon the back with such a heavy handed gesture of welcome that I stumbled.

'Brother Paolo looks feverish,' said Angelo to him.

'And with good reason. Apparently Father Abbot is remaining loyal to Rome. Any right-thinking monk in the Badia must feel as if he is split in half. Oh! Look! Do you see what I see? The rain. It is not so heavy.' Vespasiano summoned his customers to witness a miracle. 'The rain is stopping!'

As the doorway filled with the curious, I was forced out on to the street. Indeed, the rain was lighter, and all the time becoming lighter still. A gang of boys came running along the street, crying: 'Make way for the great knight! Make way!'

'What is it?' said Angelo. 'What have they got on that rope?'

'Madonna ... !' I retched at the smell.

'What have you got there?' Angelo demanded of the boys. They stopped by us to display with pride the stinking bundle which they dragged behind them, a corpse in the first stage of decomposition.

'It is Jacopo de' Pazzi. He is riding the city, calling "Freedom for the People!"' said one of the boys. His friends took up the mocking call: *Freedom for the People!*

'You have disinterred him from Santa Croce?' demanded Vespasiano, holding his nose and staring at the bundle in horror.

'We have stopped the rain!' the boys claimed. With a jerk of the rope, they ran on, dragging the corpse behind them. 'Make way for the great knight! Freedom for the People!'

Angelo's eyes were alight with wonder. For all his learning, he still hoped for miracles. 'The rain has stopped!' he said.

'If it has,' said Grazia beside us, 'it is sheer coincidence.'

'The word coincidence' Angelo retorted, 'merely means two

things occurring at the same time. In itself, the word offers no explanation for the phenomenon.'

'Very clever,' said Grazia acidly, pushing back into the shop through the crowd in the doorway. Angelo followed him to air his ideas on cause and effect. I remained where I was. With a few last drops, the week of rain was over and the sun came out to dazzle the wet streets. People emerged with relief from their homes and workshops. 'It is over,' they said, meaning the turmoil as much as the rain.

The bell of the Badia rang for Mass. I crossed and went in. A *Te Deum* was to be sung for the passing of the rain. All the monks looked as drawn as Brother Paolo. Was it only because of the abbot's loyalty to the Pope? The Badia is a charitable abbey, giving shelter to the poor, sick and homeless. Its doors are always open. I went to the cloister door and found it closed. Turning, I saw that I was being watched anxiously by every monk in the church. Those in the congregation were mostly old ladies and vagrants, but there were two of the civic guard present, though with the Palazzo della Signoria so close by, there was nothing unusual in that. But one of the guards turned to see what was attracting the attention of the monks, and I quickly left.

I stood outside, panting in breathless realisation of the obvious: at the end of the street was the Cathedral, and it had been from the south door that Antonio had bolted. He would not have gone far, yet I had searched the city to its farthest reaches. With the closeness of the Badia to the Palazzo del Podestà and the Palazzo della Signoria, Antonio must have been listening all week to the execution of his friends.

When Mass ended and the congregation left, I re-entered the church. Seeing me come, Brother Paolo unlocked the cloister door and silently ushered me through.

'Where is he?' I demanded. My voice, amplified by the barrel vaulting of the cloister, was louder than I intended.

'Here.'

I looked to the upper storey where, around the walls in a series of arched niches, ran the life of Saint Benedict in fresco. As a figure stepped out from a painting, Antonio looked down on me. 'Come, Judas. Come and kiss your brother.'

'How can you be so arrogant, even now?'

'Hush! Keep your voice down. Come up here.'

I ran to the stairs and up the narrow flights of stone two at a time. Antonio was waiting for me at the top. He caught hold of me and, against a wall depicting Saint Benedict's Holy Rule, knocked out of me all breath, and all stupidity. Throughout the long search, I had carried the hope of reconciliation, of some miraculous transcendence above the realm of differences. My chiaroscuro brother, all that I wanted of him in this, his moment of supreme failure, was for him to leave the shadows and accept the light. But instead he caught me by the neck of my shirt, and, twisting the cloth in his hand, began to choke the life out of me. How could I have expected anything else?

'I nearly had him. I nearly had him. And you interfered. One chance is all I ever wanted, and now I shall die for that which I failed to do. I need recompense, and I will have it ... ' I had no breath left to cry out. On the opposite wall was a picture of Saint Benedict receiving the vision in which 'the whole world seemed to be gathered into one sunbeam and brought thus before his eyes.' A dark-robed figure of a priest stood before the painting, his face livid and implacable: Stefano da Bagnone. Then I heard a roaring sound, as of a mighty deluge breaking through a wall, or a sea of mercenaries, bursting into a city. It was, I thought, the sound of blood exploding in my brain.

Consciousness returned in a drench of cold water from a bucket. Brother Paolo, who had dragged me from the cloisters, pulled me to my feet and shook me roughly. The air was tumultuous with the sound of men. Shouting at me to move quickly, the monk pushed me through the refectory towards a door. We emerged in a lane beside the abbey. Guards were running from the Palazzo della Signoria to the church, but too late: the people had already entered for the kill. From within the abbey came the screams of the brethren. The guards forced their way through to save them, but men in the vanguard of the mob had already found the real quarry. They had found it some minutes before. Indeed, in finding it when they did, they had saved my life.

Dazed and staggering, I was carried by the throng as a leaf in a flood. The people tried to force their way into the church, but were pushed back by the guard coming out, dragging two limp prisoners.

'Are they alive?' I shouted, but was drowned by the howling of the crowd. I caught a glimpse: it was enough. Stricken with nausea, I became blind to everything except the vision of Antonio as I had seen him, with nose, eyes, tongue gouged from his head; dark blood at his groin.

Throughout the ensuing day and night I kept vigil at the Palazzo del Podestà, sitting in the mud outside its gate; nor did I move when, in the morning, an eager multitude arrived to watch the last of the executions. I listened to the strident heckling of the crowd and the beating of the drums; I listened to the silence, to the snapping of two ropes, and the gratified moan of a people avenged.

FORTY NINE

T*HE HOUR of departure has arrived, and we go our ways – I to die, and you to live. Which is better, God only knows.*

The speech of Socrates to his friends among the Athenian judges lit a candle in the blackness of despair. I looked up at Marsilio Ficino.

'Do you understand?' he asked.

'I believe so.'

'What is the sense in mourning, when we do not know what death is?'

'But is mourning for the dead, or for the living?'

'Just so. Do you recognise, then, that your sorrow is for yourself and not for your brother?'

I nodded dumbly. We were in the solarium of his villa on the hill of Careggi. The sun poured through the windows into a room fragrant with myrrh, balsam and cinnamon. I was clothed in a robe of saffron and had to hand the finest Trebbiano wine, warmed and sweetened with honey. All these things are of Jovial character, for the power of Jove alone may dispel the melancholic humour of Saturn. Yet within me the darkness of guilt and misery persisted. Any brief moment of respite which I enjoyed was brought to a swift end by an image of my aunt Lucia staring at me, whey-faced and accusing.

Ficino read my thoughts. 'It is presumptuous to blame yourself for Antonio's death. You were not the cause of it. What man on earth is the cause of anything? We are either channels for the will of God, or we are not: that is our only choice. As God the Creator is the Supreme Architect, Painter and Sculptor, so is he the Supreme Poet. Against his plots, themes and characters, even Homer's stories are feeble imitations. God alone has the power to determine the span of a man's life. You believe that you alerted the guard to where your brother was hiding, but, in truth, the time had come for Antonio to be found, that is all. If you were present, if you were instrumental in that discovery, it was merely a device of the plot.'

'Strange – that is what Antonio desired most, to be a device of the plot.'

Ficino smiled, whether at my joke or at God's, I could not tell. It seemed that there was nothing in creation so dreadful but that he could not find some humour in it. Thus it is for a man who looks death in the face and is not afraid, a man who knows that death is but a trick of the great illusion. That we are born and that we die is nothing but sleeping and waking in the eternal life; a lifespan is but one day in our true existence. This was the truth that Ficino proclaimed, this and the unity of the soul with the soul's Creator. For how can a man die, when the essence of man is omnipotent God?

What had I expected of Ficino? A giant, perhaps, or an archangel arrayed in glory. In fact he was shorter than I, of middle age, and had a weathered face as familiar to me as any, for I had seen him many times over the years. I had even spoken to him once, mistaking him for his own gardener.

He sat in his villa overlooking Florence, a city on the brink of war, and though he was concerned for its welfare, it was its spiritual rather than its material welfare which concerned him. The more those about him grew serious, the more often he bubbled with laughter. If Lorenzo sometimes lost his temper in the face of truth, it was because of his responsibility to the untruth, the illusion, the dream which we call 'reality'.

If 'pope' means 'father', and is a term denoting a spiritual leader and guide of souls, then Marsilio Ficino was the true Pope of our time. Meanwhile Lorenzo prepared for war with that creature who claimed the title.

I stayed for a week or more in the villa, and for an hour each day I took the heliotropic cure in the solarium, either reading Plato or handling precious stones which, neither cut nor polished, remained in their natural state: rhomboid crystals of topaz, pyramidal sapphire and hexagonal beryl, each of them yellow. There was a geode, a nodular stone, which had a cavity lined with crystals of purple amethyst. Staring into this jewelled heart as if into another world, I gazed upon a treasury of polyhedra wrought by nature. The Jovial properties of these raw gems caressed my soul, and their enigmatic beauty drew me from the power of Saturn.

The discipline of the house rested on a strict timetable of activity and rest. Activity included periods of physical exercise or work in the garden; to find deep rest, Ficino taught me the method of true prayer, which asks nothing of God, but requires instead a silence of both heart and mind, for such time until you lose all sense of time, and of identity also, and know nothing but the deepest peace. Some might say that to adopt this monastic life was to avoid one's duty, that I should have been playing my part in defending Florence. But prayer can be more effective than action, and a few men inturned on the soul can bring about peace more surely than any amount of fighting.

Other members of the Academy came to the villa to find repose from the agitated world. Sometimes Ficino read to us, from Plato, Plotinus or Hermes Trismegistus. One evening Angelo arrived, wishing to be reminded of poetry. 'For I hear none in the city and my own Muse is silent now.' Ficino picked up his lyre and rested it on his hip. His hands ran gently over the strings, playing a rising octave. Then my eyes closed in ecstasy as the sacred octave flowered like amethyst crystals into music.

Never before nor since have I heard such measures. Were there harmonies? I am not sure, for I heard each note separately; each one a planet held in limitless space, with unexpected notes bursting in the firmament like comets. Then Ficino began to sing, and the words were not of an Orphic hymn, but of Psalm 18. My favourite psalm was his also:

> 'And their line is gone out through all the earth,
> and their words to the end of the world.
> In them hath he set a tabernacle for the sun.'

It was then I realised that a man who enters the Platonic Academy does not do so by accident, but is born to it. As a nobleman is born to the nobility, and a peasant to the peasantry, so the philosopher is born to philosophy; the difference is that he may come from any walk of life, and any parentage. During the recitation of the psalm, my past resentments vanished as mist in the sun. How can it matter how or where one is born, or to whom, so long as this is where one comes to: the present moment in which to rejoice.

Sometimes I had thought that, from the larva of childhood, I had become a butterfly, sometimes I thought me a moth. But I had become, like all men, a chrysalis. Now something was awakening within, responding to the call of the lyre. Gently stirring its moist, folded wings, Soul began to emerge from the husk to fly. That husk, that chrysalis which will crumble into the dust and earth of which it is formed, is named variously by various men. In my case it is named Tommaso dei Maffei. All that the world has to offer ultimately is the death of a chrysalis and a stillborn butterfly. Only Truth gives rebirth, and freedom.

Ficino laid the lyre aside and, while the last precious notes could still be heard in the air, began to speak: 'God is the soul of the universe, who inwardly nourishes heaven and earth, the moving seas, the moon's shining orb, the stars and the sun. Permeating every limb, He moves the whole mass and mingles with its vast substance. The heavenly spheres are set in motion by God, the spirit and mind of the whole universe, and from Him arise the songs of those spheres, which are called the Muses. All things are full of God, and that spirit which is called God is everywhere; He enlivens and fulfils all things. God is first, God is last, God is the head, God is the centre. The universe is born of God, God is the foundation of the earth and of the star-bearing heavens. He is the source of the ocean, the movement in the undying fire. He is the King and Prince of all. Whatever you see and wherever you move is God.'

Angelo delivered to me a letter from Lorenzo. I read it with curiosity. In his magnanimity, Lorenzo had found both the time and will to condole me on the death of my brother. In exquisite Latin, he expressed sympathy as if he were writing in impassioned Tuscan. I read it twice through before coming to the postscript, which was in the vernacular language, and almost brutal in its forthrightness.

'It is time, young man, for you to begin paying your taxes. Florence is no longer content to support you; you must now support Florence. Therefore it has been decided to grant you citizenship. Present yourself at the Palazzo della Signoria on the eighth day of May.'

'The eighth of May? What date is it, Angelo?'

'The seventh.'

'Have I missed May Day?'

He laughed and asked why it should matter; besides, May Day had not been celebrated this year. 'It was raining, if you remember.'

'Oh yes, the rain.' It seemed a year ago rather than a week.

I looked out of the window. The sky was cerulean, innocent of any deluges. It was always blue, it claimed, and the sun always shone. Heaven has no part in the clouds that roll beneath its vault and cannot be held responsible for their behaviour.

Into the sky rose a hawk. I watched it circle, then stoop. Somewhere in the fields a mouse was dying, and it mattered not. Death-life-death, nothing but the blink of an eye in the Mystery.

FIFTY

WHEN Raffaello finally left sanctuary at the church of the Friars Observant, I was there to meet him. It was a sober reunion. His childlike face had suffered from accelerated maturity: his skin was parched of its freshness, his hair lank, his eyes defensive. He too had received a letter from Lorenzo. I took it from him and became voluble in my admiration for Il Magnifico.

'Lorenzo write this? In such Latin? Only one man composes in such a fluid style: Angelo Poliziano wrote this letter.'

'Lorenzo not only wrote this,' I said, 'but in his own hand.'

'I do not believe it. Why in heaven's name should Lorenzo de' Medici wish to condole with me? What does he say – He knows how it feels to lose a brother, having lost his own? Well, his brother has gone to paradise, mine to hell. I fail to see the comparison. Giuliano is entombed in magnificence while Antonio lies in unconsecrated ground. Where is the similarity?'

Fresh from my time at Careggi, I was steadfast in the face of Raffaello's bitterness. 'That you and I are alive is due to Lorenzo. Never doubting our innocence, he has protected us throughout these days. To lock yourself up with the Friars Observant was unnecessary. I have been abroad in the city, have been recognised and left unharmed. Now he has been moved to write to us. This letter is a gesture of supreme nobility. Being noble yourself, at heart you know it.'

'A step too far and sympathy becomes condescension.'

I looked at my brother across a gulf of his own making.

'You will see things differently in time,' I offered, throwing a tentative line across to him. Disdained, the line fell limply into the abyss.

'I already do,' he replied sourly. 'I once disparaged Antonio's ideal society, but now that he has died for it ... '

'Died for an ideal? He was executed for attempted murder!'

'The murder of a tyrant who deflowered our native city. Rightful vengeance. The shame is that he failed.'

'Raffaello! What legacy is this that Antonio has bequeathed to you? Are you to continue where he left off? Have you taken up that hell-born load he carried through his life? Set it down, now, before it is too late, or you will have the devil riding on your back. For the sake of all that is true and good, let the Maffei's hatred die with Antonio.'

In response, Raffaello stated that he was to leave for Rome within the hour.

'Rome?' I cried. 'How can you go there?'

'It is where I live. And the Pope is my Lord.'

I surrendered all hope then and could fight him no longer. 'As soon as you are there, please find my document of legitimisation and then burn it.'

This softened him. 'What are you saying?'

'I am saying that I desire no family of the loins. I would be free of all ties to the past, and of any responsibility to the future, apart, of course, from that which is the duty of every man to the next generation.'

'You are my half-brother. Burning documents will not alter that.'

'True, just as the existence of them has not altered the love I have always borne you, and always will. But I would be free to love whom else I choose, and not to be so bound by family associations that I am caught up in feuds and vendettas.'

'A man's prime duty is towards his family.'

'But what is the family's duty towards the man? To restrict him, limit him, cause him to hate where he naturally loves? The family is the seed of the city, the city is the seed of the nation. Is it any wonder, when we look at our families, that our 'nation' is but a riot of fighting cocks caught up in a sack? Look north of the Alps, to where great kingdoms arise, countries unified by leadership and a common cause. Our private battles keep Italy fragmented. All that changes is the relation of one fragment to another. Alliances build up and crumble, dependent on the caprices of fortune. Now we have among us a man, one who is great enough to have a vision of nation, who puts the welfare of his family before his own, the welfare of the city before that of his family. I mean to offer myself to him, in full service.'

'Then you contradict your own argument, for to stand with the Medici is to divorce yourself from the Maffei.'

'If it appears so, it is only appearance. Before I can enjoy the unity of family, I must find the unity in myself, and that is a quest I have only just begun. We must part for a while, you to go to Rome, I to remain here. Florence is now my city and my home. For a time our cities, and therefore you and I, are at war, but there never was hatred where there was not first love, and behind difference lies unity. In time we will find each other again. Meanwhile I shall nurture in secret my love for you, and for the family, while all appearances may show the opposite. If only you would do the same, then you and I at least would have begun the work of building a nation out of the ashes of greed.'

He considered me darkly. 'You have an effective power of rhetoric, brother.'

'Give the credit to my old tutor, the Bishop Agli,' I said. 'He has a habit, even after death, of informing my speech.'

Raffaello continued to gaze at me. Gradually, as imperceptible as the opening of a flower, he blossomed into a smile. Another chiaroscuro brother, but in Raffaello the light triumphed. I leapt forward to embrace him.

The next time I rode to Careggi, I was in the company of Angelo Poliziano and wearing the crimson lucco, the gown of citizenship from which I would not be parted. My pride was, I would have thought, both forgivable and understandable.

Lorenzo, having no time for anything other than meetings of the Council of War, had charged Poliziano with the safe removal of his wife and children to Pistoia, and to care for them throughout this period of acute danger. The weighty duty he had been charged with so filled Angelo's hours that not only had his fount of poetry dried up, but that of scholarship too. He had no need of my services other than for letter-writing, which, he said, he was perfectly capable of doing himself. Thus I was being delivered to the place where I was needed most: the Academy.

Lorenzo had called me to him and asked if I were willing to serve not him, nor Florence, but all humanity. Only when I had agreed did he tell me the nature of the task, which was to assist Marsilio Ficino in a transcription of his Latin version of the *Dialogues* of Plato. 'For it must be published, as soon as possible,' Lorenzo said. 'This work, initiated by my grandfather Cosimo, is the beating heart of Florence. If I save the city but lose its heart, then all we shall have is a corpse.'

Although my own heart leapt with pleasure at this duty, I put a condition upon my agreement, saying that I could neither rest nor concentrate while I was unsure of the fate of a certain lady. I told him then of Elena de' Pazzi, the bastard daughter of Ser Jacopo, and how I was willing to marry her without a dowry, once I had established myself with a small house. Lorenzo promised to ensure that Elena did not take her vows, and said, 'As for the small house, it is yours, as soon as the Plato is published.' (And he held true to his word, even though, when the time came, he was in the middle of war against Rome.)

When we reached the villa, Angelo entered to find the master. I wandered in the garden and was drawn to a gate leading to a small grove where, among the dark, mossy wood of olive trees, vines had been set on poles. Birds darted between the trees, before a sweeping view of terraced fields.

'You must be hot in that heavy gown,' said a familiar voice. Ficino straightened up from an inspection of the vines. It was June, when the fruit is at its most vulnerable. I laughed, somewhat nervously, at this most gentle and revealing criticism. There is only one way to survive the barbs of a wise man – accept them, do not seek to protect yourself. I took the gown off. 'You are right, of course. I am melting.'

'Pride is bad enough without having to suffer for it.'

'Absolutely.'

'How goes it in the city?'

'A Bull came today from the Pope. All Florence is now threatened with excommunication, unless we give up Lorenzo, which of course we shall not do.'

'What is excommunication from a man such as Sixtus the Fourth? Has the devil the power to keep men out of heaven?'

'Our churches intend to ignore the Bull.'

'As they should,' said Ficino. More concerned with the grapes than with bulls of excommunication, he returned to inspecting them for signs of blight.

'And there is an outbreak of plague,' I said.

'Is it serious?'

'Yes. Lorenzo is sending his family to Pistoia but insists on remaining in the city himself.'

'As he must.' Ficino straightened again, looking thoughtful. 'There is no cure for plague, but you can prevent it.'

I asked him how this could be done.

'By keeping clean, scrupulously clean, both your body and your house. Certain herbs should be burnt, and I have an incense of Arabic origin which helps. I shall have some sent to the palazzo.'

The vineyard was quiet. A light breeze played with the leaves but the pendulous grapes remained unmoved. Grapes like these had inspired the pen of Virgil. Throughout the ages and in all lands, men had crushed such grapes for their juice, had drunk their way through baptisms, weddings and funerals, had raised wine-filled cups in expectation, helped drunken friends home in intoxication, slept late into the following day to their wives' indignation. Etruscans, Romans, Lombards, Italians, Spaniards, Germans and French: all the same. Individual grapes come and go, uncelebrated, unmourned, but Grape remains. So too with men, and Man. Ficino was watching me, waiting for me to speak.

'I have been here forever,' I said.

'And you shall be here forever.'

'This life – it is but the recounting of a tale.'

'You have a million others, if only you could remember them.'

'Is that all my life is – a story I happen to remember?'

'Look at me.'

I flinched and glanced away. He lifted my chin; slowly I raised my eyes to meet his clear, fathomless gaze.

'What do you see?'

'Myself ... '

'In what way?'

'By reflection, in the windows.'

'Windows are for looking through, not at. Go further, what do you see?'

There was a rushing sensation, as if all the limits of my body and world were dissolving: the observer and the observed became as one. But then, as a man learning to swim, a sudden loss of trust caused me to thrash and flounder.

Ficino smiled. 'Come, what did you see?'

'God.'

'And who is God looking at?'

I paused a little, smiled diffidently, then said it: 'God.'

I regarded him anew, as the temple of the Spirit, the tabernacle of the sun, and I the same. I looked about. Purity and innocence informed all I saw. In the grapes, in the heart of the grapes, was the same as in the heart of the leaves, the grass, the leaping crickets and the pedestrian beetles, the nearby woods and the distant hills. All things in the visible and invisible Universe have God as their essence. Most wonderful of all, I am included.

'Welcome, citizen,' said Ficino, 'to the City of the Sun.'

To Desiderio Erasmus of Rotterdam, in Paris, greetings

It is done, my friend, and here it is. I had hoped to read aloud to you the end as I had the beginning, but you denied me that pleasure by your sudden departure from England. Restless man, or perhaps not so, for it seems the world itself is home to you and no country may claim you for its own. And where a country fails, how can I, a mere individual, hope to succeed? When the wind blows from the east, I collect your greetings; when it blows from the west, I send you mine. For there is no locking up of Erasmus in the box called friendship. If I would have Erasmus as friend, then I must love all I meet, seeing him in all of them.

We survive without you, you will be happy to learn. Everyone is studying hard. There is no news and the turn of the century did not sweep us into an abyss. As you foretold, March 25th was followed by March 26th, and I did not wake up with leprosy or with all my hair and teeth gone. There has been much clamour about the sixteenth century (as the English call the cinquecento, but then, as you know, they are an eccentric people); but nothing in effect has changed.

Here is my book. All I have has been gained from the company I have kept; little or nothing is due to my own abilities. Now that time has moved on and carried me across my obsessive fears of new centuries, I am developing a new anxiety, that of the tutor who has to crane his neck to look up at his pupil. Jerome! What am I doing, writing personal histories, while my pupil embarks upon a translation of Saint Jerome? I spend hours in the confessional, admitting to a lust for history and an aversion to theology. Then, as I leave muttering my Aves, Thomas is waiting to cancel my penance. He says there are too many theologians and too few historians. Therefore, under pressure from More, I may continue with my task, for there is much yet to tell, particularly about the friar who purged Florence of the Medici and the evils which, unleashed by the Antichrist, sent me flying to England.

Will all this help us in our work of cleansing Holy Mother Church? Should I not instead be setting about a translation of Clement of Alexandria? Desiderio, I must end this letter, and return to the confessional.

To my own dearest friend, farewell. May the gods attend your days.

Tommaso dei Maffei, Florentine
April 1500

FIND YOUR PEACE IN THAT
WHICH IS NOT TROUBLED
AND IN PEACE
YOU WILL
LIVE

MF